Praise for

The Dark King series

O9-BTL-733

"Loaded with subtle emotions, sizzling chemistry, and some provocative thoughts on the real choices [Grant's] characters are forced to make as they choose their loves for eternity."   —*RT Book Reviews* (4 stars)

"Vivid images, intense details, and enchanting characters grab the reader's attention and [don't] let go."
                    —*Night Owl Reviews* (Top Pick)

The Dark Warrior series

"The world of the Immortal Warriors is a thoroughly engaging one, blending powerful ancient gods, fiery desire, and touchingly human love, which readers will surely want to revisit."   —*RT Book Reviews*

"[Grant] blends ancient gods, love, desire, and evildoers into a world you will want to revisit over and over again."
                    —*Night Owl Reviews*

"Sizzling love scenes and engaging characters."
                    —*Publishers Weekly*

"Ms   et love to
crea   *tle Reviews*

PALM BEACH COUNTY
LIBRARY SYSTEM
3650 Summit Boulevard
West Palm Beach, FL 33406-4198

ise for Donna Grant

Grant mixes adventure, magic, and swo...
...le the perfect romance!"
—Single Ti...

The Dark Sword series

"Grant creates a vivid picture of Britain centuries after the Celts and Druids tried to expel the Romans, deftly merging magic and history. The result is a wonderfully dark, delightfully well-written [series]. Readers will eagerly await the next Dark Sword book." —*RT Book Reviews*

"Another fantastic series that melds the paranormal with the historical life of the Scottish highlander in this arousing and exciting adventure." —*Bitten By Books*

"These are some of the hottest brothers around in paranormal fiction." —*Nocturne Romance Reads*

"Will keep readers spellbound." —*Romance Reviews Today*

DON'T MISS THESE OTHER SPELLBINDING NOVELS BY **DONNA GRANT**

THE DARK KING SERIES

Dark Heat
Darkest Flame
Fire Rising
Burning Desire
Hot Blooded
Night's Blaze
Soul Scorched
Passion Ignites
Smoldering Hunger
Smoke And Fire
Firestorm
Blaze
Heat
Torched
Dragonfire
Ignite

THE HEART OF TEXAS SERIES

The Christmas Cowboy Hero
Cowboy, Cross My Heart
My Favorite Cowboy

THE SONS OF TEXAS SERIES

The Legend
The Hero
The Protector

THE DARK WARRIOR SERIES

Midnight's Master
Midnight's Lover
Midnight's Seduction
Midnight's Warrior
Midnight's Kiss
Midnight's Captive
Midnight's Temptation
Midnight's Promise

THE DARK SWORD SERIES

Dangerous Highlander
Forbidden Highlander
Wicked Highlander
Untamed Highlander
Shadow Highlander
Darkest Highlander

THE REAPERS E-NOVELLA SERIES
Dark Alpha's Claim
Dark Alpha's Embrace
Dark Alpha's Demand
Dark Alpha's Lover
Dark Alpha's Night
Dark Alpha's Hunger
Dark Alhpa's Awakening
Dark Alpha's Redemption

From St. Martin's Paperbacks
HeroesandHeartbreakers.com
Original Stories, Sneak Peeks,
Exclusive Content, and
Much More!

FEVER

DONNA GRANT

St. Martin's Paperbacks

NOTE: If you purchased this book without a cover you should be aware that this book is stolen property. It was reported as "unsold and destroyed" to the publisher, and neither the author nor the publisher has received any payment for this "stripped book."

This is a work of fiction. All of the characters, organizations, and events portrayed in this novel are either products of the author's imagination or are used fictitiously.

FEVER

Copyright © 2019 by Donna Grant.

All rights reserved.

For information address St. Martin's Publishing Group, 120 Broadway, New York, NY 10271.

ISBN: 978-1-250-18291-3

Our books may be purchased in bulk for promotional, educational, or business use. Please contact the Macmillan Corporate and Premium Sales Department at 1-800-221-7945, ext. 5442, or by email at MacmillanSpecialMarkets@macmillan.com.

Printed in the United States of America

St. Martin's Paperbacks edition / October 2019

10 9 8 7 6 5 4 3 2 1

To G

Thank you for showing me
that love still exists.
You make every day brighter,
and I'm so happy you're in my life.

ACKNOWLEDGMENTS

To everyone at SMP who had a hand in getting this book ready, including the amazing art department for such a stunning cover that matches the character to perfection. To my phenomenal editor, Monique Patterson—you rock. Much appreciation also goes out to Mara.

To my extraordinary agent, Natanya Wheeler, who is on this dragon train with me. Thank you!

A special thanks to my children, Gillian and Connor, as well as my family for the never-ending support. To Charity, Jillian, and Jessica—we make a great team, and I couldn't do all of this without the help of each of you.

Hats off to my incredible readers and those in the DG Groupies Facebook group for keeping the love of the Dragon Kings alive. Words can't say how much I adore y'all.

CHAPTER ONE

"Dragons are real."

The words went through the small room of the restaurant reserved for special meetings like a pistol shot. Today's meeting was of the local cryptozoologists.

Keltan wanted to be anywhere but there. Yet Ulrik had sent him halfway across Scotland to hear whatever Dr. Bernadette Davies had to say in her highly publicized talk about dragons.

Keltan was shocked at the sight of her. He'd expected some older woman in her sixties with gray hair, glasses, and at least two chins. Instead, he was met with a vision that actually had his mouth hanging open. Straight black hair parted on one side fell just past her chin and brought attention to her incredible cheekbones. Her large, jade eyes met everyone's gaze with determination and calmness that proclaimed that she wholly believed everything she was going to talk about.

Her hunter-green button-down shirt was billowy yet molded tantalizingly to her breasts. And the black pants her shirt was tucked into made Keltan's mouth water when he caught a glimpse of her perfect derriere.

Keltan had to bite back a groan when he saw the black stilettos on her feet. He'd always been a sucker for women who wore heels.

But it was the first three words out of her mouth that made him sit up straight and pay attention. A jolt of dread and worry went through him so quickly that his stomach roiled viciously.

"As cryptozoologists, we work tirelessly to prove that such creatures exist," Bernadette continued. "Many of you know for certain that particular creatures you believe in are real. For me, it's dragons."

"Do you have proof?" someone asked.

Keltan didn't look in the direction of the voice. He kept his gaze locked on Dr. Davies. Now, he wished he hadn't chosen a seat toward the back. If he'd sat closer, he wouldn't have had to look around the various heads to keep her in view as she walked back and forth.

There was no doubt about the confidence she exhibited. And while there was a chance that she was one of the few off her rocker, Keltan didn't think that was the case. As a Dragon King, he and his brethren at Dreagan had gone to great lengths to hide their true selves from humans.

But a few years ago, the Dark Fae had taken a video of the Dragon Kings in a skirmish with them. The Dark released the footage to the world, and speculation about dragons soared overnight—and it had yet to diminish.

Now, humans looked at the sky constantly, making it harder and harder for the Kings to shift, even on the sixty thousand acres of Dreagan where they lived. On an almost weekly basis, the magical barrier surrounding the lands stopped numerous drones sent by mortals trying to see if Dreagan was the home of dragons.

It made all of the Kings wonder if it had been wise to

choose the double dragon as their logo, or the Celtic word for *dragon* as the name of their whisky.

Ryder, the King who could create and work with anything electronic, used his hacking skills to wipe the video from everything and everywhere. Yet the curiosity of the humans had been woken. They wanted answers.

Which was why Keltan was at this meeting.

He'd thought it a joke and a waste of time. Obviously, Ulrik had been right to send him.

"Fuck," he mumbled beneath his breath.

Dr. Davies smiled. And for the first time, Keltan realized that she wore a nude color on her full lips. There was something in her smile and the way she held her head that sent a chill of foreboding down his spine.

Instead of responding, she merely smiled in response.

A murmur of shock went through the group of twenty-five people as they all assumed her smile meant she did, indeed, have proof.

Keltan opened the mental link all the Dragon Kings shared and said Ulrik's name, followed by Ryder's. Both answered him immediately.

"*We have a problem,*" Keltan said.

Ulrik sighed. "*Damn. Does the woman know something?*"

"*Aye, but I doona know what yet.*" Keltan studied her as she returned to the center of the room without sharing the proof she claimed to have. "*Ryder, I need everything there is on Bernadette Davies.*"

"*Kinsey and I'll do a deep dive on her immediately. You'll have something shortly,*" Ryder promised.

Ulrik then asked, "*Has she shown you anything about us?*"

"*No' yet,*" Keltan answered. "*She did allude to some proof she had, but she's no' said what it is.*"

"Yet," Ryder added.

Keltan grunted because he'd thought the same thing. *"She's verra confident. It's no' just speculation she's peddling. Her first words were that dragons are real."*

"Keep me informed," Ulrik stated.

Keltan severed the link. Ulrik was running the shots at Dreagan at the moment. Not that any of the other Kings wanted the responsibility. After Constantine, King of the Dragon Kings had been taken by Usaeil, Queen of the Light just as the Kings were about to go to war with her, things got . . . tense at Dreagan.

And now this.

Keltan ran a hand down his face. They didn't need this. They should be concentrating on locating Con, not chasing after some mortal who might or might not have information on the Dragon Kings.

And, frankly, Keltan didn't care if Dr. Davies did. The Kings had walked and lived among the humans for millions of years, forsaking their true selves and the fact that they had once ruled this realm. Maybe it was time for the Kings to stop hiding.

As soon as that thought went through his head, Keltan knew it would never happen. The proof was in the brief time that dragons and mortals had attempted to live together. It had ended with the Kings sending their dragons to another realm and hiding away for millennia.

All because of a vow to protect the mortals without magic.

When, in fact, the dragons could have wiped them from the Earth in minutes.

But they weren't murderers. They had tried to make it work with the humans, conceding land again and again and again as the mortals bred like bunnies.

For a long time, Keltan had hated them. Con's spell to

stop the Kings from feeling hate—or love—for the mortals had helped to quell much of his anger. Now, Keltan just wanted his life back. He didn't care if the humans were there or not.

He wanted to fly during the day, feel the sun on his scales, and survey the world from the clouds for however long he wished.

He wanted to let out a roar without having to wait for a thunderstorm to mask the sound.

He wanted to be able to choose when and where he shifted instead of only doing it at Dreagan at night.

With an inward shake of his head, he ground his thoughts to a halt and returned his focus to Bernadette Davies. She was pointing at a projection screen that displayed a picture of Fair Isle.

"Some of you may not know, that not long ago some bones were found in one of the many caves of Fair Isle. An American archeologist, Faith Reynolds, claimed that they were dragon bones. Oddly enough, Faith hasn't been seen since that declaration."

A man to Keltan's left said, "Are you saying that someone silenced her?"

Bernadette shrugged. "I'm saying that I couldn't locate Ms. Reynolds in order to speak to her. When I dug deeper, the prominent and up-and-coming archeologist appears to have disappeared."

That wasn't true, but Keltan couldn't point that out. If he did, everyone—including Dr. Davies—would want to know how he knew such a thing. And right now, he didn't want any attention on himself. He was there to observe and take notes.

"What about the video?" a woman in her mid-twenties asked from the front row. "Is that your proof?"

A ghost of a smile flitted across Bernadette's face.

"For those who didn't get a chance to see it, the young woman is referring to the video that surfaced a couple of years ago that showed men shifting into dragons and fighting other beings with red eyes."

"There was magic," the young woman said.

Dr. Davies nodded as she glanced in the girl's direction. "That there was. Within days of the video going viral, it was wiped from the internet."

"That isn't possible," a man in his fifties with a heavy French accent stated.

The young woman turned around and met the Frenchman's gaze. "It's true. It's gone. You can't find it anywhere."

Another man with an English accent snorted loudly. "I agree with him. Once something is released on the internet, it's in the cloud. And once it's there, you can't get anything back."

Keltan hid his grin because there was one person who could get it back or remove it entirely—Ryder.

Before the argument could continue, Bernadette quickly interjected, "We could debate this all night long. And while it's fascinating, that's not what I came to talk about. Though it is part of the story."

Bernadette clicked something in her hand, and the picture of Fair Isle vanished, replaced with a list that made Keltan clench his teeth together.

"Here are all the things that involve dragons."

Keltan read the list.

1. The video of dragons appearing, then disappearing
2. The dragon bones on Fair Isle
3. Archeologist Faith Reynolds disappearing

No big deal. Dr. Davies had already mentioned all three.

Then Keltan read more of the list.

Bernadette touched on each one, adding dialogue next to the names. "Number 4: Known members of a mob go missing near Dreagan. Number 5: Kyle Ross goes missing only to be heard telling someone that he was going to find his sister who worked for Dreagan, then Kyle goes missing. Number 6: Renowned journalist Rachel Marek goes to Paris to cover the World Whisky Consortium and is seen with a representative from Dreagan—and has only released one new piece since then. And that piece was about Kyvor."

"Kyvor is no longer in business," someone said.

Dr. Davies nodded slowly. "No, they aren't. After a little digging on my part, apparently, the higher-ups in the company were interested in buying out Dreagan Industries."

Keltan wanted to stand up and tell everyone the truth about each of the points. He had to clench his hands into fists just to remain seated.

Based on everything Bernadette was laying out, anyone in the room who hadn't believed was slowly coming to her way of thinking. And by the smile on her face, that's exactly what she intended.

The question was why? What did she gain by all of this? What was her motive?

She continued down the list with a mention of how Dr. Sophie Martin had left her position at an Edinburgh hospital to open a practice near Dreagan. It was no surprise to Keltan when Bernadette cited the socialite Alexandra Sheridan and the Scotsman she had been photographed with in New York, only now to be seen near Dreagan.

Thank goodness Bernadette didn't know about all the others. As it was, there was a serious case for anyone to take an interest in Dreagan on a level that would keep Ryder and his mate, Kinsey, extra busy.

For the next two hours, Keltan was one of the few who didn't say anything as the room debated Dr. Davies' list, adding their own thoughts and conjecture.

Bernadette answered question after question but never revealed any of her sources. And while it appeared those sources weren't always accurate, they came close enough to make Keltan aware that someone knew the secrets of the Dragon Kings.

The problem would be discovering who it was—and silencing them.

CHAPTER TWO

It had gone better than she could've hoped. So much better. Then again, how could anyone not want to know about dragons? Bernadette said good-bye to the last person leaving the room and packed up her papers and laptop. The talk was only supposed to last two hours, and yet she'd talked for five.

The entire evening had exceeded anything she'd dared to hope for. Finally, it seemed as though others might actually begin to pay attention to the things she had to say about those at Dreagan—especially since she knew the truth.

She hadn't had to explain if she had proof or not, and she was thankful since she couldn't exactly show it. Everyone had been immersed in the discussion and the links that she had found between the various women and Dreagan.

But she knew she would have to show the proof eventually. She'd brought the dragon scale for just that. And yet she didn't want to share it. It had been something she'd kept to herself for nearly a year now. To show it to others would almost be like sharing a secret part of herself.

A part that had kept her going during the long months when her fellow anthropology colleagues thought she'd lost her mind. Though she supposed she'd feel the same thing about someone who, after a decade as an anthropologist, had decided to become a cryptozoologist.

Not that she'd had a choice. As soon as she'd seen the dragon, she'd been unable to look away.

Or think of anything else.

For weeks after, she'd stared at everyone around her, wondering how they couldn't know of the magical beings that lived among them. It boggled her mind that so many went about their lives as if they were the only creatures on Earth.

She, however, knew differently. Her glimpse of the dragon had opened up an entire world to her. It was also how she'd discovered the Fae.

Bernadette pulled her keys from her purse as she looped the strap of her laptop bag over her shoulder. Her stomach growled, reminding her that she hadn't eaten anything since lunch.

The moment she walked from the back room into the restaurant and was assaulted by the various delicious smells, she decided to eat there. It was a splurge that she couldn't really afford, but she was going to do it anyway. It was her gift to herself for carrying out such a fabulous evening.

Bernadette set her bag and purse on the chair next to her as a waiter handed her a menu. Her mouth watered as she looked at all the options. Everything sounded good, which made choosing difficult. Then she looked at the prices and barely hid her wince.

The food wasn't extremely expensive, but since she was now down to part-time at the museum so she could focus on her research about dragons, her income had taken a beating.

"Excuse me, madam. This is for you."

She looked up as the waiter set a glass of whisky on the table. "Um . . . I'm sorry, but I didn't order this."

"It's from the gentleman at the bar," he told her and motioned to his right.

Bernadette leaned around the waiter, her gaze latching on to the bearded man who lifted a small tumbler filled with amber liquid in her direction.

The waiter then said, "The gentleman said you should give it a try. It's the best Scotch in the world. And, frankly, I have to agree with him."

Bernadette swallowed hard as her gaze swung back to the glass before her. "What brand is it?"

She knew the answer before the waiter said, "Dreagan."

She closed the menu and set it before her as her heart hammered in her chest. The man at the bar was from Dreagan. She knew it with the same certainty that she knew dragons were real. There was no running from him. She'd known that someone from Dreagan would contact her sooner or later.

She just hadn't expected it to be in person.

Bernadette had never run away from anything in her life. Well, that wasn't exactly true. There was that incident when she was seven, but did that really count?

She squared her shoulders and looked back at the man at the bar. She took in his dark blond locks that were combed away from his face and fastened in a queue at the back of his neck. His gaze was still locked on her.

While she couldn't discern the color of his eyes, there was little doubt that he expected her to ignore him. The slight widening of his eyes when she waved him over had her giving herself a little pat on the back—albeit with a shaking hand. She might be sitting with a straight spine, but it would be foolish to not be at least a little anxious.

Her gaze didn't waver from him as he casually stood from the barstool. He was tall—taller than expected. And the fact that he carried himself with certainty had her anxiety skyrocketing with a vengeance.

The waiter wisely walked away before the man approached. Bernadette shoved her hair back from her face and tried not to fiddle with her hands—a nervous habit she had yet to break.

"Good evening."

Damn. His voice was as smooth and rich as velvet. It had just the right amount of husky timbre that made bumps rise on her flesh.

She had been raised along Scotland's border with England, so it wasn't as if she hadn't heard a Scots brogue before, but there was something unique about his. Something wild and untamed that made every nerve ending in her body stand up and take notice.

To her delight, her voice came out strong and clear when she gave him a nod of greeting and said, "Good evening. Please, join me." She motioned to the chair opposite her.

He pulled out the seat and lowered himself into it before his eyes met hers once more.

"Thank you for the drink," she continued. "Why do you believe that I've not drunk whisky before?"

Instead of answering, he asked, "Have you?"

"No." Damn him. She should've guessed that he'd come back with such a comment.

"Try it," he urged.

"I'm not much of a drinker. I'll occasionally have a glass of wine, but that's it."

The man shrugged one shoulder. "Please, doona feel as if you have to drink it."

Well, now she wanted to more than ever. "It's always good to try new things, right?"

One side of his mouth kicked up in a grin. Bernadette spotted even, white teeth. His eyes were the color of amber, and they blazed with a fire that mesmerized her and made her breath catch in her throat.

Her stomach clenched as she continued staring into his beautiful eyes. Finally, she lifted the glass to her lips, but just before she took a drink, he stopped her.

"Smell it first," he urged. "Let the flavors of the whisky invade your nose before they hit your tongue."

The way he'd said it made it sound so . . . sensual. As if they were about to do something sexual, not drink Scotch. She swallowed and inhaled the scent of the whisky as he'd advised.

To her shock, she quite liked it. It was nutty, and she could definitely smell the peat moss used. But there was something else she recognized yet couldn't quite name.

She looked at him over the rim of the glass. Their eyes met and held. She sat there surrounded by the smell of whisky and the presence of a man that set her on edge and made the air around them fairly crackle.

"Now, drink," he told her in a soft voice.

Without hesitation, she let the liquid touch her tongue, and her mouth exploded with flavor. She tasted the peat moss and the nuttiness she'd smelled, but she also noticed a smokiness. The Scotch was heavy and bold. It burned slightly as it went down her throat and settled into her stomach, but she went back for another sip.

The man's smile was slow, his gaze stating that he'd known she would like it. Bernadette licked the whisky from her lips as she set the glass on the table.

"Are you ready to order, madam?" the waiter asked as he walked up, seemingly out of nowhere.

She'd forgotten all about being hungry. Bernadette opened the menu again and quickly scanned the items, looking for something that was reasonably priced.

"The smoked salmon is particularly good," the man said.

Salmon was one of her favorite dishes. She hadn't had it in months. It sounded so good that she didn't even look at the price. "I'll have that," she told the waiter.

The man then turned to her table companion, who waved him off.

Once they were alone again, Bernadette leaned back in her chair and crossed one leg over the other. "I would introduce myself, but I believe you already know who I am."

"I do."

She liked that he hadn't tried to lie. She'd give him props for that, at least. Bernadette raised a brow, waiting for him to offer his name.

He chuckled and said, "I'm Keltan Dreagan, but you already knew I was from Dreagan."

"I did," she confessed. Bernadette wracked her brain, trying to remember if he'd been in her lecture, but she couldn't place seeing him. Not that she paid attention to every face—something she would need to change.

"I came to hear your talk."

She let out a sigh. "I see. For one of you to come, those at Dreagan must be worried about what I'm going to say."

His lips twisted as he lifted a shoulder. "Every business has an interest when they learn someone is telling wild tales about them."

"But they aren't so wild. They're the truth."

"You believe you know the truth?" he asked, a blond brow arched.

There was something in his words that gave Bernadette pause, yet she found herself saying "Yes."

"Hmm," he said as he took a swallow of his whisky.
"You have quite a few theories, Dr. Davies."

"Are you here to tell me I'm wrong?"

"As I said, I came to listen to what you had to say."

She laughed and reached for the Scotch once more.
"And the drink?"

"No' something I intended, but I doona regret it."

"Despite everything I said about Dreagan?"

He glanced at his hands that rested in his lap, one large
one holding the tumbler. "I was curious about you." His
lids lifted, and amber eyes caught hers.

"Curious?" she repeated, a little thrill running through
her that she didn't understand or expect.

"Something must have happened that turned your focus
to Dreagan."

"And you want to know what that was," she said with
a smirk.

Keltan shook his head. "Dig into Dreagan Industries
all you like. We give substantial sums to various charities
around the globe. You'll no' find anyone in our company
who's been arrested or given so much as a speeding ticket."

"That's just it, Mr. Dreagan. You and everyone at your
company are squeaky clean. Too clean, in fact."

He chuckled and sat up in his chair, bracing his forearms on the table. "Are you honestly telling me that the
fact we're no' breaking the law and do right by others
means we're a target? Lass, there are plenty of other
people for you to go after. Throw a stone, you'll hit one."

"So, you're not a dragon."

Her words stopped him in mid-rise from his chair. He
slowly lowered himself back down and leaned close to
her. "Do you know how daft you sound?"

"I don't care."

"You should. I dug into you, Dr. Davies. You had a stellar career, one that only a fool would throw away so nonchalantly. You were respected, and with just a few printed words from your first post about dragons, you lost that respect."

She leaned forward and lowered her voice since she saw others in the restaurant staring at them. "I don't care what others think."

"That's shite," he stated, no heat in his words.

She ignored him and continued, "If you knew something was true, that something extraordinary was real, would you keep it to yourself? Or would you tell the world?"

"I doona know what proof you think you have, but there is no such thing as dragons. They're nothing but mythological creatures."

"Then why do you have them on your logo? Dreagan is Gaelic for *dragon*."

Keltan shrugged and shook his head. "Dragons, griffons, and a host of other mythological creatures have been used for eons as logos and on family crests. Why does anyone choose such a logo? You're reading far too much into this, I'm sorry to say." With a nod, he stood. "Goodnight, Dr. Davies."

She could only watch as he walked away.

CHAPTER THREE

They were so fucked.

Keltan stood in the shadows outside the restaurant and watched as Bernadette Davies got into her car and drove away just as the rain began. There was no doubt in his mind that she would continue on her quest to expose Dreagan. They had to stop her. But how?

Nearly the entire room she had spoken to had been converted to her way of thinking. Those people would tell others, and those would tell even more people. Not to mention, Bernadette would hold more talks, write columns, and appear in more places, converting more and more people.

"Bollocks," he grumbled and walked to the white G-Class Mercedes SUV that he'd driven to Glasgow.

He climbed inside, but he didn't start the engine. Keltan was too wired to sit still for the three-hour drive back to Dreagan. He wanted to take to the sky and soar among the clouds, weaving in and out of them, all while forgetting—if only for a little while—that the Dragon Kings were nothing more than caged animals.

Except the mortals had no idea that bars held them back.

He really wished Con was there. Keltan might not always agree with every decision the King of Dragon Kings made, but in the end, they were the right ones. Now, too much was pushing against the Kings.

For thousands upon thousands of years, the Kings' secret had been kept safe, their identities firmly concealed. Then the spell Con had cast on them never to feel any deep emotion for the humans was broken, and the Kings began to fall in love.

Keltan squeezed his eyes shut. He had no problem with his brethren finding their mates and bringing them to Dreagan to live. What he did have an issue with was those same mates now being the focus of an investigation into Dreagan.

And it wasn't as if they could haul out any of the women Bernadette had listed to say anything against her, because Dr. Davies would surely be prepared for that. No matter how good any of the mates were at answering questions, one of them would get tripped up. And that's all it would take for anyone previously skeptical about Bernadette to begin to wonder and entertain the idea that those at Dreagan were more than they said they were.

That was the last thing the Kings needed. Not when they were still searching for Con.

Keltan opened his eyes and slammed the heels of his hands against the steering wheel. He still couldn't believe that Constantine was unable to get free of the Queen of the Light. Con was the strongest, most powerful of all Dragon Kings. And the Kings' magic was more formidable than any other on the realm.

But if Con could get free, why hadn't he? Why was he

staying with Usaeil? All the Kings knew that Con had no feelings for her.

"We're missing something," Keltan said.

But, for the life of him, he couldn't figure out what it was.

There was Rhi. Keltan blew out a breath. Of late, the Light Fae hadn't exactly been someone the Kings could count on. She was going through her own problems involving Usaeil. Rhi and Con were supposed to attack the Light Queen together, but it had been pushed back again and again. And now look where they were.

A flash of lightning filled the sky the same instant a man appeared before the SUV. Keltan's enhanced senses allowed him to see the Fae's silver eyes in the dark.

The man was a giant with short, black hair. He wore dark denim and a white shirt that molded to his upper body. The man said nothing, simply stared at Keltan through the windshield while standing in the rain. But this was no ordinary Fae. The Light didn't mingle with the Kings, preferring to keep their distance.

The Dark Fae, well, they were another matter entirely with their red eyes and the silver in their black hair. They had been actively attacking the Kings ever since the Fae Wars. And while both the Light and Dark could use glamour to alter their appearance, the Kings could see through such magic.

The man before Keltan was a Light Fae. And Keltan was curious as to what he wanted.

Keltan exited the vehicle and stood in the rain that now came down in thick sheets. He shut the SUV door and walked toward the man. The closer Keltan got, the surer he was that this wasn't just any Light Fae. He stood like a warrior, like someone who had seen plenty of battles.

Though Keltan didn't have much interaction with the Reapers when they came to Dreagan, he knew of them. Could this be one of them? And if so, why was he here?

"Cautious," the man said with a slight smile, his Irish accent thick. "You scared of me?"

Keltan snorted loudly. "The day I'm afraid of any Fae is the day the Dragon Kings will no longer be."

The man smiled widely then. "I knew I'd like you. I'm Rordan."

"Keltan."

Rordan nodded. "I know who you are."

"How's that?"

"I was sent by Eoghan."

Now that was a name Keltan knew. Eoghan had been part of the original seven Reapers, but he now led another group. "Why? Should you no' be talking to Ulrik or one of the others?"

Rordan shrugged. "You'd have to ask Eoghan or Death that. They told me to come here and speak with you."

"What can I do for you?" Keltan asked.

"We just learned what happened to Constantine."

Keltan clenched his teeth. If the Reapers knew, then it was good odds that all Fae knew. "How did you find out?"

"Eoghan. He went to visit Con at Dreagan and learned that Con had been taken by Usaeil."

Keltan let out a breath. That was good news, at least. There was a chance that the Fae didn't know about Con. Not that they would be stupid enough to attack. With or without Con, the Kings could—and would—defend not only Dreagan but also the world.

"Can Death find Con?"

Rordan shrugged as rain dripped from his face. "She has the ability to find any Fae, but Con isn't a Fae."

"Then she can locate Usaeil. Once we find her, we'll find Con."

Rordan glanced away. "I'm not here about that."

"Then why are you here? To piss me off? Because you're doing a bloody good job," Keltan said tightly.

"I'm here to let you know the Reapers are monitoring the situation."

Keltan's brows rose in disbelief. "Monitoring? Wow. That's . . . shite. Death, who I might add befriended Con hundreds of years ago and has given him gifts, willna do anything? What is that friendship for then?"

"I knew he needed guidance," said a feminine voice from behind Keltan.

He turned around to see a beautiful, petite woman with long, black hair hanging to her waist and lavender eyes. She was clothed all in black, a curious and sensual mix of leather and chain mail. Keltan knew in an instant that he was speaking to Death—aka, Erith.

Death wasn't alone. Beside her was someone Keltan did recognize, Cael, the leader of the first group of Reapers. Though Cael's eyes were no longer silver, but instead a dark purple.

"Some things have happened," Cael said.

Keltan could sense the strength of Cael's magic. It now matched Death's. If there was anyone who could destroy the Kings, it was Death herself.

"I'm not here to harm you," Erith said. "I'm here because of your anger."

Keltan crossed his arms over his chest as he glanced at Rordan. "Was your messenger no' doing his job?"

"No, you're being an ass," Cael stated as he blinked through the rain.

Erith put a hand on his arm as they shared a look. Then her lavender eyes swung back to Keltan. "I can feel the collective pain, worry, and anxiety of the Kings. Each of you is connected to the magic of this realm, and all those emotions beat through the magic—and straight into me. I couldn't ignore it any longer."

"Con needs help."

"Does he?" Death asked, a black brow raised.

Keltan dropped his arms and looked away, shaking his head. "You think the same as everyone else."

"You mean, the same as you." Erith smiled faintly. "You know Con's might and power. You know he could get away if he so chose."

"Is that why you willna tell me where Usaeil is?"

For the first time, Keltan saw uncertainty cross Death's face. She swallowed loudly and lowered her eyes to the ground, ignoring the rain that soaked them. Several seconds ticked by in silence before she finally returned her gaze to him.

"I don't know where Usaeil is."

The statement floored Keltan. Death, the one being who could find *any* Fae, was unable to locate the Light Queen? "How is that possible?"

"Usaeil is using more than Fae magic," Cael said.

Keltan nodded. "Aye. We recently learned she incorporates Druid magic, as well."

"Whatever she's doing, it's hindering my ability to locate her," Erith said. "I told Rhi that Usaeil was hers to destroy, but she's waited too long."

"So, you went after Usaeil yourself," Keltan guessed.

Death nodded. "Only to come up empty-handed."

"There has to be a way."

"There is," Rordan stated.

Keltan looked at him for a long moment before his gaze slid back to Erith and Cael. "Tell me."

Death drew in a deep breath and then released it. "There is much about Usaeil none of you know. Many things I've only recently discovered. Rhi was right. I should've sent the Reapers to claim Usaeil long ago."

"What? What did she do?" Keltan asked, the pit in his stomach growing.

"She was damn smart," Cael said.

Rordan moved to stand on the other side of Erith. "She knew the Dragon Kings would be focused on Ulrik and his uncle, Mikkel. That bought her the time she needed."

Keltan shook his head. "I doona understand. As much as it makes me gag to even think about Con and Usaeil as lovers for a brief time. He knew her every movement."

"That's what she led him to believe," Erith said. "But she had her own agenda. We've all underestimated her. And I fear she might very well win this war."

Keltan felt the anger rise up in him, but he tamped it down. "No' when so many stand against her. The Kings are with Rhi, and Balladyn with his Dark Army will be, as well."

"The King of the Dark would follow Rhi anywhere," Cael said. "Balladyn is good for the Dark."

Keltan let out a bark of laughter. "Good? You're telling me that he's actually good for the Dark?"

Death's lavender eyes turned icy as she narrowed them on him. "Every being on every realm has the opportunity to be either good or bad. Which is right, which is wrong? Who are you to make that decision?"

"I know evil should be destroyed," Keltan replied.

"And replaced with what, exactly?" Death retorted. "There is a balance. You know this, but it's convenient to blame evil for everything."

"Because it is to blame!" Keltan drew in a breath,

hating his outburst of anger. But he couldn't help how he felt. The fact that the Reapers were standing there telling him that there had to be evil as well as good infuriated him.

Erith blinked, fat drops of water falling from her eyelashes. "You sound as rational as a Dark blaming the Light for their misfortunes."

"How can you not see that evil is bad?" Keltan demanded.

"I never said it was good. I said there's a balance. You can't have one without the other. It's the way of the universe. Fighting against it is like hitting your head against a wall. You will never be rid of evil. Just as evil will never be rid of you."

Keltan didn't reply because he had nothing to say.

"As I was saying," Cael continued. "Balladyn is good for the Dark Fae because he focuses on them, not what power he might amass."

Erith then said, "However, Usaeil will go after Balladyn. He knows this, but he's ignoring it because he wants to help Rhi."

As much as Keltan hated to admit it, that bit of news changed his views on Balladyn greatly. "Will the Reapers join us in this war?"

"That isn't possible," Death replied.

Keltan should've known. "Then why did you come?"

"To warn you," Rordan said.

Death and Cael vanished in the next instant. Rordan remained. He let out a long breath as he looked at Keltan. "If I had any say, I'd be standing with you, fighting Usaeil. She's Fae, so in my opinion, she's the Reapers' problem."

"But you doona call the shots."

Rordan grinned. "But I don't call the shots. Good luck, Keltan."

With that, Keltan was alone once more. He ran a hand down his face to wipe away the water and then got back into his vehicle.

CHAPTER FOUR

"Keltan Dreagan," Bernadette said aloud as she typed the name into a search engine on her computer.

Just as she expected, nothing came up. She shouldn't be shocked by the outcome. Every person tied to Dreagan that she attempted to look up somehow had very little information—if any—available on the internet.

She swiveled in her chair and opened the file from the World Whisky Consortium a few years back. She ran her finger down the page, looking for the name of the individual who had been sent by Dreagan.

"Aha," she said with a smile. "Asher. No last name. Surprise, surprise."

She gave a shake of her head. "How are these people getting around without using surnames? I mean, they aren't Madonna or Usher."

"I thought I showed you enough."

Bernadette stilled at the sound of the Irish voice behind her. It had been weeks since she'd last encountered the Fae, and while she had opened Bernadette's eyes to many things, there was something about her that frightened Bernadette.

It wasn't as if Usaeil had done anything in particular or had said anything off, but Bernadette couldn't squelch the growing feeling inside of her.

She swallowed and turned her chair around to face the Fae. "Of course, you did, Usaeil."

"Then why are you still digging?"

"I thought that's what you wanted me to do."

Usaeil rose from the sofa clothed in an all-red ensemble, the jacket buttoned but left open enough to reveal no shirt beneath and providing an ample view of her cleavage. "I wanted you to tell the world about those at Dreagan."

"I did. I have," Bernadette hurried to say. "Tonight, even."

For some reason, Bernadette didn't tell the Fae that one of the men from Dreagan had been in attendance. She didn't understand why, but she instinctively knew she shouldn't impart that bit of information. At least, not yet.

Usaeil flicked her long, black hair over her shoulder and strode to Bernadette on four-inch red stilettos. "I like you. I knew you were the right one to show the truth to."

"Why me, though? Why not expose them yourself?"

"I have other matters to attend to. Do you think being Queen of the Fae is easy? I have millions of Fae to keep in line."

Bernadette nodded.

"Did you have to show your proof?" Usaeil asked.

"I mentioned it, but everyone got to talking about all the links I had to Dreagan, and they forgot about it."

Usaeil smiled. "Good. I'd like to hold off showing it for as long as you can. As soon as you do, someone from Dreagan will contact you. Remember what I said they'd say about me?"

"That you're a liar who can't be trusted."

"But you know the truth."

Bernadette smiled, though her mind was on Keltan. He hadn't seemed like a bad guy. He'd been gracious and kind when he could've been anything else. He hadn't threatened her or demanded that she stop saying things about Dreagan. He hadn't asked anything of her, actually. Even though that's exactly what Usaeil had said those from Dreagan would do.

In fact, the only one asking anything of her was the queen.

Usaeil leaned down and peered closely at Bernadette. "So, tell me why you're still digging into those at Dreagan?"

"I may know they're dragons, but I don't know anything about them. People like that I can link the women to them, but if I can show specifics about individuals at Dreagan, it will help to convince others. The quicker they believe, the quicker word spreads."

"You don't need individuals," Usaeil said as she straightened. "Anyone associated with Dreagan will be a target once the world focuses on them. That's all that matters."

Bernadette knew that wasn't true, but she was also keenly aware that trying to convince Usaeil of that would be suicide. She hadn't actually seen Usaeil hurt anyone, but the queen had magic, and that was enough for Bernadette.

The Fae had started out sweet and giving, practically bending over backwards to get Bernadette to believe. And once she had, once Usaeil had her utterly enthralled, the Fae had changed. She had become curt, talking down to Bernadette, and had even threatened her once.

If Bernadette weren't so immersed in Dreagan, she'd walk away and tell Usaeil to kiss her ass. No, actually, she wouldn't, because Bernadette wasn't entirely sure the Fae would let her live.

Usaeil turned and walked around the small cottage. Bernadette missed her roomy house, but it was something she'd had to sell in order to keep paying the bills. She hadn't needed such a big place anyway. What she had now sufficed. Though she still missed some of the furniture she'd had to sell.

"You need to have another lecture," Usaeil said as she faced her.

Bernadette raked a hand through her hair. "I intend to. It's already scheduled for next month."

"It'll be next week."

"I-I don't have the time to find a venue or get the word out."

Usaeil shrugged. "I'm sure you'll figure something out. Do it next week."

"You've never demanded such a thing before. Why now?"

"Because I'm a queen, and I'm telling you what to do."

Bernadette almost told Usaeil she wasn't *her* queen, but that likely wouldn't go over too well, so she kept her mouth shut. "I'll see what I can do."

"You'll do it."

The *or else* hung silently between them.

Bernadette wondered what she had gotten herself into. Then again, having the knowledge Usaeil had imparted to her was worth this small amount of discomfort.

Dragons and Fae on the same planet as humans. And for millions of years. How in the world had mortals been

so blind? They hadn't been, actually. One look at the my-
thology of various cultures proved that.

Fingers snapped in front of her face. Bernadette jerked
back and looked up into Usaeil's face, the Fae's silver
eyes narrowed in anger.

"I was talking," Usaeil said.

"Sorry. My mind wanders."

The Fae rolled her eyes. "That's not something you
should admit to anyone, let alone me. Your goal is to have
the world banging on the door of Dreagan Manor. It's
been nearly a year since I first showed you the truth. You
need to get moving."

"I didn't know there was a timetable for this."

"There is now."

Bernadette squeezed the bridge of her nose. "I've got a
friend who owes me a favor. She edits an online column.
I'll write up something and get it to her."

Usaeil raised a brow. "An online column? What is that
going to do?"

"She has over a million readers. Even if only a fraction
read my piece, it's more than was there tonight."

"Hmm. You might be onto something. See if you can
put something in for the next few days. And make sure to
mention your next lecture. You'll be showing your proof
then, so be prepared."

Bernadette nodded and forced a smile, suddenly very
uneasy about everything. Usaeil hadn't made the dragons
out to be scary. In fact, she hadn't shaded Bernadette's
view one way or the other. But somewhere along the way,
something had changed. And Bernadette had yet to figure
out what it was.

Could it be that Usaeil had used her all along?

No, that couldn't be the case. Usaeil was a Fae with
magic. She could do whatever she wanted.

Then why does she want you *to tell the world about Dreagan?*

Bernadette didn't have an answer for the voice in her head.

Usaeil cocked her head to the side as she studied Bernadette. "You're pretty."

"Um . . . thank you." The compliment hadn't just come out of the blue, Usaeil had said it as if she were just now realizing it.

The Fae tapped a finger against her chin. "Someone from Dreagan will come to talk to you. No doubt he'll be amazingly handsome and charming. Don't believe a word he says."

"I'm sure it won't be long before everyone at Dreagan realizes I know the truth. They'll want to talk to me. They'll want to ask how I know."

"Don't tell them anything," Usaeil ordered. "And never mention my name."

Bernadette jerked back as if slapped. "I wouldn't dare. But I don't see how talking to them will hurt. Maybe I can convince them to show themselves to the world."

"Right," Usaeil said sarcastically. "You have as much chance of that as Hell freezing over."

"As long as it happens, what does it matter who does it?"

"Because no one at Dreagan will do it."

Bernadette frowned. "You sound sure of that."

"I sound that way because I am. I know them. They will continue hiding."

"You said the dragons were beautiful, and they are." Well, they were once she'd gotten over her initial terror at seeing the size of them.

Usaeil's gaze narrowed once more. "What does that have to do with anything?"

"When you first told me about them, you made them out to be something I should accept, not fear. Now, I hear hatred in your voice."

"If you feared them, you would never have been interested in learning about them."

Ice went through Bernadette's body at the realization that she had been used. She didn't know why or even how, exactly, but she had.

Usaeil laughed, the sound cold and hollow. "As for hating the dragons, they're an obstacle that needs to be overcome."

Everything in Bernadette rebelled, but she held her tongue. She had seen Usaeil's magic. She knew how powerful the Fae queen was, and she didn't want to piss her off. But at the same time, she no longer wanted to be a part of whatever the Fae had planned.

Because it couldn't be good. Anyone who spoke like that and held such anger within her couldn't be up to anything noble.

"No questions?" Usaeil asked.

Bernadette felt the weight of the Fae's probing stare. She shook her head, twisting her lips. "I don't need to hear more. You're the one who showed me this new world. I'm helping you, and if you say you need this, then I'll do my best to help."

Usaeil's smile was slow as it filled her face. "I knew you were the right person."

"Why me, though? What was it that made you pick me?"

Usaeil shrugged one shoulder nonchalantly. "You had a look about you."

Naïveté, Bernadette wondered? All these years, she'd believed herself intelligent and worldly. She hadn't even been able to tell when someone used her.

She laughed and cracked her knuckles. "I better get to writing that article."

"Remember, don't trust anyone from Dreagan. They're going to lie to you. They'll say whatever they need to in order to get you to believe them."

The same thing you did. Bernadette grinned. "You don't need to worry. I won't fall for that."

"If that fails, they'll try and seduce you."

Bernadette laughed, thinking about Keltan. He hadn't done any such thing. "I'll be prepared, don't worry. But what if they try and kidnap me or something?"

"They're dragons with magic. Expect anything."

Bernadette stared at Usaeil for a long minute. "Isn't this when you tell me that you'll protect me?"

"Of course," the queen said, her entire demeanor and voice seeming offended that Bernadette would even mention otherwise.

"Is there some magic you can do?" Not that Bernadette actually thought the Fae would do it, but it would look weird if she didn't ask.

Usaeil grinned. "I already have."

"Thank you. I knew I could count on you."

The queen blew out a breath. "Well, I must get back."

"To a movie set?"

"There's something else I'm occupied with at the moment. I won't be making any movies for a while. I'll drop by soon."

Bernadette wanted to sigh the moment Usaeil was gone, but she didn't. Instead, she faced her computer to begin writing the column. It would be just her luck if Usaeil hung around for a few minutes, invisible, to spy on her.

An hour later, when Bernadette felt it was safe, she

looked up the address to Dreagan. Then she packed an overnight bag and her laptop and got into her car. It was more than a three-hour drive to Dreagan, but she wasn't going to wait until dawn.

CHAPTER FIVE

Keltan stuffed the remainder of the roast beef sandwich into his mouth and looked out the kitchen window into the night. He'd just gotten off patrol, but his mind was working overtime since his jaunt to Glasgow.

"Still upset, huh?" Ulrik asked as he walked into the kitchen.

Keltan glanced at him, noting the lines of strain on the King's face that hadn't been there a week ago. Con's absence affected everyone, but since Ulrik had stepped in to lead while Con was gone, he likely felt more of the pressure than most. But Ulrik would never complain. He would carry on.

Because that's what Con always did.

"Aye."

Ulrik raked a hand through his long, black hair before he put the kettle on to heat water. "About which part? Dr. Davies or the Reapers?"

"Both," Keltan replied and faced the King of Silvers. "Are you no'?"

"Oh, I am. There's nothing that can be done about

the Reapers. We can no' force anyone to join our war. Frankly, I'm pleased with who we have."

Keltan shrugged, his lips twisting in doubt. "We willna know for sure until we're on the battlefield."

"Good point. However, as far as Bernadette Davies is concerned, we can no' do anything. If we threaten her, she'll use that against us."

"You're no' seriously suggesting we do nothing?" Keltan asked in disbelief.

Ulrik sighed loudly. "That's the only move we have. She's going to put us in a spotlight. I think sooner rather than later, and we need to be prepared for that."

"We'll be in the middle of a damn war, most likely."

"No doubt, we will. Regardless, we can no' give Dr. Davies or the world anything that will make them take a closer look. I've already spoken to both Henry and Esther to see what they can find out from MI5."

The brother and sister had exemplary careers in the domestic counter-intelligence and security agency. Esther was now mated to Nikolai, King of Ivories, and Henry was immersed in locating Usaeil. Yet the siblings were also part of an ancient line of Druids who kept other Druids in line. Esther was the TruthSeeker, and Henry the JusticeBringer.

Keltan's thoughts were pulled from the brother and sister as the kettle started to scream. He watched Ulrik lift it from the burner and pour the steaming liquid into two mugs before adding the teabags. "Did either of them learn anything?"

Ulrik shook his head as he set aside the kettle, his gold eyes locking on Keltan's. "Nothing as of yet, but both will keep checking. If Bernadette continues having successful lectures, then it willna be long before the press, as well as the government, takes a look at us."

"This is when we should've had friends in the government."

"Con thought it was better no' to have others know our secret."

Keltan had to agree. "They might help us for a little while, but sooner or later, they'd attempt to blackmail us."

"That's what the mortals do. Well, no' all of them, but more often than no', that's the case."

"We can no' have our attention divided. We need to be focused on Usaeil and taking her down so we can find Con."

Ulrik added some sugar to his tea and handed the other mug to Keltan. "That's the reason Con put off going after Usaeil with Rhi in the first place. He wanted everyone focused on me and my uncle."

"On Mikkel, no' you."

Ulrik didn't reply. Even after finding love with Eilish, a powerful Druid, and returning to Dreagan, it was apparent Ulrik still felt as if he had things to make up for.

Each Dragon King had spoken with Ulrik separately, hashing out issues and bonding once more. But the one most pleased with Ulrik's return was Con. They had been closer than brothers. Now, Constantine was gone.

"I've been trying to think what Con would do if he were here," Ulrik said after he'd finished stirring his tea.

Keltan reached for the honey and poured it into his cup. "What have you come up with?"

"A fat lot of shite."

They looked at each other and shared a laugh.

Ulrik sobered first. His lips flattened, and he shook his head. "It's going to take all of us in the war with Usaeil. I thought that before. Now, I know it for certain."

"We've never left Dreagan without a Dragon King here."

"I know. If it's decided a few Kings should remain to protect Dreagan and whatever happens from Dr. Davies, we'll have to draw straws or something to see who stays."

Ryder walked in then and said, "Kings should definitely remain, no matter what. Four at the most."

Keltan watched as the King of Grays and the guru of all things electrical fixed himself a mug of tea. "Why four?"

Ulrik twisted his lips as he tilted his head to the side for a moment. "The magic of Dreagan will do a lot. Then there are the spells and wards that have been added over the years. Three could hold Dreagan, but four would be better."

"I'll remain," Ryder said. "I've spent too much time protecting Dreagan. And then there's Kinsey."

Keltan nodded at the mention of Ryder's mate. It wasn't surprising that he wanted to stay behind to protect her. In fact, Keltan assumed the other mated Kings would feel the same.

"Eilish has already told me she's fighting against Usaeil," Ulrik stated.

While he and Eilish hadn't officially performed the mating ceremony yet, everyone considered them mated. Except that without the ritual and the dragon eye tattoo that came with it, Eilish was still mortal. She could be killed.

One look at Ulrik confirmed that he was thinking the same thing.

It was just one of many reasons Keltan was glad that he hadn't fallen in love. It might be a glorious thing—at least that's what he'd been told by those who had done it—but it freed him from the worry that came when the Kings were attacked.

"You willna stop Eilish," Keltan said.

Ryder snorted. "Kinsey said she wanted to fight. Bloody hell. All the mates do."

"Can you blame them?" Ulrik asked. "Look at what Usaeil has done."

"More to Con and Rhi than any others," Keltan pointed out.

At the mention of the Light Fae, Ryder's gaze lowered to the floor while Ulrik focused on his tea.

Keltan looked between the two. "What's going on?"

"Rhi's pushing for us to go after Usaeil now," Ulrik said.

Keltan shrugged. "Why no'? Why give Usaeil more time? Let's go at Usaeil before we have the mortals beating down our door."

Ryder's hazel gaze turned to Ulrik. "Keltan has a point."

"I'm no' ruling it out. We need to finalize our plans first," Ulrik replied.

"You two go do that," Ryder said. "I'm going back to do more digging on Bernadette Davies."

That got Keltan's attention. "I thought you already did a deep dive on her."

"I did, but there's something that doesna make sense."

Ulrik quirked a black brow. "And that is?"

"She has never been involved in cryptozoology before. Why now?"

Keltan sipped his tea. "You mean, what did she see?"

"Or who did she meet?" Ulrik added.

Ryder nodded to both of them. "Exactly. It could be one or the other, but I think if I can figure out what happened, we might be able to flip it to our advantage. We can turn things around to make her sound as if she's daft."

"Hmm," Ulrik said with a nod. "That would certainly get the attention off us and onto her."

Keltan shifted feet, uncomfortable with the direction this was headed. "I spoke with her. She's no' deranged. She's intelligent. And more importantly, she has proof. Of that, I'm sure."

"Then we need to get it from her. I'll send Dorian in to get it. If she doesna have it, then she has nothing to support her claims," Ulrik said.

Keltan briefly looked away and cleared his throat. "I doona want this attention on us, but do we have to harm her?"

"We're no' harming her," Ryder said, a frown marring his brow. "We're marring her reputation. There's a difference."

"I know," Keltan said.

Ulrik peered closely at him. "You spoke with her. You're the one who returned telling us that we should be concerned. Now you want to back off?"

"I just wish there was another way. Despite what Bernadette is doing, she seemed nice," Keltan explained.

Ryder nodded, sadness clouding his face. "Sometimes, our options are limited. I doona want to destroy a person professionally or otherwise, but she came after us."

"Why, though?" Keltan asked.

Ulrik jerked back, frowning. "It's obvious."

"Is it? No' to me." Keltan ran a hand down his face. "I think Ryder's right. We need to know what she saw or who she spoke with."

"We doona have time for that," Ulrik stated.

Ryder quickly said, "I'll be quick. Give me a few hours. If by dawn I've no' found anything, then we can send Dorian to steal whatever proof she has."

Keltan didn't point out that they needed to know what the proof was. No doubt Ryder would find that out, as well. Give Ryder a computer, and he could hack into anything in seconds. He was that good. And that didn't even take into consideration the gadgets he created.

Ulrik released a sigh. "Fine. Dawn it is."

When the King of Silvers' eyes landed on him, Keltan nodded. "I'm in agreement. Ryder has until dawn. No matter what he discovers, I'll agree and help out with whatever is decided."

"Then I better get to work," Ryder said as he walked out, cup of tea in hand.

Keltan hurried after him. "I'll come with you. An extra set of eyes could help."

There was also the fact that Keltan wanted to see for himself what all Ryder and Kinsey could pull up on Bernadette Davies. He didn't want to like her. In fact, he wanted to hate her. But he couldn't.

She had known he was a dragon, yet she hadn't seemed frightened of him. Guarded and hesitant, but not scared. Keltan had to give her props for that.

He sat in an empty chair in the computer room and faced rows and rows of monitors. Kinsey sat at one end, the few screens she was focused on changing as she typed. Ryder sank into his chair and set his hands over the glass table.

A holographic keyboard appeared that was attuned to his body. Ryder's hands hovered over the keys as his gaze swept from side to side, taking in what the monitors showed him. As soon as he saw something on one screen, he'd hit a few keys and tightened the search.

Keltan saw dozens of pictures of Bernadette pop up, from the time she was a little girl, all the way through to the present day. She hadn't changed much. The smile she wore was always wide, always genuine. As was the light that shone in her eyes.

She wasn't evil. Of that, he was certain. But he didn't

know her motives yet. Well, other than wanting to draw attention to Dreagan. She'd mentioned dragons, but she hadn't said anything about Dragon Kings.

Could it be that she didn't know all of it? That was certainly a possibility. But she knew enough to be dangerous. And she'd done her homework on several of the mates. If she dug any deeper, things could get even hairier.

Thirty minutes later, Ryder leaned back in his chair and laced his hands behind his head.

Kinsey looked over at him and grinned. "You found something."

Ryder smiled at her then looked at Keltan. "I found something."

CHAPTER SIX

The closer she got to Dreagan, the more anxious Bernadette became. Was she doing the right thing? God, she really hoped so.

There was a very good possibility that Usaeil had told her the truth, and those at Dreagan couldn't be trusted. In fact, she could go missing, and no one would know what had happened to her. The authorities might look into those at Dreagan, but with the wealth and power the corporation had, nothing would help her.

After all, they *were* dragons.

She slammed on the brakes, skidding on the road as her car came to a jarring halt.

"What am I doing?" she asked herself aloud.

Bernadette was shaking so badly that she pulled off to the shoulder and turned her hazard lights on. Then she sat there and tried to get herself under control. She was less than forty minutes from Dreagan, but it was the middle of the night. It wasn't like she could go to the door and demand to speak to Keltan now. They really would think she was a lunatic.

She hadn't thought about why she felt the need to go to Dreagan and speak to them herself.

"Liar," she mumbled and blew out a long breath.

She'd driven over three hours because of the way Usaeil had acted, along with the things the queen had said. Something had changed the Fae queen, and it bothered Bernadette greatly. Or maybe Usaeil had always been like that, and Bernadette just now saw it.

Either way, the more she thought about it, the more it felt as if she were some pawn in a game that she had no idea was being played. And that didn't sit well with her at all.

It was time she found out the truth from the dragons. If they didn't eat her. The thought made her giggle, she was so exhausted.

Bernadette grabbed her phone and located the nearest rest station, which happened to be just a few miles away. She pulled back onto the road and drove to it before she turned off the ignition and leaned her seat back to get a few hours of sleep.

Except as soon as she closed her eyes, Keltan's face flashed in her mind. It was soon replaced by Usaeil's angry expression. Bernadette cleared her thoughts and turned on some music. It wasn't long before she drifted off.

The sound of a horn startled her awake. It felt as if she'd just closed her eyes, but a look at her phone told her she'd slept for nearly five hours. She'd hoped that the rest would revive her. Instead, she felt worse than before.

"Isn't that just wonderful?" she muttered.

She twisted and reached into the backseat for her toothbrush and toothpaste. She brushed her teeth, rinsing with the bottle of water she'd had for the drive before opening the door and spitting.

Then she pulled down her visor to check her image in the mirror. She winced when she saw the dark circles under her eyes. Thankfully, she had concealer that could help with that. For the next ten minutes, Bernadette put on a little makeup. And for once, her mascara went on beautifully.

"That's irony for you." She laughed at herself, shaking her head. "There might seriously be something wrong with me, seeing as I have no qualms about talking—and answering—myself."

She packed everything back into her overnight bag and then drove to the nearest café to get some tea and breakfast as well as to use the toilet.

With her bladder empty, her belly full, and fortified with tea, she headed toward Dreagan. She marveled at the beautiful scenery. She'd been near here before, but she didn't remember it being so stunning. Part of her couldn't wait for the drive home so she could see everything that she'd missed in the dark.

All too quickly, she saw signs directing her toward the distillery. As she drove through the village, she looked at the people and saw them happy, and the place well-kept. No doubt the tourism from the distillery helped, but if the dragons were dangerous, then surely that would show in the people. Wouldn't it?

With her heart thumping once more, she took the turn-off toward Dreagan, driving down a winding road with soaring trees on either side of her.

When she came out the other side, the white buildings and red roofs of the distillery met her. She had to tear her gaze from them to park. Once the engine was off, she simply looked around her, taking it all in.

Bernadette had looked up Dreagan online, of course, but those searches did nothing to prepare her for what she beheld. She knew that Dreagan was made up of several thousand acres. As the world's bestselling Scotch, she hadn't expected the place to feel so . . . cozy.

The one thing no picture had shown her was Dreagan Manor. While those at Dreagan did host a few parties, only their closest personal friends were ever invited to the manor. And finding any of those people was as difficult as finding the Ark of the Covenant.

It was early in the morning, but people were already lined up for tours and tastings. This was Bernadette's last chance. She could turn around and drive away. No one would ever know she was there. No one had to know.

But she would always wonder about the truth. It had been niggling at the back of her mind for months, but she'd been focused on other items, which made it easy to ignore. Then, last night, Usaeil had brought it to the forefront—unintentionally, of course. Yet now that it was there, Bernadette couldn't make it go away.

There was only one way to find out what would happen. She grabbed her purse and opened her door. She stepped out before she changed her mind and headed toward the gift shop.

Bernadette walked in and found herself surrounded by dragons. The double-dragon logo of Dreagan was on everything. And the sheer number of bottles of Scotch lining the walls was wondrous to behold.

"Good morning."

Bernadette turned at the friendly voice and found herself staring into dark brown eyes. The woman was pretty, her smile welcoming. "Good morning."

"Are you here to take a tour?" the woman asked.

Bernadette heard the accent. "You're American?"

The woman chuckled, her long, brunette hair moving with her. "Guilty. I've been here a few years now, and I keep thinking I'll pick up the Scots accent, but my husband thinks I'll be waiting awhile."

"Oh, so you married a Scotsman and moved here?"

"Actually, I met him after I came for a visit. We married soon after. I love this country, though."

Bernadette kept the smile in place, but it was difficult. "You don't, by chance, happen to be married to one of the owners of Dreagan, do you?"

The woman's smile faltered just a little. "If I was, would I be working here?"

That was a good question, but Bernadette couldn't help but notice that the woman hadn't actually answered.

The American cleared her throat. "I apologize. I don't think I heard you. Are you taking a tour?"

"No," Bernadette said. "I was just driving through. I'm not much of a whisky drinker. I thought I'd stop and give it a look over."

"I'll be here if you change your mind." The woman turned to the next visitor as the bell over the door chimed when it was opened.

Bernadette slowly moved around the store. She tried looking for cameras, but as far as she could tell, there were none in the shop. Then again, why would there be? Dreagan was run by dragons with magic. They didn't need mortal technology to keep thieves at bay.

That's when it hit her. Magic. She'd been interacting with a Fae—and not just any Fae, but a queen—for almost a year now. Not once had she thought twice about the fact that Usaeil could've probably killed her with a snap of her fingers. Because Bernadette had been too intent on learning about dragons.

She felt like such a fool. She'd been so blinded by what Usaeil had shown her that she hadn't realized the danger that surrounded her. Danger that had grown every day.

To top it off, Bernadette had let those at Dreagan know of her intentions after the lecture the other night. What had she said or done that'd put her on their radar enough for them to send someone down to hear what she had to say?

And then she'd thought it was a good idea to drive to Dreagan to try and talk to immortal dragons. That would be like telling a lamb it was safe to be in the same pen as a tiger.

Bernadette turned on her heel and strode from the shop. She dug into her purse with shaking hands, searching for her keys. She ran into a car and dropped them. After she'd retrieved them, she straightened and lifted her head—only to lock eyes with none other than Keltan.

He leaned against the side of her vehicle with his arms crossed. He didn't smile, just watched her.

"So much for me getting away," she whispered.

And though she was a good twenty feet from him, she could have sworn that she saw a ghost of a smile.

"I didna expect to find you here," he said.

She shrugged and jangled her keys, thankful that there were others in the parking lot. "I felt like a drive."

"That's a long drive. If you were curious, all you had to do was ask. I would've shown you around myself."

She snorted. "Right."

"I'm no' lying."

Bernadette eyed him. "If you say so."

He pushed off the car and walked to her. When he was a few feet away, he halted. "Ask me. If you dare," he said after a pause.

She raised her chin. "You assume I want to see."

"Oh, I *know* you do. You think you know Dreagan, but you know nothing. I'm offering to give you what you want. But . . . you have to ask."

Damn him. He knew how much she wanted to see, and he was giving her the option. But what would it cost her? She didn't bother to ask because it wouldn't matter what he said. She was willing to pay any cost to get her answers.

"Will you show me?"

He smiled and nodded. "It would be my pleasure."

"Will I get to leave whenever I want?"

His grin faded. "No one at Dreagan will ever harm you. You have my word."

There were millions of reasons she shouldn't believe him, but she found that she did. "I didn't mean any offense."

"I would've thought you a fool no' to ask. Follow me."

Bernadette took one last look at her car. She kept her keys in her hand as she turned and followed Keltan back into the gift shop. The brunette she'd spoken with before looked from Keltan to her but didn't say a word.

Keltan took Bernadette behind the registers and through a doorway to another, private part of the shop. They walked down a corridor a ways before he opened a door and waited for her to walk through.

Bernadette found herself outside once more. She determined that they were behind the gift shop. When she looked back at Keltan, he was headed toward some hedges that soared up to the sky. She hurried to catch up with him.

Once they passed through the thick hedgerow, she gasped and came to a stop. She took in the mountains and glens and the sheep and cattle that dotted the landscape. The clouds passed over the sun, casting huge shadows on the mountains. And while she had no magic, she sensed that it was here, on this land.

"It is a sight, is it no'?" Keltan asked from beside her.

"You get to wake up every day and see this."

He drew in a breath. "Aye. But this is only a small part of Dreagan."

She could look at the view all day, but she knew he wanted to show her more. Bernadette turned, her mouth falling open. Dreagan Manor stood before her, a mountain rising up directly behind it.

Suddenly, she grew nervous. She glanced at Keltan. "Why are you showing me this?"

"Normally, I wouldna. But seeing as you already know so much, we thought it would be wise to show you who we really are."

"In order to change my mind about continuing my lectures?" she asked, even though that was her very reason for being here. Though she hadn't realized it when she drove from Glasgow.

All she knew was that she wanted to talk to Keltan and discover the truth.

He shrugged and clasped his hands behind his back. "That is for you to decide."

Keltan walked toward the manor without looking back at her. Bernadette hesitated for a few seconds before following him. She might be stepping into an abyss that she couldn't get out of, but something had pushed her to Dreagan. It was time she found out what that was.

CHAPTER SEVEN

Surprise didn't even begin to describe what Keltan felt when Ryder informed him that none other than Bernadette Davies was at the distillery.

He hadn't gone to the shop to intercept her. Instead, he'd waited at her car because he'd had a feeling she wouldn't stay long. He'd been right. Because five minutes later, she walked from the shop.

The astonishment on her face when she saw him was well worth his plan. Even now she was hesitant, uncertain of where he was taking her. And yet, she followed him. That shocked him a little.

He reached the front door of the manor and paused for a heartbeat as he listened for the sound of Bernadette behind him. As soon as he heard her, he hid his smile and opened the door. He stepped aside and waited for her to enter.

Keltan kept his eyes on her face, watching as her gaze darted from one object to another. It wasn't hard to miss the many dragons depicted throughout. And she saw nearly all of them.

He shut the door behind them and walked with her into

the wide foyer. Her mouth slightly opened as her head tipped back to look at the ceiling. He didn't say anything, preferring to just let her take it in until she wanted to talk.

Another five minutes passed before she stopped and turned toward him. "Why did you bring me here?"

"You think you know us. When, in fact, you know verra little."

"But I looked into Dreagan. I know that you don't bring strangers here."

He shrugged. "We made an exception for you."

Bernadette licked her lips. "I see."

"Are you scared?"

"I'd be a fool not to be."

Keltan shook his head. "If we wanted to hurt you, we could've done it at any time. No one is going to harm you. I told you that at the restaurant."

"That was before I showed up here."

He crossed his arms over his chest. "Why did you come?"

Her gaze briefly darted to the side. "I could come up with some plausible lie, but the truth is that I wasn't sure what made me come. I only knew I had to."

"You said, '*wasn't sure.*' Does that mean you know now?" he pressed.

She nodded slowly. "I don't regret discovering what I know about you. I don't feel bad about the things I uncovered about Dreagan over the last few months."

"Nor do you regret telling others about us."

Bernadette didn't answer. Instead, she said, "But I realized last night that there are two sides to every story. I've been told one side. And I don't know how much truth there is to it."

"And you came here thinking we would tell you the truth?" he asked, his brow quirked.

She blew out a breath and twisted her hands. "I know you must think I'm an idiot. I've come to the very people I'm investigating and telling others about. Who in their right mind does that?"

"Someone who wants answers."

Her jade eyes met his. "But how do I know if what you tell me is the truth?"

"You're just going to have to trust me."

Her smile was fleeting, and she turned her head away. "Of course.

"Would you like something to drink? Tea, perhaps?"

She shook her head. "No, thank you. I don't think it's wise to put anything in my stomach at this point."

If she were nervous enough that she was nauseous, she hid it well. She didn't fidget or do any of the other things people often did when uneasy.

"Perhaps you'd like to sit. Follow me," Keltan said.

He couldn't remember a time when he'd been so aware of a woman beside him. He noted every movement of Bernadette's body, every glance of her eyes. As she fell in step beside him, he pointed out different rooms as they walked past. She nodded as he spoke, and while he felt her curiosity and need to look into each room, she didn't ask anything.

Keltan took her to the library. The room was spacious and yet could be closed off to others. He pulled the doors shut once they were inside, closing them off. And the idea of them being alone was something he found he liked.

A lot.

"Please, have a seat," he said, indicating the sofa and chairs set before the fireplace. She wasn't a woman he should be interested in. She was someone who had the ability to cause havoc, and he needed to remember that.

"There are quite a few books here," she said with a little laugh before sitting against the arm of the sofa.

He grinned. "That there are. And before you ask, nay, I've no' read even half of them. I'm sure I'll get to all of them eventually."

Her eyes widened.

Keltan laughed out loud as he took the chair nearest her. He knew he should probably put some more distance between them, but he couldn't seem to make his body listen. "What was that for?"

"You said that because you're immortal."

He lifted one shoulder. "And if I am?"

"How old are you?"

Keltan sighed loudly. "I doona think we should begin with that question."

"Why?" she pressed.

"Because you willna accept the answer."

She gave him a flat look. "I accept that you and the others here are dragons. I accept that you have magic and that you're immortal."

"Accepting that and hearing how old I am are two verra different things."

"Try me," she dared him.

Keltan narrowed his eyes. He'd never been one to pass up a challenge. "I'm millions of years old. So old, that I stopped keeping track some time ago."

"Millions?" she asked in a whisper, her face losing some of its color.

"My exact age doesna matter. I've seen empires rise and fall. I've seen so many wars that I can no' believe you mortals are still alive. I've seen the human race come from no' knowing how to make a weapon to hunt with, to your kind creating nuclear weapons. I have, in fact, seen it all."

Bernadette sat there for several minutes in silence before she murmured, "Bloody hell."

"I told you that you were no' prepared for the truth."

She ignored his statement. "Are you the oldest?"

He shook his head. "Nay. Nor am I the youngest."

"I see. Tell me more. Please."

"You realize that if you tell anyone how old we are, no one will believe you."

"Who said I would tell anyone?"

It was Keltan's turn to give her a flat look. "After the lecture you just gave, you really want me to believe that?"

"Look, I don't know what I'm doing anymore. At first, after I came to realize that dragons were real, I wanted to find out everything I could about you. I didn't understand why everyone at Dreagan hid. The more I dug, the more questions came up. Women disappearing and relocating, changing their jobs and such. I began to wonder if nefarious things were going on here. Last night . . . well, let's just say I had an eye-opening experience. I wish I would've had it months ago. But if I hadn't spoken with you after the lecture, I'm not sure I'd be here."

Now that was interesting to hear. Keltan had never expected that his need to talk to her last night would bring her to him now. "What did I say that changed your mind?"

"Nothing in particular. You didn't threaten me with legal action or any harm. You didn't even ask me to stop. I've been wondering ever since why you didn't do those things. Then I remembered you had magic. You could stop me in other ways. Which, I assume, was your intention."

Keltan sat forward, placing his forearms on his knees and interlocking his fingers. "Dr. Davies," he began.

"Bernadette, please," she said.

He grinned. "Bernadette."

She smiled, her gaze dropping to her lap for a heartbeat.

Keltan had to remind himself who she was and why she was there. He inwardly shook himself before he continued. "We've remained hidden for dozens of millennia for a reason. And we've gone to great lengths to make sure things remain the same. You put a spotlight on Dreagan, and we can no' allow that to happen. We doona harm mortals. Nor do we want to discredit you professionally. We've discussed a few options."

Bernadette set her purse down and rubbed her hands together. "I should've seen that coming."

"Any company would do the same."

She nodded slowly. "I suppose I seem like a fool to you."

"I didna say that."

"You don't have to. I can see it in your eyes."

Keltan frowned at her. "I apologize if it appears that I've judged you. That isna my intent. I'm merely doing what I must to protect my home."

"You've not asked me how much I know."

He shrugged, his lips twisting as he sat back in the chair. "I doona need to. If you knew everything, you would've stated that at your lecture. You know enough to make life difficult for us."

"I'm not asking you to tell me what it is, but how much knowledge am I missing about you?"

"Quite a bit."

She blew out a breath and looked at the ceiling.

Keltan could see her mind working. He wondered how long she would go before she gave in and told him who had shared the Kings' secret with her. "What is it?" he pressed.

Her gaze returned to him. "You haven't asked how I found out about you."

"Nay, I have no'."

"Why not?"

"Would you tell me?" he countered.

She drew in a deep breath as a frown formed on her brow. "It's not that I don't want to. It's that I'm not sure what will happen to me if I do."

Keltan closed his eyes for just a heartbeat. Damn. He'd hoped that Ryder had been wrong, but it seemed that the computer guru had struck gold again. The problem was, he had no idea how Usaeil was interacting with Bernadette. Was it as a Fae? Or as the movie star that the world believed her to be? Or was it something else entirely?

Usaeil could've changed her appearance, so he couldn't even describe her. Fuck! And if Bernadette wouldn't tell him, then he had no way of arguing his side.

"I'm surprised you haven't offered me protection."

Her words jarred him out of his thoughts. He gave her an apologetic smile. "If you believe you need it then, of course, we will."

"Even for someone like me?" she asked.

"It's what we do."

Surprise flickered in her jade depths.

Keltan chuckled. "You doona believe me."

"I . . . I'm trying to sort through everything."

"You were brave enough to come here, and you had the courage to walk into the manor. Based on what I know of you, I think once you have the facts, you can figure things out."

"Facts," she said and glanced at her hands. "I believed what I was shown was fact. I also believed what I was told."

"In case you have no' already guessed, we have enemies."

She raised a brow. "Hard to have enemies if people don't know who you are."

Keltan held her gaze without saying anything.

"You don't trust me," she said and pressed her lips together. "Not that I blame you."

"It has nothing to do with me trusting you."

She jerked back as if struck. "You don't think I trust you?"

He lifted one shoulder in a shrug. "That's exactly it."

Bernadette gave a small shake of her head and got to her feet. She walked around to the back of the sofa and paced from one side of the room to the other. Keltan watched her struggle with what to tell him. He could make it easy on her and tell her that it was a Fae who had given her the information on them, but he wanted Bernadette to tell him the truth.

Because once she did that, then she would be open to learning the real facts. Something must have happened between her and Usaeil that'd sent Bernadette to Dreagan. He should thank the queen for that.

Then a horrible thought filled Keltan. What if Usaeil had sent Bernadette to them for exactly this reason?

The moment Bernadette walked into the shop, Ryder had turned off her phone and made sure that she had no other recording devices. But that didn't mean Usaeil didn't have a hand in Bernadette showing up at Dreagan.

Not that Keltan was worried. Guy was nearby to wipe her memories before she left. No matter what happened, Bernadette wouldn't be shining the spotlight on Dreagan any more after today.

CHAPTER EIGHT

She had to calm down, or she was going to get sick. And Bernadette really didn't want to ruin the rug she now paced on.

Her blood felt like ice in her veins. Her hands were sweating. Her stomach roiled violently, alternating between pain and nausea. And her mind was jumbled so tightly that she wasn't sure she would ever sort anything out again.

Her life had been sedate and boring—and she'd liked it. She enjoyed waking up at the same time every day, having a cup of tea and toast as she read the news on her mobile before getting ready for the day. She'd loved going into work and being good at her job, having friends, and even eating at the same places for lunch every week. She liked stable and constant. There hadn't been any surprises.

But all of that had changed one fateful, rainy night. With one image, she'd kissed her peaceful life good-bye without a second's hesitation. She'd given up her home, her belongings, friends, and even her career. For what? To chase something *she* knew to be real, but the rest of the world didn't?

She stopped and leaned her hands on the back of the sofa. The leather was cool to the touch. She drew in a breath and slowly released it in an effort to calm herself, but it didn't work. Finally, she lifted her gaze to Keltan, who watched her patiently.

The recent fad with men sporting beards hadn't been her favorite. In fact, she'd always preferred men to be clean-shaven, but she quite liked the beard on Keltan. It accentuated his strong jaw and his wide lips.

Bernadette hastily looked away. She didn't know why she kept looking at his mouth. It wasn't as if he were attracted to her or anything.

She cleared her throat and dropped her chin to her chest. "I was once a respected anthropologist. I had a great career."

"I know. I looked into you."

Her head snapped up. His gaze caught and held hers. "I gave it all up the night I saw one of you."

"In Glasgow?"

"Yes," she said with a nod.

Keltan swallowed, regret tightening his face. "You didna see one of us."

"I know what I saw. It was a dragon."

"Remember when I told you we've gone to great lengths to hide ourselves? Why would we be somewhere a mortal could see us?"

She opened her mouth to reply, but she realized that she had no answer. Finally, she shrugged. "I don't know."

"Because it wasna us. You were tricked."

Bernadette's mind rebelled at the thought. She barked with laughter and straightened, folding her arms across her chest defensively. "I'm not a fool. I know what I saw."

"Magic can appear real, but I give you my word that it wasna one of us."

"Then there are other dragons you don't know about."

Keltan shook his head before she finished talking, which only infuriated her. Bernadette's nerves were quickly switching to anger, and she didn't like that any better.

"Stop," she said and held up her hands. "Just stop."

"You wanted the truth. I'm giving it to you."

Her arms dropped helplessly to her sides. "Are you? For all I know, you're lying."

"What color was the dragon?" he asked.

She was taken aback by his question. Of all the things she'd thought he might ask, that hadn't been one of them. "Um . . . gold."

Keltan chuckled softly, and she could've sworn that he said "bitch" beneath his breath. "And the date?"

"Eleven months ago."

"There is only one gold dragon. Constantine. And Con wasna in Glasgow eleven months ago."

Bernadette hated that she immediately became defensive again. "You can't keep up with everyone all the time. And it was nearly a year ago. You can't tell me that Constantine wasn't in Glasgow."

"I can. And the date was actually the fourth of June."

Her mouth fell open. "So, you were there. Why did you lie?"

Keltan sighed loudly and shook his head. "You're no' listening to me. I know the date because we searched the CCTV feed and found you trying to get a cab that rainy night. A woman fell, and you went to help her. The two of you struck up a conversation, and then both of you went into a nearby bar to have a couple of drinks."

The apprehension was back. Bernadette couldn't quite

catch her breath—or look away from his amber gaze. She wanted to grab her purse and leave, but she couldn't. She wouldn't. She was there and getting the answers she needed.

She swallowed hard and asked, "How do you know all of that?"

"We have magic, remember? We can do a lot."

She really would have to remember that she wasn't talking to a human. She was chatting with a dragon who looked human.

Keltan hadn't risen from the chair. He remained calm and spoke to her softly, which kept her from running from the room. She nearly laughed at herself. She might try to run, but she wasn't getting away from the dragons. She'd accepted that the moment she followed Keltan from her car.

That's not why she was scared. She was frightened because, in the back of her mind, she knew there was a good chance Usaeil had fed her a few grains of truth and a lot of lies.

If that was the case, she'd given up her entire life. For what? Knowledge that she couldn't do anything with?

Bernadette grabbed the back of the sofa again to keep herself standing. Acknowledging the truth to herself had released a flood of adrenaline that caused her to be nauseous once more.

She closed her eyes. "She was the one who offered to buy me a drink since I helped her. I'm not much of a drinker, but she was nice, so I went. Before I knew it, two hours had passed. She felt like an old friend."

"She did that on purpose."

Bernadette's eyes snapped open as she looked at Keltan. "You know her?"

"She made sure we couldna see her face on any of the

CCTV screens, but aye, we know her. Who did she tell you she was?"

"She said her name was Usaeil."

Keltan harrumphed. "I'm surprised she didna lie."

"She said she was Queen of the Fae."

He shook his head. "That's what she's aiming for. She's a queen all right, but she's Queen of the Light Fae. How did she show you a dragon?"

"I don't remember how the talk turned, but the next thing I knew, she was telling me that she's a Fae. She showed me some magic. I was"—Bernadette paused and shook her head—"I was blown away with what she showed me. Then she said that there were other magical beings on the planet. I asked her if she could show me. We left the pub and got a cab to a field on the outskirts of Glasgow. We waited for another hour before the dragon appeared."

"What did the dragon do?" Keltan asked.

Bernadette shrugged as she pulled up her memories from that night. "He flew down from the sky and landed in the field. He was there for only a short time. It appeared as if he were looking for something. Then he flew off again."

"That's when your fascination with dragons began?"

She rolled her eyes. "You can't see a mythological creature come to life and not become obsessed. I asked Usaeil a million questions. She told me all about Dreagan and how this is where the dragons live. She said that it was imperative the world know who you are."

"Did you no' stop to think that you had never seen a dragon yourself until that night? That no one had? That perhaps it was a little odd that she wanted you to expose us?"

"Now that you put it like that, yes." With every minute

that passed, Bernadette felt like an even bigger fool than before.

Keltan gave a small shake of his head. "It's no' your fault. Usaeil used you."

"Why?"

"She's had her sights on Con for a while. When he didna return the sentiment, she became unreasonable. Usaeil isna exactly stable, but then again, we've only recently discovered that little tidbit."

It was obvious that there was a mountain of information Bernadette didn't have. How was Usaeil able to get her to do everything that she'd done with just a few words? That's when it hit her. Usaeil must have used magic.

"Your kind has been hiding for thousands of years," she murmured. "And I just told a roomful of people things in the hopes that others would begin looking into you."

"Doona blame yourself. Usaeil wants our attention divided."

"She didn't ask me to look into the others involved with Dreagan. Faith and Rachel. Those were all me."

Keltan tilted his head to the side. "Why did you look into them?"

"I've spent every waking moment that I wasn't at work digging into anything and everything to do with Dreagan. It wasn't easy finding anyone who worked here, but what I did discover were women somehow associated with Dreagan that suddenly all but vanished."

"Each of those women is alive and happy," he told her. "I'll be happy to introduce you to them later."

She frowned and snorted. "Why are you being so forgiving and forthcoming?"

"I'm being polite. What happened to you wasna your fault. It was Usaeil. We're at war with her and, unfortunately, you were pulled into the middle of it."

"She told me I'd be visited by someone from Dreagan. She told me not to believe any of you."

Keltan shrugged. "I think you're smart enough to figure things out for yourself. If it's really you I'm talking to, and no' someone Usaeil has commanded with magic."

Bernadette was immediately offended. Then she realized that Keltan was right. "As far as I know, I'm me. I'll admit, I've done things over the past year that weren't even remotely me. Whether Usaeil was just a really smooth talker or she used magic, I had no idea I was being used."

"So, you believe me?"

Bernadette shrugged. "I'm still getting the facts, remember? I've told you what she showed me."

"When was the last time you spoke to Usaeil?"

"Last night. She was different. Intense and very focused on Dreagan."

Keltan rested his ankle on his knee and laced his fingers over his stomach. "The dragon she showed you wasna Con, and I know that because he's the last one of us who would ever do anything where a mortal could see him."

"All right. Maybe you're right about that. Will you tell me your story? I have this need to know the truth. It's like something is pushing at me, and I can't stop it."

He smiled and nodded. "I'll tell you the whole story."

"Really?" she asked, shocked that he would give in so quickly and easily.

"Aye, lass."

Bernadette smiled as she thought of her grandfather. He used to call her that all the time.

"You should probably get comfortable. It's a long story," Keltan said.

She walked around the couch and lowered herself onto the cushion. "Aren't you worried about Usaeil?"

"She can no' get through the barriers around Dreagan. Con made sure of that."

"He hates her that much, huh?"

Keltan shrugged one shoulder. "She left him no choice."

"Wait. Before you begin. You said, 'Light Fae.' Are there other kinds of Fae?"

"There are the Dark."

A shudder ran through her. "That sounds ominous."

"Stay away from anyone with red eyes. The Dark eat the souls of humans by having sex with them. All you'll feel is pleasure, but you'll be dying the entire time."

"There are worse ways to go, I suppose," she muttered.

"There certainly are."

Bernadette sat back. She couldn't believe that she was actually going to get the facts that she'd been searching for. The last year hadn't been a waste. She wasn't exactly thrilled with the idea of being used—if that's what had happened—though she was sure she had. But to know about the Fae and the dragons!

To be privy to such secrets. That made it bearable.

"First," Keltan began, "you need to understand who we are. We are no' just dragons, Bernadette. We're Dragon Kings."

CHAPTER NINE

Keltan bit back his smile when his statement caused Bernadette's face to go slack.

"Dragon *Kings*?" she asked.

"Aye."

Bernadette swallowed audibly. "Usaeil left that part out."

"She left out a lot."

"I'm beginning to see that."

Keltan had made his point. Now, it was time to tell his story. Not that he was looking forward to it. It was the past—though what had occurred had made him—and all the Kings—who they were.

"This realm was ours," he told her. "For untold eons, we ruled here. Until you humans appeared."

Jade eyes widened a fraction. "Appeared?"

He tried not to notice how her voice wobbled, but it bothered him nonetheless. "One day, a small group of mortals arrived. We doona know how or from where, and they were unable to tell us. They had no memory of anything before coming here."

"You didn't send them away?"

"We're no' monsters, Bernadette. The Kings checked each human for magic to be sure none were lying. We took pity on them. We vowed then and there to protect the magic-less beings. And the magic of the realm allowed us Kings to shift into your form so we could communicate. We each gave up a small portion of our lands for the mortals. We helped them build structures and taught them about this planet. We showed them which creatures were dangerous, and which could be tamed."

Bernadette crossed one leg over the other. "I'm surprised, but only because I'm fairly certain that we humans wouldn't do the same."

Keltan knew they wouldn't, but there was no use pointing that out. "We discovered how quickly your kind reproduce. It takes dragons much longer."

"Because you're immortal, perhaps?"

"Dragons themselves are no'. They can live for several thousands of years, but they do die. Kings are immortal. To an extent. The only thing that can kill a King is another Dragon King."

Bernadette nodded slowly. "I take it from your comment that the human population expanded."

"Verra quickly. Those who first arrived here understood how perilous their situation was, but those born here didna feel the same. They took for granted their freedom and what we had given up for them. And, as in such cases, both sides crossed a line. A dragon or two killed a human, and that dragon was immediately punished. The mortals, however, didna just take one or two dragons. They hunted the smaller clans for food, much as your kind does with deer."

"Please tell me the humans in charge put a stop to it," she said, a frown creasing her brow.

Keltan drew in a deep breath. "I wish I could. Constantine w—"

"Why him?" Bernadette interrupted. "Why not you or one of the others?"

"Because Con is King of Dragon Kings. He is the strongest of us, the one with the most magic."

Her mouth formed an *O*.

Keltan then continued. "Constantine met with the mortal leaders each time one of the smaller dragons was killed, but it became an almost daily occurrence. Truces were broken time and again. Tensions grew worse when the humans wiped out the smallest of the dragon clans—the Pinks."

Bernadette closed her eyes and shook her head. "I'm so sorry."

Keltan waited until she looked at him before giving a bow of his head to acknowledge her apology. "During all of this, many Kings lived among the villages in their domain. Some Kings even took human females as their lovers."

"Did you?"

Keltan wasn't surprised by her question. It was the way her fingers fidgeted when she asked the question that drew his attention. She was nervous. Because she didn't like the idea of a human and dragon together?

Or was it because the idea intrigued her?

To his dismay, his cock twitched as blood rushed to it at the thought of her as his lover. This was the last thing he needed. Recognizing her beauty was one thing. Becoming attracted to her was something else altogether.

But it was too late to stop himself from feeling . . . drawn to her. The ties had formed quickly and without him being aware of them. Or maybe he was aware and didn't want to stop it.

No. That couldn't be true. Becoming involved with her was risky at best.

"I took a few as lovers, aye," he replied. "What we noticed was that none of the humans were able to carry a babe. Most miscarried within weeks. A handful made it to term, but the bairns were all stillborn. Despite that, Ulrik, the King of Silvers, fell in love with a mortal. They were to be married."

Bernadette uncrossed her legs and leaned forward, intrigued. "He didn't care that he couldn't have children?"

"Love is what Ulrik sought. He was verra giving. I've no doubt that he would've rounded up all the orphans—both human and dragon—and reared them himself."

Her head tilted. "You say that as if Ulrik didn't marry his woman."

"Because he didna. His uncle, angry that he hadna been chosen as King, poisoned the woman against Ulrik. Mikkel convinced her to murder Ulrik."

"Did she not know that the Kings couldn't be killed like that?"

Keltan shook his head. "There wasna a reason for her to know. Just like she had no idea that when a King takes a mate, no' only is it for life, but the female becomes immortal, as well. Mates live as long as the Kings do."

"Oh, God," Bernadette mumbled as she sat back. "If humans knew that, they'd be lining up at your door, trying to get you to marry them."

"We know," Keltan stated ruefully. He licked his lips. "I doona think that would've swayed the female. Mikkel did a good job of convincing her that Ulrik had to die. She never got a chance to do anything, however, because Con discovered that she was going to attempt to kill Ulrik. He sent Ulrik away so he didna have to face his lover. And we Kings tracked her down."

Bernadette leaned forward, her brows raised. "And? Don't stop there."

"What do you think we did?"

She opened her mouth. A heartbeat later, her brow furrowed. Then her face smoothed out. "You did the only thing you could do. You killed her."

"Aye. We did. When Ulrik returned, and we told him, it broke him. He turned his anger to those he believed responsible—the humans. We didna know until a few months ago that his uncle had been a part of it."

"Humans," she said.

Keltan nodded. "It was a bloodbath on both sides. Dragons slew thousands. The other half of the Kings kept to the oath we took and set up dragons around villages to protect the mortals. But the humans wanted no part of it. They killed the dragons sent to keep them safe."

"Stop," Bernadette said as she got to her feet and turned her back to him.

She wrapped her arms across her midsection and went to stand in front of a bookcase to gather herself. Keltan didn't need to see her face to know that his words had troubled her. Hell, telling her the story was forcing him to relive events he'd rather forget.

Bernadette sniffed loudly and ran her fingers through her black hair, smoothing it back from her face. After a moment, her arms dropped to her sides, and she faced him. Keltan was shocked to see that her eyes were red-rimmed as if she had been crying—or trying *not* to cry.

"Your kind had magic. Why didn't you wipe out the humans?"

"Because we're no' monsters. We made a vow, and despite what happened, we kept to it. Con convinced all the Kings who had joined Ulrik to return to him. When Con couldna get Ulrik to stand down, Con did the only thing he could. He forced the Silvers to come to him. All but four of the largest did as commanded. Ulrik with his four remaining Silvers annihilated hundreds more humans. No amount of talking, from Con or anyone else, could calm the mortals down. That's when we all knew that the war would continue. And if something wasna done, the dragons would be wiped out one by one. Or we would go back on our vow."

"What did you do?" Bernadette asked in a soft voice.

"We used our magic and opened a dragon bridge to another realm. The Kings stayed behind, but we sent our clans away."

Bernadette stared at him for a moment in silence. "Do you know where they are?"

Keltan shook his head. "We had no time to see where we sent them or even if it was safe. We only knew they needed a fighting chance somewhere else because this realm was no longer safe."

"It could've been. It probably should've been. You were within your rights to defend what was yours and get rid of us."

Keltan ran a hand down his face. "Trust me, there isna a King on Dreagan who hasna thought that verra thing."

Bernadette leaned back against a bookcase. "What happened after the dragons left?"

"We trapped the four Silvers and made them sleep. Then Con called for Ulrik. When he still wouldna back down, Con bound his magic, forcing him to live as a mortal. Then Ulrik was banished from Dreagan."

"That was harsh," she stated.

"If you knew Con and how close he and Ulrik were, you would realize how difficult all of that was for Con. It nearly killed him, though he would never admit it to anyone. There was no other choice for us. We had to disappear. The humans needed to believe that all dragons were gone, and if Ulrik wouldna stop attacking, that couldna happen."

She shrugged, her face scrunching. "I can see your point. But banishment? That's a bit much."

"Is it?" Keltan asked. "Ulrik couldna shift into his true form. Was it kinder to send him out into the world to live as one of you or to remain here, constantly reminded of how others could shift and he couldna?"

Bernadette grinned and nodded. "Point taken."

"In truth, there wasna a good option. Being unable to shift, Ulrik went mad. And being immortal, he couldna die to end his torment. So, his fury turned to us. Specifically, Con. He began plotting our ruination while we each took to our mountains and slept away the centuries."

"You have mountains?" she asked curiously, pushing off of the bookcase.

Keltan grinned, liking her interest. "Aye. Each of us has one that is ours alone. We stayed there while Con remained awake, keeping up with the changes of the world. Every decade, he would come to each of us while we slept and fill us in."

"That was a brilliant idea. That way, when you did wake, you would fit in."

"That's right." Keltan hadn't wanted to tell her their story, but he quite liked how she accepted all of it as well as added her own opinions. He hadn't looked at what had happened to him through anyone else's eyes before.

Bernadette walked back to the sofa and sat. "But you all woke?"

"Eventually. We did it in shifts. Some didna like what they saw and returned to their mountains. Others remained awake for a few hundred years and then chose dragon sleep again. The only two who never slept were Con and Ulrik."

"I'm guessing that no one bothered Dreagan because of the . . . What do you call what's around the land?"

"The magical boundary. Aye, it deters humans from wanting a closer look. We know the difference in an animal crossing and a human."

She nodded, smiling. "That's amazing. Then you made whisky? Why Scotch?"

"It was Con's idea. It was inevitable that we would mix with the mortals again, and because we had such a huge swath of land, they would no doubt be curious about us. The whisky allowed us to hide what we wanted, show what we needed, and live as we have."

She smiled and looked around the library. "It was a brilliant idea. Not only to have such a thriving business that allows you secrecy, but I'm sure the wealth is nice, as well."

Keltan shrugged one shoulder. "I'll no' lie and say I doona like it."

Bernadette blew out a breath and pressed her lips together. "And then I came along and ruined it."

"Nay, lass," he said with a shake of his head. "There is much that happened before you came into the picture."

Her eyes glittered. "There's more to the story, then?"

"There is."

"Please," she begged. "I want to know it all."

CHAPTER TEN

It was a dream. It had to be. For the last year.

Bernadette squeezed her hands together as excitement and more than a little trepidation ran through her as quick as lightning. But nothing—not even Usaeil—could've made Bernadette get up and leave.

She'd been enthralled from the first words out of Keltan's mouth. Dragon Kings. It boggled her mind, and yet, at the same time, it made so much sense. These men at Dreagan weren't just *dragons*. They were kings!

"All of it, aye?" Keltan asked with a grin. "I'm no' sure I can remember it all."

She knew he was teasing her, but she didn't care. The fact that he didn't seem angry was a win, in her estimation. Because he had every right to be furious. Everyone at Dreagan did. She could say that she didn't know, but that wasn't much of a defense. Regardless of whether she'd known that Usaeil was using her, Bernadette knew better than to go barreling into something without doing research.

Though she had done it. Nearly a year's worth. She hadn't watched the tele, gone to a movie, visited with friends, or done anything other than work, research, and sleep. That's how obsessed she'd become.

It wasn't healthy. She realized that now. But at the time, she'd felt like it was her destiny. It might very well be. Otherwise, she likely wouldn't be sitting in the opulent library at Dreagan talking to Keltan.

"What were you thinking just now?" he asked.

Bernadette glanced at her hands, embarrassed. "How fixated I've been on Dreagan and everyone here. I've never done anything like this in my life. And even now, I'm not sure how it happened."

"You saw a dragon. No' one of us, but one created by Usaeil in our image, I'm guessing."

"That might be true, but I'd say the majority of people in my place might have kept to themselves."

"Or run away in fear," Keltan added. He gave her a pointed look. "Were you scared?"

She laughed, thinking about it. "Terrified. I shook so badly that I thought my knees would give out. Part of me screamed to get as far away as I could, but another part just stared at the creature in awe. The idea that something could exist alongside us that we didn't know about intrigued me."

One side of Keltan's lips turned up in a grin. "I'm glad you didna run. Did Usaeil hold you?"

"Not that I'm aware. She kept staring at the dragon as if mesmerized."

"Interesting," he murmured.

Bernadette thought that he might tell her not to beat herself up about the year she'd wasted of her life or the damage she'd done to Dreagan, but she realized that she should condemn herself. She hadn't thought things through carefully enough. She'd let Usaeil talk her into giving that lecture instead of continuing her research.

Though the Fae queen had made it seem as if Bernadette had finished her research. She still couldn't understand why she had believed everything Usaeil told her. It wasn't like her. Bernadette wasn't exactly mistrustful, but she tended to err on the side of caution. Usually.

She nearly rolled her eyes at the thought. *Usually* wasn't something she could say anymore. She was anything but her usual self.

It was then that she realized how quiet the library had become. Keltan stared at her again, and she shot him an embarrassed smile. "I apologize. I'm here to listen, not get lost in my thoughts."

"Actually, I find it interesting to watch you while you think. Emotions pass over your face as you do."

Dear Lord. Was he able to tell what she was thinking?

Bernadette realized too late that her face showed her shock. She quickly tried to smooth it away, but the damage had been done. They shared a laugh, making the moment more bearable.

"I didna mean to embarrass you. I like trying to discern what you're thinking, but I shouldna have pointed it out," he told her.

"Actually, I'm glad you did. Apparently, I need to work on schooling my features." She chuckled, shaking her head.

Keltan scratched his jaw. "Where was I in the story?"

"You told me how you came to make whisky."

"Right," he said with a nod. "One thing I forgot to mention was that before we found our mountains, we worked magic so we would never feel any strong feelings for humans again. No hate or love."

Bernadette swallowed, thinking how Ulrik had felt both keenly, and look where it had gotten him. "Did it work?"

"Aye. For many, many years. Magic can do a great many things, but it can no' stop love. Ryder didna tell anyone that he met and fell in love with Kinsey. When he realized what had happened, he ended the relationship."

Bernadette blinked in shock. "What? He fell in love and walked away? Why would he do that?"

"Because the spell was supposed to prevent it."

"Still," she argued.

Keltan shrugged. "It wasna long after that Cassie came, and she and Hal fell in love. That's when we all realized the spell was broken. We had no way of knowing that Ulrik was the one who broke it without even knowing it had been cast."

Bernadette frowned. "How did he do that?"

"Ulrik wanted his magic back. All the millennia that he'd been stuck in human form, he'd been searching for some way to unbind his powers. He came to realize that Druids held the key."

"Druids?" she asked, taken aback. "There are Druids?"

"Aye, lass. The magic of the land found certain mortals and gave them the ability to use it. They're Druids. There isna many of them left. Years of diluting their blood with humans who had no magic at all made it difficult for them to sustain their magic."

Bloody hell. Just when she'd thought she knew everything. Obviously, she knew only a thimbleful. "Go on," she urged.

"Each time a Druid attempted to touch Ulrik's dragon magic, they died."

That news made Bernadette nervous. "I'm guessing Ulrik still sought them out?"

"He did," Keltan said with a single nod of his head. "Ulrik was desperate to unbind his magic and attack us."

"Has he succeeded?"

"He did find a Druid who was strong enough to withstand the dragon magic and do what he wanted."

Bernadette gaped at him. "So, Ulrik is out there now with his magic? He's going to attack?"

"He's here, actually."

Fear pooled in Bernadette's belly, making her sick. Then she really looked at Keltan. Her eyes narrowed as she stared. "You don't seem worried."

"I'm no'. Ulrik did attack individual Dragon Kings, several times, but he found out that his uncle never left with the other dragons. Mikkel remained, intending to kill Ulrik and become the King of Silvers."

"Oh," Bernadette murmured.

Keltan shrugged and glanced out one of the windows near him. "It took some doing, but Ulrik and Con talked and joined forces against Mikkel. Ulrik destroyed his uncle, fell in love with a Druid, and was able to return to Dreagan, where we welcomed him."

Just when she thought the stories couldn't get any better . . . Bernadette now had a dozen more questions she wanted to ask, but she held back. While she was curious, this wasn't the time to get details. There was more to the story.

Keltan cleared his throat. "When your kind came to this realm, and we vowed to protect you, it wasna just against outside threats. It was against anyone who tried to harm humans."

"Even after the war?" she asked with a shake of her head. "I don't think I could've done that."

"It wasna always easy," Keltan confessed.

She twisted her lips. "The spell not to feel strong emotions for us helped, I'm sure."

"It certainly did. When the Fae came, we didna hesitate to defend this realm."

Bernadette liked Earth being called a realm. It would likely sound odd coming from her, but it sounded right when Keltan said it. "The Fae haven't always been here?"

"The Fae lived on another realm. Their civil war destroyed their world. Humans brought them here."

Bernadette tried not to shudder when she recalled what she'd been told the Dark Fae did to her kind. "Do the Light harm us?"

"They have strict rules to only have sex with mortals once, but that's all it takes for the damage to occur. Once a human has sex with a Fae, no one of their kind will ever live up to the pleasure they received."

Bernadette drew in a breath and held it for a second before she released it. "I suppose I should be thankful that it was Usaeil who found me rather than a male."

"Fae doona discriminate. If she had wanted you as a lover, Usaeil would've had you."

Should Bernadette be relieved, or insulted that the Fae didn't want her? She inwardly laughed at herself since it was a thought she'd never imagined having.

"Count yourself lucky," Keltan said as if reading her thoughts.

Bernadette flashed him a quick smile. "I do, of course. I take your story to mean that you didn't stop the Fae from coming here either?"

"It was a mistake we all acknowledge. They chose Ireland as theirs with the Dark on the bottom half and the Light on the top. But they didna stay. The lure of the mortals was too much for them. We stepped in to stop the killing and instantly clashed with the Dark. The Light stayed out of it, preferring to watch because of their civil war that had lasted generations.

"The Fae Wars went on for years without the humans realizing it. We managed to hide most of the battles, but it was easier back then. The technology wasna the same, nor were there nearly as many mortals."

Bernadette couldn't imagine the lengths the Kings went to in order to keep the humans from knowing what was going on. "I admit, I'm surprised the Light didn't attack you."

"They accepted what the Dark couldna."

"What was that?"

"That we have the strongest magic of any beings on this realm," Keltan replied.

Bernadette snorted as she shook her head. "Now it makes sense."

"What does?" he asked with a frown.

"Something Usaeil said last night. She told me that she needed the world to know about all of you being dragons. She said it was imperative. She knows she can't beat you on her own."

Keltan scrubbed a hand over his mouth and then down his beard. "There is much about Usaeil you doona know. She's dangerous. The fact that she didna harm you surprises me more than I like to admit."

"But she's a Light Fae. Doesn't that mean she's good?" His hesitation made Bernadette uneasy. "So, Light doesn't mean good, and Dark doesn't mean evil?"

He shrugged and leaned forward. "It does, mostly, but Usaeil isna so black and white. Before I get into her story, let me finish the other."

"Right," she said with a nod.

Keltan looked at her a moment and then blew out a breath as he got to his feet. He held out a hand to her. "Are you hungry?"

"Famished, actually." She couldn't hide her grin as she took his hand, and he helped her to her feet.

"I'm rubbish with computers, but I'm a decent cook."

Her smile grew. "I'm not going to pass up that offer."

"Good."

They remained standing, inches from each other, their gazes locked. The last year had been backwards of anything Bernadette had known before. She was sure she should be nervous or, at the very least, wondering if Keltan or someone else would harm her.

But she didn't feel anything even remotely like that. It could be the magic of the Dragon Kings. Or it could be real. She couldn't distinguish between the two, and at the moment, she didn't want to.

She might regret it later, but for now, she was going to enjoy herself.

CHAPTER ELEVEN

Usaeil stood in the tiny place that Bernadette called home as she fumed. "I gave you a chance, you stupid mortal," she said into the empty abode.

She looked around, sickened at how quickly Bernadette had given up her lavish lifestyle after a quick peek at a dragon. Usaeil rolled her eyes. Humans were so easily manipulated. Usaeil never grew tired of seeing how far she could push one.

She turned in a circle and looked about the cottage. Bernadette could be anywhere, but Usaeil knew where she was—Dreagan. Not once had Bernadette made Usaeil question her. She had done and said everything Usaeil expected of her.

It went beyond Usaeil's magic to find anyone, much less a mortal. That didn't mean she hadn't prepared for just such an instance.

She narrowed her eyes. The moment she had seen Keltan at the lecture with Bernadette, Usaeil had known that her plan was falling into place perfectly. The only thing that bothered her was that Bernadette hadn't told her about Keltan.

While she needed the mortal at Dreagan, she didn't want Bernadette to remain there. Women had a habit of falling for the Kings, and while that was Usaeil's plan, she didn't want to make it easy for the couple.

"Don't worry, Bernadette. I'll soon have you right where you belong," Usaeil said as she walked to the desk and grabbed Bernadette's favorite pen.

With one wave of her hand, Usaeil scattered the items that were on the desk, sending papers, files, and notebooks flying across the room to land haphazardly on the floor.

With the desk cleared, she set the pen in the middle of it. Usaeil then summoned a dagger and pricked the end of her finger, letting three drops of her blood fall upon the pen. The wound closed up immediately with some magic, ensuring that no more blood touched the writing instrument.

Usaeil then held her hand over the pen, her fingers splayed. "I summon thee, Bernadette Davies. For every hour you don't return, your body will begin to wither."

With the spell done, Usaeil lowered her arm to her side. "It's time you remember who you serve, human. And if I have to give you pain to make you recall that, then I'll gladly do it."

She smiled because the one person who could've helped Bernadette was no longer at Dreagan. Usaeil thought about Con, her heart leaping. That's what he did to her. It still infuriated her that he didn't see the love that was between them. He didn't realize that they were destined to be together.

But he would.

In the end, he would do whatever she wanted.

Usaeil looked down at the pen. She could tap into the Druid magic coursing in her veins to locate Bernadette. It wasn't a feat even the Druids had mastered, but with her magic mixed with the Druids', it just might work.

But if it didn't, that meant she'd used up the Druid magic she'd taken. And she'd have to go and find another—and Druids weren't that easy to find anymore.

That wasn't precisely true. She could go to the Isle of Skye. The Skye Druids were some of the most powerful, but Usaeil was hesitant to go there. Corann, the leader of the Skye Druids, kept to himself. Because of that, he had no idea what was going on with the Dragon Kings or the Fae. She needed it to stay that way for a bit longer. She had a plan for Corann and his Druids, and it wasn't time for that yet. If she began taking their magic, then when it came time for her plan, she'd have to spend time ensuring that they did as she commanded.

So, while she wanted to make sure Bernadette was at Dreagan, she wouldn't. But the moment the mortal was back in her ugly cottage, Usaeil was going to let her know just how angry she was to not only be lied to, but because Bernadette had run off on her own.

Usaeil was about to teleport away when she felt something in the air. The first time had been a few weeks ago on a tiny isle off the coast of Scotland. It had happened twice more since then.

She might not know what it was, but she knew it wasn't good. The moment she felt it, she left. She wanted to know who or what it was, but she wasn't sure she wanted to stick around to find out.

Usaeil made sure that she rarely lost a fight. The few times she'd gone into battle without knowing every detail of her opponent, she'd lost. She couldn't afford another such mistake.

If you're going to defeat whatever this is, then you need to know what it is.

The voice in her head wasn't wrong, but the urge to flee pressed her. She fought against giving in, fought against the primal need to protect herself.

"I'm a queen," she said. "Soon, I'll be queen of this realm, and then the entire universe. My days of fleeing should be over."

Then don't run away.

It was easier said than done. For each second she remained, that odd feeling doubled. It was tenacious, pressing in on all sides of her as if closing in.

"Uuuusaeillllllll."

The eerie voice saying her name made her take a step back. "Who are you?"

There was no answer. Usaeil turned her head one way and then the other as she cast magic out to force whatever was hiding to show itself. Nothing appeared. And the voice didn't return.

Yet Usaeil knew without a doubt that she wasn't alone.

"Who are you?" she demanded in a firmer tone.

Only silence met her, which made chills race along her skin. It seemed more sinister that there hadn't been an answer to her question.

Perhaps you should run.

Usaeil wanted to hit the voice in her head. Instead, she teleported away.

Rhi stood at the door, staring at it with narrowed eyes. She didn't know what had brought her to this house in Glasgow. She'd dreamed about it last night, and it had plagued her mind since then.

For the past few hours, she'd walked the streets of the city, trying to find it. Now that she had, she was more confused than ever as to why she was there.

She was about to turn away when she thought she

heard a voice. She couldn't make out what had been said, however. Rhi walked around the small building, glancing in the windows.

It didn't appear as if anyone were home. Rhi put her hand on the outside wall and felt for magic. No spells protected the place. She frowned and shook her head. The more she tried to figure out why she was there, the more baffled she became.

With just a thought, she teleported inside the house. A quick look inside the bedroom confirmed that a woman lived there. Yet there was nothing that would cause Rhi to dream about such a place.

Then her attention landed on the papers in disarray. She slid her gaze to the desk and saw the pen with the three drops of blood. Instantly, she put up some protection around her.

Rhi cast out another spell to make anyone reveal themselves if they were hidden. Unfortunately, no one appeared. But the pen and blood confirmed that magic had been done. The question was, who had worked the magic and why?

She walked closer to the desk and squatted down so her gaze was level with the pen. Her mind went through the various reasons a pen had been used. Then Rhi glanced around her to find another pen or pencil, but there wasn't one in sight.

Her head swung back to the instrument. That meant it wasn't the woman who lived here who had done the spell. The pen could belong to someone else, but Rhi would bet her best Jimmy Choos that the pen was the homeowner's.

It was the blood that disturbed her. The Fae didn't use blood in their enchantments. There was no need since their magic could do just about anything.

Except locate someone.

Rhi slowly got to her feet. A Druid could do a locating spell, though they rarely worked because the Druids didn't possess enough power. Someone like Eilish could probably do it without the use of blood.

Blood tied the person doing the spell to the one they were putting the spell on. It meant that severing such an enchantment would take an exorbitant amount of magic.

This could be a Dark Fae. It could be a Light. It could also be a Druid. Or Usaeil. The fact that Rhi wasn't able to distinguish who had done the magic made her angry. And with that rage came the tantalizing voice of the darkness within her.

It begged her to give in to it. It told her that once she did, she would be able to do all the things she wished she could. Like finding Usaeil and locating Constantine.

Rhi closed her eyes. Each time the darkness called to her, it became harder and harder for her to turn away. She was being beaten down, and she wasn't sure she had the courage or the will to continue for much longer.

No! she bellowed in her mind.

The darkness didn't care. It kept talking. *"You've suffered enough. It's Usaeil's turn. She took away the love of your life. She betrayed your best friend, turning Balladyn over to the Dark. She lied to you. She banished you. She deserves everything that's coming to her."*

Rhi couldn't disagree with that. Usaeil had done all those things to her, but the queen had done so much more to so many others.

"She's part of the Others," the darkness said. *"How much longer will Usaeil go before she tells Balladyn and the Dragon Kings that your father was also part of that group? What do you think your friends will do?"*

"This isn't about my father," Rhi said.

The darkness laughed. *"This is about you, Rhi. It's al-*

ways been about you. The only way you can win against Usaeil is by accepting what I have to offer."

"I won't turn into a Dark. I won't."

"Then you will die. That hope in your heart? The one you try to deny regarding getting back with your Dragon King? That will be gone forever. If you let Usaeil win, then she will conquer the Fae."

Rhi shook her head. "No, she won't. Death won't let her."

"This isn't Death's battle. It's yours. Even Death said so."

"Usaeil will never win against the Dragon Kings or Death. She'll lose whatever way you look at it."

"Are you sure of that? Really, really sure?"

Rhi wanted to say that she was, but she couldn't. There was doubt there. Usaeil's power had increased with the use of the Druid magic mixed with hers. No doubt there were things she could do that Rhi didn't even know about.

"Face her now. Alone," the darkness urged. *"If you wait for the others, they will die. Some might live, but a great many will be killed. Think of your friends."*

"I'm not waiting for them." And she didn't like that the darkness said otherwise.

There was a beat of silence. *"Then why haven't you gone after her?"*

Rhi had no answer.

"I can ensure you'll win. You'll be a Dark Fae, yes, but there are worse things."

"I'll lose my Dragon King."

"There's Balladyn. He loves you more than anything. You know it."

"I do. But he's not my Dragon King."

"Was your King ever really yours? If he was, he never would've let you go."

The words pierced Rhi's heart like a blade. "No!" Rhi bellowed.

She looked down and found herself glowing. By trying to fight the darkness, she had given a little more of herself to it. Maybe she was a fool to fight it. Perhaps she should give in to it.

But not yet. There was still more to do.

CHAPTER TWELVE

Keltan had surprised himself when he offered to cook for Bernadette. He wasn't sure why he'd done it. Maybe it was because he wanted her to relax more. She'd been tense since first running into him in the parking lot. Not that he could blame her.

Some of the anxiety had left her while he was telling his story, and he liked it. Food had always been something that made him relax. Whether he was cooking a meal or partaking in one, the setting held a kind of ease that he thought they needed.

To his delight, Bernadette had readily taken him up on his offer. Every Dragon King had expertise in something. For some, those skills were put to use to further the success of Dreagan Industries. For others, like him, it was a much more personal talent. Because Keltan could cook. Anything.

All he had to do was look at some ingredients, and the entire meal formed in his head. He was able to put together any type of dish and have it come out perfect.

"What are you hungry for?" he asked Bernadette when they entered the kitchen.

She looked around the grand room while turning in a slow circle. "Umm," she said without glancing at him. "Whatever you want to cook, I suppose."

Keltan chuckled. "Anything you doona like? Anything you're allergic to?"

"Nothing." She finally looked at him. "I don't particularly like peas. Or cauliflower. Oh, and I can't stand beets. Nothing I'm allergic to, however."

"Vegetarian?"

Her smile spread over her face. "I tried it once. I realized within two days that I loved meat too much to ever give it up."

"Sit back and get comfortable then."

"Anything I can do to help? I don't want to feel like a bump on a log."

Keltan usually did all the cooking, but he quite liked the idea of sharing some of the task with Bernadette. "Want to mince some garlic and chop an onion?"

"I'd be happy to."

Within minutes, he had her set up at the table with a cutting board, a knife, bowls, an onion, and some garlic. He liked how she began without any hesitation, proving that she knew her way around a kitchen.

"You liked Usaeil when you first met her, didn't you?" he asked as he pulled one of the freshly caught salmon fillets from the fridge.

"I did," Bernadette said. "She was so nice. We instantly clicked. Things like that don't happen too often. At least, not to me."

Keltan put the salmon on a tray and began seasoning it. He glanced at Bernadette and shot her a wry grin. "I wish I could tell you it was genuine."

"Is everything Usaeil does a lie?"

"We used to believe we could take her at her word.

That she was a friend. It hasna been too long since we discovered the truth."

Bernadette paused in her chopping. "She's a movie star. I was awestruck for a moment. I can't believe she has time to do everything. Being in movies and being a queen."

"She's no' been a queen in a long time," he stated. "A verra long time. The Light are floundering, and Usaeil doesna care."

"She's powerful, though. Isn't she?"

Keltan met Bernadette's jade gaze and nodded. "Verra. More now than before."

"How is that possible?"

He shrugged and finished with the salmon. He readied the oven before turning to get out some cheese and crackers for them to snack on. "We learned about the Fae when they came here. When Usaeil brought her Light Army to us and helped us fight the Dark, we believed we had an ally. That was one of the main reasons we didna force the Fae to leave. In hindsight, it's exactly what we should've done."

"You would've thought you'd learn your lesson after the humans." Bernadette winced, wrinkling her nose. "Sorry. That was harsh."

"Aye, but the truth. We could've forced the Dark to leave, but Con knew then that they would return if we allowed the Light to stay. We didna need the Light to win against the Dark, but it helped to bring the war to a close sooner. Looking back now, I think Usaeil timed it all perfectly. But we didna see that back then."

Bernadette grunted. "You're too trusting."

"I'd like to think we're fair, but you're right. Again. Because we only made the Fae sign a treaty promising they would remain in Ireland and no' kill humans. We didna make them leave. We did try to get all the humans out of Ireland, but no' all would listen to us. Usaeil promised to help keep the Dark in check. We kept a strict eye on both the Light and Dark for decades, and it all went according to plan. Until it didna.

"The Dark hated us, as you can imagine. During the Fae Wars, they trapped a couple of Kings and drove them mad. We lost both of those Kings, so there is definitely strife between us and the Dark."

Keltan set the plate of cheese and crackers before her. Bernadette grabbed one of each and popped them into her mouth as she nodded.

He leaned his hands on the back of a chair as he watched her. "The Dark began killing in such a way that we didna see it immediately. And when we did, Usaeil swooped in and stopped it. Once more, she proved we could take her at her word. The ties between the Light and Kings tightened."

"I'm surprised none of you fell in love with a Light, or even Usaeil, for that matter."

"One of us did fall in love." Keltan looked out through the kitchen window. "Her name is Rhiannon, but everyone calls her Rhi. She's got a wicked sense of humor. She's fearless, dedicated, and loyal to a fault. She's also one of the strongest Light there is."

"Who fell in love with her?"

Keltan shot Bernadette a smile and shook his head. "You should've seen them. Their love was . . . there are no words, really. It was true love. The kind that spans time and space. It awed all of us."

Bernadette smiled wistfully. "It sounds beautiful. So, they're still together?"

"Nay."

Her eyes widened as the smile faded. "What? Why? Tell me she didn't die."

"Rhi is verra much alive, and she still comes to Dreagan. She is an ally, and someone we've counted on multiple times to help us."

Bernadette drew in a deep breath and released it. "Did the Dragon King die?"

Keltan shook his head.

A frown marred Bernadette's forehead. "I'm confused then. If they're both still alive and they had a love that most everyone hopes to find, why aren't they together?"

"That is something we all still ask. The Dragon King called it off. He wouldna tell us his reasons then—or now."

Bernadette's face crinkled with disgust. "Rhi is a better woman than I am. I never would have returned here."

"She didna for years, but she has many friends at Dreagan. She and Rhys are extremely close. I doona know how she does it, though. I asked her once, and she said that she was able to compartmentalize things. It was the only way she could go on with her life. So, when she's here, she doesna let the past invade. She focuses on why she's here and what she's needed for."

"That's . . . pretty damn amazing. I don't think I could do that."

"Me, either. But back to Usaeil. You're right. It seems like more Kings should've begun interacting with the Light, but it didna happen. What we learned from Usaeil was that all her family died or disappeared, so she was left with the throne. The fact that she had ruled the Light longer than any other king or queen seemed good to us. There was nothing out of the ordinary that made us question anything."

Bernadette raised her brows. "Obviously, that changed. When?"

"Nothing happened until a year or so ago. She went out of her way to help Kiril, who had fallen in love with a Dark Fae."

"A Dark?"

Keltan shook his head. "Shara was raised as a Dark, but she didna want to be one. It was Usaeil who helped Shara become a Light."

Bernadette stopped chopping again. "They can go from one to the other?"

"All Fae are born Light. They make the choice to kill to become Dark. But, aye, apparently, a Dark can change to a Light."

"Wow," Bernadette murmured.

Keltan smiled in agreement. "A few things began. Mostly, it was between Rhi and Usaeil. They were no' only close friends, but Rhi was also the only female in the Queen's Guard. Yet Usaeil began acting out against Rhi. There were lies, and Rhi uncovered one. It seems that Usaeil is the one who tore Rhi and her King apart."

Bernadette gasped. "How?"

"We doona know the details. It devastated Rhi, though."

"I bet," Bernadette agreed with a nod. "To discover that your friend and queen did something so despicable."

"Centuries ago."

Bernadette went back to chopping. "Damn."

"Rhi left the Queen's Guard. During that time, Con became lovers with Usaeil."

"Yikes. Not sure that was a good move," Bernadette said.

Keltan happened to agree. "Con isna perfect. He's made a few bad choices, but for the most part, he's never led us astray. We all thought he'd lost his mind, and he told us it was because he couldna bed just anyone. That was part of it, but Con also had a plan—one he didna share with anyone."

"Did it work?"

"Usaeil was obsessed with Rhi. The queen blamed her for everything bad that happened. When Con tried to call off his affair with Usaeil, she blamed that on Rhi, as well."

"Did Rhi have anything to do with it?" Bernadette asked.

Keltan shook his head. "Con had his own reasons for ending it. But it wasna long before Usaeil banished Rhi from the Light as her way of revenge. Then Rhi discovered that the queen had begun making movies with the humans."

"I don't understand why Usaeil would do any of that. She's not only beautiful, wealthy, and has magic, but she's also a queen."

"There are those who never have enough. They always want more. Usaeil could get Con, but eventually, she'd want something else. Nothing will ever fulfill her."

Bernadette shrugged. "I suppose not."

"During our battle against Ulrik's uncle, we discovered a new enemy. Actually, a group of them. They consist of Light and Dark Fae, as well as *mie* and *drough* Druids. *Mies* are the good Druids."

"And *droughs* the evil ones?" Bernadette finished.

Keltan nodded. "None of them on their own or even paired up could come close to our magic. But the four groups together is enough to match, and in some cases, exceed our power."

Bernadette slowly lowered the knife. "Do you know why this group wants to hurt you?"

"We're working on that. They call themselves the Others, and Usaeil is part of them." Keltan paused when he saw Bernadette's face pale. He wanted to reassure her, but it would be hollow. Instead, he sighed and turned back to put the salmon into the oven. "Rhi, along with Con and the rest of us, were getting ready to attack Usaeil, but she went into hiding. None of our magic was able to locate her. We even went to some friends, the Warriors." He paused and looked at her. "Sorry. The Warriors are humans who agreed to allow primeval gods from Hell into their bodies in order to fight Rome when they invaded. The Warriors who survived are here, in Scotland, living with their Druid wives. One of the Warriors can find anyone, anywhere, but no' even he could locate Usaeil."

"Dragon Kings, Fae, Druids, and now Warriors. Are there any others?" she asked.

"No' that I'm aware of."

Bernadette nodded slowly. "All right. Has Usaeil been able to hide herself like this before?"

"We're no' sure. We've never tried to look for her before. Con devised a trap using himself as bait to lure her out. It worked perfectly. Right up until she managed to kidnap him."

CHAPTER THIRTEEN

"She did what?" Bernadette was too shocked to think beyond that point.

Keltan glanced at her over his shoulder as he continued picking up one item after another. Bernadette wasn't even sure what he was making, and she didn't care at this point. Her attention was focused solely on the story.

"I'm pretty sure we all wore that exact same expression you're wearing now," he said ruefully. "There's a debate between us. Some of us believe Con has the power to break free of Usaeil, but is biding his time until he finds out what he wants to know. Others think that Usaeil's magic has increased to the point that she can hold Con."

Bernadette swallowed and touched her throat. Before she could even ask for a glass of water, Keltan set one before her. She drank deeply, but nothing could stop the dread that continued filling her stomach.

Finally, she finished the water and set aside the glass. "I know nothing about magic, so I'm not sure I could tell you anything. I know Usaeil is fixated on all of you. She never let on that she knew Con, but then again, why would she?"

"Verra true, lass."

"You're telling me that Con's gone? That Usaeil has him?"

"I am," he said with a nod.

Bernadette hadn't even met Con, but she knew from Keltan's story that he was important to the Dragon Kings. A part of her wondered if she could believe Keltan. In all actuality, he could be lying to her, as well.

She didn't consider herself able to read people. In fact, she had been played by others a time or two when she hadn't listened to her intuition. The feeling of unease she'd gotten from Usaeil hadn't been felt around Keltan. She couldn't swear on it, but Bernadette felt that he was telling her the truth.

"In other words, Usaeil isn't what she led me to believe she is?" Bernadette asked.

"It's worse than that. Usaeil killed her family in order to take the throne. Rhi's best friend and leader of the Light Army, Balladyn, was betrayed by Usaeil to the Dark. Usaeil left him for dead on the battlefield, believing that the King of the Dark would honor their deal and kill Balladyn. What he did was turn Balladyn Dark. And now, Balladyn is the King of the Dark."

"I didn't see that coming," Bernadette said with a shake of her head.

"Neither did Usaeil. She's no' happy about it at all."

"I bet not." Bernadette licked her lips and put the minced garlic into one of the small bowls before reaching for the onion. "She really killed her entire family?"

Keltan nodded and wiped off his hands before facing her. "Aye."

"Wouldn't that make her a Dark?"

"That it does, lass. Fae have the ability to use glamour to change their appearance. Usaeil has been using it for quite some time, I believe. Normally, we can see through a Fae's glamour, but for whatever reason, we can no' with her."

Bernadette frowned, a shiver racing down her spine. "That's not good. I could be her for all you know."

"You're no'," he replied with a lopsided smile. "We have spells in place that prevent her from coming here, remember? Even if she did use glamour, our magic would stop her."

Well, that was good to know. Bernadette filed that knowledge away. She shifted, suddenly not feeling all that well. It was probably because she hadn't eaten properly in several hours. She ignored the discomfort and went on chopping. "You said something about Con and Rhi attacking Usaeil. Are you all still going to do that?"

Keltan stared at her silently for a long time.

Bernadette laughed and nodded. "And here I thought you trusted me."

"I do. To a point," Keltan said.

"I understand. I could be working for Usaeil, taking this information back to her."

He shrugged one shoulder. "You want to know if we intend to attack her? Aye, we do. And we willna be alone."

A part of Bernadette realized that something was off for Keltan to suddenly tell her such details. That's when it hit her. The Dragon Kings had magic. No doubt they could make sure she didn't remember anything once she ate or drank something here. Or it could be just a little swish of their finger to wipe her mind. Either way, it was the same result.

She set down the knife. "I wasn't sure why you were so ready to tell me so many of your secrets. I thought maybe it was because you trusted me, but that's difficult to do when I'm not exactly giving you the same courtesy. But now I know. I won't leave here remembering anything about our conversation."

Keltan walked to her and pulled the cutting board to him. In seconds, he had chopped the whole onion and put it in the second bowl. Then he took the bowls of garlic an onion and turned to walk to the counter.

She continued watching him, waiting for him to tell her she was wrong. The fact that several minutes passed without him doing such a thing gave her all the answers she needed. She thought she should be angry at something like that being done against her will, but instead, she was sad. Because she wanted to remember all of this. Otherwise, she would always be curious about the Dragon Kings.

She shook her head as the truth of it hit her. They wouldn't just wipe her mind of what she learned today. They would take everything she knew about them, Usaeil, and anything to do with magic. Maybe that would be for the best. If she wasn't so obsessed, then she might be able to get her old life back.

That thought didn't appeal to her as much as she'd thought it would. Actually, it made her break out in a sweat. She'd been living in a dream world most of her life. It was just this past year that she had been woken enough to see everything without a filter.

It was terrifying and horrible and beautiful. And she couldn't imagine life without the knowledge she'd gained.

"It's for your safety as well as ours," Keltan finally said.

The irritation in her abdomen increased enough to make her shift in the chair. She grew nauseated and scooted down in the seat so she was half-reclining, which helped to ease the discomfort.

Keltan faced her as he wiped his hands. "You do understand that, I hope."

"Usaeil could find me again and tell me everything once more. For all I know, this has happened multiple times," she argued.

He grinned and used his arm to move the hair back from his face. "I promise, lass, that isna the case." He frowned as he looked at her with narrowed eyes. "Are you feeling all right?"

"I think I'm just tired. I drove all night and only slept for a few hours in my car."

"When was the last time you had a good meal?"

She shrugged. "Sometime yesterday."

He jerked his chin to the cheese. "Eat some of that while this finishes. Would you like some tea?"

"That sounds great, actually."

Bernadette closed her eyes as she munched on the cheese and crackers. Her belly began to feel better, which she was happy about. It never took much to upset her stomach, but to do it today when she was at Dreagan was more than embarrassing. But with all the anxiety and stress, she wasn't at all surprised.

To her further embarrassment, she jerked awake at the sound of the kettle. She hadn't even realized she'd drifted off. She hadn't thought she was that tired, but obviously, she was.

Bernadette straightened in the chair and ate another piece of cheese as Keltan brought her a cup of tea. She declined the sugar but said yes to the milk. The first sip was just what she needed to bolster herself.

"Better?" Keltan asked.

She flashed him a bright smile. "Much. Thank you."

"We've plenty of rooms if you need to lie down for a bit."

Bernadette waved off his words. "I'll be fine."

He sighed and returned to the oven where he checked

on the salmon. "I would've thought you'd argue with me about leaving here without the knowledge of us."

"What good would it do? You have magic. I don't. It doesn't matter what I want. You'll do whatever you feel you must."

"If it makes you feel any better, I doona like erasing your memories."

She held back her wince as he took out a pan and put it on the stove. It didn't take her long to realize he was making risotto, one of her favorite dishes. "That does help some."

"Your life was disrupted, Bernadette. That wasna fair to you."

"Maybe. I could argue that I've woken up or pulled the covers down or whatever analogy you'd like to use. Knowing about the Dragon Kings, Druids, and the rest is . . ." She paused, searching for the right word. "Sublime. There is so much more to this world I live in. It's been going on all around me this entire time, and now that I've seen it, I don't want to be left out of it."

Keltan stirred the rice as he turned to look at her. "You've only seen the good parts. You've no' had to witness the horrible side, and I honestly hope you never do. The destruction, the betrayals, the . . . deaths."

"In case you've missed it, you just described life. All life. Look at the wars we humans engage in. It's in real life as well as our entertainment. It has desensitized most people to what war really is. And don't even get me started on betrayals."

"Bernadette," he said softly. "You're comparing human war to our wars. It's no' the same. You can no' comprehend what it's like. The Dark Fae use orbs of magic. Think of it as a ball of acid. It burns through anything it touches."

"Have you seen what some of our weapons can do?" she countered.

He didn't reply. "And if a Dark takes you, they'll torture you, slowly killing you all the while."

Bernadette didn't bother to say that at least she'd feel pleasure, but that wasn't really an argument.

His amber eyes locked on hers. "Think of the most horrifying thing you've seen on the tele or heard about during a war and multiply that by a hundred. Nay, a thousand. Then you can understand what our war is."

"You're immortal, so you can survive it. Do the others?" she asked.

He lowered his eyes to the pot. "The Warriors are immortal unless you take their heads. But the Fae and Druids can be killed."

"And any mortal that's around will be in the way."

"It's no' that." He swiveled his head to her. "We protect you, so we would spend our time shielding any and all humans that were near us instead of fighting. That would allow our enemies to get the upper hand."

Bernadette wrapped both hands around the mug of tea. "And Usaeil knows this, doesn't she?" At Keltan's nod, she said, "Then the queen will use that against you."

"She'll try."

"I'd offer to help, but I know you won't take it."

His smile was soft and genuine. "I appreciate you saying that. If there was even a hint that you could help, we would take you up on the offer."

That made her feel better. Bernadette drew in a breath and grinned. "My mouth is watering from the smells coming my way."

"It's nearly done. Just a couple more minutes."

"Can I get the plates or anything?"

Keltan shook his head of dark blond hair. "You stay right there, lass."

Bernadette had no problem doing that. She quite liked watching him move around the kitchen with such skill. Not to mention the sight of all his hard sinew shifting beneath his tight shirt. He was certainly handsome.

It was easy to see how someone would think the Dragon Kings weren't dangerous in such a setting. But if the image Usaeil had crafted for her was anything even remotely close to what a Dragon King actually looked like, then the world would tremble before them.

And yet they hadn't wiped out the mortals. They probably should have. It didn't matter why they didn't, and she didn't think the fact that they'd sent their dragons away made them weak. In fact, their actions proved just how strong they were.

Which is why she couldn't understand how stupid Usaeil was, going up against them.

CHAPTER FOURTEEN

It was good to have Bernadette like his food. Keltan watched as she devoured the salmon and risotto on her plate. He liked that she dug in and didn't pick at her food.

"This is delicious," she said after swallowing another bite. "You should be a chef."

He shrugged, not bothering to tell her that a few hundred years ago, he'd done just that. "I like cooking for those here."

"Do you do all the cooking?"

Keltan finished off the last of his salmon and risotto. "No' all of it. I like it, so I do the majority, but several of the mates also enjoy being in the kitchen."

Bernadette smiled after cleaning her plate. She sat back and blew out a breath. "Is it difficult to prepare a meal for so many? And that begs the question, how many Kings are there?"

He hesitated.

"Oh, come on," she said. "You're wiping my memories anyway. What does it matter if I know?"

"True. It doesna matter. There are twenty-three mated Kings."

Her jade eyes widened. Bernadette shoved a black lock behind her ear. "Just those Kings and their mates make forty-six. That's not including you or Con. And I suspect there are others."

"It's rare when we all sit down to eat together. There's just too many."

"And you'd be in the kitchen all day. Then again, I get the feeling you enjoy it."

Keltan grinned, unable to deny it. "I do. Every Dragon King has a specialty."

"Yours is cooking?" She let out a soft whistle. "Wow."

He had to laugh out loud at her impressed look. "It's no' that great. Con can heal anything but death. Ryder can hack any computer and work or build anything electronic in his sleep. Vaughn knows all legal systems like the back of his hand."

"Those sound nice, but you can feed people. Have you never heard that there is no more sincere love than that of food?"

"As a matter of fact, I have."

Her eyes narrowed as she tilted her head. "What's that little smirk for? Don't tell me. . . ." Her eyes suddenly widened. "You coined that phrase, didn't you?"

"Does it matter who said it first?"

She placed her hands together on the table. "I suppose not."

"So, Dr. Bernadette Davies, I've told you a great many of our stories. I think it's your turn to share."

Bernadette glanced down nervously and cleared her throat. "I already told you."

"A fraction of it, but I'll no' push you." He didn't need to hear anything from her. He knew most of it from the deep dive Ryder and Kinsey had done on her, but that didn't mean Keltan didn't want Bernadette to tell him something herself.

"No, no. You're right. I should share. You bared your soul. Though, I'm not sure I can really say that if I'm not going to remember any of it."

She laughed, but Keltan didn't. It bothered him that she was taking it so well that her memories would be wiped. For a moment, he'd thought she had magic that would prevent Guy from taking the memories. But that worry didn't last long.

Her smile died, along with her laughter. "You want to know why I'm not angry about it."

"You already told me."

"But you still don't understand."

He shook his head. "Nay, I doona."

"What good would it do for me to fight the inevitable? All that would happen would be an ending to this day. I may not remember what you've told me or anything about the supernatural world around me, yet I believe that somewhere inside me, the things we've shared will live on somehow. I might not remember your face, your words, or the sound of your voice, but deep inside my soul, I'll always remember that I had a special day with someone."

Keltan leaned back in his chair, one arm on the table. "If there was another way . . ." he began.

She lifted a hand, halting him. "You don't need to say it. Whether you're sincere or not, I appreciate the sentiment. You welcomed me into your home and your world for a few hours. Whatever happens, I'm grateful for that. I also want you to know that I realize now why everyone here is so secretive. There will be others out there that look into you and Dreagan in the future."

"We know."

"You might find out about some. Others you won't. You can only hide for so long."

Keltan looked down. He fisted his hand before flexing his fingers and resting his palm back on the table. Then he raised his gaze to her. "What do you think would happen if the world found out about us?"

"I could sit here and tell you lies. I could say that you'd be welcomed, but you know better than that. All you have to do is look back through history to see what we'd do. Humans have a nasty habit of searching for something new, then instead of trying to understand it or learn from it, we destroy it because we fear it."

"We willna engage in another war with mortals."

"No matter how hard you try, no matter what kind of magic you use, eventually, you'll be found out."

"Let's hope that by then, we can all share this world."

Bernadette gave him a sad smile. "We both know that will never happen."

"Then what do you suggest we do?" Keltan was curious as to what solution she might come up with.

She shrugged. "You can rid the world of us."

"That goes against the vow we made."

"True, but it might be for the best."

He stretched his legs out under the table and crossed his ankles. "If your kind continues to rape this planet at the speed with which you've done for centuries, you'll end yourselves."

Her lips twisted. "Ouch. But true. We probably will. You'll survive?"

"Who knows. We might. I hope we do."

"You'd get your world back."

He lifted a shoulder.

She drew in a deep breath. "You have the choice to force us to live with you."

"Because that worked so well last time," he replied cynically.

"We've become more advanced."

"Aye, you have. I've no doubt some leaders would love to drop a nuclear bomb on Dreagan. All that would do is kill millions. It wouldna kill us."

Bernadette wrinkled her nose. "Sadly, I think that's exactly what my kind would do."

"That leaves the option for us to leave."

"It's your world," she argued.

Keltan chuckled wryly. "If it was, we wouldna have sent the dragons away, nor would we be hiding our true identities."

"If you don't want to wipe us out or leave, then you only have one option left. Hide."

He raised his brows. "Precisely."

"You must think I'm incredibly stupid. Here I am, thinking I might know something more than a Dragon King who is millions of years old."

"I doona think you're stupid, lass. I think you're hopeful. It's no' something I've been in a verra long time. It's refreshing to see it in someone else."

She smiled, pleased with his comment. "Thank you for not thinking I'm some silly child. I'd love to hear all about your life. All the times you've lived in and the things you've seen. I could think of no one better to teach me about the true history of things."

"But would it be true?" he argued. "It would be colored by what I felt, saw, and did at that particular time. There is no accounting of history that isna colored by the one who wrote it."

"Regardless, I'd love to learn from you. If only there was time," she said wistfully.

Keltan wished he could give her what she asked for. The fact that she wasn't railing against what Fate had dealt her and what she would lose when she left Dreagan made him want to find another way to protect her from Usaeil. The problem was, there wasn't another way.

"I'm boring," she said. "I take the same route to work every day. Or I did until I moved."

Now that got his attention. "Why did you move?"

"I spent all my time researching everything to do with Dreagan. I went from a full-time position at the museum to part-time so I could devote more time to looking into dragons. That came with a huge cut in pay, and I could no longer afford my house. I sold it and most of my belongings."

Keltan shook his head, baffled that she would go to such extremes. "All because Usaeil showed you a dragon?"

Bernadette shrugged and wrinkled her nose. "It sounds utterly daft, trust me, I know. But that's the truth. All I could think about was discovering every detail about dragons and Dreagan and who lived here. I'm embarrassed to say that it became an obsession. What else can you call something that makes a person completely change their lives on a whim?"

"I've seen a lot of things in my time, lass. And while I agree, it is out of the ordinary, I doona think I'd be embarrassed about it."

She gaped at him. "I would! I gave up a career I had worked hard to obtain. I lost the respect of my peers and friends as well as the living I had. And for what? To finally get to the truth, only to have it taken away. So, I'll be able to get back to work, except I don't have my position anymore. I spent years getting to where I was, and I'll have to start all over. If I even can. Not to mention, I'll not be able to tell anyone why I did what I did for the past year."

Keltan's stomach tightened in dread at hearing all of this. He hadn't thought about the repercussions once Bernadette went back to her life. And he should have. "Things happen for a reason."

She made a sound at the back of her throat. "I don't believe that."

"I do," he insisted. "Whether you believe it or no', Fate or destiny or whatever you want to call it is real. I believe you were destined to learn about us. Just as you were meant to come here and have me tell you our story."

"Only to then take it away from me? I don't buy it."

Keltan straightened and grabbed the empty plates to take to the sink. He washed them off and glanced Bernadette's way. That's when he saw a flash of pain move over her face. "Are you all right?"

"I have a sensitive body. When I'm stressed or anxious, I don't feel that great."

"And you've been both for a while now." He wiped his hands and returned to the table. "Is there anything I can get you?"

She waved away his words. "I'll be fine."

"Let me know when that changes."

"This may sound incredibly rude, but I don't have to leave now, do I?"

He smiled and shook his head. "I hope you doona. I've yet to hear more about you. I also thought I'd take you for a tour around Dreagan. There's something I think you might like to see."

Her eyes brightened. "Really? That would be great."

"If you're up for it. But we can wait."

"Now sounds good," she said with a smile.

"Come then. I'll take you now."

Bernadette jumped up and followed him as he walked from the kitchen to the conservatory. He kept his gaze on her when he went to the hidden door and opened it.

"No way," she said with a grin.

Keltan waited for her to go through the door first before he followed. "You're in Dreagan Mountain now. We built the manor into the side of the mountain so we had access. The back of the mountain has a huge opening that we fly in and out of."

"You say that as if it's an everyday occurrence."

"We do patrol at night."

Her head whipped around to look him. "Amazing."

Keltan led her through the tunnels. When she pointed out that the lights along the way didn't have any wires, he explained that their dragon magic kept them lit.

"I love this place," she replied.

Which made him smile. That grin was still in place when he brought her to the cavern that held the four sleeping Silver dragons inside the cage.

He couldn't take his eyes from her as she walked with reverence to the huge cage and squatted beside a head of one of the Silvers.

"Touch him," he urged her.

To his delight, she reached out her hand and laid it upon the dragon's scales.

CHAPTER FIFTEEN

Bernadette was touching a dragon. A real dragon!

She could hardly believe it. The scales looked metallic and were as hard as she expected, but they were also warm—something she hadn't anticipated. The even sound of the four massive beasts breathing was calming.

She moved from dragon to dragon, touching each of them, all while marveling at how surreal it was. These Silvers, as Keltan had called them, looked much different than the gold one she'd seen.

Her gaze lifted to look across the dragons and through the bars to where Keltan stood watching her. "All of you look different, right? Like these have the spines down their backs. The gold one didn't. Do you?"

"We all certainly look different, aye. And no' just in spines and horns and such. In color, as well."

She was keenly aware of how he didn't answer her second question. "What color are you?"

He grinned. "I can tell you. Or . . . I can show you."

Bernadette slowly got to her feet, shock running through her so fast that she got a little dizzy. "Are you serious?"

"Aye," he stated.

She was about to ask if that went beyond what they would normally do, but then again, everything he was showing and telling her was different. Then there was the little fact that she wouldn't be able to remember any of it.

Remembering that they were taking her memories dimmed some of her excitement, but she refused to let it all be taken away. Maybe, just maybe she could find a way to remember some of it. Even if it was just Keltan's smile.

He cocked his head at her. "What were you just thinking?"

"Why?"

"An odd look came over your face."

She swallowed and shrugged. "I just can't get over what I'm seeing and touching. Dragons," she said with a shake of her head. "I mean, you tell me you're one, and I believe you, but then I *see* these."

"It's easy to believe what you see. You're taking what I tell you on faith."

"I am."

"And you believe every word."

She heard the incredulity of his words and wondered at them. "Why wouldn't I believe?"

"Most wouldna, though I suppose you had a little more of a head start than others because of what Usaeil showed you and the research you did. Still, you were no' skeptical."

"Who says I wasn't?" she asked with a grin. "I might keep that to myself."

Keltan laughed, his eyes crinkling in the corners. "Touché, Bernadette."

She sobered and put her fingers in the front pockets of her jeans. "I believe what you tell me not only because

I've believed for a while, but because you don't have any reason to lie. Not if you're going to wipe my memories."

"I've more to show you."

Bernadette hurried around the cage and caught up with Keltan so they could walk from the cavern together. She liked that he moved slowly so she could take it all in.

She kept hoping they would run into others, but it was almost as if everyone knew that she was there and stayed away. Not that she blamed them. Now that she knew the truth, she realized just what a predicament she'd put the Dragon Kings in. If there were a way for her to fix it, she would.

"Keltan, when I leave here, will you make sure I do something?"

He glanced and nodded. "If I can. What is it?"

"Make sure I right the wrongs I've done to you and everyone here."

"We can take care of that."

She shook her head. "It'd be better coming from me. I won't remember anything, but I'll still have people asking me about the lecture and what I've spent the last year doing. If you can come up with some explanation for me to give as well as reversing the damage I've done, I'd feel better about all of this."

He looked away and nodded. "I'll see what I can do."

She couldn't really ask for much more than that. Bernadette knew that when it came to fighting against magical, immortal creatures, she didn't stand a chance. Hopefully, her request would be considered fully.

Her thoughts halted when she and Keltan emerged from the tunnel into another cavern, this one so huge she couldn't fathom it. Bernadette walked toward the center and slowly turned in a circle, taking in the various etchings and drawings of dragons on the walls and ceiling. Some of the artwork was as big as the Silvers she'd just seen, while others were much smaller.

"It's so beautiful," she murmured.

Keltan nodded as he looked at the walls. "That they are."

"Who did them?"

"The largest was done by Ulrik when we first began building here. We all contributed in some way. I guess you could say we left our mark on the place."

Bernadette's gaze landed on him, watching the way he looked at the cavern with reverence and happiness. The Kings had something special here. Dreagan was their home, sure, but it was also their sanctuary. The only place on Earth where they could be themselves without fear or worry.

His head turned, and their gazes caught. A frown furrowed his brow. "Doona blame yourself."

"But I did it."

"Nay, lass. Usaeil did it. You were just dragged into the middle of it. Others would've done the same thing you did."

She twisted her lips, unconvinced. "I'm not so sure. I dove headlong into this without thinking of or considering the consequences. That's not like me at all."

"No doubt Usaeil used magic on you."

"That doesn't make it any better."

"It should," he argued. "You have no control in that instance. Someone decides for you."

Bernadette wrapped her arms around herself. "Is there anything I can do to prevent Usaeil or another Fae or Druid from using such magic on me?"

Keltan quirked a brow. "You doona want to have a guard up against us?"

"The Dragon Kings haven't hurt me. In fact, you've been kind and immensely generous when you didn't have to be."

He walked closer to her. "We're no' brutes. But we can be."

"I know."

"Nay, you doona. We could have—and still could—wipe out all mortals in a matter of hours."

Bernadette suppressed a shiver. "If you think I believe you weak, you're wrong. It takes a strong being to stand by their vow, to go against every instinct they have to fight for what is theirs . . . to continue living with the humans who ruined your life."

Keltan looked away and swallowed loudly. "I doona know what the future holds. In many ways, we've had a decent life. We live in grandeur and are left alone, but you're right, that willna always be the case. I hope we're always able to make the right choices, but there may come a time when there *are* no good choices."

To her surprise, he took her hand and led her to the edge of the entrance. She gawked up at the opening while trying to imagine dragons flying in and out of the mountain.

"Do you regret staying behind?" she asked and turned her head to him.

He blinked, seemingly confused by her question. "No one has ever asked me that before."

"If I recall correctly, you didn't really have a choice, did you? The dragons were sent away, but the Kings stayed."

He nodded.

She raised her brows. "Surely, some of you thought of going with the others."

"There was so much going on that day. The battles,

the decisions, the blood. I remember fighting an internal battle to join Ulrik and fight the mortals while still remembering the vow I made. I remember being so verra angry and bitter at watching my clan fly over the dragon bridge to another life. Right after that was the sadness that came with the quiet. No dragons meant no roars, no flapping of wings. That silence was like a knife to my heart, the blade turning when I went to my mountain to sleep while my clan was—hopefully—setting up their new lives. But I worried for them. Did they find a safe place? Were there other beings on the realm? Were they happy and fed?"

It physically hurt her to hear him talk of such things because she could see the pain in his eyes, hear it in his voice. Even after so many thousands upon thousands of years.

He flashed a sad smile at her. "I remember all those things as clearly as I see you. But I doona remember anything else. I'm sure there was more."

Keltan drew in a breath, causing his shoulders to rise as he looked out at the mountains. "I doona think I told you, but magic chooses us. It's the magic of this realm that looks deep into our hearts. It sees how strong we are physically, mentally, and magically. And it's that magic that decides if we'll lead. The magic did that because every clan had to have someone keeping the others in line. It's like you mortals no' having leaders for your countries."

"That makes perfect sense. So, you were chosen?" Somehow, that made Keltan being a King even more special.

He glanced at her and then slowly nodded. "I'd felt it inside for some time, but I didna act on it."

"Why not? Didn't you want to lead?"

"Our society wasna like yours. In today's world, if there is a monarchy, the next in line waits until the current king or queen either dies or steps aside. That's no' how things work with us. Occasionally, a Dragon King was killed in battle, and the next one would step in. But more often than no', we were supposed to challenge the current King."

She blinked, taken aback. "But I thought only a Dragon King could kill another King."

"When the magic chooses you, whether you accept it or no', you are a Dragon King."

"Bloody hell," Bernadette murmured.

Keltan chuckled and faced her. "Some Kings rule for thousands of years, while others only rule for a few hundred. Some lead for even shorter periods of time."

"You had to challenge your King, didn't you?"

His smile faded. "I did. He wasna just my King, he was my mentor and friend. My father and the King were close friends, so when my father died in battle, the King stepped in to help our family. I was the oldest of four. My mother was strong, but losing my father broke something in her. My sisters took up that slack while I tried to do the rest.

"For nearly a year, I ignored the call I felt from the magic. I studied my King, watching him to look for any weakness or something to prove that he wasna exactly what my clan needed. And I found nothing. Yet the overwhelming desire to challenge him grew every day."

"Obviously, you did it," she said.

Keltan's gaze dropped to the ground. "I did. He told me he'd been waiting for such a challenge, and that he was glad it was me."

Bernadette reached for his hand and squeezed it. "I know that couldn't have been easy."

"It's a fight to the death." His gaze lifted to hers. "He didna go easily. He made me earn it, and when I struck the killing blow, he smiled at me and told me he was proud."

She blinked back her tears. "He sounds like a good man. I mean, dragon. I would've liked to have met him."

Keltan suddenly smiled. "He would've liked you."

"Really?" she asked, surprised by his words.

"Oh, aye," Keltan said with a nod. "He would've said that you were meant to push me, to make me think outside the box. And you know what, he'd have been right. You have done that."

Bernadette couldn't stop the smile. "All this time, I thought I did something irreversible, and I probably have. It would be nice to think that I might have done something good, too."

"You have."

She got lost in his amber eyes. There was no lie there, only truth. And she felt it all the way to her soul.

Along with the desires that fanned to life.

CHAPTER SIXTEEN

Try as he might to ignore the desire that grew the longer he was around Bernadette, it became impossible. Keltan couldn't look away from her jade eyes. He wanted to run his fingers through her chin-length black hair and pull her against him to feel her body against his.

He couldn't feel this.

He *shouldn't* feel this.

But there was no stopping it. It'd happened without him even realizing it. Bernadette's wit, her charm, her honesty all complemented her beauty until he was utterly mesmerized, completely enthralled.

Yet his attraction was doomed. The moment she decided to leave Dreagan, her memories would be wiped. He couldn't do that to either of them. It wouldn't be fair.

But she was so close, her eyes so captivating. He could get lost in their jade depths, exploring the simple beauty that was her soul. When he first heard of her, he'd thought the worst. Even when he sat in her lecture, he hadn't given her the benefit of the doubt.

It wasn't until she came to Dreagan and he spent time with her that he'd seen her. Really seen her. He didn't even think she was aware of how open she was. And that was exactly why Bernadette had been chosen by Usaeil.

Bernadette was trusting and honest and open regarding the unknown. Some might call her a fool or naïve, but Keltan saw her as something precious. She had something pure that everyone else lost at some point during childhood. Somehow, she had kept hers.

And he didn't want her to lose it. Not now. Not ever.

An embarrassed smile pulled at her lips as she briefly looked away. "Thank you."

It took him a second to remember why she would thank him. Then he recalled that he'd told her she had done some good. "I only speak the truth."

"Whatever the reason, I appreciate it."

He smiled at her and found himself taking a step closer. She still had a hold of his hand, and he was glad she hadn't let go. Never in all his long years had he believed that he would be showing a mortal around Dreagan. Yet, it seemed right that it was her.

Fate.

He laughed inwardly. It wasn't that long ago that he'd told her that destiny had led her to him. Now, he was getting a dose of it himself because, without a doubt, he knew she was supposed to be there.

With him.

"When do I have to leave?" she asked suddenly.

Keltan shook his head. "You can stay as long as you like."

She laughed. "I'm serious."

"So am I."

Bernadette bit her bottom lip. "As long as I stay, I can retain my memories?"

"Aye."

"I know I'll have to leave sometime, but I'm not ready yet."

He grinned, happier than he could show. "Good. I'm not ready for you to leave."

"Because you have more to teach me?"

"Because I like being with you."

He hadn't meant to be that honest. It came out, but once the words were loose, he was glad he had said them. He wanted her to know that while he hadn't liked her lecture, he also didn't blame her.

Her fingers tightened a fraction on his hand. "I like being with you, as well. It might sound stupid, but I feel as if I can be myself with you. With others, I've always tried to be who they wanted me to be."

"You're special just as you are. You doona need to prove anything to anyone."

"You keep saying things like that, and I may never leave," she said with a teasing grin.

But all Keltan could think about was her doing just that. It was like being hit with a bolt of lightning. He wasn't prepared for such a revelation, and in fact, he didn't like it. At all.

The one thing he didn't want—ever—was a mate. Things were hard enough as it was without adding someone else to his life. He saw what Ulrik and the others who were mated went through. That wasn't going to be him.

Even as he vowed that to himself, he couldn't let go of Bernadette's hand. Or look away from her sweet face.

Or stop thinking about tasting her tempting lips.

"It's supposed to rain later. If you're up for it, I can take you around Dreagan," he offered.

There was a bit of hesitation in the tightening of her

mouth. "I'd love to see it all, but my stomach still isn't feeling well."

"How about we return to the manor? I can take you to a room if you'd like. Or we can go back to the library."

"The library for now," she said.

He liked her smile. But he was concerned that she wasn't feeling well. Yet she didn't show any symptoms. It must not be too bad, but he'd keep an eye on her just the same.

They turned together to go back through the tunnel, past the cavern with the Silvers, to the conservatory—all while holding hands. He liked the feel of her palm against his. It was a connection he hadn't had in ages, and it did something to him inside.

He tightened his fingers a fraction while noting that he and Bernadette had fallen in step with each other. He glanced at her, and a second later, she looked at him. They shared a smile. The moment was nothing momentous, but it touched Keltan deeply.

"I gather everyone is keeping their distance from me," Bernadette said as they walked to the library.

Keltan glanced at her and shrugged. "No one really knew what to expect. We thought it better if you saw just me until we knew where you stood. I've already told Ryder that it's fine for the others to come to the manor."

"Wait," she said as they stepped over the threshold into the library. "You've not left my side or spoken on a mobile. How did you tell Ryder anything?"

Keltan grinned and tapped his temple. "Dragons speak telepathically. That's why we had to shift when the mortals arrived in order to communicate."

"That's pretty cool," she replied with a grin.

The happy expression quickly vanished, replaced with a flash of pain as she put her hand on her stomach.

"Sit," Keltan ordered. "Do you need anything?"

"I've got some ginger gum in my purse. That always helps to settle my stomach."

He got her to the sofa and sat helplessly as she fished out the gum. He'd never heard of ginger gum, but he saw on the package that it helped with nausea and motion sickness. He hoped it did as stated because, otherwise, he didn't know what to do.

Con, who was able to heal anyone, wasn't at Dreagan. Eilish with her Druid magic, and Shara with her Fae magic were there, but there was no guarantee that either of them could help.

Keltan had never been faced with such a situation. It was just another reason he didn't want a mate. Already, he was thinking of who he could contact that might be able to help if Bernadette became too ill. Unfortunately, he could think of no one. Not even the Druids and Warriors at MacLeod Castle could help him.

"I'll get you some water," Keltan said, needing to do something.

He walked to the door and paused to look back at Bernadette. She leaned her head back on the sofa with her eyes closed. It seemed like it was nothing, but the knot forming in Keltan's stomach said otherwise.

When he reached the kitchen, he spotted Thorn. The King of Clarets stood looking inside the fridge for something to eat. He glanced Keltan's way. "How are things going?"

"I doona know."

Thorn straightened with a frown and closed the refrigerator door. "I thought you told Ryder that she was fine to meet others."

"Bernadette isna our problem."

"Bernadette now, huh?" Thorn said with a chuckle.

Keltan didn't smile. "Usaeil used her. And from what I've gathered from Bernadette's story, I believe that Usaeil did more than just show her an image of Con. I believe the bitch also made Bernadette give up her life to become obsessed with us."

"Fuck me," Thorn mumbled.

"Exactly."

Thorn crossed his arms over his chest. "We have that knowledge now, so we can make sure Usaeil never hurts Bernadette again once she leaves here with her memories wiped."

"She's no' going anywhere," Keltan stated.

Thorn's dark brows shot up on his forehead. "Whoa, brother. What's going on?"

"Bernadette isna feeling well."

Thorn shrugged. "That happens to mortals sometimes."

"I've got a bad feeling. Con isna here to help her."

"Shite," Thorn mumbled as his arms dropped to his sides. "Usaeil might have sent Bernadette here knowing exactly that. What is hurting her?"

"She says her stomach. She got some ginger gum when I left. I came to get her water."

Thorn shook his head as he went to the stove. "Some tea might help, too."

"Good idea."

"Bring the water. I'll get the tea," Thorn told him.

Keltan grabbed a glass and filled it with water before returning to the library. Bernadette lifted her head as soon as he walked in and gave him a smile. That helped relieve some of the growing panic, but not a lot.

"Don't worry about me," she told him as she accepted the glass. "My stomach has always been sensitive. It's why I try to stay away from stressful situations. I guess it was just too much all at one time."

He took the chair from earlier. "I scared you."

She chuckled and drank some of the water. "It was the unknown that made things worse. I imagined all sorts of things. Things Usaeil told me, things I learned about the women who have disappeared, and then my imagination filled in the rest. Not to mention that when Usaeil visited me last night, she made me uneasy. I'm not afraid to admit that she scares me. I don't know what she'll do if she finds out I came here."

"She willna bother you again. We're going to make sure of that."

"You can do that?" Bernadette asked with a frown.

He gave a firm nod. "Absolutely."

"Even with her mixing her magic with Druid magic?"

"We can keep her out of Dreagan. We can keep her away from you."

Bernadette's smile, full of gratitude and beauty, made his heart skip a beat. "Thank you."

"Do you think there's any way that she sent you here?"

Bernadette shook her head, her black hair swinging with her movements. "She was adamant that I keep away from those at Dreagan. She warned me that someone would come to talk to me, and she made it clear that I shouldn't succumb to any charms or seductions."

Keltan laughed with Bernadette, but all he could think about was kissing her.

"I don't know," Bernadette said with a shrug and took another drink. "The impression I got was that she wanted me to stay away from all of you. She kept pushing me to release an article online. She wanted one every week. She was just so . . . different last night."

"How, exactly?"

"Like she was close to getting what she wanted, but there were a few things not lining up. She was angry that I had waited so long to do a lecture. She wanted me to set up another soon, as well as write the articles. It was like she was impatient for the world to know about you."

Keltan sat back. "That could make sense. If she knows we're going to attack her, she wants to make sure that everything is lined up to divide our attention."

Bernadette started to say something, but her head turned to the door when Thorn walked in with a cup of tea in his hand. He flashed her a smile.

"I hear that some tea might be in order," Thorn said as he stopped before her.

Bernadette set aside the water on the table next to her, and graciously accepted the tea. "That is very kind of you. Thank you."

"Bernadette," Keltan said. "This is Thorn. Thorn, Bernadette."

Her smile was bright as she held out her hand so they could shake. "It's a pleasure to meet you. I'm so sorry for what I did. I'll do whatever it takes to fix it. I've asked Keltan to make sure that when you take my memories, something is added in about that."

Thorn glanced at Keltan in surprise. "You're . . . all right with us taking your memories?"

"No," she said with a small laugh. "But I understand why it needs to be done. This place is very special. All of you are. It should be hidden for as long as possible."

Thorn smiled at Bernadette before he looked at Keltan, and using their link, he said, "*I like her. A lot.*"

Keltan knew just what he meant. Because he felt the same.

CHAPTER SEVENTEEN

Bernadette tried to think of something other than her upset stomach. And it wasn't difficult to find something. She closed her eyes, and an image of Keltan popped into her head.

She smiled as she recalled how he'd made her lunch. And what a meal it had been. No man had ever cooked for her before. It was definitely something she could get used to.

Chills raced over her skin when she thought about how he'd taken her hand earlier. His fingers had been long and slender, firm and gentle at the same time. He'd held her hand not like he wanted to control her, but as if he needed to touch her.

Then she had done the same with him. It had been unconscious, really. She'd seen that he was hurting and wished to comfort him. She'd never expected his fingers to wrap around hers so quickly. It made her think that he desired her touch.

Oh, how easily she could let herself fall for Keltan. He was . . . well, *everything*. Sure, it helped that he had magic and came from a powerful family, but that's not what drew her to him. Thorn was the same, yet she didn't feel any kind of pull to him.

No, it was all Keltan. She sighed when she thought about the way he smiled. And, oh, God, the way he looked at her. His eyes were so damn beautiful. There were more secrets there, or perhaps it was just his years of living that she saw, but it was so easy to become lost in them.

Bernadette wanted to believe that he liked her company, and perhaps found her somewhat attractive. But a man like Keltan—gorgeous, wealthy, and immortal—probably already had a woman. In any event, he could have his pick.

She knew she was being rude by closing her eyes with Keltan and Thorn in the room, but she didn't have a choice. It was embarrassing to feel so poorly, and she wasn't going to make matters worse by vomiting. Just thinking about it made her wince.

A large hand came to rest gently on her brow. Then Keltan said in a soft voice, "You shouldna stress in such a way. I apologize if I had anything to do with it."

Bernadette forced open her eyes and found him squatting next to the arm of the sofa. "You didn't do anything."

"I'm sure I'm partly to blame after confronting you following the lecture."

She shook her head and swallowed, her mouth dry. "I'll be fine."

"Why no' let me take you to a room to rest? Maybe all you need is some sleep," he offered.

The idea of lying in a bed sounded amazing, but it meant that she would have to stand and walk. And that simply wasn't something she could do right now.

As soon as she started to argue, Keltan said, "And before you say you can no', you can. Because I'll be carrying you."

"That's worse," she whispered and squeezed her eyes closed.

"I'd rather see you get better. Now, put your arm around me."

She didn't have a choice as he lifted her. Bernadette wrapped her arm around his neck. The feel of his thick muscles beneath her hands made it difficult for her not to rub her palm over his chest to feel more of him.

Keltan got to his feet with ease, her body cradled in his arms. He smiled down at her. "I've always wanted to carry a woman to bed."

His teasing made her chuckle. She managed to keep her head up, but her eyes wouldn't focus properly when he carried her from the library. Bernadette spotted Thorn on the stairs and smiled his way. There was someone with him, but she couldn't tell who it was. And, honestly, she didn't care at the moment. She likely would later, but right now, she just wanted to feel better.

She laid her head on Keltan's shoulder and closed her eyes. Bernadette hated that she was missing this part of the manor, but maybe she could ask Keltan to take her through it once her stomach settled.

"You're going to be fine, lass."

Bernadette smiled at his comforting words. She didn't know if he was saying that for her or himself, but she liked it either way. She let out a deep breath. "I know. I'm safe with you."

"Aye, you are. Never forget that. No matter what, I willna let anything happen to you."

She almost told him that he shouldn't make promises he couldn't keep. Then she remembered that he was a Dragon King. Perhaps he could keep this promise.

Neither of them said anything else as he walked her to a bedroom. Bernadette was having a hard time keeping her eyes open. When she woke, she would likely be really embarrassed, but at the moment, she just wanted to sleep.

She sank into the blackness that called to her. She didn't know how long she was there before she felt a hand on her forehead once more. A soft blanket was wrapped around her, warding off the chill. She was no longer in Keltan's arms, but she knew he was near.

"Sleep, Bernadette. All will be well," Keltan whispered.

She could've sworn that she felt his lips on her cheek, but most likely it was just her imagination. She wanted to lift her lids and look at him, to smile and let him know that she liked him being there, but her body wouldn't obey her.

Then she stopped trying.

"Something isna right," Keltan whispered to Thorn and Sebastian at the doorway as he stared at Bernadette.

Sebastian shrugged. "She told you that she gets ill when she's under stress. I'd say the past few days have been extremely stressful."

Thorn nodded in agreement. "You confronting her at the restaurant might have begun it."

"Then Usaeil last night," Keltan said.

Bast's brows rose on his forehead. "Then coming here to face us. The girl has got some kind of courage."

Keltan had to agree. He took a step back when Bernadette shifted on the bed. He didn't want to wake her, so he motioned for his friends to follow. He made sure he could still see into the room. He didn't know why he was so worried about her, but he was. It was the same concern that drove him to think that something might not be right.

"I agree with Bast," Thorn said. "And I already told you, I like Bernadette."

Fever   135

Keltan shrugged. "I didna know what to expect when she arrived, but she's taken things pretty well."

"Aye," Sebastian said. "And you can no' take your eyes from her."

Keltan swung his gaze to Thorn and Sebastian. "What are you saying?"

Thorn threw up his hands. "All Bast is saying is that we can see how much attention you're paying her."

"Do you know what would happen if she died here? Or became seriously ill?" Keltan shook his head. "We'd be blamed."

Thorn crossed his arms over his chest. "You have a point."

Bast held Keltan's gaze. "It isna a weakness to think a lass is pretty. Or to want to be around her."

"Or to be worried," Thorn added.

Keltan ran a hand down his face. He didn't want to talk about this right now. "I need to find Shara. Or even Darcy or Eilish."

Sebastian's brows drew together. "You think Usaeil used magic on Bernadette?"

"I want to find out."

Bast nodded. "That's a fine idea. I just let Kiril know we needed Shara."

Before Keltan could let Ulrik and Warrick know, Thorn said, "Ulrik and Warrick will get Eilish and Darcy here as quickly as they can."

"I'm probably overreacting," Keltan said. "I used my magic to look for anything, but I could find nothing out of the ordinary."

Thorn shrugged. "It's better to be safe than sorry. And we can no' underestimate Usaeil again. We have a Fae and Druids here. Use them."

"Our magic is stronger," Bast said. "We should be able to detect something."

Keltan spotted Shara coming toward them. "Aye, but V and Hal couldna see through Usaeil's glamour last time. She's upped her game significantly. We need to do the same."

Shara smiled as she greeted them in her Irish accent. "Kiril said our guest isn't feeling well."

Keltan walked Shara to the door to look in on Bernadette. He briefly explained what had happened, including Bernadette's last encounter with Usaeil.

Shara's silver gaze slid to him, worry etched on her face. "I'll look, but Usaeil's magic has always exceeded mine. If you couldn't sense anything, I probably won't either."

"Please," Keltan urged.

Shara shoved aside the thick silver lock in her mane of black. "Of course."

He stared as Shara walked to the edge of the bed and held her hands over Bernadette. The minutes passed slowly. Darcy and Eilish arrived while Sebastian filled them in. Keltan didn't know when Thorn left.

Shara lowered her hands and turned to Keltan before she shook her head. Eilish and Darcy walked into the room to stand on the opposite side of the bed.

Keltan knew from the Druids at MacLeod Castle that sometimes all it took was the combined magic of others to give them what they needed. Darcy's magic was slowly coming back, and while she couldn't come close to matching either Shara or Eilish in power, every little bit helped.

At least, he hoped.

Shara stood silently as Eilish and Darcy searched for any spells placed on Bernadette. When they couldn't find anything, the three of them tried together.

But in the end, the result was the same—nothing.

Eilish was the first out of the room. She stopped in front of him and smiled. "I don't think there's anything there."

There was still a hint of an Irish brogue in her American accent. Keltan wanted to believe her. After all, he'd looked himself and found nothing.

"We did help to facilitate her getting better," Shara told him.

Darcy's fern green eyes crinkled as she smiled at him. "Bernadette will be better before you know it. I'm looking forward to meeting her."

"Thank you," Keltan said.

The three walked away, but he didn't budge from his spot.

"You still think something is going on," Sebastian said.

Keltan nodded. "I can no' shake the feeling."

"Then doona ignore it."

He snorted. "What good does it do me? We've all had a look at Bernadette and found nothing that suggests a spell has been placed on her."

"Did you ever think it's because you want there to be something wrong with her?"

Keltan jerked back as if struck. "Have you lost your mind?"

"Think about it. You were sent to see what she had to say. You spoke with her, hoping to nudge her in the right direction. Instead, she came here. You spent some time with her, got to know her. And you learned that Usaeil used her, that none of this is Bernadette's fault. She deduced that we would take her memories, and she accepted it graciously." Sebastian snorted and shook his head. "More graciously than anyone before. You opened up to her, told her your story. That in itself is a big step. You've never done that before."

"So?" Keltan stated irritably, not liking Bast's words at all.

"So . . . you showed her a side of yourself you've probably no' looked at before. The same thing happened to me with Gianna. The thing is, brother, Bernadette got inside you. Maybe just a speck, but no other woman ever has before. And it's gotten under your skin. You standing guard now? That's being protective."

"She's under my care," Keltan argued.

Sebastian blew out a breath. "Call it whatever you want. Deny it to me for the rest of time. But when you're alone, be honest with yourself. There's nothing wrong with being attracted to someone and giving in to that attraction."

Bast smiled and slapped Keltan on the shoulder before walking away.

Keltan waited until Sebastian was out of earshot before he whispered, "Maybe no' for you. But it is for me."

CHAPTER EIGHTEEN

Something was wrong. Henry could feel it in the pit of his stomach. He stopped pacing in the cavern of Dreagan Mountain and pressed his hand to his abdomen.

His skin felt too tight on his body, as if something were trying to get out of him. Feelings he couldn't put a name to churned inside, urging him to . . . he didn't know what. He only knew that something was prodding him.

If only he could figure it out.

"Fuck. It's you, as well."

Henry spun around at the sound of his brother-in-law's voice. Worry filled Nikolai's baby blue eyes, and there was only one person who could cause such a reaction from the King of Ivories. "Esther."

Nikolai nodded. "She's been staring into the fire for the past two hours."

"Fire?" Henry asked with a frown. "In May?"

"She started a fire in our bedroom and has been sitting in front of it since then." Nikolai shook his head. "This is about the two of you, is it no'? Esther being the Truth-Seeker and you the JusticeBringer."

Henry ran a hand down his face. Neither he nor his

sister had any magic, but they'd recently learned that they came from a line of Druids who used to make sure no Druids got out of line. It was always a brother and sister duo.

Esther had embraced her heritage immediately. Henry, not so much. He'd railed against it and questioned it from the beginning. But deep inside, he knew the truth. He just wasn't ready to accept it.

Though that may be out of his hands now.

While his sister was more than merely human now as a mate to a Dragon King, Henry was still very much mortal. He'd been assured by those at Dreagan, even Con, that he had a part to play in the war, but all Henry saw himself as was a liability.

"What do you feel?" Nikolai asked. "Please, tell me something. Because Esther willna speak to me. It's like she doesna hear my voice."

"She hears you. She just can't answer."

Nikolai raised his gaze to the ceiling and sighed before turning back to Henry. "I urged her to follow wherever her path led, but I'm no' sure where it's taking her. She's no' supposed to be on it alone. You're supposed to be with her."

It rankled Henry that Nikolai was the one pointing that out. He squeezed his eyes closed. He was working up to accepting what he was, but he wasn't there yet.

"Henry. Esther needs you."

"No, I don't."

They both jerked at the sound of Esther's voice. She walked into the cavern and stopped beside her husband. She smiled up at Nikolai and took his hand. "I'm sorry I scared you. I think . . . I think, for the first time, I was able to access exactly what our ancestors used to see."

Henry fisted his hands. He didn't want to hear this. He

had to search for the weapon that had been stolen from Dreagan. The very thing the Dark Fae had tried to obtain for years because it was the only thing that could kill the Dragon Kings. He'd promised himself that he would find it for Con.

"Henry," Esther called.

He shook his head and turned away. "I'm not ready. I've not found the weapon yet."

"The more you try and ignore what's calling you, the more you'll hurt. Let it out. Let it show you. Or maybe it shows me and does something else to you," she said. "Just stop fighting it."

Henry looked into his sister's nutmeg eyes. "You were always the stronger of the two of us."

"We're a team," she told him. "We work together. I seek the truth. You bring the justice."

"And you found the truth?"

"I know where we need to go."

Henry glanced at Nikolai to find the Dragon King wearing a deep frown. Henry then said to Esther, "And where is that?"

"Madrid. Lily is preparing the helicopter now," Esther informed him.

What else was he to do? Henry nodded. He'd follow his sister to see where this took them. He couldn't deny her. And she was right. The moment he stopped fighting the feeling, the pain dissipated.

Esther smiled and turned to walk out of the cavern, but Nikolai stepped in her way.

"You're no' going without me," he told her.

Esther took his hand. "It never crossed my mind, love."

Henry followed behind the two. Seeing them together made him think of Rhi. He hadn't seen her in weeks, and when she had appeared, she hadn't so much as looked in his direction. He knew there could be nothing between them. That didn't make it hurt any less.

The kiss they'd shared had changed him forever. But even he had to admit that it had done nothing to her. That was because her heart belonged to another. Everyone at Dreagan had tried to tell him. Henry hadn't wanted to believe them. It had taken years for him to finally see the truth.

There was a lot of that coming at him lately. Frankly, he didn't like it. He barely dealt with one thing before another truth came at him. It was like having his arse kicked repeatedly. If only he could handle things as well as his sister.

Then again, Esther had always had that kind of knack. When he'd joined MI5, Henry had believed he'd finally found his calling. Then they'd recruited Esther, and he discovered just how good of an agent she really was. But it was nothing compared to her role now.

She had truly come into her own. The love she and Nikolai shared made her glow. She was stronger for Nikolai's love, and for being the TruthSeeker.

Henry wanted to know more about their past. Not so much their ancestors, but why he and Esther had been adopted. He wanted to know who his birth parents were, and why it was so important that his and Esther's identities be kept secret. But not even a trip to Eigg had given him that.

In fact, it had only given him more questions.

Esther looked back at him over her shoulder as they left the mountain and headed toward the chopper that waited. Lily had already started the motor. The blades whirled above them with a deafening growl. Nikolai got Esther into the luxury helicopter before climbing in after her. Henry hesitated. For just a moment, he wondered if he should stay behind.

But a hand shoved him in the back. He glanced behind him, only to find that there was no one there. He flattened his lips and walked to the helicopter and got in. The moment the door was closed, Lily took off.

Henry buckled himself in and then looked at his sister and Nikolai. The Dragon King had his arm wrapped around Esther and she had her head on his shoulder. Henry turned and stared out the window to see the buildings of Dreagan growing smaller as the aircraft ascended into the sky.

His mind was an abyss that he was tired of being in. Every time he attempted to unravel some problem—and there were many—it seemed to make things worse. It was hard to bear because solving issues had always been his specialty. Why was nothing working now?

He tried to sleep. As soon as he shut his eyes, he fell into the dream. It was the same nightmare he'd been having ever since Usaeil disappeared.

In the visions, he works day and night tracking the queen. He finds her and gives the location to the Dragon Kings and Rhi so they can go kill Usaeil and hopefully find Con.

Except that's not what happens. Instead, Usaeil kills Rhi and the Kings. Then she breaks the barrier around Dreagan and slaughters the rest of the Kings. With their Kings dead, the mates fall all around him. Only one remains—Esther. She reaches out to him.

"Henry. You were supposed to save us. You promised Con you would find the weapon."

He runs to her, but no matter how fast he feels his legs pump, he doesn't move an inch.

"*Henry.*" A tear runs down his sister's face just before she falls dead.

Henry woke with a start. No matter how many times he'd lived through that nightmare, it still affected him the same each time.

"You all right?" Esther asked.

He cleared his throat and nodded while wiping the sweat from his brow. Henry straightened in his seat. "Where are we?"

"Spain," Nikolai said. "We'll be arriving in Madrid in about twenty minutes."

Henry tried to prepare himself like he used to do before a mission with MI5, but this wasn't the same. Still, he had to do something. The moment they landed in Madrid and got out of the chopper, he felt something in the air.

"I sense it, as well," Esther said from beside him. "This way."

He followed her and Nikolai, still unsure about all of it—especially his role in things. They walked the maze of streets for what felt like hours until Esther suddenly stopped and looked up at the second floor of a residence.

"This is where it happened."

Henry exchanged a look with Nikolai, but when he lifted his gaze to the window, he saw something shining out of it for just a split second.

"What happened?" Nikolai asked.

Esther looked at him. "This is where Usaeil killed a Druid and took his magic."

Henry's knees went weak at her words because he knew they were the truth. He didn't have to ask anyone if a murder had taken place. He knew it to the depths of his soul. It was a truth unlike anything he'd ever experienced.

"That's great, but what good does that do us now?" Nikolai asked.

Henry walked past them to the door. He didn't knock, just pushed it open and went inside. The moment he crossed the threshold, the entire scene of Usaeil's arrival and short-lived battle with the Druid played out before him like a movie. The man and Usaeil weren't solid. He could see through their bodies, almost like they were ghosts.

He walked around the area, watching as Usaeil easily killed the Druid. It was while she transferred his magic to herself that Henry got a glimpse of the real Usaeil.

Her face was still beautiful, but her eyes were blood red, and her hair was almost entirely silver. Evil radiated from her to such a degree that Henry took a step back.

When the scene finished, he squatted down next to the spot where the Druid had lain dead and touched the wood. "You will be avenged, brother," he whispered.

Henry got to his feet and found Esther and Nikolai watching him. He waited for them to say something, but all his sister did was smile. He gave her a nod. Whether he wanted this mantle of JusticeBringer or not, it was his. And he was going to do what he had been born to do.

"Now what?" Nikolai asked.

Henry licked his lips. "We search for Druids all over the world. Usaeil will go to the strongest first."

"The Skye Druids," Esther said.

Henry shook his head. "If she's not killed them yet, then she won't until she has to."

"That doesna make me feel better," Nikolai said.

Esther said, "Corann knows about Usaeil now. He and the Druids on Skye are prepared."

"No one can prepare for Usaeil." Henry ran a hand over his chin. "You didn't see what she did to the Druid."

Esther's mouth fell open. "You saw it?"

Henry nodded, his gaze sliding to Nikolai. "All of it."

"Shite," Nikolai murmured.

"Did she say anything to him?" Esther asked.

Henry blew out a breath. "Unfortunately, no."

"Then we're done here?" Nikolai asked.

Esther looked around them. "I think so."

Henry stayed behind a moment after his sister and Nikolai had left. He went to the door, and once more hesitated. He lifted his gaze and, through the people walking the streets, he saw her. She stood as still as a statue and was more beautiful than anything he'd ever laid eyes on.

And she was staring at him.

CHAPTER NINETEEN

It was amazing what a few hours of sleep could do. Bernadette woke refreshed and feeling much better. She was mortified that she'd gotten so bad that Keltan had to carry her to the room, but she couldn't forget how good it had felt to be in his embrace.

She stretched her arms over her head and then sat up. Her gaze went to the windows, where she could see that it was well into the afternoon. Her only hope was that she hadn't slept for more than twenty-four hours. She'd never done that before. But then again, she'd never felt so horrible before that a man had to carry her to bed.

Bernadette threw off the covers and swung her legs over the side of the mattress. Her shoes were set on the floor neatly, waiting for her. She smiled, wondering if Keltan had removed them and tucked her into bed. Bernadette got to her feet and looked around the room. It was done up in various shades of gray and off-white. The colors were soothing. She particularly liked the black headboard, side tables, and dresser. They added a touch of elegance to the room.

As she scanned the space, her eyes landed on an open

door. She spotted the pale gray tile within. She looked inside, found a bathroom, and quickly made use of it.

After relieving herself, she checked her hair in the mirror and winced when she saw how pale she was. She really did need to take better care of herself. Perhaps she needed to start meditating again. That always helped to keep her stress levels even.

She walked from the restroom to find Keltan standing in the doorway of the bedroom. His amber eyes crinkled at the corners when he spotted her.

"You look better," he said.

Bernadette smiled. "I feel much better. Thank you."

He waved away her words. "You're welcome to stay in here as long as you like."

Her gaze swung to the windows. "Would you mind showing me a little more of Dreagan?"

"It would be my pleasure."

Bernadette hurried to put on her shoes, and then they walked from the room together. As they descended the stairs, they ran into Thorn, who had a woman with him.

"Glad to see you're up and about," Thorn told her.

Bernadette chuckled. "I'm hoping my embarrassment over this will disappear someday."

The women elbowed Thorn in the side. "Ignore him. I'm Lexie, by the way."

Bernadette heard the American accent and shook Lexie's outstretched hand. "It's nice to meet you."

"There's a lot to see here. Don't let Keltan overwhelm you," Lexie warned with a wink.

Keltan put his hand to his chest over his heart. "I'm wounded you would even suggest such a thing."

Bernadette was amazed that they could tease and go on with their lives as if their King weren't missing, and the Queen of the Light weren't gunning for them.

Thorn and Lexie walked away, hand-in-hand. And as if reading her mind, Keltan said, "It would be easy for us to let the anxiety and weight of it all crush us. We carry on as normal to remind us of what we have and what we are."

"It's a reminder of what you have to lose."

He nodded. "Precisely."

This time, he took her out of the manor using a side door. Bernadette looked around at the splendor before her. The grounds around the domicile were gorgeous, but not overly done. The hedges were manicured, and there were sections where flowers bloomed bright and glorious.

And while the manor was beautiful, it was the view of the mountains, wild and untamed, that drew Bernadette's attention. She had no problem imagining a dragon flying over them.

"If others could see the beauty of Dreagan, they'd be clamoring to get here," she said.

Keltan nodded slowly. "That's another reason we make sure visitors can no' see more than they do when they come for a tour."

"No one has tried to get past the distillery buildings?" she asked as she turned her head to him.

He grinned. "I didna say that. They try daily, but no' only do we have magic that prevents them, there are also Dragon Kings walking around to stop anyone they find."

"It would be easier if you didn't allow anyone to visit the distillery."

"Aye, but that isna something we can do. Besides, we're closed in the winter months. It's only a few months out of the year, and we can handle it. It's no' always easy, but it's something we must do."

She had to agree. "If you tried to keep hidden, it would only make people crazier to get in and see what's going on."

"So, we open our gates, take them on a tour, let them taste the whisky, and give them the impression that they've gotten to see Dreagan."

Bernadette grinned, looking into his amber eyes. "When all they've really seen is a few buildings of the distillery."

"And the gift shop," he added.

She busted out laughing. "And the gift shop."

Their gazes held as the laughter died. They stood alone, the magic of the land swirling around them. Bernadette couldn't feel it, but she knew it was there. She could imagine it. And while that was amazing, it was the man before her that she couldn't look away from.

He stood tall, his dark blond locks brushing the tops of his shoulders. She wondered if the thick strands were as soft as they looked. And his beard. Damn. She didn't think facial hair could look as sexy as it did.

Between his hard body, penetrating eyes, sensual mouth, and beard, she couldn't pull her gaze away from him. She wanted to believe what she saw and felt was real, but she couldn't help but wonder if magic had something to do with it. Especially after realizing that Usaeil had used it on her.

Her behavior for too much of the past year had been so unlike Bernadette that it made her realize that something had been done to her. It wasn't a good feeling, and she didn't want the same thing to happen here.

"I believe everything you've told me," she said.

A frown passed quickly over Keltan's face. "I didna say otherwise."

"I just wanted you to know that. You don't need to use any kind of magic to make me think that everything here is beautiful and good."

"Lass, do you think I or someone here is using magic on you?"

Well, when he said it like that, it sounded preposterous. "Just in case you were, I wanted you to know that you don't have to."

He took a step closer. "No one here is using magic on you. Everything you're feeling and seeing and hearing is all you. I give you my word."

Chills raced over her. She didn't doubt him for a moment. Keltan had been open from the very beginning. If anyone should be distrustful, it was him about her.

"What do you feel?" he pressed.

Bernadette thought of herself as a woman who spoke her mind. Except when it came to her feelings about men. In any relationship, she found it difficult to tell the man how she felt. Now was no different.

Keltan moved close enough that she could feel the warmth coming from him. If she lifted her hands, they would rest upon his chest. She had to tilt her head back to look into his eyes.

"Doona be afraid," he urged. "You can tell me anything. What are you feeling?"

She shrugged her shoulders. "Lots of things. It's different than I expected."

"What's different?"

"You." There, she'd said it. And oh, God, that was terrifying.

One side of his lips lifted in a grin. "Good different? Or bad?"

"Good," she replied.

Keltan reached out his hand and looped his pinky with hers. "Then I can tell you that you're no' someone I was expecting." He grinned. "In a good way," he added.

She smiled, unable to hold it back. "I like how easy it is to talk to you."

"I'm glad. Then will you tell me what you're feeling?"

The nervousness returned with a vengeance. Getting out that he was different had taken all of her courage. How in the world could she tell him that she found him attractive?

"How about if I start?" he whispered.

She nodded, drowning in his amber eyes. "Yes."

His palm caressed her cheek before sliding around to the back of her neck. He leaned forward, his face lowering toward hers. Bernadette's heart slammed against her ribs as her lips parted. Without even realizing it, her free hand lifted and rested on his waist.

The moment his mouth met hers, the world vanished. It was just the two of them. His lips moved softly over hers, nibbling at her lips. She responded, and he wrapped both arms around her, pulling her against him.

She sighed at the contact of their bodies. Her hands moved up and over his broad shoulders, learning the feel of his hard muscle.

His tongue slid into her mouth, tangling with hers. Desire erupted, sending heat rushing through her veins. She clung to him as he held her tightly, as if he couldn't imagine letting her go.

It was the type of kiss she'd dreamed about experiencing. The kind she'd never thought she would get to experience. And here she stood—with a Dragon King, no less.

Keltan ended the kiss, forcing her to open her eyes. It took a moment for Bernadette to focus on him. When she did, he was grinning.

"Bloody hell," she murmured.

He nodded. "Aye. I want more."

All she could think was *thank God* because she wasn't done kissing him.

The next kiss was fire and passion. Keltan deepened the embrace as his hands tangled in her hair. She shivered, wondering how he knew just how to touch and kiss her to send her spiraling into an abyss of pleasure.

This time when the kiss ended, they were both breathing heavily. Their foreheads rested together. She kept her eyes closed because it took too much energy to open them. Her body pulsed with a desire she'd never experienced before. She wanted—no, she *needed*—his hands on her.

"Please don't stop kissing me," she told him.

"I'll kiss you for days." He lifted his head and tilted her face up.

She knew he was waiting for her, so Bernadette opened her eyes. As soon as she did, his gaze snared her.

"I'll kiss you everywhere," he said. "I'll gladly bring you pleasure and expect none for myself."

That idea didn't sound good to her at all. "I want you to have your own."

"Let me give you this," he begged her. "Let me pleasure you. You doona even have to take off your clothes if you doona want to."

Oh, she most definitely wanted to. Bernadette knew this was an opportunity she might never get again. She nodded, putting her trust in Keltan as she had from the moment she walked with him to Dreagan.

He took her hand and led her back inside. His steps weren't hurried, but he didn't linger either. Thankfully, they didn't meet anyone on their way to the bedroom she'd occupied earlier.

She entered first and turned to watch him shut and

lock the door. Then he pulled her toward the bed. They stopped at the foot as he kissed her again. Then he sat.

Bernadette pulled away from him and removed her shoes and her shirt. Then, with his gaze on her, she reached around and unhooked her bra. The moment it was gone, his eyes darkened as he took in her breasts.

"Beautiful," he said and pulled her toward him.

Bernadette found herself surrounded by his arms again. He kissed her and laid them back on the mattress.

She sighed as he kissed her senseless, then let his lips travel down her neck. He cupped her breast, massaging it gently before pinching her nipple.

The pleasure traveled straight to her sex.

CHAPTER TWENTY

This was not what he'd intended. Keltan tried to tell himself that lie once more as he held Bernadette. Because if he admitted that he'd been thinking about tasting her lips, then he would have to admit that he wanted her.

And that was a path he didn't dare walk.

He could pleasure Bernadette without putting himself in a position that he couldn't get out of. Keltan didn't wonder why it was so important that he bring out the carnal nature he suspected lay dormant within her. That was for another time—when he was alone with his thoughts and drinking heavily.

Now was for basking in the beauty of the woman who was kissing him as if there were no tomorrow. Bernadette's pale skin was in direct contrast to her black hair. Her body was slim, but she had the full curves he liked on a woman. And her breasts . . . By the stars, they were stunning. They were large, spilling over his hands.

Her back arched when he pinched her nipple. Sharp nails dug into his skin through his shirt. Her hips rocked against him, connecting with his arousal. He kissed her deeply, thrusting his tongue inside her mouth, wishing it was his cock.

Bernadette was a sweet spirit and a beautiful woman, but unleashing the siren she kept hidden was a find, even though he'd known it was there. It had been in the way she looked at him, as if she could picture them doing just this.

He wanted to see more of the sensual woman he'd found. Keltan kissed down her neck to her chest and then to her other breast. With his hands teasing one nipple, his mouth found the other.

Her moan was music to his ears.

He teased her ruthlessly, pushing her to give in to the pleasure that pressed in on all sides of her. Her hips rocked in a steady rhythm against him in her own kind of tantalizing torment.

Keltan couldn't remember ever being so hard. Or wanting to be inside a woman so desperately. The need pounding through him was so overwhelming that he was thankful there were clothes between them.

Though a little voice in the back of his head reminded him that he could remove it all with just a little magic.

That was like a punch to the gut. He lifted his head and looked at Bernadette. Her head was thrown back, ecstasy contorting her face. Her chest heaved with her breaths. Slowly, her eyes opened.

She said nothing, just pulled at the hem of his shirt. He took it off and tossed it away. Then she shoved at him, rolling him onto his back. She straddled his waist and caressed her hands down his chest.

Her movements paused when she spotted his tattoo. Her gaze jerked to his, her eyes widening a fraction.

"Every King has one," he told her.

The pads of her fingers skimmed over his abdomen to his tattoo that covered his right rib cage where it looked as if the dragon were hovering. Her fingers traced the wings that were stretched out and then down the tail.

"It's exquisite," she whispered. Her gaze met his. "Just like you."

Keltan reached up and cupped her face before he rose up and kissed her. It was meant to be a quick one, but after a taste of her, he needed more.

This time, she was the one who ended it. She smiled seductively at him as she ran her hands over his shoulders, arm, and chest. Then down his stomach. Keltan lay back, giving her access to his body. He liked her hands on him. In fact, he wanted her to touch every inch of him.

When she leaned forward and flicked her tongue over his nipple, his cock jumped, and his balls tightened. He gripped her hips, fighting not to grind against her. He was winning the battle until she rotated her hips, rubbing against him.

"You want me."

The fact that she sounded surprised shocked him. "Of course, I want you."

"I don't want this day to ever end."

"It doesna have to." He knew it was a lie, even if it was one he also wanted to believe.

She smiled and skimmed her nail over his nipple. "I like touching you."

"Then doona stop."

Her fingers spread out as she smoothed her hands down his abdomen and then moved them back up again. She leaned over him, placing soft kisses over his chest. With each touch of her mouth, his desire grew until he was burning with it.

When he could stand it no more, he flipped her onto

her back and settled his leg between hers, right against her sex. They stared at each other for a heartbeat before he focused on her breasts once more.

It wasn't long until she began moving against his leg, which added friction. Her moans turned to small cries. Her hips moved faster and faster. He knew she was on the brink of an orgasm. He'd hoped she could get there on her own because if he had to touch her, he wasn't sure he'd be able to stop.

"Please," she said on a whimper. "I need to feel you."

Keltan didn't hesitate. He was so happy to hear her words that he didn't even think of using magic. He quickly divested her of her jeans and panties.

The moment he touched her and felt how wet she was, he nearly climaxed right then. She sighed loudly when he cupped her sex.

He pushed a finger inside her and closed his eyes at the feel of her wet heat. She felt so good. Keltan forced his eyes open. He pulled out his digit to circle it around her swollen clit.

She jerked, her hands fisting the covers. He wanted to hear her scream, to be so overcome with pleasure that she lost herself in it. He shifted between her legs and filled her with his finger once more. Then he licked her.

"Keltan," she whispered, the bliss she felt evident in every syllable of his name.

He watched her as he swirled his tongue over her while thrusting his finger inside her. She rocked against him, giving in to the desire. It wasn't long before her body began to tighten, alerting him that she was close to orgasm.

Keltan redoubled his efforts. And then she climaxed.

The sight of her was stunning. Her body jerked as she opened her mouth on a silent scream. The pleasure on her face made his heart skip a beat. He'd never seen anything so pure in all his life.

He brought her down softly, extending the orgasm until her body went limp. Keltan then moved up beside her and pulled her into his arms.

"Oh, my God," she whispered.

He smiled as he looked at the ceiling. "I think I enjoyed that nearly as much as you."

She chuckled and put her hand on his erection. "I doubt that."

"I enjoyed watching you."

"And if I want to pleasure you?"

He put a finger beneath her chin to tilt her head up so he could look into her eyes. "You doona need to do that."

"What if I want you inside me?"

How could he refuse? He was holding a very beautiful, very naked woman in his arms. Only a fool would decline such fun. "Bernadette," he began.

She put a finger on his lips. "I know you didn't expect this. No one has ever made me feel like you just did. I'd like to give it back to you."

He started to open his mouth, but she squeezed his cock through his pants, and Keltan forgot what he was going to say. Without a thought, he removed his clothes. He would let her choose what they did and how far things went.

She moved her hand up and down his length slowly a time or two before she increased her tempo. He closed his eyes as the pleasure enveloped him.

He felt her shift, and then she wrapped her lips around him. Keltan forgot to breathe as she took him deeply into her mouth. It felt so good that he knew he wouldn't last long—but he also didn't have the wherewithal to stop her.

Just when he thought she would finish him in her mouth, she moved to straddle him. This time, she took his cock in hand and led him to her entrance.

He watched as she lowered her body onto his arousal. Keltan cupped her breasts and pinched her nipples as she began to rock her hips. She held on to his arms and dropped her head back. Their moans filled the room as she moved faster and faster.

Keltan lifted his hips, driving into her. She called out his name and raised her head to look at him. He grabbed her hips and moved her up and down on his length as she braced her hands on his chest.

The moment he felt his orgasm, he pulled out of her. She took hold of him, milking him. He let out a shout as the bliss took him. He'd never experienced a climax so deeply before, and he knew he would always remember this day.

When he was able to, Keltan materialized a towel in his hand and wiped himself clean. Then he pulled Bernadette into his arms. She nestled against him, her head on his chest. He wound his arm around her and simply held her, thinking over what he'd just experienced—what they had experienced together.

"That was . . . I have no words," he told her.

He felt her smile against him. "Now you know how I felt."

"Can we do that again?"

"I was hoping you'd say that."

He kissed the top of her head and let out a deep breath. It wasn't long before her breathing evened into sleep. There was much Keltan had intended to show her that afternoon before he cooked for her again. But they always had tomorrow.

There was a moment of alarm as he realized where his

mind had gone. Then he rationalized it by saying to himself that he couldn't make her leave now after just making love to her. She would leave tomorrow.

And with her departure would come the removal of all her memories of him.

That saddened him greatly, but he would never forget their time together. Besides, it would be better if she didn't know anything about him, the Dragon Kings, Usaeil, or any of it.

The queen had used Bernadette for her own purposes. If anyone deserved to get out of this world and continue on the path that they'd deviated from, it was Bernadette. But he would miss her.

Keltan could admit that to himself—and only himself—because she would only be in his life for a short time. He held her tighter. He noticed that her body was still warm. Then again, maybe it took her longer to cool off than it did him. He didn't think anything about it as he closed his eyes and let his thoughts drift.

He must have dozed because when he woke, he was drenched in sweat. He was confused about it until he realized the one sweating was Bernadette.

Keltan put his hand on her forehead and felt the heat against his palm. In a heartbeat, he realized that she had a fever.

He rolled her onto her back. "Bernadette, lass. Wake up."

But no matter how many times he called her name or shook her, she wouldn't open her eyes. Worried, Keltan jumped out of bed and hastily dressed. He walked around to the side of the bed and sat to once more try and wake her.

Finally, he gave up and used his mental link to contact Darius, who was mated to Sophie, a doctor. He covered Bernadette with the blanket. In moments, there was a knock at the door.

Keltan rose to open it and found Darius and Sophie, as well as her nurse, Claire, along with V.

"What happened?" Sophie asked in her British accent.

"She was unwell earlier. Stomach problems related to stress," he explained. "Shara and Eilish looked at her because I thought Usaeil might have spelled her."

Claire walked to the bed and put her hand on Bernadette's forehead. "She's running a high fever."

Sophie rushed to Bernadette and began examining her. Keltan looked at both V and Darius. V said nothing, just watched the women with Bernadette.

"Sophie will know what to do," Darius said.

But Keltan feared that this was something major. And what had he done? Made love to Bernadette instead of recognizing that she was ill. What did that make him?

He ran a hand through his hair and stared at Bernadette, willing her with his mind and magic to wake up.

CHAPTER TWENTY-ONE

A secret place ...

"Oh, I can't wait for you to see what's coming." Usaeil stared at her prisoner, lying prone on the bed.

She walked from one side to the other, trailing her hand along the mattress. It gave her immense pleasure to torture her nephew as she was. Xaneth had thought to deceive her, but as always, she had come out on top.

And when she finished with him, his brain would be mush.

She leaned down so that her mouth was by his ear. "It's what you deserve. How dare you think you could escape me? Worse, you tried to betray me. For that, you will suffer untold pain. You see, nephew, only a few weeks have passed for me, but for you, it has been decades."

Usaeil smiled as a tear ran from his closed eye into the hair at his temple. "And I'm not nearly finished with you yet. It's only just begun."

She laughed and straightened. It was so much fun tormenting Xaneth. She had trapped him in his own mind. If he were strong enough, he could break through. But she knew he wouldn't be able to. He was weak. Her entire family had been weak.

It was why she'd killed them all and took over.

Without her, the Light would have been decimated by the Dark. Without her, the Fae would've been wiped out by the Dragon Kings during the Fae Wars.

She had seen it all and did what any ruler would have—she helped her people survive.

It was what she was still doing, though few would understand.

"There's one who does," she whispered.

Usaeil turned on her heel and strode from the room. She walked to the other end of the structure and opened the door. Her eyes landed on his tall form and wavy, blond hair. Her stomach quivered in anticipation.

"Constantine."

He turned at the sound of her voice and met her eyes with his black ones. "How long will you keep me here?"

"Not much longer."

"I need to get back to Dreagan."

She walked to him and placed a hand on his chest before gazing up into his face. "Just a little longer. I promise."

"Usaeil," he said, irritation deepening his timbre.

The sound caused a shiver to run through her. Damn, but the man had a voice she could listen to until the end of time. Which is exactly what she intended.

It wouldn't be long now before Rhi was dead. The time she gave the Kings to turn Rhi over was running out quickly, and Usaeil could hardly contain her excitement.

"I give you my word, Con. Only a little longer."

"And how are my brothers?"

She lifted a shoulder. She hated when he wished to talk about them. It was the last thing she wanted to do, but she indulged him. "They're fine. They understand that I need you right now."

"Do they?" he asked, a blond brow quirked.

"I would never lie to you. They've even asked if they could help, but I told them I only need you."

Con nodded slowly. "I should've spoken with them."

"They understand how important it is for you to keep away from Rhi. Especially since she and Balladyn are trying to kill you."

Con's lips flattened as they always did when she told him that. So far, he'd believed the lie. And she knew that, with her magic, she could keep it up for as long as it took for her to kill Rhi. Once the meddling bitch was out of the way, then Usaeil could have Con once and for all.

"I still doona believe it. Rhi is a friend," he argued.

Usaeil stopped short of rolling her eyes. She couldn't wait for the bitch to be out of her life forever. "You know that rulers like us can't really have friends. Everyone envies our power and position. They try to be our friends, but in the end, they betray us."

"I didna do anything to Rhi."

"But you did, my love," she whispered.

Con's eyes grew distant as he went back through his memories. Then he turned his back on her to once more look out the window. "I didna have a choice."

"There is always a choice. You made the right one, by the way. Look how far you and the Dragon Kings have come. Do you really believe you could've achieved that any other way?"

He crossed his arms, his black tee pulling tightly across his shoulders. Usaeil smiled and fisted her hands so she wouldn't touch him. She'd made it impossible for him to wear any of his suits in her presence. She wanted a constant view of his great body.

"I've always done what I had to for the Kings," Con said.

"Which means you don't regret your decision about

Rhi." When he didn't immediately reply, she walked to stand before him. "Right?"

His black eyes glanced her way before he gave a quick nod.

"Good. You should live your life without regrets."

He snorted loudly. "I have a great many regrets. Letting the humans stay, vowing to protect them, sending the dragons away, banishing Ulrik, and, most of all, allowing the Fae to remain on this realm."

She gawked at him. "You can't be serious? Had you sent us away, we never would've found each other."

"And we wouldna be where we are today. Rhi has a great many friends at Dreagan. It's going to kill them to see her destroyed."

Usaeil did roll her eyes this time. "It's you or her. Do you really want to give up your life just so Rhi can have her revenge?"

"I willna willingly lay down for anyone to kill me."

"You're damn straight, you won't," she declared. "You're Constantine, King of Dragon Kings."

He blew out a breath. "Tell me again how Rhi was able to contact the Others so she could kill me?"

"I'm not ready to leave."

At Henry's declaration, Esther and Nikolai stopped walking and turned to him. Nikolai didn't utter a word, his baby blue eyes giving nothing away.

Esther's forehead furrowed with a deep frown. "What's wrong?"

Henry shrugged. "Nothing."

"You're lying," his sister said. "I know it."

Henry swallowed and shot her a quick smile. "I want to spend more time in Madrid. I want to investigate more of what I saw at the house."

"Perhaps we should remain, as well?" Nikolai said.

Henry shook his head, his gaze moving from his brother-in-law to his sister. "You found this place for us. You did your job. Now, it's time for me to do mine."

"Perhaps you're right, but we're a team. We should stick together," Esther replied.

Henry should've thought of that. By the smirk on Nikolai's face, Henry realized that his brother-in-law had. Thinking quickly, Henry said, "You've accepted your gifts. I haven't. I need some time. I don't want anyone looking over my shoulder, questioning me, or following me."

"I don't know," Esther hedged.

Nikolai put his arm around her. "Henry's right. He needs time to himself."

"How are you going to get back to Dreagan?" Esther asked.

Henry laughed and shook his head. "You do remember I worked for MI5, right? I know how to get home from anywhere in the world."

Nikolai gave him a nod. "There's no doubt you can take care of yourself, but our enemies are vast. Those foes may now know of you. I'm no' going to be the one who returns to Dreagan to tell everyone that I lost you."

"You're not losing me," Henry said irritably.

Esther licked her lips, the frown still firmly in place. "How long do you need?"

Henry threw up his hands. He, like everyone else at Dreagan, was keenly aware that their time to deliver Rhi to Usaeil was running out. "I've no idea. I want to look at my leisure."

"We'll be close," Nikolai offered.

"Yes," Esther said, brightening. "Close."

Nikolai twisted his lips as a form of apology. "I'm

sorry, Henry. I must look out for my mate, and this allows both of you to compromise and get what you want."

There was no way for Henry to get out of this. Finally, he nodded. "Fine. I'll agree to that."

"I'm a phone call away," Esther said.

She embraced him, and Henry held her tightly as he looked at Nikolai. The Dragon King knew something was up, and he was giving Henry what time he could to figure it out. Henry gave him a nod of thanks before releasing his sister.

Esther smiled at him before she and Nikolai walked away together. Henry didn't wait for them to leave. He turned on his heel and went back to the house to find the woman. He didn't know why, but it was important that he locate her. He'd known the moment he saw her that he needed to talk to her. About what, he wasn't sure.

All he knew was that going against his instincts had brought him nothing but trouble. Now more than ever. Maybe it was because he'd discovered that he was the JusticeBringer. Hell, for all he knew, he'd had the same instincts his entire life but hadn't been listening for them.

Or maybe he had. There were many instances when he should've been killed out on a mission, yet somehow, he'd always managed to get out of it and make it home.

By the time he reached the house where the murder had taken place, the woman was gone. He went down many winding streets, but no matter how hard he looked, he found nothing. He didn't give up, though. She was there, somewhere. He was sure of it. She had looked right at him as if she were staring, waiting for him to notice her.

Henry walked the streets until it grew dark. Then he

went to find something to eat. He passed numerous cafés and restaurants, but he kept walking.

He had no idea where he was going, only that he'd know it when he reached it. Another fifteen minutes later, he turned a corner and saw the bistro. Without knowing how, he *knew* this was the place he'd been searching for. His gaze scanned the people sitting outside as well as inside, but he didn't see the woman.

With a sigh of regret, he made his way inside and found a table. A waiter took his order and brought him some wine.

Henry took a drink then set the glass down, holding it by the stem and slowly swirling the dark liquid inside. His thoughts were centered on the woman. He could recall every detail of her.

Her long hair was the most beautiful silver color and faded to pitch black at the ends. She was tall and held herself with confidence. While he didn't know the shade of her irises, he knew her face. The high cheekbones, the large eyes, and lips that would bring any man to his knees.

As if his thoughts had conjured her out of thin air, the woman appeared out of the shadows beneath the light of a streetlamp. She halted the moment she saw him.

Henry wanted to go to her, but he made himself hold still. It paid off because she slowly came to him. There was something about her that was so familiar. As if he knew her somehow. But that wasn't possible. If he'd met her before, he certainly wouldn't have forgotten her.

"Did you follow me?" she demanded.

He heard the Scots brogue, but he didn't mention it. Instead, he shook his head. "I admit I looked for you, but I gave up finding you."

"You just happened to come here to eat?"

"I did."

She took a deep breath and stared at him as if trying to decide what to believe.

Henry held out his hand. "I'm Henry."

For a count of three, she did nothing. Then she gripped his hand. "I'm Melisse."

CHAPTER TWENTY-TWO

The minutes ticked by with torturous deliberateness. And with each one that passed without either Sophie or Claire lifting their heads to tell Keltan what was wrong with Bernadette, he became more worried.

"Something isna right," V said.

Keltan had been telling himself that for a while now.

Darius didn't reply. He walked to his mate and leaned close to Sophie, whispering something in her ear. She didn't even stop examining Bernadette as she replied.

Keltan's stomach clenched when Darius's gaze landed on him. "What is it?" Keltan demanded.

V put a hand on his arm. "Give them time."

Keltan turned away and walked a few paces as he ran a hand down his face. Then he faced the bed once more. "We need Con. Everyone is thinking it, so I'll say it. And the fact that we need Con means that Usaeil is a part of this. She knows Con isna here. She knows . . ."

He couldn't finish the sentence.

"I need Bernadette at my clinic," Sophie suddenly said.

In seconds, Ulrik was there. Keltan hadn't had time to notify him, which meant that either Darius or V had.

Keltan was thankful, but before he could utter the words, Ulrik walked to the bed, lifted Bernadette in his arms, and waited for both Claire and Sophie to put their hands on him before he touched the silver cuff at his wrist and teleported them all away.

It was the first time that Keltan wished he had such a bracelet. He didn't like being left behind.

"I'm driving," Darius stated as he turned away.

Keltan quickly followed him with V falling in step beside them. It wasn't long before they were at the garage and pulling away in one of the Range Rovers.

There was no need for Keltan to tell Darius to hurry because he was already zooming down the drive and through the streets. Though it only took a few minutes, it felt like an eternity before they pulled up to the clinic.

The three of them said nothing as they jumped out of the SUV and rushed inside. Keltan had only visited the center a handful of times, so he followed V and Darius into the building and toward a back room. Only to have to wait some more as Darius came to a halt.

"They'll be out in a moment," he said.

Keltan raked a hand through his hair and leaned back against a wall. He thought back to the past few hours, remembered making love to Bernadette. She had shown no signs of feeling unwell. He hadn't been so wrapped up in pleasure that he would've missed something like that.

Surely.

He closed his eyes because he couldn't help but wonder if he might very well have done just that.

"It might be nothing," Darius said.

Keltan opened his eyes to look at his friend.

V nodded. "Humans get ill all the time. Sophie is an experienced doctor. If anyone can help Bernadette, she can."

He knew what they were doing, and Keltan wanted to tell them that their words helped. But in truth, they didn't. "I should've noticed something."

"We might be magical creatures, but we're no' all-knowing or all-seeing," V stated.

Darius snorted, nodding. "No truer words have ever been spoken. This isna your fault, Keltan."

"I beg to differ," he argued. "I should've known something was wrong."

V crossed his arms over his chest, his ice blue eyes landing on Keltan. "You think because the two of you were having sex that you did something?"

Though none had said anything or asked, Keltan knew that everyone had guessed that he and Bernadette had been together. It wasn't hard to deduce when she'd been lying nude in a bed of tangled sheets.

"I might have. Usaeil warned her against us," Keltan said.

Darius rolled his eyes. "I've no doubt that Usaeil's hand is in this somehow. We will figure it out."

"Can we?" Keltan asked, truly wanting to know. "Because without Con, I'm worried."

Neither V nor Darius got to answer that because the door flew open, and Claire appeared. Her face was pale, her eyes wide as she looked at the three of them.

"Ulrik just took Sophie and Bernadette to the hospital," Claire announced.

Keltan pushed away from the wall. "Why? What happened?"

Claire swallowed and walked to V, who put his arms around her, offering her comfort and strength. "Her organs are failing."

"Shite," Darius mumbled.

A muscle ticked in V's jaw. "Usaeil."

"But why?" Claire asked and raised her face to look at V. "Why would she do this?"

And that's when it hit Keltan. "Because she didna want Bernadette to talk to us."

Darius's dark brown eyes narrowed on Keltan. "Or Bernadette has stayed too long."

Keltan couldn't think about any of that right now. He just wanted to get to Bernadette. "None of that matters. What we have to figure out is how to stop whatever is happening to Bernadette."

V lifted a shoulder. "Maybe getting away from Dreagan will help."

Claire shook her head. "Afraid not."

"The clinic is still part of Dreagan," Darius said.

Keltan cut his hand through the air. "If Usaeil did this to Bernadette, then no amount of human medicine will stop what's happening to her."

"What do you suggest, then?" V asked.

Keltan shook his head as he went through his conversations with Bernadette. That's when it dawned on him. "We need to bring Bernadette home."

"That could work," Darius said.

Claire gaped at them. "Or, it could kill her."

"She's dying as it is," V said.

Keltan didn't want to waste time arguing. "We need answers, and Ulrik can give them."

Keltan opened the mental link and said Ulrik's name. In the next heartbeat, the King of Silvers stood in the room with them.

Ulrik's black hair was pulled back at the base of his neck in a queue. His gold eyes moved around the room until they landed on Keltan. "It's no' looking good."

"The medicine needs time to work," Claire said.

Keltan ignored her and kept his gaze on Ulrik. "Usaeil did this."

Ulrik's head tilted to the side. "It sounds like something the queen would do. You think this is Usaeil's revenge?"

"I do." Nothing else made sense, but Keltan still hoped that he wasn't wrong.

Ulrik blew out a breath. "She's going downhill fast. If you have a theory, then tell me now."

"Bring Bernadette home."

Surprise flickered on Ulrik's face. "If she's back where she needs to be, then Usaeil's magic may stop hurting her."

"It's a guess," Keltan admitted, his gut clenching with fear and helplessness.

V made a sound at the back of his throat. "A damn good one."

"I agree," Darius said.

Ulrik nodded. "I just got the address from Ryder. I'll take her home, then I'll come back for you."

Claire began locking up the clinic, and Keltan understood why she wasn't totally going along with them. Claire was a great nurse. She knew mortal medicine, but this was magical and needed to be treated as such.

"Do you want us to go with you?" V asked him.

Keltan shrugged. "Whatever you want to do."

"I think the fewer Kings that are there, the better," Darius said.

V's brows shot up on his forehead. "Unless that's exactly what Usaeil wants."

"Bloody hell. I hadna thought of that," Keltan said.

Darius ran a hand through his long blond hair. "She'll know if we're there. Either way, we're playing into her hand."

"Maybe none of you should be there," Claire interjected.

Keltan was about to argue when he realized that Claire was absolutely correct. "Usaeil doesna want Bernadette talking with us, and if we're at Bernadette's house, it'll push Usaeil to possibly hurt Bernadette even more."

No sooner had he finished speaking than Ulrik appeared and looked his way. "Ready?"

Keltan took a step back. "Is she doing better?"

"We just got her there," Ulrik replied. "Sophie is monitoring her, but we need more time."

V caught Ulrik's gaze. "Keltan thinks that any King at Bernadette's may only hurt her."

Ulrik frowned for a moment, then he nodded. "Usaeil. She could verra well have set a trap for us, waiting to see if any Kings take the bait."

The idea of Bernadette as bait infuriated Keltan. But the moment he felt that anger, he let it go. It was fury that would lead them straight into Usaeil's hands. He wasn't going to fall for that. Usaeil believed she was smarter and stronger than them. She wasn't.

And he was going to prove it.

Ulrik's gold eyes swung back to him. "You're no' going?"

Keltan shook his head, unable to say the words.

It was Darius who said, "When Bernadette wakes, she's going to want to see you."

"I know," Keltan replied.

"If Usaeil is responsible for Bernadette's pain, then Bernadette may never be able to return to Dreagan," V said.

A cry of outrage welled within Keltan. "No' if we kill Usaeil."

"Sounds good to me," Darius said.

Claire put a hand on her stomach. Keltan had been so wrapped up in Bernadette that he had forgotten the lengths Usaeil had gone to in order to ensure that Claire carried V's bairn in her womb.

"I'm sorry, Claire," Keltan said.

She gave him a sad smile. "You're worried about Bernadette. There's no need to apologize for anything. I'm fine."

"I've got you, love," V said as he kissed her forehead.

Keltan looked away as he thought of Bernadette opening her eyes and him not being there. It was for the best, though. Hadn't he said how wrong it was that she'd gotten pulled into their world simply because Usaeil had picked her out of a crowd?

This was Bernadette's way of getting out of it all.

"We need to wipe Bernadette's memories," Keltan said. He looked up at Ulrik. "That was the plan anyway."

Claire shrugged. "What does she know that Usaeil doesna already? Maybe we don't need to do anything."

"Nay, we do," Darius said.

Ulrik nodded slowly. "It isna just Usaeil we need to worry about. It's the Others and what they could do with what Bernadette has learned."

Claire sighed loudly. "Again, what did she learn that Usaeil—and most likely the Others—don't already know?"

V gave Claire a squeeze. "It's no' a chance we can take."

"I'll have Guy ready," Ulrik said to Keltan. "Are you sure you doona want to see Bernadette once more?"

They all assumed that Bernadette would recover, and right now, Keltan had to hold on to that. "It's for the best if I doona see her again."

"That's a mistake," Darius said.

Keltan quirked a brow. "Why? Because I slept with her?"

"Because of the way you look at her," V replied.

Ulrik's lips twisted. "V's right. I've no' ever seen you look at a woman like that before."

"Bernadette is nice, honest. She was used by Usaeil and tossed into our world to try and bring us down. Bernadette's life was destroyed. I like her, aye, but that's where it ends. There's nothing developing between us. I know many of you found mates, and that's all well and good, but it's no' my turn."

Darius shrugged. "Suit yourself. I'm heading back to Dreagan."

V and Claire followed Darius, leaving Keltan alone with Ulrik.

"It's no' a weakness to care for someone," Ulrik said.

"It is for me." Keltan turned on his heel and walked out before he changed his mind and had Ulrik bring him to Bernadette. It was better this way.

Especially for Bernadette.

CHAPTER TWENTY-THREE

Bernadette put a hand to her head the moment she woke and turned on her side. It felt like that one time she had gotten roaringly soused at University. She'd spent the next few hours in the toilet, and Bernadette had sworn she'd never do that again.

She searched her mind for what she had done before she went to sleep. Almost immediately, an image of Keltan—gloriously naked as he lay beneath her while she rode him—flashed in her mind.

Her eyes flew open, and she held still to determine if he was still in bed with her. She blinked when she found herself staring at one of her favorite pictures—a black-and-white photo of a chandelier.

A quick look around showed her that she was in her own room. Which couldn't be possible. She'd been at Dreagan. In bed with Keltan. Then why was she back at her house?

Bernadette sat up and winced. Her entire body was sore, making her frown even more. Worse, there seemed to be no sign of Keltan. Then she heard the voices.

"Her breathing isn't as shallow. Keltan was right that

we bring her here," a female with a British accent said. "It didn't take long for her to begin improving."

So Keltan was responsible for her being here. But did that mean she'd gotten sick? The last thing she recalled was feeling glorious pleasure before she went to sleep in his arms. Bernadette didn't move as she waited to see if whoever the woman spoke with would reply.

A deep Scottish voice said, "If she's improving, then I should go ahead and wipe her memories. I'd rather do it now than when she's awake. It's no' a process I particularly enjoy."

"I know, Guy," the woman said, regret in her voice.

"It has to be done." Guy paused. "Then we need to leave."

The woman made a sound. "I'm not going anywhere until I know for sure that Bernadette is out of the woods. Whatever Usaeil did to her was horrid."

"Keltan believes that a Dragon King or anyone involved with us might make things worse if we remain," Guy stated.

"A Dragon King I can see."

Guy sighed. "Sophie, I doona like this any more than you do, but what if this is a trap for us? The longer anyone from Dreagan is here, the more we give Usaeil the chance to take another of us. And, frankly, I doona want to have to tell Darius that the queen captured you."

"Ha," Sophie said, though there was no mirth. "He'd be nothing compared to Elena. Your mate would tear the world apart looking for you."

Bernadette closed her eyes as she listened to the two of them. Both had found love. Honestly, she'd wondered if that kind of love existed. Sure, people wrote about it and portrayed it in film. But in real life? It was as much a fantasy as finding a pot of gold at the end of a rainbow.

And yet, those at Dreagan seemed to have discovered the elusive emotion. Bernadette didn't think she'd ever find that kind of partnership with someone. Though, hearing someone else speak of the lengths the one they loved would go to for them made Bernadette's heart ache for it.

She'd once been addicted to romance novels. She had hundreds of them and devoured every word on the page as she dreamed of finding the love of her life.

That longing, that fantasy got in the way of real life and destroyed a promising relationship she'd had with a guy. The books were only a part of the problem, but it made her take a hard look at herself. She turned her focus from the stories to her studies and gave away all the books. It had been years since she'd read one.

Bernadette threw back the covers and swung her legs over the edge of the bed. She wanted to know what Usaeil had done to her, but she wasn't going to ask. Perhaps it was better if she didn't know. Like it was easier not to think that she would ever find the kind of love romance authors wrote about.

She pushed to her feet and looked down to find herself in a nightgown that wasn't hers. Bernadette licked her lips and began slowly walking to the bedroom door as Guy and Sophie continued talking.

When she got to the doorway, she looked out into her kitchen to find Guy sitting at the table. He had hair the color of honey that hit his shoulders. He wore a form-fitting navy tee shirt with a cream-and-blue-striped button-down over it, hanging open. He, like the other Kings she'd met, was handsome.

Sophie leaned back against the kitchen cabinets, her hands resting on the counter. Her thick, straight, golden hair was pulled back in a French plait. She was poised and beautiful. And for some reason, Sophie had helped Bernadette.

"I don't want anyone hurt," she said.

Sophie's and Guy's heads snapped in her direction. Guy got to his feet, while Sophie rushed to her.

"You shouldn't be out of bed," Sophie said, worry in her olive eyes.

Bernadette held up a hand, stopping her. "I feel fine. Tired and sore, but fine. I don't want to know what happened. What I do want is for everyone at Dreagan to be safe. I'm responsible for this, and if wiping my memory will help, then please do it." Her gaze moved to Guy. "It's all right. I've known this was coming."

"That doesna make it any easier," Guy said.

She gave him a smile, though it wasn't much of one. "I don't want Usaeil using me anymore. She's done enough."

"Usaeil will just use someone else. For all we know, she already has them lined up," Sophie said.

Guy let out a string of curses beneath his breath as he turned away and paced a few times. Then he halted and looked at Bernadette. "Sophie's right. For all we know, Usaeil will use someone else. At least with you, we know it."

Bernadette frowned, not understanding him at first, then her eyes widened. "You want me to retain my memories and let her continue using me?"

"That might work," Sophie said, looking between the two of them. She met Bernadette's gaze. "Think about it. You know what she's done, but she doesn't know what you've learned. You can use it against her."

"While that sounds good in theory, I should let both of you know that I actually failed acting class at University. I was so bad the instructor asked me to drop the class, which I did."

Guy waved away her words. "That was University. This is your life, Bernadette. You can take back control."

It all sounded great, but Bernadette wasn't sure she was strong enough for that. She, a mere mortal, going up against the Queen of the Light? Right. Like that would go over well.

"We'll protect you," Guy added.

Sophie nodded, smiling. "This does help us, but it helps you more. Guy can wipe your memories and let you go back to your old life. We can ward your home and you to make it near impossible for Usaeil to use you again. She might give up and find someone else."

Bernadette drew back at that. "You really think Usaeil will go and interfere in someone else's life?"

"Without a doubt," Sophie said.

Guy nodded, remorse in his pale brown eyes ringed with black. "Usaeil wants to hurt us. Divide us. She spent a year working with you. She willna hesitate to find someone else to control."

Bernadette rested her head against the doorjamb. "I was an anthropologist minding my own business. I'm not used to fighting in some magical war."

Sophie gave a bark of laughter. "You could've fooled me. It took some pluck for you to drive to Dreagan and walk into the distillery. You didn't know what awaited you or what we would do."

"She's right," Guy said. "The fact that you came to get answers on your own says a lot about your strength of character."

"I don't want to be anyone's pawn. Not Usaeil's, not Dreagan's." Bernadette closed her eyes briefly as she blew out a breath. "I want to make my own decisions without worrying about a Fae tracking me down or if it might harm Dreagan."

Guy made a face. "Doona worry about us. We've survived for untold millennia. We will continue to do so. My reasoning for you doing this is twofold. One, you help us catch an enemy so Con can return. And two, you get your life back."

"What about my memories?" Bernadette asked.

Guy shrugged and exchanged a look with Sophie. "If Usaeil is dead, I see no reason you could no' keep them. Though, I will say it isna my decision alone to make."

"Of course," Bernadette said.

She started toward the sofa, only to have Sophie hurry over to help. Once she was seated, Bernadette reached for the blanket she always kept near and covered her legs.

"Think about what we said," Sophie begged.

Bernadette smiled sadly at them. "We don't have that kind of time, and both of you know that. I appreciate you giving me the option, but we all know I need to make the decision now. If Usaeil did make me ill, then she'll be dropping by soon. I'll do it. It helps me as well as everyone at Dreagan."

"I'll let the others know," Guy said.

Sophie gave Bernadette a bright smile. "You're not in this alone. I hope you know that."

Bernadette laughed softly and shrugged. "I'm going to believe I am. It's easier that way."

Sophie put a hand on her arm and squeezed. "If you start to feel bad in any way, call me. I won't write down the number, but all you need to do is look up the clinic. It's the only one near Dreagan. I'll get your message and be here as soon as I can."

"I promise," Bernadette said.

Guy then said, "I've told the others. We can no' ward your home because it would alert Usaeil that we've been here, but I am putting up a border that will tell us if any Fae shows up."

Bernadette swallowed, hoping she made the right decision. "Will you come if she shows up?"

"Nay," Guy said. "It just lets us know when Usaeil comes to you."

"So that I can then tell you what she wants," Bernadette guessed.

Sophie licked her lips and dropped her arms to her sides. "We want you to help us, but we're not going to demand it. What you choose to share is up to you."

Bernadette was taken aback by the doctor's words. "You could easily make me do whatever you want."

"We're no' Usaeil," Guy said, anger tinting his statement.

Gone was his easy expression. In its place was a face hardened with determination and resentment.

"I didn't mean to imply that you were," Bernadette said hastily. "I'm merely pointing out that you could make me tell you everything."

Sophie walked to stand next to Guy. "We're your friends, Bernadette. We have a common enemy in Usaeil."

"We have to go," Guy said.

No sooner were the words out of his mouth than a stunning woman with black hair and greenish-gold eyes appeared. She smiled at Bernadette then clicked silver finger rings together before the three of them vanished.

Bernadette put her hand over her eyes and tried to come to grips with everything that had happened. She was sure she'd made love to Keltan. That hadn't been a dream. What had happened between falling asleep on his chest and waking in her bed was another matter altogether. And she might never know the answer.

The one thing Bernadette did know was that Keltan wasn't there. She had no reason not to believe what the Dragon Kings told her, but when she was trying to sort out the truth from fiction, everyone was a potential enemy.

It would be easy to think that the Kings were manipulating her. They'd had ample opportunity. Her entire time at Dreagan could have been nothing but a ruse.

But she knew that wasn't true.

The only one who had used her was Usaeil. The queen had controlled Bernadette for a year, causing her to do things she never would have done otherwise.

Even when Keltan had the chance to use his magic on her after the lecture, he hadn't. He'd done nothing but talk. No, the only enemy Bernadette had was Usaeil. Sophie was right, they would get more done by working together.

Bernadette moved her hand and happened to catch sight of her desk. Everything was gone from it except her pen and some dark spots on the instrument. No doubt that was blood.

Usaeil had been in control for a long time. Now, it was Bernadette's turn.

CHAPTER TWENTY-FOUR

"You did what?" Keltan bellowed as he glared at Guy.

"It wasn't just him," Sophie hurried to say. "I was there and a part of talking to Bernadette."

Keltan looked away from both of them. He felt Ulrik's gaze on him but didn't turn the Silver King's way. Ulrik wasn't the only one staring. So were Darius and V.

"She's up and walking around, by the way," Guy stated sarcastically. "You know, if you're interested at all."

Keltan swung his head to Guy and met his gaze, their anger clashing and filling the room.

"Enough," V said as he walked between them. He looked at Guy first before turning his attention to Keltan. "We told you to be there, but you refused. Perhaps if you had been, you could've spoken to her about this."

"She can still change her mind," he said.

Guy crossed his arms over his chest. "It's the best move, and you know it."

"Keltan," V said to get his attention. "Bernadette is recovering nicely. You can stop worrying."

His brows shot up on his forehead. "Stop worrying?

Are you daft? She's going to try and play Usaeil. If anything, we've put Bernadette in more danger."

"I doona think so," Ulrik said before anyone else could speak.

Keltan didn't hold back his loud sigh. "Bernadette is one of the most honest people I've ever met. I'm sure she can lie, but is it good enough to fool Usaeil?"

"There's also the fact that we can no' protect her," Darius added.

Keltan nodded as he glanced at Darius. "Especially that. We're handing her over to Usaeil."

"She knew the risks," Guy said.

Keltan threw up his hands. "How could she? She just learned that Usaeil used her. Bernadette has no concept of the lengths Usaeil will go to in order to get revenge. I want Usaeil as badly as any of you, but I'm no' willing to put an innocent in the crosshairs to achieve it."

"Bernadette might not know what Usaeil is capable of, but Bernadette isn't stupid either," Sophie said. "Her life was turned upside down by Usaeil, and the one thing Bernadette doesn't want is for that to happen to someone else."

Keltan looked to Ulrik. "Bernadette doesna deserve to be put in harm's way, and that's exactly what we've done."

"Actually, it was Usaeil who did that," Ulrik replied.

Keltan knew Ulrik was right, but he still didn't like hearing it. "That doesna mean that we have to do it, as well. Look what Usaeil did just to get Bernadette back to her home."

Ulrik nodded. "I saw the blood on the pen. The fact that Usaeil used blood magic confirms just how important Bernadette is to her."

"I willna have Bernadette hurt."

"What do you suggest then?" Darius asked.

Keltan had no clue, but he'd come up with something.

"We can no' use dragon magic," V said.

Guy shook his head. "Usaeil will be looking for that."

"Same with Fae magic," Sophie added.

Ulrik lifted his chin. "There's a chance we could use Druid magic."

Keltan shook his head. "She knows some of us have mated Druids."

"Aye, but she's also using Druid magic. I'd ask the Warriors, but they can no' do spells. They can only use the magic the primeval gods inside them grants them."

Guy twisted his lips. "The Druid magic could work."

"Maybe Keltan is right," Sophie said. "Maybe someone else should go talk to Bernadette and lay it all out for her."

Everyone looked his way. Keltan snorted. "You think I doona want to see her? I do, but I willna. Usaeil will be looking for a Dragon King to show up."

"Aye, she will," Ulrik replied with a bright smile.

Keltan frowned at him. "Why are you smiling?"

"Like you said, Usaeil will expect us to make an appearance. If we doona, then that looks strange, and she could begin to suspect that Bernadette is lying to her."

V slapped his hands together and rubbed them eagerly. "I can no' believe none of us thought of this."

Keltan blinked and shook his head. "Thought of what?"

"It's a way for us to check in on Bernadette without giving anything away," Ulrik explained.

Keltan ran a hand over his jaw. "It can no' be me."

"It has to be you," Sophie said.

Darius smiled at his mate. "She's right. You were the one who went to the lecture. It makes sense that you would visit her again."

"All of you assume Usaeil knows I was at the lecture. And if she knows that, then she knows I spoke with Bernadette."

Guy shrugged as he crossed his arms over his chest. "It doesna matter if Usaeil knows or no'. You should still go. You spent the most time with Bernadette. While neither of you will be able to come out and say what you want, you know her better than any of us. You will be able to pick up subtle nuances one of us might overlook."

Fuck. Guy was right. And Keltan wasn't happy about it. If he were honest, he would admit how badly he wanted to see Bernadette. The problem was he didn't think he would be able to keep his hands off her.

In between worrying about her sudden and inexplicable illness were memories of their stolen hours making love. Keltan felt responsible for her because he had promised her that she was protected at Dreagan. That's all it was.

The strange feelings inside him were tied to his concerns—and maybe a little with the fact that he had enjoyed sex with Bernadette.

Enjoyed. Keltan inwardly shook his head. He'd had an amazing orgasm. There was no way he could forget that when he was with her. But he'd have to. For her safety. He'd told her that he would keep her safe, and that's exactly what he was going to do.

"When do you want me to go see her?" Keltan asked.

Ulrik released a breath. "Tomorrow. Give her some time to recoup after today."

Keltan turned on his heel and walked to the door. "I'll drive down there today and scope out the city."

"Smart," V said. "It's what we'd do."

Keltan made his way to his room and changed clothes before he threw together an overnight bag. Then he walked down to the garage. He bypassed the sports cars and supercars owned by others at Dreagan and went to his favorite mode of transportation: his motorbike.

He pulled the keys from the pocket of his leather jacket and put the backpack on. Then he threw a leg over the gray-and-black BMW R1200GS. After he started the engine, he put on his helmet and gloves and revved the throttle.

He glanced up to see Ulrik standing in the garage. Keltan gave him a nod before taking off. He had no issues driving a car, but there was something truly freeing about riding a motorbike.

For him, it was the closest thing to flying in his true form that he'd found. To some of his brethren, they could achieve that by being in a helicopter or plane, but Keltan disagreed.

Only a motorcycle allowed him to move the machine similarly to how he moved his own body when he took to the skies. It was a poor substitute, but it was something.

Though he wasn't in a hurry, Keltan opted not to take the scenic route to Glasgow. He drove straight there as fast as he could, the pavement flying by beneath him. He only stopped for petrol before he was back on the road again.

In less than three hours, he made it into the city. The Dragon Kings had houses in all parts of the world. Even in Edinburgh. But that wasn't the case in Glasgow. Keltan didn't mind. In some ways, he blended in better by staying in a hotel.

Keltan made his way to Mar Hall outside of Glasgow. He'd always enjoyed the gothic architecture of the estate. He checked in and booked one of the suites that gave him a great view of the Kilpatrick Hills.

He stayed long enough to remove his backpack and

check out the room. Then he returned to his motorbike and headed into the city. He had Bernadette's address, but that wasn't where he went. There were places he needed to check before he went to see her.

Any Fae—Light or Dark—who saw him would expect such actions. He was going to give everyone exactly what they anticipated, even though it was killing him not to go directly to Bernadette.

It was even difficult for him to steer clear of the section of town where her cottage was. He drove through the city streets and stopped off at a few pubs. He ordered drinks, but never drank them. He was looking for Fae or any sign of Usaeil in the area.

To his surprise, he found very few Fae in the hours he searched. One section at a time, he cleared Glasgow until he reached Bernadette's neighborhood.

He parked the bike and decided to walk the streets on foot instead. He checked every face he passed. Though he was aware that Usaeil could use glamour without the Kings discerning it, he still prepared himself for each person he encountered to be her.

After forty minutes, he found a café and ordered some food. He ate a few bites but mainly pushed it around on his plate. His unease grew when he didn't see even one Fae.

He opened the mental link and said, *"Ryder."*

The Dragon King answered almost immediately. *"I'm here. What is it?"*

"You need to tell Henry that I've only spotted three Fae in all of Glasgow. Two Light and one Dark, and all three disappeared when they spotted me."

"Damn," Ryder said. *"That's odd."*

"Aye. I'm in Bernadette's neighborhood now."

"Any sign of Usaeil?"

Keltan snorted. "*I wish. I hate that we can no' see her glamour. She could be anyone.*"

"*Which means you need to watch your back.*"

"*Why do you think I searched the city these past hours? If she's here and watching, she'll have seen me.*"

Ryder blew out a long breath. "*I know you doona agree with Bernadette helping us, but I think it's a verra courageous thing she's doing. We'll keep her safe. Somehow.*"

"*That's the same thing I keep telling myself, but we both know that's a lie. She'll be alone for the most part. We have no idea what Usaeil will do or say to her. Or worse, what the queen will force her to do.*"

"*About that,*" Ryder interjected. "*Ulrik, Eilish, and Shara have been brainstorming ideas. I think they've come up with something. Be on the lookout for them.*"

"*They shouldna come.*"

"*Right. You tell them that,*" Ryder said with a laugh. "*I'll send your message to Henry, though he's no' at Dreagan at the moment. Still, he'll want to know.*"

"*Thanks.*"

Keltan severed the link before he tossed down enough money to pay for his meal. He was keenly aware of the time ticking down on the deadline Usaeil had given them to deliver Rhi. But one issue at a time.

He walked outside and breathed in the night air. He was counting down the hours until he could see Bernadette again. He looked one way, then the other. All he spotted were mortals. He'd thought he'd find numerous Fae milling about since Usaeil was there. Or maybe that's why none of the Fae were in Glasgow.

Keltan was pretty sure the Light didn't know what Usaeil was up to, but there was a good chance that some of the Dark did. Especially if Balladyn, King of the Dark, had informed his people. There were reasons Balladyn might keep that to himself, though.

Usaeil had spies at the Dark Palace, and if Balladyn wanted to go against the queen, he'd have to keep things secret for as long as he could.

Keltan fisted his hands. He was tired of waiting on this battle. It was time that it happened. For better or worse, the tension had been brewing long enough. It was so bad that even the humans could sense it. They looked around furtively as if waiting for something to jump out at them.

"Your time is coming to an end," Keltan said, speaking about Usaeil.

And he planned to be right there with his brethren, fighting to end the queen once and for all.

CHAPTER TWENTY-FIVE

The next morning, Bernadette stood beneath the spray of the shower so long that her fingers began to turn pruney. She didn't care, though. It felt too good.

Her mind drifted, thinking about Keltan's kisses, his hands on her body, and the way he'd so easily pleasured her. It was all she could think about, actually.

Not even contemplating Usaeil or the fact that Bernadette was going to attempt to deceive the queen entered her mind. She was utterly, completely filled with thoughts of Keltan.

And it hurt her more than she cared to admit that he hadn't been there when she woke.

He must have had his reasons, though. At least that's what she kept telling herself. Not that she would ever get to hear what that reasoning might be. She was under no illusion that she would see Keltan again, even if the Dragon Kings had allowed her to keep her memories.

That thought bothered her more than the idea that she could lose her life while going up against Usaeil. It was silly, really. She knew very little about Keltan, but she knew that she liked being with him. And she enjoyed how he made her feel when they were together.

She was no great master of reading people, but she got the sense that he had been nothing but honest with her from the very beginning. And she, in turn, had given him the same honesty.

It was so refreshing, that it might very well be the reason she was infatuated with him.

Bernadette shook her head, rolling her eyes at herself. It was just like her to start to have feelings for a man she couldn't have. To make matters worse, she couldn't even get angry thinking Keltan had used her—because he hadn't. If anything, she had used him.

She leaned forward and put her forehead on the shower wall. There was too much going on. She needed to stop thinking about Keltan and get her head straight for when Usaeil came because she knew the queen would come very soon.

And it would take everything Bernadette had to try and outwit and outsmart Usaeil. In truth, she wasn't sure she could do it, but after what the queen had done to her, she was absolutely going to try anything to get back the self-respect she'd lost. Even if that meant going up against a powerful supernatural being.

"Are you going to get out sometime soon? Or am I going to have to make you come out?"

Bernadette's head snapped up at the sound of Usaeil's voice. She looked through the steam and out the glass to see the queen standing in the middle of the bathroom. "Can I have some privacy?"

"I don't like to be kept waiting, and you're not doing anything but standing there."

"I'll be out in just a second," Bernadette said and turned her back on Usaeil.

There was a loud sigh and then nothing. Bernadette glanced out the glass to find the room vacant. She turned off the water, wrung out her hair, and then reached for the towel. She dried off and stepped out of the shower to get dressed in a pair of thin, baggy sweats and a tee shirt.

Bernadette raked her hands through her hair and winced at the sight of the dark circles under her eyes. She quickly put on some eye and face cream before walking out of the bathroom. There, she found Usaeil sitting in her office chair, one long leg crossed over the other.

The queen smiled a knowing smile at her. "How are you today?"

"Not good, actually."

Usaeil laughed and turned the chair from side to side. Then she looked directly at the pen and the dried blood on it. "Want to know what I did?"

"I'd like to know why you did anything at all."

The smile vanished as Usaeil uncrossed her legs and sat up straight. "You left without telling me."

"I didn't know I had to tell you my every move."

The queen narrowed her silver eyes at Bernadette. "Where did you go?"

"Driving. I tried to go hiking since that clears my head, but everywhere I went there were too many people. So, I drove," Bernadette said, proud of herself for saying the lie without stuttering.

And she hadn't even thought about any of this before-hand.

Usaeil quirked a black brow. "And where did you drive?"

"North. I got on a road and just drove."

"Is that right?" Usaeil slowly sat back, staring at Bernadette with uncertainty in her gaze. "Why did you need to think at all? I gave you an assignment."

"That's just it. You've let me follow my own timeline of things this past year. It . . . bothered me that you put such pressure on me."

Usaeil barked with laughter. "So, you ran away?"

"I went to think things through. I couldn't do it here because I kept looking at the laptop. I needed to get out." Now came the time for Bernadette to test just how close an eye Usaeil had been keeping on her. "Surely, you knew exactly where I was and what I was doing."

"Of course, I did."

"Then why did you do that?" Bernadette asked and pointed to the pen and blood.

Usaeil glanced at the writing instrument and shrugged. "To remind you that I can bring you home anytime I want."

"What did you do to me?"

The queen's lips curved into a wide smile. "I made sure that for every hour you were away from your home, your organs would break down."

Bernadette's knees nearly gave out. She walked to her desk and grabbed hold of it to keep on her feet. "Why would you do that? You could've just come and got me and told me to return."

"What would be the fun in that?" Usaeil asked in puzzlement.

"You're the Queen of the Light. You don't hurt people."

Usaeil shrugged and got to her feet. "You're right. I am the queen. You need to remember that. The next time I tell you to do something, I expect you to do it."

Bernadette slowly nodded. There was a light in the queen's eyes that frightened her. The kind of light that warned others that someone was about to come unhinged.

"Now, then. You need to pick up your desk. There is someone from Dreagan in town."

Bernadette's heart leapt at the news. She prayed it was Keltan. Then, in the next breath, she hoped it wasn't. If Usaeil knew that there was a King in Glasgow, then the queen would want to stay behind and spy on them.

It took a moment for Bernadette to realize that Usaeil was staring at her, waiting for her to comment. Bernadette quickly let surprise contort her features. "Someone from Dreagan? Are they here for me?"

"Who knows?" Usaeil said with a shrug. "I'm betting they are. After all, I know one was at your lecture the other night."

Bernadette really needed to sit down if she was going to continue having this conversation because at the rate things were going, her legs were going to give out from beneath her. Usaeil hadn't said anything before about knowing that a King had been at the lecture. "Are you sure?"

"Without a doubt."

All Bernadette could think about was if Usaeil knew that Keltan had approached her during dinner. This would be twice now that she hadn't said anything to the queen about it, but Bernadette figured it was better to keep with the lie than to try to talk her way out of something she might not even need to do.

Because while Usaeil was powerful, she wasn't all-knowing. The fact that she hadn't known it was Keltan at the lecture or that Bernadette had been at Dreagan spoke volumes. She would never have known that had she not tested things.

Bernadette didn't know how far she was willing to push things, but she would do whatever she had to in order to win back the life that had been taken from her. And she hadn't even known it had been taken until Keltan told her. What a fool she must seem to those at Dreagan.

Now was her time to make up for it and ensure that Usaeil didn't ruin anyone else's life.

Usaeil rolled her eyes dramatically. "Do you have nothing to say?"

"I don't know what to say."

"Did anyone talk to you after the lecture?"

Bernadette laughed. "Just about everyone."

"Did anyone seem . . ." Usaeil waved her hand, searching for the right word. "Different?"

Bernadette shot her a dry look. "I spoke about dragons and magic. Everyone there was a bit different, including me."

Usaeil moved closer, her silver gaze staring intently. "Are you sure you're telling me everything?"

"I wouldn't dare lie to you," Bernadette said in a convincing voice. "You have magic. Look what you did to bring me home!"

The queen relaxed and smiled. "Never forget that."

Even though Bernadette had lied to Usaeil and had gotten away with it, she was all too aware of how close to death she'd come, simply because she had left the house without telling the queen. The only way Bernadette would ever be free would be if the Dragon Kings killed Usaeil.

"Are you going to clean up this mess?" Usaeil asked as she motioned to the contents of Bernadette's desk that were scattered on the floor.

She almost told Usaeil that she could clean it up in seconds with magic since she was the one who'd destroyed it, but Bernadette somehow kept her mouth closed.

Bernadette walked to the scattered papers and other items and began gathering them. She could feel Usaeil's gaze on her the entire time, and Bernadette knew that it pleased the queen that she was on her knees doing exactly as Usaeil had ordered.

When she finished, Bernadette put the items back on her desk. That's when she realized that her car and her belongings were still at Dreagan. How would she explain that to Usaeil?

Then she realized that the queen had driven there, so she couldn't know that Bernadette's car wasn't in the drive. The laptop, however, was another matter entirely.

"For someone who wanted to get away from the laptop, why did you take it with you?" Usaeil asked.

Bernadette's heart jumped into her throat. She jerked her head up to the queen and then followed Usaeil's gaze to the tote she used for her laptop. One of the Dragon Kings must have brought it with them. Bernadette would have to thank them whenever she saw them again.

She shrugged at Usaeil and grabbed the pen before she went to the kitchen to rinse off the blood. Bernadette then cleaned the blood off the desk and replaced her laptop in the middle.

No sooner had she finished than there was a knock at the door.

Usaeil smiled and waggled her eyebrows. "Your visitor from Dreagan is here."

"What do I say to them?"

The queen gave her a look of disinterest. "Whatever you need to in order to keep them from stopping you. Remember, this is a free country. You can say and write whatever you want."

"Right," Bernadette said, inwardly rolling her eyes.

Suddenly, Usaeil stood right before her, fury in her silver depths. In a heartbeat, the orbs flashed red before returning to silver. "The most important thing is to not fall for them. The men from Dreagan like to use their charms on women. You won't succumb. Are we clear?"

"Crystal," Bernadette replied, thinking about how her hands had stroked Keltan's amazing body.

"Then answer the door."

Bernadette raised her brows. "Are you staying?"

"Oh, I'll be close," the queen said before teleporting away.

Bernadette blew out a breath and made her way to the door. She looked through the peephole, her heart jumping to her throat when she saw Keltan.

Her hands shook as she unlatched the door and opened it to stare into his amber eyes. She wanted to smile in welcome, but she held it back, remembering that Usaeil could be near.

"Hello, Dr. Davies. I'm Keltan, a representative from Dreagan. I was wondering if I could have a few minutes of your time?"

She nodded and stepped back to allow him entry. As he passed, his hand brushed hers, sending a jolt running through her.

CHAPTER TWENTY-SIX

Seeing her was like a punch in the gut. For a moment, Keltan couldn't breathe. When her lips curved into a quick little smile, he'd wanted to reach for her and pull her into his arms. It was all he could do to keep his hands to himself.

How he got the words out to introduce himself, he'd never know. When he walked into the house, he couldn't help but make sure their fingers brushed. It might be the only contact he had with her, and he wasn't going to let such an opportunity pass him by without taking advantage.

He was overjoyed to see her on her feet. There was still some fatigue in her eyes, but the fact that she was alive was amazing considering what Usaeil had done to her.

"Would you like some tea?" Bernadette asked as she shut the door behind him.

"That would be nice, thank you."

She didn't look at him again as she filled the kettle and set it on the stove to heat. "What brings you to my home?"

He stared at her, waiting for her to look at him. He'd

been thinking of her jade eyes all night, and he desperately wanted to look into them again.

Keltan cleared his throat, remembering his role. "I'm here about the lecture you gave in regard to Dreagan. You made some pretty large leaps."

"Did I?" She faced him and leaned back against the counter. "Are you willing to go through my data and give me answers?"

"And what data would that be?"

"Let's begin with the women that have all but disappeared after visiting Dreagan."

Kelton shook his head. With every word that fell from Bernadette's lips, he knew that Usaeil was near. He wanted to send out magic to look for her, but he held back. Let the queen eavesdrop and get whatever she wanted so she'd leave, and he could talk to Bernadette as he wished.

"I'm no' able to divulge information on private citizens," he replied.

Bernadette gave him a pointed look. "So, you admit that the women are at Dreagan."

"I'm no' admitting anything. If you've done any research, then surely you hired some private investigators to locate those you're looking for."

She propped her foot against her ankle and gave a shake of her head. "You don't plan on telling me anything, do you?"

"Dreagan is an international company. We're a multi-billion-pound, euro, dollar, or whatever currency you wish to use corporation. No business willingly sits back and lets someone make such accusations against them. In fact, we could sue you for slander."

Bernadette's gaze narrowed on him. "You would sue me?"

"I've been sent to talk with you in the hopes that it doesna come to that."

The kettle let out a loud whistle in the prevailing silence. Bernadette turned and put two teabags into the teapot before she poured in the hot water. She then set a timer for five and a half minutes.

"You've come to threaten me," she said before she faced him once more.

He shrugged. "I call it talking, but you can call it whatever you want. The point is, Dr. Davies, the things you're saying need to stop."

"This is a free country. I can say whatever I want."

Keltan wanted to applaud her acting skills. He was, in fact, surprised that she hadn't said many of these things when they spoke at Dreagan. If he hadn't heard from Guy and Sophie that Bernadette had agreed to this charade, Keltan might actually think she meant every word.

"Actually, that isna entirely true. Especially when it comes to slander. We at Dreagan pride ourselves on our good name. Your lecture has besmirched our reputation, and that, in fact, is slander. Now, I'm sure you've no interest in going to court over these wild allegations you're throwing at us."

She crossed her arms over her chest and held his gaze. "You said wild."

He shrugged. "Aye. What of it?"

"You didn't say they were false."

Keltan glanced away. "Wild. False. Same difference."

"Actually," she said, using the same tone he had moments ago, "they aren't. I believe you're hiding something."

"You really want to go down this road? We have unlimited funds, Dr. Davies. We can spend decades dragging you to court. No one wants to do that."

She licked her lips and stared at him for a long moment. The timer went off for the tea, and she turned to pour it into two cups before setting his on the table with some milk and sugar.

After she'd fixed her tea, she held her mug between her hands and looked his way once more. "I want the truth."

"Why do you believe what you're saying is true? Is this the proof you spoke of at the lecture?" Keltan couldn't believe he'd forgotten to ask her about that while she was at Dreagan. He'd been otherwise occupied.

She took a sip of tea. "Perhaps."

"Care to show me this *proof*?"

It was her turn to snort. "No, I don't. And you can search my house if you want, but you won't find it here."

He narrowed his gaze at her. "You're one individual, Dr. Davies. Someone who has lost her main position with the museum and is now only working part-time. Your income has severely dwindled, and you want to go up against Dreagan? You'll lose."

"Maybe. But the rest of the world will hear about why you're taking me to court. They'll read my articles. They'll hear from the ones who attended the lecture. And the attention you're so anxiously trying to avoid will be on you."

Damn, she was good. Keltan fought to hold back his smile. As good as Bernadette was at this game they were playing, he was tired of it. But for her safety, he would continue in this vein for however long it took for the Kings to bring down Usaeil.

"No witty comeback?" she asked, her brows raised.

Keltan reached for the tea and lifted it to his lips for a drink. "This is good."

"I'm glad you like it."

"Let's work out an agreement, Dr. Davies."

She shook her head. "I'm going to have to pass on that offer."

For the next twenty minutes, they continued in the same way, each getting in a dig as often as they could. That's when Bernadette set aside her empty cup, a small frown forming between her eyes. She left the kitchen and made her way to the bathroom, where she closed the door.

Keltan walked around the small home, seeing Bernadette in her private setting. There wasn't much in the house, but there were a few items, like a bronze statue of a red deer with its head tilted back as it let loose a call.

He knew Bernadette had given up almost everything to dig into Dreagan, but the few things she'd kept were obviously the ones that were important to her for one reason or another. And Keltan wanted to know the story behind each of them.

Unable to resist, he touched the bronze buck, letting his finger run down the back of the beast. It was a large statue and probably hefty.

The sound of the door opening drew his attention. He dropped his hand and faced Bernadette. She looked haggard and spent as if it had cost her everything just to talk to him.

"Perhaps I should return another day," he said.

"She's gone."

Keltan frowned, unsure why Bernadette would dare say such a thing. "I'm sorry. I must have missed something. Who is gone?"

"Usaeil. She's gone. And I know you don't think I should be saying her name, but it's fine," Bernadette said as she walked toward him and sank onto the sofa.

Keltan glanced around furtively as he walked to stand before Bernadette. "Dr. Davies—"

"She came to me in the bathroom, Keltan. She said she

couldn't stay but wanted to let me know that I was doing a good job."

Keltan hung his head for a minute. "It could be a trick."

"It's not."

"Bernadette," he said and raised his head.

She gave him a pointed look. "I don't care if it is a trick. I can't keep talking to you the way I have been. It's not . . . us."

He sat beside her and took her hand. "How are you feeling?"

"Oh," Bernadette said with a frustrated shake of her head. "You mean how am I feeling since Usaeil used magic to make my organs begin shutting down unless I came home? She got great joy out of that one. I'm feeling fine, though."

"It was close."

Her jade gaze darted away as she tucked her black hair behind an ear. "She's lost her mind."

"We've known that for a while now."

Bernadette swung her eyes back to him. "She doesn't know when I'm lying, though. I told her I went driving. She has no clue I was at Dreagan."

"She'll figure it out eventually."

"Unless you kill her before then."

Keltan squeezed Bernadette's hand. "There is a way for you to keep her out of your home, but if you use it, she'll know we told you."

"What is it?"

"A symbol. You can carve it or mark it anywhere in your home. Most people put it on the doorway or even a door."

She shifted to face him. "Do you think I should use it?"

"It'll keep her and any Fae out, and it'll ensure that she can no' hurt you. I doona like the position you've put yourself in. The symbol can help."

She cocked her head to the side as she smiled at him. "She'll know it came from you. It's the same as if you used your magic to protect me. All of which defeats the purpose of me gaining information from her that could help you."

"I'd rather you stay alive. We'll get Usaeil another way."

"She's hurt enough people, Keltan. Her eyes turn red on occasion."

He nodded slowly, his lips twisting. "We've known for some time that she's using glamour to hide her true visage. She's killed her family, and even her own children. There's no telling how long she's been Dark and hidden it."

"I understand that, and I'm also aware of how dangerous she is. But I can do this."

"It's no' a matter of whether you can. It's more of if you *should*."

Her brow furrowed as she shot him a dark look. "Are you saying you don't think I can do this?"

"I'm just getting to know you. You have a strong character, and I know you want to make up for what you think you did."

"What I *have* done," she interjected.

Keltan drew in a deep breath and released it. "You mean what Usaeil made you do."

"I wasn't strong enough to withstand her."

"No human could," he told her. "That's magic for you. Unless the Druids know to be wary, Usaeil has gotten a jump on them, as well. That's why she's been able to hide her glamour from us. She's combining her magic with that of the Druids."

Bernadette gave him a flat stare. "All the more reason that Usaeil needs to be brought down."

"It doesna have to be by you."

"I'm the person she used. Who better than me? She thinks I fear her. After she listened to us today, she believes I'm completely on her side."

Keltan sat back while keeping his hand linked with Bernadette's. "There are few Fae who can remain veiled that long. I didna believe Usaeil was one of them. I suppose the Druid magic helps her with that."

"And you think if she can do that, then she can come back at any time and find us."

He nodded slowly. "Which means we can no' keep talking like this. If Usaeil caught us, she'd wait until I left, then she'd kill you."

"Is there nothing you can do that would ensure she can't spy on me like that?"

Keltan suddenly smiled. "There is. And now that I've been here, I have every reason to put it in place."

CHAPTER TWENTY-SEVEN

She was back at the house in Glasgow. This time, Rhi was going to find out why she felt the need to be there. She veiled herself and was about to enter the house when she spotted movement in the window. That pleased her because now she might get some answers.

The moment Rhi entered the house, she spotted Keltan walking away from the sofa where a pretty mortal sat. Rhi could drop her veil now, but that might scare the human. Though why should she care? If a Dragon King were there, then this somehow involved Usaeil.

Rhi lowered her veil. The moment she did, Keltan's gaze swung to her.

"Rhi," he said. There was a moment of surprise immediately replaced by worry. "What are you doing here?"

"I could ask you the same thing." Rhi's gaze slid to the mortal. "Is this your house?"

The woman nodded her head of black hair. "It is."

Keltan returned to the sofa and said, "Bernadette, this is Rhi. She's the Light Fae I spoke about. Rhi, this is Dr. Bernadette Davies."

"Hello," the female said.

Rhi forced herself to smile, though there was nothing for her to be happy about. "I was hoping you might tell me why someone used blood magic here."

The human glanced at Keltan, but before the King could speak, Bernadette said, "It's Usaeil."

Rhi wasn't sure if she was happy about the news or not. "How is Usaeil involved?"

"She used Bernadette," Keltan explained. "Usaeil approached her a year ago and showed her a dragon."

Rhi's eyes widened. "She did what?"

"She showed Bernadette Con," Keltan said.

Bernadette got to her feet. It didn't go unnoticed by Rhi that the mortal moved closer to Keltan. The mortal trusted the King. And by the way the two kept looking at each other, they had already shared their bodies.

Rhi released a breath. "There is no way Con would've shown himself to anyone."

"He didna. It was all a hoax," Keltan said.

Bernadette shrugged as she crossed her arms over her chest, hunching her shoulders. "It worked. As soon as I saw the dragon and Usaeil told me they were real, I was hooked. She explained that she was Queen of the Fae. After I learned that, I started asking more questions about the dragons. She told me that they lived at Dreagan."

"She told you about the Dragon Kings?" Rhi asked in surprise.

Keltan made a sound at the back of his throat. "Usaeil left that part out. Just as she let Bernadette believe that she was the queen of all Fae. Usaeil simply said that there were dragons—and they lived at Dreagan."

"Why not tell Bernadette that you're Dragon Kings?"

Keltan and Bernadette both shrugged.

Rhi flicked her hair from her shoulder. "I can't figure out why Usaeil wouldn't want her to know about the Dragon Kings."

"I didn't need to know that part," Bernadette said. "I was intrigued enough to start digging into Dreagan. I was an anthropologist who loved her job, but all I could think about all day long was finding out more information about Dreagan and the dragons.

"It started as something I did once I got home from work. I'd stay up until the wee hours of the morning and only get a few hours' sleep. Then it bled into more research during my lunch hour. Finally, I was taking vacation days. That was when I got the most done—not having to go into work or deal with anyone interrupting my research."

Rhi looked at Keltan to find the Dragon King staring at Bernadette as if he couldn't get enough of her. She wondered if Keltan knew that he was falling for the mortal. Probably not since Keltan had always made it clear that the Kings shouldn't be mating until the dragons were back.

"What happened then?" Rhi asked.

Bernadette smiled sadly and dropped her arms to rub her hands together. "I gave up my position at the museum. I wanted to quit, but I needed some form of income, so I only work part-time now. I had to sell my house and most of my belongings."

Rhi blinked and jerked back. "All because Usaeil showed you a dragon?"

"It wasna just that. Usaeil used magic to push Bernadette to dig into us," Keltan said.

Rhi rolled her eyes and cocked out a hip. "Now that I can definitely see. That must be why I was drawn here."

"Drawn here?" Keltan repeated, his brow furrowed in a deep frown.

Rhi shot him a half smile. "A few days ago, I dreamed about this house. I knew it was in Glasgow, but not where. It took me almost an entire day to locate it. I heard someone inside, but when I came in, no one was here. That's when I saw the pen and the blood on the desk."

"A spell by Usaeil to make sure I returned home," Bernadette stated angrily.

That got Rhi's attention. "What kind of spell? The fact that Ubitch used blood means she was trying to track you."

"Bernadette was at Dreagan," Keltan explained.

Rhi looked between the pair. "And both of you believe Usaeil doesn't know that? Fae don't need to use blood spells. That is something Druids do. What blood magic *does* do is link the person casting the spell to the one they're casting it on."

"Meaning what?" Bernadette asked, her expression growing worried.

"That Usaeil may know more than she's letting on."

Keltan vigorously shook his head of dark blond hair. "If Usaeil knew that Bernadette was at Dreagan, then she would've pushed her for more information at the verra least. More likely, she would've killed her."

"Usaeil has Con," Rhi stated flatly. "And she intends to keep him. The rest of the Dragon Kings and the mates matter little to her. Based on what we've learned so far, Usaeil wants all of you out of the way, and she'll do whatever she needs to in order to get that done."

"Including making me believe in dragons," Bernadette said. Her head whipped around to Keltan. "Rhi's right. Usaeil knows I was at Dreagan. She was using me. Not to tell the world about you, but to get close to someone at Dreagan."

"And to get a Dragon King to trust her," Rhi said.

Keltan ran a hand down his face. "Why? What does that get Usaeil?"

"She's not making any moves that I'd have expected," Rhi said. "Everything she's done so far has been completely different than what I've known her to do in the past."

Bernadette slowly sank back onto the sofa. "What if Usaeil has been setting this up for hundreds of years? Making the Fae and even the Dragon Kings believe one thing while she's waited to put this plan into motion."

Rhi considered that for a second and then shook her head. "Usaeil is crafty and smart, but she doesn't have the patience for something like that. She has an agenda, of that I'm sure, but what it is exactly, I've yet to figure out."

"She wants you," Keltan said.

"She wants to kill me, and she'll get her chance soon."

Bernadette tilted her head to the side, causing her black locks to fall away from her face. "Do you often dream of places? I'm still trying to figure out why you came here."

"The answer is no," Rhi explained. "I don't dream of places. I think I was brought here because of Usaeil. Our showdown is coming sooner rather than later, thanks to the deadline she gave the Kings."

Keltan narrowed his amber eyes at her. "I know you're ready for it."

"Very. I'm tired of this. She wants me. Why not let her have me?"

"Usaeil has hurt enough people," Bernadette said.

Rhi smiled at the mortal. "The fact that you can stand here, knowing what Usaeil has done to you and say that says a lot about you. I like you, Bernadette. When this is all over, if we both survive, we'll go get a manicure. My nail tech, Jesse, is the absolute bomb."

"I'd like that," Bernadette said, returning her smile.

Keltan squeezed the bridge of his nose. "Rhi, you can no' do anything rash regarding Usaeil. You need to think about things."

"It's all I've been thinking about, Keltan. If Con had attacked Usaeil when I wanted, we wouldn't be in this mess."

"You can no' know that for sure," he argued.

Rhi pointed to Bernadette. "She wouldn't be dealing with this now. Ubitch wouldn't have kidnapped Con or used her magic to ensure that Claire became pregnant with V's child."

"What?" Bernadette exclaimed.

"Oh, you didn't know about that?" Rhi asked her and then rolled her eyes. "Usaeil knows that no mortal has birthed a live Dragon King's baby. She also knows what the strain of a mate becoming pregnant and waiting each day to see if she'll lose the bairn does to a couple. Usaeil used glamour to appear as me and spelled Claire so that she'd become pregnant. Now, Usaeil threatens Claire's life if any King goes to the Light Castle."

"A King?" Bernadette asked, her gaze fierce.

Rhi nodded, unsure of what wasn't clear. "That's what I said."

"What about a mortal?"

"Nay," Keltan stated angrily.

Rhi blinked, looking at Bernadette with new eyes. "No mortal goes to the Light Castle."

"But can I get there?"

Keltan threw up his hands. "Did neither of you hear what I just said?"

Rhi cut her gaze to Keltan. "Bernadette is a grown woman. She can make her own decisions."

"No' when it comes to our world," he argued.

Bernadette calmly put her hand on Keltan's arm.

"Thank you for looking out for me, but even I can see that you all need every advantage you can get."

"We have an advantage," he replied.

Bernadette's jade eyes moved to Rhi. "Are you sure that we're even talking to Rhi? You said yourself that you can't see through Usaeil's glamour."

Rhi snorted loudly. "Oh, doll. Trust me. I'm me. Usaeil might be able to pull off looking like me with someone who doesn't know me, but Keltan knows me."

He nodded at Bernadette. "Rhi is one in a million. Usaeil knows better than to try and pull something like that on a King. The Dragon Kings are unstoppable when we fight together, and that's what Usaeil is trying to avoid."

"But you won't be fighting together," Rhi said.

Keltan blew out a loud breath. "Nay. Some will have to stay behind at Dreagan. We willna leave our home undefended. But we'll have you, Balladyn, and the Dark Fae army."

"Damn right you'll have me. Any chance one of you spoke with Death?" Rhi asked. "It'd be great if she and her Reapers made an appearance." Keltan wouldn't meet her gaze, which was all the answer she needed. "I see."

Bernadette's eyes went wide. "Reapers? Death?"

Rhi took pity on Keltan and said, "Death is a goddess who makes it her mission to be judge and jury to the Fae. Her Reapers . . . well, they reap the souls she's judged."

"Oh," Bernadette murmured, frowning. "Why wouldn't Death and the Reapers join in? They're Fae. Doesn't this pertain to them?"

Rhi looked pointedly at Keltan. "That's exactly my question."

His lips flattened. "The night I went to hear Bernadette's lecture, I had a run-in with Rordan. It wasna long after that Erith and Cael showed up."

"Erith is Death's real name," Rhi told Bernadette. "And Cael is her main squeeze."

Bernadette smiled her thanks.

Rhi looked back at Keltan. "You going to tell me what was said, frowny? Or do I get to guess?"

"Erith said this was your fight. She willna join in, and neither will the Reapers."

"Well, isn't that just peachy?" Rhi said, not bothering to hide her sarcasm. Or her anger.

All this time, Death had been telling her to go after Usaeil and not wait, or else Death would do it herself. Looked like it was all just talk to get Rhi moving.

Rhi forced a smile. "I've waited on Con to make a move against Usaeil, and that was a mistake. I've let others make all kinds of decisions while I sat on the sidelines waiting and planning. I'm done with that. I've offered myself up to the Kings so you could bring me to Usaeil as she asked. I suggest we do that."

"Rhi," Keltan began.

She held up a hand to silence him. "The time has come. Take a look at the clock, stud. Time has nearly run out for you."

"I know," Keltan said with clenched teeth.

"Ward this house against Usaeil. Then take Bernadette to Dreagan. I just warded her. Add in yours and Eilish's, as well. That might be enough to keep Usaeil from forcing Bernadette back to her."

Rhi gave a thumbs-up to Bernadette as well as a smile she didn't feel. Then she teleported away.

CHAPTER TWENTY-EIGHT

"Rhi did what?" Rhys demanded, his voice rising with shock and outrage.

Keltan tossed back a shot of Scotch and set the glass on the table before he turned to face the others. When he called for Ulrik to bring him back, he hadn't realized that others were waiting to hear what had happened.

No one said a word as they stared at him. Keltan ran a hand over his face and tried to find the words. His brain could barely process all of it, and somehow, the others wanted him to spell it out in a way they could understand.

"She's demanding we bring her to Usaeil as we planned," Keltan told the room. "If we doona, she'll go after the queen herself."

"Damn," Ulrik said as he rested a hip on the corner of Con's desk.

It was rare that Ulrik sat at the desk. They might conduct business in the office, but no one wanted Con's chair.

"We can no' let her go alone," Rhys stated.

Anson shrugged, twisting his lip. "Rhi's right. There's no use in continuing to wait for the final minutes of the countdown. Look what Usaeil has done to V and Claire and now Bernadette. No' to mention taking Con."

All the arguments Keltan had in mind died when he looked into Anson's black eyes. "Anson's right."

Rhys gaped at him. "What?"

"Rhi can win," Kellan said as he pushed away from the doorway.

Keltan turned his attention to the Keeper of History. It was Kellan's job to see everything that happened in each of their lives and record it. There was so much that he didn't retain it all, and didn't always understand what he wrote down. He just got it out of his head as fast as he could.

Ulrik nodded as Kellan moved to stand beside him. "He's right. Con put off the battle for a long time, even though Rhi wanted it. The time Usaeil gave us is nearly up anyway. We doona have a choice."

Not all the Dragon Kings were in Con's office, but the ones who were nodded in agreement. Including Rhys. Keltan swallowed and thought about Bernadette. He hadn't wanted to leave her behind, but she had been adamant. He'd tried to force her to return to Dreagan with him, but Ulrik had stepped in and prevented that. Thankfully.

Keltan had taken Rhi's advice and warded not just Bernadette but also her house. Eilish was, at that moment, adding her magic to both his and Rhi's. And Keltan would make sure several other Kings did the same for Bernadette—and all the mates.

"There's one thing we've no' mentioned," Banan said, his gray gaze sweeping through the office. "We doona know where Usaeil is holding Con."

"And we doona have time to find out. Usaeil made sure of that." Keltan blew out a breath. As much as he wanted to fight against the road he somehow found himself on with Bernadette, there was no way he could.

And if he couldn't change the course, then he would walk it with purpose.

Ulrik gave him a nod. "Kellan, get everyone gathered in the mountain. Keltan, Guy, Rhys, and Anson stay behind."

Keltan could hardly maintain his patience as he waited for everyone to leave. Once he and the King of Silvers were alone, he turned to Ulrik and lifted his brows in question. Ulrik gave a nod for him to proceed.

In short order, Keltan explained to the others about Rhi warding Bernadette. That's when he asked them if they would each add their magic to it as well, before they returned and repeated the process with every mate at Dreagan, including Eilish.

"It's come to this, has it?" Rhys asked.

Anson crossed his arms over his chest. "I'd rather be safe than sorry. Usaeil is continually unpredictable."

"What we need is Gemma," Guy said. "After what she did to Usaeil, she'd be handy in battle."

Ulrik shook his head. "I agree, but Cináed will fight that. As would any of you if it were your mate who could stop Usaeil from using Druid magic."

"I know I would," Rhys said.

Guy's nose wrinkled as he winced. "You're right. I wasna thinking about her being a mate."

"You were thinking of her helping us win. No harm in that," Anson said.

Keltan licked his lips. "I want to get back to Bernadette."

"You can no' help us there," Ulrik said.

"Then convince her to come here."

Rhys caught his gaze. "Then she can no' help us."

Keltan glared at all of them. "Did I no' just hear all of you say that we couldna force Gemma to help us? But now you want to make Bernadette?"

"First," Ulrik said softly, "no one is forcing Bernadette to do anything. This was her idea."

"She doesna know better," Keltan said.

"I'd say she knows better than most of the mates did when they first found out about us." Ulrik paused and took a deep breath. "Second, Gemma is Cináed's mate. I didna think Bernadette was your mate. Is she?"

Keltan's breath locked in his throat. For a moment, his mind went completely blank. He couldn't talk, couldn't even form words. Ulrik's question went around and around in his head.

Anson cocked his head to the side. "You obviously care about her, or you wouldna be fighting so hard to get her out of danger."

"I promised I would keep her safe," Keltan finally managed to get out.

Rhys raised a brow. "You didna answer Ulrik. Is she your mate?"

"I doona want a mate." It was the last thing Keltan wanted.

Guy chuckled. "There are few of us who went looking for our mates, brother. You know this. When it happens, it happens."

Keltan shook his head. "I didna say she was my mate."

"If you say so." Ulrik straightened from the desk. "If she isna your mate, then that changes things."

"How?" Keltan didn't stop the word from falling like acid from his lips.

Guy made a sound at the back of his throat. "Keltan, mates are cherished above all else. You've seen those of us who have found our mates."

Keltan shook his head, furious that his friends were acting like this. "We made a vow to protect humans. We even sent our dragons away and hid for centuries so the mortals would forget about us. It isna Bernadette's fault that Usaeil picked her to toy with."

"Nay, it isna," Anson said. "I applaud Bernadette for standing up to Usaeil. That takes an insane amount of courage. We're going to help her by adding our magic to yours, Rhi's, and Eilish's."

"Help? You can help by talking her into forgetting this foolish idea of hers and coming here," Keltan replied.

When he finished, the four of them simply stared at him. He shrugged. "What?"

"I wish you could see your face and hear your voice," Rhys said.

Guy nodded. "You need a mirror, pronto."

Keltan rolled his eyes. "If any of you says that Bernadette is my mate, I'll punch you. All of you knew immediately upon meeting yours. I like Bernadette, sure. I slept with her, and I promised I'd keep her safe. That's where this is coming from."

"You're lying to us and yourself," Ulrik stated in a soft voice.

Keltan threw up his hands before letting them fall against his thighs. "It doesna matter what I say, all of you will continue arguing with me."

"Because we see what you do no'," Anson told him.

Keltan raised his brows. "And what is that? Someone worried about another?"

"Someone willing to do whatever it takes to protect another," Guy answered.

Keltan squeezed the bridge of his nose with his thumb and forefinger. "You four are making my head ache."

"If anyone knows what Keltan feels, it's him," Rhys

told the others. "We're so used to Kings finding their mates that we're forcing it on him."

Finally! Keltan dropped his arm and shot Rhys a thankful look.

Ulrik lifted a shoulder. "You may have a point. We're going to war, and I suppose we're all grasping on to normal things."

"Take us to Bernadette," Anson told Ulrik. "We need to get this finished. I agree with Keltan. Usaeil shouldna be allowed to hurt the doctor like she did."

Keltan moved to touch Ulrik so he could go with them to Bernadette, but Ulrik shook his head. "Since you were a part of this with Bernadette, you should be the one to tell the others."

"I want to see Bernadette," Keltan said.

Ulrik held his gaze. "You said she wasna your mate."

"That doesna mean I'm no' concerned about her."

"We doona have time for this," Guy said.

Ulrik held out his arm, and Rhys, Anson, and Guy touched him. The next instant, they were gone.

Keltan was furious. There was nothing he could do about it, however. He turned and stalked from the office, making his way to the stairs before descending them to the main floor. He was almost to the conservatory when someone called his name. He turned and found Eilish walking toward him.

"How is Bernadette?" he asked.

The Druid smiled and shoved her long, dark hair back from her face. "She's amazing. I can't believe how well she's holding up under all of this."

"Because she doesna know the true danger."

Eilish raised her brows and tipped her head to the side briefly. "I think she's very aware of it. She keeps going despite the fear. Not many could do that. Hell, even I have reservations about going up against Usaeil, and I have magic."

The overwhelming need to get to Bernadette and make sure she was all right pounded through Keltan. "Take me to her."

"Ulrik and the others are with her. She's fine. And we've warded her."

"I need to see her."

Eilish stared at him for a long second. "You care about her."

He fisted his hands. "That's what I've been saying."

"Is she your mate?"

Keltan turned away to pace a couple of steps, raking his hand through his hair. "Why does everyone keep asking me that?"

"Because, normally, when a Dragon King acts the way you are right now, it means they've found their mate."

Keltan slowly turned to the Druid. "And you're an expert on Dragon Kings now?"

"Not at all."

He knew how harsh his words were, and he hadn't meant it. "I'm sorry, Eilish. I just want to get back to Bernadette and I can no'."

She laughed then, shaking her head. "You act as if you need permission."

"I doona want to spend hours driving to Glasgow," he snapped.

Eilish shrugged. "Who said you had to?"

It was all he could do not to lose his temper. "That's why I asked you to take me."

"Keltan, you're a smart dragon. Why aren't you seeing it for yourself?"

He opened his mouth to reply when he realized what she was saying—or not saying. "I can no' fly there. It's daylight. Someone would see me."

"Then I don't know what to tell you."

She walked away before he could say anything else. Keltan debated throwing away the rules that Con had put into place for thousands of years. That was how desperate he was to get to Bernadette. He turned and looked at the hidden door in the conservatory that led into Dreagan Mountain.

The other Dragon Kings were there with Kellan. All of them knew some of what was going on with Bernadette and Usaeil, but few knew all of it. If he left now and flew to Bernadette with the chance of being seen by a human, he would be putting Dreagan in the spotlight more than Bernadette ever had with her lecture.

Keltan's hands itched to hold her, but he had a duty to his brethren. They had all survived so much loss and loneliness. He owed them patience. And, as Eilish had said, Bernadette wasn't alone. She had Kings with her.

Keltan drew in a deep breath and slowly released it. Then he squared his shoulders and walked into Dreagan Mountain to find Kellan and the rest of the Kings.

CHAPTER TWENTY-NINE

Seeing magic would never get old. Bernadette was mesmerized by it all, especially the Dragon Kings. Eilish had been stunningly beautiful, and while Bernadette might not be able to feel power, she knew Eilish had plenty of it as a Druid.

She had been warded by a Fae, a Druid, and now several Dragon Kings, including Keltan. Bernadette didn't feel any differently, but that didn't mean she didn't appreciate what everyone had done for her.

Now, if only it worked.

Dragon King magic was supposed to be stronger than any other. Yet Bernadette still hadn't quite worked out why Usaeil was able to continue thwarting them. Keltan had said she'd mixed Druid magic with her own Fae power. Bernadette wanted to ask Guy or Ulrik about it, but then again, she was only human. They had been born with magic and knew all about it. Her question would be foolish.

"What is it?"

She turned her head to the tall King beside her. Rhys's aqua-ringed dark blue eyes stared at her intently as she sat in her office chair. Bernadette started shaking her head, ready to say, "nothing," but something stopped her. She took a breath and held it for a moment, weighing her options.

Then she blurted out, "How can Druid and Fae magic combined be greater than dragon magic?"

Rhys crossed his arms over his chest and leaned his hips against the back of her sofa. "That's a verra good question, lass. It's one I've been asking myself for some time."

"Which one has the least magic?" she asked.

Guy chimed in and said, "That would be the Druids."

Bernadette nodded quickly. "That's right. Keltan said they have been losing magic each generation as a result of diluting their blood by mating with humans."

"Still, there are some Druids who have a considerable amount of magic," Anson said.

Ulrik gave a single nod. "Eilish is one. The Isle of Skye is home to a large number of Druids. Some of them have a good amount of magic. Then there are the Druids at MacLeod Castle. They are some of the strongest."

"No' as powerful as Eilish," Rhys stated.

Ulrik smiled. "Aye. My woman is something special."

Bernadette looked between the four of them. "Are you saying that the Druids Usaeil has been taking magic from aren't that powerful?"

The Kings looked at each other, but it was Ulrik who nodded. "That's right."

"And even that weak Druid magic has allowed her to hide her glamour from you?" Bernadette asked, shaking her head. "I don't believe that."

Anson lifted a shoulder in a shrug. "Usaeil's magic is considerable. That has never been in question. With her potent power, it probably doesna take much Druid magic to give her an added kick."

"Or what if it does?" Guy asked.

Ulrik's black brows snapped together. "What are you saying?"

Guy met Bernadette's gaze. "I think Bernadette is onto something."

"How so?" Rhys asked.

Guy shifted his feet to widen them. "We all imagined that Usaeil was powerful all these years simply because she is the queen. None of us saw that she was really Dark."

"Fuck me," Rhys mumbled and straightened to walk around the house.

Anson closed his eyes and sighed heavily.

A muscle jumped in Ulrik's jaw. "We've all been so focused on the here and now. We just discovered that she could hide her glamour from us, but obviously, she's been doing it for a verra long time."

"How long has she been Dark?" Bernadette asked.

Guy snorted. "From the verra beginning, I imagine. A Fae's eyes turn red with their first kill. Each after that turns their hair more and more silver."

"All this fucking time," Rhys mumbled.

Disbelief overtook Anson's expression. "She's really been using Druid magic all this time?"

"It's the only thing that makes sense," Guy said.

Ulrik's gold eyes flashed with anger. "We all believed that Druids were becoming rarer because the magic was fading. It wasna the magic, it was Usaeil all these centuries."

"She's no' taken any from Skye," Anson declared.

Rhys halted and said, "That anyone knows of. It's no' like we've kept track of the Druids."

"Gemma's ancestors stood with her against Usaeil," Guy pronounced.

Bernadette shrugged, confused. "What does that mean?"

Ulrik looked her way and said, "Some Druids have the unique ability to talk to the Ancients. They are past Druids who help or guide in certain ways. Gemma comes from a long line of extremely powerful Druids that were all but wiped out by another Druid. Her ancestors came to her during the battle with Usaeil and stood with her."

Bernadette was floored. "That's . . . Wow. Would they help again?"

"The Ancients have never stood with a Druid before," Anson explained.

Rhys shoved his hands into the front pockets of his jeans. "Ancients. Ancestors. Whatever they're called, they helped Gemma and Cináed. They might help this time."

"We can no' count on such a thing," Ulrik replied.

Guy looked at Ulrik. "Nay, we can no'."

"It still begs the question: Where is Usaeil getting her Druids from? Because they must have a decent amount of magic for her to have the power she does when she combines it with hers," Rhys said.

Ulrik's frown deepened as his body went rigid. "How many of us have mated a Druid or someone who has a blood connection to the Druids?"

"You can no' seriously think . . ." But Rhys couldn't finish the sentence.

Anson swallowed hard. "Warrick and Darcy were the first couple."

"Darcy was a Druid," Ulrik said.

"Then there was Dmitri and Faith," Anson continued.

Rhys chimed in. "Faith has a connection but no magic."

Anson kept going. "Nikolai and Esther."

"She may no' have magic, but she and Henry are blood relatives of the Clachers, just like Gemma," Guy said.

Anson nodded. "Cináed and Gemma. Ulrik and Eilish."

Rhys snorted and shot a quick grin at Ulrik. "We all know Eilish is definitely a Druid."

Ulrik's smile was fleeting as his gaze returned to Anson.

"Then there is Devon and me," Anson said softly. "She has a connection."

"A deep one that allows the two of you to link your minds," Guy stated.

Bernadette's eyes went wide. She wanted to ask all about Anson and Devon, but she decided that now wasn't the time. "That's six mates."

"That we know of," Rhys said.

Ulrik flattened his lips. "Ryder looked into every mate's past."

"Maybe no' deep enough," Anson replied.

There was a minute of silence before Ulrik said, "Ryder and Kinsey are going back through each of the mate's pasts."

"Why does it matter who is a Druid and who isn't?" Bernadette asked.

"It doesna," Guy told her. "But if more of the mates have a connection to the Druids, it could be useful information."

She could understand that. "Usaeil can't harm any of the mates, right?"

"No' the ones who have gone through the mating ceremony," Rhys said, his gaze going to Ulrik.

Ulrik slid his gold gaze to Bernadette. "My and Eilish's ceremony was postponed when Con was taken."

"Usaeil wouldn't dare go after Eilish." Bernadette shook her head in bewilderment. "That would be insane. Besides, Usaeil can't get on Dreagan land."

Anson's lips twisted. "Usaeil might no' be able to step foot on Dreagan, but there are other ways for her to get to Eilish or any of the other mates."

Bernadette's stomach clutched. "Eilish came here."

Ulrik waved his hand through the air, cutting off her words. "Eilish isna stupid. She protected herself when she was here. But there are other ways."

"It's why we've got to make sure no' all the Kings are at the battle with Usaeil. Some need to remain behind to guard Dreagan and the mates," Guy said.

Bernadette wished they were whisking her away to Dreagan. Even though she wanted to stand against Usaeil, to be included in such a family, to be protected and cherished in such a way, was something she'd always yearned for. But she wasn't an idiot. She wasn't Keltan's mate.

They'd had sex—amazingly wonderful sex—but she knew that's all it was. To think there might be more—to *hope* for more—was akin to believing that Usaeil would just forget about her.

"You doona have to do this," Rhys said, pulling her attention from her thoughts and back to them.

Bernadette shrugged and forced a smile. "I'm the type of person who likes to solve problems. I also tend to be someone who always helps others. I'm not saying I'm not utterly terrified of what could happen, but even I see this is a unique chance for you all. Usaeil already has me in her crosshairs. I'm not getting out anytime soon. If I can get you any type of information, no matter how little that could help, then I want to make sure that happens."

Ulrik's smile was soft and kind. "You truly are one in a million, Bernadette. We can no' thank you enough."

"Sure, you can. Kill Usaeil."

They all laughed, but it died quickly.

Suddenly, Eilish appeared in the house again. She held

out her hands, which were filled with small electrical items. "Ryder sent these for us to install. He wanted to make sure that we caught everything."

The Kings immediately went to Eilish and each took a piece from her hand, disbursing them throughout the house. As Bernadette watched, she realized that they were tiny cameras. She had to admit, that was smart.

It also took a huge burden off her not to have to remember every detail or word Usaeil said to her.

In less than twenty minutes, she was surrounded again. Eilish and Ulrik spoke softly to each other. Eilish then flashed Bernadette a quick smile and a wave as she left.

Ulrik turned his head to her. "The spells and wards used on you and the house will ensure that Usaeil willna be able to hurt you again. She will still be able to get in, though."

"Because we need her inside," Bernadette interjected.

Ulrik nodded. "Precisely. Ryder sent over cameras that we've hidden throughout the house. They will livestream to Dreagan, where we can see and hear everything in real time."

"All right." Bernadette rubbed her hands on her thighs and got to her feet. "I don't know when she'll show up again."

Rhys snorted loudly. "It could be in the next second."

Anson gave him a dark look.

"It's all right," Bernadette told Anson. "Rhys is only speaking the truth."

"Bernadette."

At the sound of her name, she turned to Ulrik. His face was serious, which meant that whatever he said next would be important. "Yes?"

"Our time is running out with Usaeil. We only have a few more hours. When those are up, you are welcome to make your way to Dreagan. We would be honored to have you."

His words warmed her heart because she knew he meant every one of them. "Don't worry about me. You all do what you do best."

Ulrik gave her a nod and backed away. Rhys shot her a wink, while Anson bowed his head. It was Guy who walked to her and took her hands.

"Please make sure you come to Dreagan. Keltan wants you there, as do all of us," he said.

She smiled up at him. "I'll be there."

CHAPTER THIRTY

Madrid, Spain

He'd never been at a loss for words before, but as Henry stared across the small table at Melisse, he found he couldn't string two syllables together.

"Why are you here?" she demanded.

He sat back and rested his hands on his thighs. "Why are *you* here? Your accent is Scottish, so you aren't a local."

Her white eyes, ringed with black and speckled with silver, were steady as she stared at him. "I'm not pretending to be."

Henry scratched his forehead and briefly looked away. "I don't know what we're dancing around here, but perhaps you should just come out and tell me."

A silver brow arched regally. "Why should I be the one to do it? Just because I'm a woman?"

"That's not what I meant."

"Why were you in the house?"

He didn't need to ask which one she was referring to. Henry stretched out his legs at an angle and crossed his ankles. "I came to see where the murder took place."

"You aren't with the authorities."

"No, I'm not. Your turn. Why were you there?"

"I also came to see the place of the killing. Why did you want to see it?"

He lifted one shoulder. "I was drawn there. You?"

"Curiosity."

Henry knew she wasn't telling him the entire truth, but he didn't point that out. Not now, at least. She didn't trust him. Not that he could blame her. He didn't exactly trust her either.

Well, that wasn't true. There was something about her that he almost recognized. He couldn't put his finger on what it was, but it was like he *knew* her.

That couldn't be true because if he had met her before, he wouldn't have forgotten. Her beauty alone would have been branded on his mind. So, what was it? What had drawn his gaze to her when he walked from the murdered Druid's house?

"Who were the people with you?" Melisse asked.

Henry wasn't surprised by the question. It was one he would've asked had he been her. "My sister and her husband."

"Where are they now?"

"Gone."

Melisse turned her gaze out to the road as people walked past. "You should leave."

"Why?" he asked, frowning.

Instead of answering, she looked back at him. "It was nice getting to meet you, Henry North. You aren't what I expected."

The moment he heard his last name, he froze. He hadn't told it to her, so she either had been following him for a while or . . . she had magic. Before he could ask her about it, she rose and turned to walk back the way she'd come.

Henry stood and jogged a few steps to catch up with her. "Melisse, wait."

"Henry!"

The sound of his sister's voice behind him stopped him cold. He turned and saw her and Nikolai running toward him. Henry glanced back at Melisse, but she was gone. He wanted to try to find her, but Esther and Nikolai wouldn't have tracked him down if it weren't important.

Henry returned to the table and tossed down enough money to pay for his coffee. Then he walked to meet his sister.

"We have to get back to Dreagan. Now," she said breathlessly.

Henry looked at Nikolai to find the Dragon King on high alert, his gaze moving around, looking for threats. "What's going on?"

"We'll explain on the way to the chopper," Nikolai replied.

Henry fell into step beside them. Just before he turned the corner, he cast one more look back to where he'd last seen Melisse.

The three of them walked fast through the streets. Each time Henry wanted to ask them to tell him what was going on, there were too many people near. None of them could take the risk of someone overhearing anything they said.

It wasn't until they met Lily at the chopper that Henry finally got to hear what was going on.

"We're gearing up for war," Nikolai stated.

Henry had been looking outside, but he jerked his head around as they ascended. "What?"

His sister nodded. "Apparently, this thing with Bernadette and Usaeil has progressed significantly."

"Aye, but it's really Rhi," Nikolai explained. "She dreamed about Bernadette's house and went to visit. She got there after Usaeil had used a blood spell."

Henry shook his head. "Wait. What? A blood spell?"

"Something Druids use to locate someone. Fae are no' able to just find someone, no' even with their magic," Nikolai said.

Henry took in that bit of new information. "I gather that Usaeil found Bernadette."

"Not exactly." Esther then proceeded to fill him in on everything that had been happening with Keltan and Bernadette.

"Bloody hell," Henry murmured when she finished. "It's amazing she's alive."

Nikolai nodded. "Verra."

Henry looked to the front of the chopper and Lily. No wonder everyone had been in such a rush to find him. They all wanted to get back to Dreagan.

"That's not all."

He slid his gaze to his sister. "What else is there?"

Nikolai released a long breath. "Rhi returned to Bernadette's place and spoke with her and Keltan."

"What is it about Bernadette that keeps drawing Rhi?" Henry asked.

Esther gave him a pointed look. "That's something I'd really like to know."

"That's no' the point now." Nikolai took Esther's hand and brought it to his lips to kiss. "It's no' just the timetable Usaeil gave us that's running out. Rhi intends to attack her. Rhi said that we can pretend to bring her in to Usaeil, but if we doona, she's going after the queen herself."

"Fuck." Henry ran a hand through his hair.

Esther nodded. "Exactly."

And they had wasted time looking for him. "I'm sorry. I didn't know. I shouldn't have taken the time alone in the city. I thought I had a few hours."

"So did we." Esther gave him one of her sisterly smiles. "Lily is getting us home quickly. The Kings aren't heading out immediately."

Nikolai twisted his lips. "It'll be soon, though. Ulrik called everyone back so we could finalize plans. I'm guessing we'll be headed to the Light Castle by morning."

"So soon?" Esther asked with a frown.

Henry turned his face away from them. He was worried about the battle, but like his sister. It might be different if he were actually going to war with the Kings, but that wasn't his path.

However, all the new information he'd gotten on Usaeil might help them locate where she'd been hiding. At the very least, he might be able to find Con.

His thoughts moved to Melisse. Henry wished he'd gotten to talk to her more. She was hiding something. Then again, so was he. It wasn't as if he could come out and ask her if she had magic.

The fact that she was interested in the murdered Druid's house was interesting. Though there were humans who were curious about such things. They usually worked for the authorities, but a few followed such things as a hobby.

Melisse didn't look like a hobbyist. And if she weren't, then there had to be another explanation for her being at the house. Did he want to dig into that? Especially when he had so many other things on his plate—including learning his new abilities?

Henry swallowed and glanced at his sister and Nikolai to find them both watching him. "What?" he asked.

"What are you thinking so hard about?" Esther asked.

He shrugged nonchalantly. "We have a lot going on."

"There's something you aren't telling me," she insisted.

Nikolai put his arm around her and drew her close to him. "Sweetheart, your brother is working through accepting his role as JusticeBringer as well as keeping track of the Dark Fae and trying to locate Usaeil. Let the man keep some secrets."

Esther narrowed her gaze on Henry. "Fine, but I want you to promise that if it's something bad, you'll come to me."

"We're a team, sis," he told her.

"That means you have to tell me what's on your mind."

Henry glanced at Nikolai, who was gazing at his boots. "Really? Do you tell me everything? Or do you go to Nikolai?"

"You walked right into that one, lass," Nikolai said before he kissed Esther's temple.

She rolled her eyes. "Bloody hell."

Henry laughed and reached across the way to playfully slap at her leg. "I promise I'll tell you if it's something important."

"Good." She flashed him a wide smile.

He returned it while noticing how Nikolai couldn't take his eyes from her. Henry wondered how bad the war would be. The Kings hadn't gone into a battle like this with mates before. No one knew what to expect, especially the women.

It was no wonder Nikolai was staring at Esther. This might be the last time they could joke and laugh for a while. Henry hoped to hell he was wrong, but Usaeil had blindsided them too many times for him not to think she might do it again.

Esther yawned and closed her eyes as she rested her head on Nikolai's shoulder. Henry met his brother-in-law's gaze. He saw the Dragon King's worry. Henry gave him a nod, a silent promise that Esther would be looked after. Always.

But Henry had another fear. Esther might be mated to a Dragon King who made her immortal. Therefore, she could live forever and never get sick as long as her mate was alive and well. Yet if Nikolai died in battle, Esther would die, too.

Henry's mouth fell open as he realized another reason Usaeil had taken Con.

"Aye," Nikolai whispered.

Henry leaned forward and dropped his head into his hands. If Usaeil somehow managed to either turn Con to her side or use magic on him, then he might very well fight each of the Kings. And since Con was King of Kings and the strongest of them all, the odds were in his favor.

It took several moments before Henry was able to lift his head and look at Nikolai. Obviously, his brother-in-law hadn't told Esther any of that, and neither would Henry. Esther would have her own weight of worries to carry. She didn't need any more. Henry would carry this for her.

He glanced at Esther to make sure she was asleep, then asked Nikolai, "Is there a plan?"

"To win," the King replied.

Henry should've known that would be the answer. "How worried is everyone?"

Nikolai looked away and swallowed thickly, which was answer enough.

"I would gladly go into battle with all of you," Henry said.

Nikolai slowly turned his face to him. "And we would be honored to have you beside us."

"But I'm useless."

The King shook his head. "You are the JusticeBringer, Henry. You and Esther are a force that the Druids have no' encountered in ages. The two of you together are just now figuring out your strengths and learning your way. That needs to be protected. And so does Dreagan. We need you there with Eilish, Shara, Esther, and Denae to fight whoever and whatever attacks. Because Dreagan *will* be attacked."

Henry sat back and nodded. "We will hold Dreagan for you."

"We know," Nikolai said with a smile. "Some Kings will remain behind because Dreagan must always have Dragon Kings there."

"Do you know who is staying?"

Nikolai glanced at Esther and shook his head. "No' yet. That's being decided once we get home."

Which meant Henry would need to be close in case Esther learned that Nikolai would be going to fight Usaeil.

"Henry. You need to know that you are my brother. You are a brother to everyone at Dreagan. The fact that you doona have magic means nothing to us."

Henry blinked, shocked and astounded by Nikolai's words. "Thank you."

"You are one of us. Now and always."

When Henry looked out the window, he felt peace he hadn't in a very long time.

CHAPTER THIRTY-ONE

Things could go wrong. Keltan understood that fact. Hell, every person who went to war was cognizant of that, but this was different. This was nothing like the Fae Wars, where the Kings protected the humans.

This was the Kings fighting for themselves—something they hadn't done since the clash with the mortals so long ago.

"You look worried," V said as he walked up next to him in the cavern.

Keltan looked out over the crowd of Dragon Kings. "Are you no'? You and Claire have a lot to lose."

V's lips flattened at the reminder. "Am I sorry that Claire is carrying my bairn? Nay, I'm no'. Do I know that the odds of us losing that babe are great? Aye, I do. I want my mate, and I'll do whatever it takes to break the hold Usaeil has over her and my child. Everyone at Dreagan has a lot to lose, Keltan. My pain willna be greater simply because I've found my mate."

Keltan didn't point out that V and Claire hadn't gone through the ceremony yet, so Claire, like Eilish, Sabina, and Gemma was still very much mortal.

Just like Bernadette.

Keltan took a deep breath to control the bellow inside him at the thought of her being alone.

"You're a fool."

Keltan jerked his head to V. "Excuse me?"

"You're a bloody fool."

Keltan blinked, trying to think why V would say such a thing. "About?"

"Bernadette. Are you so afraid to love that you can no' see what is right before you? Everyone else can see it."

Keltan didn't know how to respond. His first instinct was to refuse that he felt anything for Bernadette, but that was a lie. He'd admitted to caring about her. But . . . love?

"Love doesna make you weak," V continued. Anger sparked in his ice blue eyes and dripped from every syllable. "It makes you stronger."

Keltan could argue that. "Stronger? You think you're stronger when you're worrying about Claire and the babe she's carrying thanks to Usaeil? You think you're strong having your mind split between the battle and the safety of your mate?"

V's eyes went cold as he faced Keltan. "Like I said, a bloody fool. I worry no' just for my mate and our unborn child. I worry for every soul living here, including your dumb arse. I worry about Con, about our dragons, about the future. Worry is always there, but I doona let it rule me. If I'm one of those called into battle, I will trust that the Kings who remain behind to guard Dreagan and the mates will do their job. And if I'm asked to stay behind and defend Dreagan, I will do it knowing that those fighting with Usaeil will do their best. That's what we do. Because we're Dragon Kings."

"Even you have to admit that Claire will always be on your mind," Keltan argued.

V gave a slight nod. "Always. She's in my heart, which means, she is forever with me. But I know in order to defeat our foe, I have to focus. Just like every King who has a mate. Just as you will."

Keltan frowned as he snorted. "Me?"

"Tell me you're no' thinking of Bernadette. Tell me you doona wish she were here."

Keltan looked away, unable to deny V's words.

V let out a loud sigh. "Regardless of what Bernadette did that brought our attention to her, she is more than making up for it. There isna a soul on Dreagan that doesna realize that."

"She could die."

"We all could."

Keltan swallowed and looked away before V saw just how torn up he was about Bernadette's involvement. "She didna ask for this. Usaeil forced her into our world."

"Perhaps. Did you no' tell Bernadette that it was her destiny to come to Dreagan?"

Keltan shook his head as he dropped his chin to his chest because he couldn't refute that.

"Then that means it's her destiny to be right where she is, helping us. Even if it kills you no' to interfere and stop her."

Slowly, Keltan lifted his head. "I'm no' sure who is more to blame for Bernadette. Usaeil or me."

"It's Usaeil," V stated. "You can rest assured about that. Now, here comes Ulrik. He should be able to tell you how Bernadette is."

Keltan slid his gaze to the side and spotted Ulrik, who was looking right at him. When Keltan started to go to him, Ulrik shook his head slightly.

"Anson is headed our way," V told him.

As soon as Anson was near, Keltan asked, "How is Bernadette?"

"She's fine," Anson assured him. "She's well, and we've warded her and her home. Ryder also sent cameras that we placed throughout her house so we could see when and if Usaeil shows up."

"I assume Ryder is recording audio and video?" V said.

Anson nodded. "That way, Bernadette doesna have to remember everything."

Keltan took in all of that with interest, but he couldn't dispel the disappointment. "Bernadette is still in Glasgow."

"Aye." Anson's black gaze met his. "She will head to Dreagan when she can."

"How is she supposed to know when?" Keltan asked, his anger rising up.

V put a hand on his arm to calm him as he frowned at Anson. "Keltan has a point. We willna have time for anyone to notify Bernadette that she can come to Dreagan."

Anson shrugged. "We didna talk specifics. She knows she's welcome. Whether she comes or no' is another matter entirely."

The knot inside Keltan tightened significantly. He glanced at the tunnel that led back to the manor. Perhaps he could talk Eilish into getting Bernadette. It would take seconds instead of the hours it would take if Bernadette drove.

"I'd do the same," Anson said.

Keltan sighed as he swung his gaze back to his friend.

Anson shrugged. "Everyone with a mate would ask Eilish for help whether they admit it or no'."

"You think I should talk to her?"

"I think you should make sure Ulrik knows what you're going to ask his mate to do."

Anson was right. Especially since Eilish didn't have the dragon-eye tattoo from the mating ceremony that meant she was bound to Ulrik and he to her.

Keltan suddenly frowned. "This might be a stretch, but do you think there is any way Usaeil might verra well know Bernadette is working with us? That by me asking Eilish to help her, I would, in fact, be sending Eilish straight into a trap?"

"At this point, I think anything is possible."

That didn't make Keltan feel any better. "I can no' do that to Eilish or Ulrik. No' after all they went through." Nor could he leave Bernadette in Glasgow. But there might be another way. . . .

Anson raised a black brow. "What are you thinking?"

Keltan looked around the cavern at the Kings. "Ulrik is about to tell us who is going to the Light Castle and who is to remain behind."

"You want to stay here," Anson guessed.

"No' exactly. Usaeil chose Bernadette for a reason. We've all thought that it was just to put us in the spotlight. What if there is another reason?"

Anson considered that for a moment. "This ties back to you believing Usaeil knows about Bernadette working with us."

"Aye. What if that was her entire point? She kept telling Bernadette to stay away from us, but we all know that wasna going to be possible. Usaeil knew one of us would find Bernadette and talk to her."

"A King that wasna mated," Anson said with a knowing look. "I'll be damned. Usaeil could've done that hoping a King would fall for Bernadette."

"She couldna know that whoever went would develop feelings for Bernadette."

Anson shrugged, one brow raised. "Are you sure? Look what Usaeil did to get Claire pregnant."

The idea that what Keltan felt for Bernadette wasn't real infuriated him. Then his thoughts halted. Wasn't that what he wanted? To be free? To not have anyone or anything clinging to him?

Before he could answer, an image of Bernadette in his arms as they made love flashed in his mind.

"If Usaeil used magic to get both of you to feel something, then you're off the hook," Anson said, unaware of Keltan's turmoil. "You didna want to have a mate, and now we know for sure that you doona."

"Aye. It's what I want." Wasn't it? Keltan couldn't be sure anymore.

He fought against the idea of having a mate, but now that there was a good possibility that Bernadette wasn't his, he was . . . disappointed.

"That doesna mean Bernadette still shouldna come here," Keltan said.

Anson shrugged. "Perhaps it does. We doona know how deep Usaeil's magic has gone. In fact, we can no' believe anything Bernadette has told us."

Before Keltan realized it, he'd stepped closer to Anson with his fists clenched in anger. "She hasna lied."

Anson stared at him for a long minute. "Is that right?"

"You didna hear her words. You didna look into her eyes."

"And I didna hold her during sex."

The need to shift and challenge Anson poured through Keltan as hot as lava. Movement out of the corner of his eye stopped him. He glanced to the side and saw others watching. When he took a second and looked around him, he realized that every King in the cavern had stopped what they were doing to watch and listen to him and Anson.

"Are you sure you doona want to revise your thoughts about Bernadette from earlier?" Rhys asked.

Keltan returned his gaze to Anson before he took a step back. His anger lessened to the point that he could control it once more.

Anson shook his head. "I provoked you. I'm sorry, brother, but you needed to know."

"Know what?" Keltan asked.

Ulrik walked through the crowd then. "That no matter how much magic a being has, no one can make another fall in love. Desire and infatuation, aye. But no' love."

Keltan began to shake his head to deny that he had that depth of feeling for Bernadette, but then he stopped himself. He'd been ready to beat the shite out of Anson for speaking ill of her. Keltan was prepared to put Eilish in danger just to get Bernadette to Dreagan. And all Keltan could think about was the beautiful doctor.

Ulrik put his hand on Keltan's shoulder. "Usaeil might have made sure to get a King to Bernadette, and she might have ensured that the two of you were attracted to each other." He paused for a heartbeat. "But she couldna have made you react the way you just did because of the feelings inside you."

"Fuck," Keltan murmured as he ran a hand through his hair.

"Many of us have been right where you are," Rhys said, which caused the other mated males to laugh.

Ulrik dropped his arm as he grinned at Rhys's words. "Let me catch everyone up on what happened at Bernadette's."

Keltan hung on every word, the scene playing out

in his head as he imagined Bernadette talking with his friends. The need to see her continued to grow until it became an ache. He rubbed his chest as the pain swelled and spread to every nerve in his body.

"That brings us to now," Ulrik finished. "Since we've no' located either Con or Usaeil, we will be going to war."

Merrill snorted. "It's about time."

"I agree," Rhi stated as she appeared beside Ulrik. She took a moment to move her gaze from one side of the cavern to the other, looking at the Kings. "I know I don't need to remind all of you because you're skilled warriors, but be prepared for anything. Usaeil will try to surprise you, causing you to hesitate. When you do that, she'll go in for the kill."

"You really think she can kill us?" Ulrik asked.

Rhi shrugged, her lips flattening. "I honestly don't know. She's doing things I've never known a Fae to do."

"The fucking Others," V said with a growl.

Roman put a hand on V's shoulder. "One enemy at a time."

"Actually, destroying Usaeil might make more of an impact with the Others than we think," Ulrik said.

"No time like the present to find out." Rhi smiled in anticipation.

Ulrik nodded. "Let's determine who is remaining at Dreagan and who is going to the Light Castle."

CHAPTER THIRTY-TWO

Dark Palace

It was nearly time. Balladyn could practically taste it on the air. Today, as he had for most of the past month, he stood staring out the windows of his quarters overlooking the vibrant green of the Irish countryside.

He hadn't wanted to love this land.

But he did. It had claimed him slowly, silently until one day he realized that it had seeped into his soul. Ireland wasn't the Fae Realm. But it was as close as anything would ever come.

At one time, he'd prayed that the Dragon Kings could kick the Dark off the Earth. That was when Balladyn had been Light. Now, as a Dark—and king—he was glad that the Dragon Kings had allowed the treaty to be signed so all Fae could remain.

Looking back, Balladyn realized that it was all Constantine. That infuriated him, but he was man enough to admit when someone had done something decent. And that's exactly what Con and the Dragon Kings had done.

Con had realized that the Fae had nowhere to go. The Kings could've easily forced the Fae from the realm, but they didn't. Some might say that was a weakness on the part of the Kings. Balladyn would argue that it was their greatest strength.

The Dragon Kings knew their ability to protect the realm and the mortals. They had proven it time and again. It was because of that, that they gave sanctuary first to the humans, and then to the Fae.

For hundreds of years, Balladyn had been the right-hand man to Taraeth, the previous King of the Dark. He'd worked with Taraeth to bring about the downfall of the Dragon Kings. Balladyn would've gladly done whatever was needed to hurt the Kings any way he could.

Of course, that was because of Rhi. He'd loved her for so long, only to lose her to a Dragon King. Actually, she hadn't really been his because he'd never told her of his feelings. That had been a mistake he'd never thought to fix, but then he'd had the chance.

Rhi had been his for a short while. Those had been the best—and worst—days of his long life. She might have been in his arms, but her heart still belonged to another.

Now, he was willing to stand with the Dragon Kings in order to help Rhi. That was how much he loved her. Besides, he owed her much more than that after chaining her in the Dark dungeon and putting the Chains of Mordare on her.

Balladyn still couldn't believe he'd done such a thing. Sure, he'd been angry with her, blaming her for the fact that he'd turned Dark, but even then, he knew it hadn't been her fault. Rhi was a great many things, but she wasn't someone who would have left him on the field of battle if she'd thought he was alive.

No, the real culprit was none other than Usaeil. The same bitch responsible for him now being Dark since she had asked Taraeth to kill him. Balladyn was thankful that

Taraeth had kept him alive so he could bring his army against Usaeil.

Balladyn wanted to call to Rhi, but he knew she wouldn't come to him. It didn't matter where he was. She hadn't answered him in months, and he wasn't entirely sure she would be happy to see him on the battlefield. But he didn't care. He'd go through ten kinds of Hell for her.

He turned his back to the window. Since Usaeil had spies in his palace, he couldn't put his army on alert. He had to wait to hear from the Dragon Kings before he called for them. Fortunately, the Fae answered quickly.

Balladyn had been keeping a close eye on his generals to make sure none of them was spying for Usaeil, but that wasn't her way. She tended to go for the lesser ranks, someone who could blend in well and wouldn't be noticed if they went missing.

The problem with the Dark was that no one trusted anyone else. Balladyn couldn't tell anyone what was going on or even have his generals or guards keep watch for potential spies because someone might use the information against him.

Balladyn had never dreamed of being king when he was Light or even when he first became Dark. He'd been happy as a general in the Light Army. He'd been damn good at his job, and he'd won many skirmishes during the Fae civil war.

Once he turned Dark, he'd used those same skills to climb the ranks. His goal had been to get close to Taraeth and discover the ins and outs of the Dark. Once he achieved that, Balladyn saw for himself how weak and uncaring Taraeth was. Taraeth could've easily beaten the Light and won their civil war, but he only cared about himself.

Balladyn had stood by and watched Taraeth for thousands of years. He saw the previous king betray one ally after another, but what Balladyn *did* learn was that if the Dark were ever to have a fighting chance, they needed a stronger king. Unfortunately, Balladyn didn't trust that somebody else wouldn't be taken in by the power of the position. So, he killed Taraeth.

Of course, that was after he'd learned that it was Usaeil who had betrayed him to the Dark. That sealed the deal for Balladyn. For him to get to Usaeil, he had to be in a position of power.

He walked toward the shelves of books that he'd accumulated throughout his life. He'd never imagined that he'd care so much about his subjects once he became King of the Dark. He didn't see them as evil beings—though they were.

Balladyn just saw them as Fae who deserved to be governed and have laws, just like the Light. The Dark were used to fear and betrayal. It was how they'd lived for so long. Few understood what it meant to trust or to have someone believe in them.

Not that Balladyn was stupid enough to think it was something he could achieve overnight. The Dark were programmed one way. It would take eons to change them. But for that to begin, the first step had to be taken.

The Dark didn't even realize that he'd already implemented small changes in the months he'd been king. In order for this to work, things had to start small and build up. And it was going to take patience. If only he had someone he could trust enough to help him on this quest.

He would've turned to Xaneth had Usaeil not taken him. Xaneth wasn't Dark, but he'd been the only Fae who had worked equally with both the Light and Dark, so he had an advantage Balladyn would've loved to use.

Xaneth was a good man. Balladyn said that of few beings, but he'd recognized it instantly with Xaneth. While he wouldn't call the Light a friend, Balladyn was friendly with him. They'd made a pact to kill Usaeil.

Hell, Balladyn and Ulrik had made that same pact.

That made Balladyn snort. Ulrik. He'd never thought to team up with a Dragon King, and if he hadn't trusted Ulrik then, he wouldn't be considering joining forces with all the Kings now.

Looking back, so much had changed in such a short time. He wasn't unhappy with the situation. In fact, he was quite pleased with things. He'd discovered the Reapers and had even teamed up with them. Though he wouldn't assume they called him an ally, he did consider them allies.

Death was something special. He still didn't know why she had such an interest in Rhi, and if he were honest, he doubted that he'd ever find out. That was fine. Knowing that a goddess as powerful and good as Erith had an eye on Rhi made him feel better.

Rhi was in a dark place. He'd helped put her there thanks to the Chains of Mordare, but it was Usaeil who pushed her closer and closer to the edge. Balladyn had once thought to turn Rhi Dark. Now, his stomach churned each time he thought of Rhi becoming that way.

If the Light Fae had any hope, it was with Rhi. Though there were others who could take the throne. Xaneth, if Usaeil hadn't killed him yet. There was also Phelan, the Warrior who was part Fae.

But Rhi was the one Balladyn would choose. The Fae adored her. They knew her and trusted her. The Light might come to accept Xaneth and Phelan—both of which had a direct line to the throne through blood—but they would welcome Rhi with open arms.

First, however, Usaeil had to be killed.

Balladyn turned away from the bookshelves. His gaze landed on the set of four chairs in the middle of the room, but it was the white-haired Fae staring at him that made Balladyn shake his head.

"One day, I might actually know when you arrive, Fintan," he said.

One side of the Reaper's lips lifted in a grin. "What would be the fun in that?"

"Dare I hope you're here for a friendly chat?" The first moment Balladyn had seen the Reaper on the streets of Galway, he'd wondered if he was the infamous assassin.

To his delight, Fintan had been. Though Balladyn didn't find that out until much later. Fintan dropped by occasionally, but it was never just because. It always had something to do with the Reapers.

"One day, I'm going to say yes," Fintan replied. The smile dropped. "But that isn't today."

Balladyn walked over, taking the chair opposite the Reaper. "What's going on?"

"You're going to hear from the Kings soon."

Balladyn nodded. "Usaeil's time limit is running out for them to bring Rhi."

"Rhi is more than ready to face Usaeil."

"But can Rhi win?"

Fintan gave him a flat look. "I can't predict the future."

"That's too bad."

The Reaper's head tilted to the side. "Why? Would you change your mind about fighting if you knew the outcome?"

"No," Balladyn said with a snort. "I'm going to fight Usaeil no matter what. That bitch has this coming."

"Are you sure your army will fight?"

Balladyn quirked a brow. "I'm their king."

"You might bear the title, but you know as well as I how fickle the Dark can be."

Fintan had a point, though it rankled Balladyn to admit it. Still, if he were going to gain the respect of his people, he needed to listen to the advice of others. And Fintan knew a lot.

"I might not have been Dark during our civil war, but even I know that every Dark out there will relish the opportunity to strike back at the Light. Particularly Usaeil."

Fintan grinned slowly. "You're not wrong, my friend."

Balladyn didn't so much as twitch at Fintan calling him friend, but Balladyn liked it. No one had called him that since he'd been a Light many, many thousands of years ago.

"You have a suggestion for me?" Balladyn asked.

Fintan twisted his lips and lifted one shoulder nonchalantly. "Perhaps."

Balladyn leaned forward, his forearms on his knees. "I'm all ears."

"You need to know that not all the Dark in your army will join you."

"I expected that."

"But they'll be there watching the battle."

Balladyn hadn't considered that. He nodded slowly. "To see who is winning. If it looks as if I am, they'll join me. If it's Usaeil, then they'll leave."

"Aye. They'll also want to know who you're fighting with."

Balladyn wrinkled his nose and sat back. "I wasn't going to tell them about the Dragon Kings."

"You should."

"It would certainly be a change of pace from what they're used to." Balladyn scratched his jaw. "Many won't like the idea of standing alongside a Dragon King."

Fintan made a sound at the back of his throat. "You don't."

"No, but I'm doing this for Rhi."

"Exactly."

Balladyn got it then. "I need to give them a reason other than just fighting Usaeil."

Fintan smiled widely. "I knew you were smart."

Balladyn held the Reaper's red-rimmed white gaze. "I don't suppose you'll fight with us."

"If I could, I would. Death has decreed otherwise."

"It would be pointless to ask for a reason, so I won't. But all of you were once Fae."

Fintan drew in a deep breath and released it. "We haven't been Fae in a very long time. I'll be watching the battle. Good luck, Balladyn."

To his shock, the Reaper leaned forward and held out his hand. Balladyn didn't hesitate to shake it.

Then, with a nod, the Reaper disappeared.

CHAPTER THIRTY-THREE

Bernadette couldn't sit still. She'd cleaned her house, but it was so small that it hadn't taken her long at all. She couldn't even go through her closet and toss out old clothes since she'd done all that before she'd moved.

She finally decided to take everything out of the cabinets in the kitchen and rearrange them. Only she put everything back exactly how she had it. She hadn't seen that while she was doing it because her mind was on Keltan and the Kings' approaching battle with Usaeil.

Every little sound made her jump since she was expecting Usaeil to make an appearance. She had mixed feelings about it, though. On one hand, she wanted to give the Kings some information to help them. But on the other, she'd be happy never to lay eyes on Usaeil again. Not to mention she wasn't sure that Usaeil would tell her anything useful for the Kings. She was merely a mortal, after all.

Bernadette wiped the hair from her face with her arm as she scrubbed a plate for the third time. It wasn't even dirty, but if she didn't occupy her hands, she might go insane. This waiting was dreadful.

She finally gave the poor dish a break and rinsed it. It was while she was drying it that a knock on the door startled her enough that she lost her grip on the tableware and it crashed to the floor, breaking into pieces.

The door flew open, and Keltan stood there. She was so happy to see him that she couldn't stop smiling.

"I thought you might be hurt," he said.

He could've busted through the door for all she cared. "My nerves are just stretched thin."

"Let me help you."

Before she could stop him, Keltan was standing before her, picking up the largest pieces. Together, they cleaned up the mess. Then they were standing in the kitchen, staring at each other again.

"Oh," he said and turned to shut the door that he'd left open.

"I didn't think any of you were supposed to be here."

He turned to face her. "I began to suspect that Usaeil's interest in you was more than just bringing attention to us."

"She used me for something else?" That was all Bernadette needed.

Keltan shot her a heart-stopping grin. "Me."

She blinked, confused. "You?"

"Well, to be honest, any King who came to talk to you."

Bernadette still didn't get it. "What do you mean? She kept telling me to stay away from you."

"That's what Usaeil *said*, but she knew we'd come. She knew one of us would try to dissuade you from your task."

Bernadette wanted to sink to the floor. "Are you telling me that she used her magic to make me attracted to you?"

"Aye."

"Just perfect." All this time, Bernadette had believed

that the one real thing in her life at present was her feelings for Keltan. Not that she even understood the fierce and strong emotions.

Now, to find out that none of it was real . . .

"Attraction is something a Fae knows well," Keltan told her. "They also like to use it with unsuspecting humans. I believe you mortals call it Cupid."

This was just getting worse and worse. Bernadette walked past him to the table and pulled out a chair before she placed her elbow on the surface and propped up her head with her hand. "Cupid. Great."

"What I'm trying to say, badly," Keltan said with a grimace, "is that magic can manifest attraction and even desire. It can no', however, force anything deeper."

He meant love, but she couldn't understand why he didn't just say the word. Bernadette lowered her hand to the table. "Are you saying that we had sex because of Usaeil?"

"No," he stated unequivocally.

Relief poured through her. Then she paused. "How do you know?"

"Usaeil was able to set the stage. She could use a spell for desire, and she could even make sure you came to Dreagan. She could ensure that you did whatever she wanted, but she doesna have that same power over a Dragon King."

Bernadette swallowed heavily. "Are you trying to tell me that you weren't spelled but that I was?"

"I think she sent you to Dreagan, and she might have made sure you found me attractive."

"As if I needed help. You know how handsome you are."

His grin made her heart skip a beat. "You find me handsome?"

"Yes. But it was the way you put me at ease that really drew me in. You didn't seem to judge me, though I'm sure you did."

"No' in the way you think. The fact that you came to Dreagan told me you were open to learning the truth."

Bernadette was pleased with his words. "You gave it to me without hesitation. You trusted me, which helped me to trust you."

"Usaeil couldna have had a hand in any of that. Like I said, she can set the stage and move one component, but she can no' move me."

Still, Bernadette wasn't entirely convinced. "What I felt, what I'm feeling for you now, is it real or magic?"

Keltan looked up at one of the cameras, reminding Bernadette that they weren't completely alone. Then he cleared his throat. "What do you feel?"

"I don't really know. I . . . well, I think about you all the time."

"Is it because of the war and the fact that you're in the middle of great danger?"

She shrugged. "That has something to do with it, but it's not all of it. When I think of you, I'm not thinking of the war. I'm thinking of you and me. Together."

His amber eyes darkened with desire, causing her stomach to quiver. "What else?"

Normally, Bernadette wouldn't dream of speaking so freely, but there was something about Keltan that made it easy to do. She didn't fear his reaction or being laughed at.

"I think about your lips on mine, the way your hands moved over my body. I think about the way you looked at me right before you kissed me. I think of how it felt to have you inside me, to feel you moving." She swallowed, growing bolder. "I think about the pleasure you brought me, and the way it felt to be held in your arms afterward."

"That's desire," he whispered hoarsely.

She could see the ridge of his arousal in his jeans, but she didn't mention it. Bernadette rose to her feet. "It's more than that. I can feel it. Here," she said as she put her hand to her chest over her heart. Then on her stomach. "And here."

Without another word, he closed the distance between them and pulled her into his arms as his mouth descended upon hers. The kiss was scorching, the intensity blistering.

It was so easy to fall into the pleasure again, but in the back of her mind, a little voice warned Bernadette that it wasn't safe. Somehow, she managed to pull her mouth from Keltan's.

"What of Usaeil?" she asked between breaths.

He put his forehead against hers. "Shite. I forget everything when you're near."

That made Bernadette smile. "So, I'm not the only one?"

"Nay, lass," he said as he lifted his head to look at her. "I doona know what's happening with us. I doona know if it's real or no'."

"You mean you don't know if my feelings are real or because of Usaeil's magic."

Keltan's lips flattened as he nodded.

The elation Bernadette felt diminished instantly. But she couldn't blame Keltan. Usaeil had used her in more than one way. For all she knew, the things she felt for Keltan were nothing more than a spell.

"You said that love can't be forced, right?" Bernadette asked.

He gave a single nod. "Aye. Are you saying that . . . ?"

"No," she quickly said. "I'm just making sure."

"Oh."

Was that disappointment she heard in his voice? She really hoped it was. Just as she hoped that what she felt was real. If it wasn't, she didn't think she'd be able to stand it. Not after everything Usaeil had done to her.

"When will we know?" she asked.

Keltan lifted one shoulder in a shrug. "I doona know."

She wanted to ask him about his feelings because, obviously, his were real. But she couldn't gather the courage. The fact that he was there, kissing her, said something.

"Did you come just to tell me all of this?"

He smiled at her and tucked a strand of hair behind her ear. "I needed to see you. Also, because I believed that there should be a King here guarding you. Usaeil would expect it."

"No," she said, fear and outrage making her voice louder than she intended. "It could be a trap."

"I'm sure it will be."

"Keltan, please. The Kings need you."

He grinned and kissed the tip of her nose. "Lass, if she's here, then we know where she's at."

"Ohhh," Bernadette said. "I see. But it's still dangerous. You said she already has Con."

"And she might take me to him."

"You're playing with fire," she warned.

Keltan briefly raised his brows. "We'd hoped to find Con before we went to war, but that isna going to happen. Usaeil's connection to the Others has us worried because we've seen what their magic can do to a King."

"Is it the Others? Or is it just Usaeil you'll be fighting?"

"I doona know. None of us do. We have to be prepared for anything because the Others have come at us in ways we never expected."

Bernadette ran her hands up his chest and over his shoulders. "That's because you've been the biggest, baddest force on this planet."

He laughed at that. "You have a point, but we've always known there was the potential for something else to come that could be stronger."

"I'm scared for you."

"Doona be, lass," he told her and smoothed a hand down her cheek. "We're Dragon Kings."

"You said yourself, the Others have been able to use their magic on you. All of this," she said, sweeping her arm out in front of her, "including everything Usaeil has done to everyone, might have all been a trap to get the Kings to attack."

"You might be right. We doona have a choice, however. If we want to get Con back, then we have to bring Rhi to Usaeil."

Bernadette shook her head. "I don't think that's a good idea."

"Trust me, Rhi can take care of herself. We'll be backing her. And we willna be alone."

"I know. You told me the Dark Army would be there, and it seems that the numbers are in your favor. Maybe it's because I'm new to this world, but I can't help thinking that Usaeil has something up her sleeve."

Keltan took her hand and led her to the sofa. "No doubt, she does. We can guess all day what it might be, but in the end, we just need to be prepared for as many outcomes as we can. She's powerful, I'll give her that." He stopped and sat, then he pulled Bernadette forward so that she straddled him. "But she's no match for the Kings when we fight together."

"Am I ever going to get to see you?" She quite liked being in his lap like this.

"Do you want to?"

"Very much so," she whispered while gazing into his eyes. "I want to know all of you, Keltan. The man . . . and the dragon."

His gaze intensified. "Then I'll show you."

She didn't stop him when his hand splayed upon her back, and he pushed her forward. His lips were firm and soft as they moved over hers. The moment his tongue slid into her mouth, she moaned, her body quickly heating again after their last kiss.

"I want you," she said between kisses.

Keltan stood, still holding her, and walked into her room. By the time they were on the mattress, their clothes were gone. She sighed as they moved, skin-to-skin.

Then his hands were on her body, and her mind went blank as pleasure consumed her.

CHAPTER THIRTY-FOUR

"Con?" Usaeil called. She'd been keeping a close eye on him because as much as she wanted to believe he was hers, she wasn't a fool.

He turned in the all-glass shower, water dripping down his rock-hard body. "Aye?"

"You started without me?" she asked in a teasing tone.

He shrugged and grinned playfully. "I grew tired of waiting for you."

How she loved his Scots brogue. It sent chills across her skin. He had no idea how he could make her melt with his voice alone—and she didn't intend to tell him. Ever.

"I'm sorry. I had things I had to see to." There was stuff Usaeil still needed to take care of, but she hadn't been able to stay away from Con. He was her Achilles' heel. And if any of her enemies ever found out, it would be the end of her.

Con's grin widened as he opened the door. "What are you waiting for?"

With a thought, her clothes were gone, and she stepped into the shower. The rainfall showerhead pelted her skin, but she ignored it. Her attention was on the magnificent body of the King of Dragon Kings.

She ran her hands over his sculpted chest, admiring the hard sinew. "I can't ever get enough of your body."

"Nor I yours," he murmured as his hands ran down her arms to her hips before grabbing her ass and yanking her against him.

Usaeil gasped as she felt his arousal. "You have no idea how long I've loved you."

"I'm glad you helped me see the light."

"We're not done. There's still much to do."

He ground against her. "That can wait."

How she wished it could. Every fiber of her being wanted to forget about everything else and stay right here with him. But she couldn't. Not if she wanted to win. Everything was so close. If she didn't stay on course, then it could all fall apart. And she'd suffered for too long, lied for too long, and pretended for too long to let that happen.

A frown formed between his brows. "You're leaving."

"It won't be long before you come with me."

"I'm tired of being left behind," he said and leaned back. "I'm powerful, Usaeil."

She patted his chest. "I know you are. And I want you with me. Remember when we discussed everything? You were on board with things then. I need you to trust me."

"I do, but if any of my Kings harm you, I'll never forgive myself."

Usaeil wrapped her arms around him and folded herself against his thick chest. "Knowing that you have my back makes this easier."

"You've done things on your own for too long."

"I couldn't trust anyone."

He kissed the top of her head. "You're no' alone now."

"Never again," she whispered.

Then, reluctantly, she stepped out of his arms. "Know that I want nothing more than to stay here and wash you from head to toe before taking you to bed and making love to you all night."

"Isna that my line?" he asked with a lopsided grin.

She laughed. "I'll be back as soon as I can."

"Doona keep me waiting, lass."

Usaeil rose up and gave him a quick kiss before she teleported out. When she appeared in her room at the Light Castle, she was dry and clothed as her people expected a Queen of the Light to be—in all white with accents of gold.

She was so tired of pretending to be someone she wasn't. It was time she became who she'd always known she was. It was time she let everyone else know, as well.

And it all began with Rhi.

Usaeil drew in a deep breath and walked from her chambers. At one time, Balladyn had stood at her door, waiting for orders. His loyalty had been unflinching, but his love for Rhi had made Usaeil realize where his allegiance truly lay—and it wasn't with her.

She'd seen the way Balladyn watched Rhi when the Fae wasn't looking. Balladyn wasn't just smitten. It was love. Balladyn could've had any woman he wanted, but he'd set his sights on Rhi. Unfortunately for him, Rhi had fallen head over heels for a Dragon King.

Usaeil halted her thoughts there. She didn't want to go down that road. It made her too angry.

She gazed at the empty spot at her door. Inen had once occupied that post, but she'd discovered his betrayal of her when he'd gone to Rhi. Usaeil knew they were conspiring against her, and that wasn't something she could stand by and let happen.

Though she'd wanted to take her time and make Inen suffer, she hadn't had the opportunity. Instead, she'd killed him quickly. Though she'd had him on his knees before her, he hadn't begged for his life.

In fact, there had been defiance there. If there had been any mercy within her, it'd vanished the moment he'd said that Rhi would be the end of her.

Usaeil realized then that the only one who could captain the Queen's Guard was herself. She couldn't trust anyone else to do it.

She walked down the long corridor, turning corners and travelling down several flights of stairs before she entered the great hall. The moment she appeared, the crowd of Light Fae fell silent. She expected that. It was what they always did.

What she didn't expect were the side looks, the Fae with doubt on their faces instead of the awe and fear she was used to. Something had happened here, and somehow, she hadn't known about it.

She needed to find out what it was and fast so she could put an end to it before things got out of hand. Usaeil took a deep breath and stood tall. She let the Light have their look at her because she wanted to remind them of who she was—and why they should fear her.

"I notice some of the looks I'm getting. What is the cause of this?" Usaeil demanded.

No one answered her. Not that she expected anything different.

"You," she said and pointed at the woman to her left, who looked anywhere but at Usaeil. She waited for the female to finally raise her gaze. Then she asked, "What do you know that you don't want me to find out about?"

The woman swallowed and glanced at the man beside her, but he offered no help. Finally, the woman said, "We know."

Usaeil wanted to roll her eyes. "I'm sure you know a great many things. What are you referring to now?"

"A-a-about the movies. We know you've been masquerading as an American actress."

So. Someone had been among the Light telling her secrets. And she could imagine just who it was—the Reapers. They were too afraid of her, which was made obvious by their actions. She would have to do something about them soon. They were next on the list, and when she got to them, she planned to show them something they'd never seen before.

Usaeil slowly let her gaze move among the Fae. She dared any of them to say something more. When they didn't, she shrugged. "So what? I got bored."

The gasp that went through the hall made her grin.

"You're surprised by this admission?" she asked them. "Since our war with the Dark came to an end, I've had nothing to do. I can only walk these halls so many times, talking with all of you, before I want to tear my hair out. Like many of you, I went out to see this world of ours. And I found something that interested me."

"You didn't tell us," someone in the back shouted.

Usaeil raised a brow. "I don't owe any of you an explanation for anything I do. *Anything.* I'm your queen. I rule you, not the other way around. Perhaps you need to be reminded of that. Or have you all gotten so lax on this realm that you've forgotten my strength and power?"

The fear that ran through the hall pleased her greatly. That's how she wanted them.

"There have been a great many changes over the last

few years, and there are more coming. First, I am calling up the Light Army."

The Light began to talk among themselves, shock making their voices grow louder as each second passed.

"We're going to war!" she bellowed.

The quiet that followed was eerie.

"That's right," she said with a nod of her head. "We're about to be attacked. I could've stayed away and let all of you fend for yourselves, but I did what any ruler does—I returned to stand beside you."

"Who would dare attack us?" someone asked.

Usaeil kept her smile from showing. "Rhi."

The second gasp was louder than the first. It was like a shock wave moving through the castle. Several Fae could be heard saying, "No. Not Rhi."

"She won't be alone," Usaeil said over their voices. "Some Dragon Kings will be joining her."

Wide-eyed fear gripped the Fae.

This was entirely too easy. Usaeil nearly laughed at it all, but she managed to hold it together. "The Kings will be stopped."

"How?" another Fae asked.

Usaeil paused for effect, then she said, "Because, Constantine, the King of Dragon Kings, and I are together. He stands with me. Together, we will defeat Rhi and prevent the Kings from harming any of us."

Smiles of relief met her gaze. She soaked all of that in before she delivered the biggest bomb of all.

"There's one more thing all of you should know. Balladyn, our brother that we mourned so long ago and knew as one of the bravest warriors and generals the Light ever knew, isn't dead. In fact, he defected to the Dark and is now their king."

The stunned surprise had the hall so silent that you could've heard a pin drop. Usaeil inwardly smiled. She had the Light just where she wanted them. It didn't matter what anyone told them now, they wouldn't believe a word from anyone else.

"Be prepared if you see or hear that Balladyn also stands against me. He wishes to start our civil war up again, and I'm not going to let that happen. We've had years of peace, and I will ensure that continues."

"Hail Queen Usaeil!"

The chant went through the hall, becoming louder and louder until the castle rang with it. How dare the Reapers, Rhi, Balladyn, or anyone else think they could take the Light away from her? These were her people.

It didn't matter that she didn't care a fig about them. They didn't need to know that. Nor did they need to know that the plans she had would ensure that half of them died. It was time the Light were culled. It was something that had been needed for a long time.

The same with the Dark. All Fae had been left to grow weak and complacent. She was about to shake everything up.

"The battle will happen here at the castle," she told the crowd. "Those in the army need to get to their commanders and prepare. I expect the arrival of our enemies any minute."

"Where is Constantine?"

She snapped her head to the right, but she couldn't tell who had asked the question. "He'll be here soon. Don't worry about him."

"Why isn't he with the Dragon Kings now?"

Her gaze narrowed as she searched the crowd for where the voice had come from, but no matter how hard she tried, she couldn't pinpoint who had said it. She had the Light on her side, and as much as she wanted to lash out at whoever was asking the questions, she couldn't. Now.

But she would later. Once she found out who it was.

"Con has been with me. The Dragon Kings aren't thrilled with our union."

"But isn't one of them mated to a Fae?"

Usaeil fisted her hands in an effort to keep her cool. "None of that matters. We're about to fight for our lives. I advise that anyone not in the army return to their homes. The Light Castle isn't going to be a safe place."

They stood staring at her until she slapped her hands together. Then chaos broke out in the castle as everyone rushed about.

Even then, she tried to see who had asked the questions earlier, but once more, she was denied.

Rordan walked through the doorway of Death's realm and sighed as his gaze moved to the tall, white tower. He wound his way through the maze of flowers. He'd only gotten a few hundred yards in when he saw Eoghan.

"How did it go?" Eoghan asked.

Rordan raised his brow for a moment. "As bad as we all thought it would."

"So, Usaeil showed up just as Erith said she would." Eoghan blew out a breath and shook his head.

"It's worse than that. She got the Light to think that Rhi and the Dragon Kings are coming to attack her. Usaeil also told the Light that she and Con are together and that he is going to protect them."

"Fek," Eoghan said and ran a hand through his hair. "Let's get to Death and tell her. No doubt she'll want to try and find Con again."

"I wish she'd let us join in the battle."

"We'll be there. Mark my words."

Rordan cocked his head to the side. "Aye, but will we be fighting?"

Eoghan lifted one shoulder in a shrug. "I doubt it. For whatever reason, Death is holding back."

"I sure wish we knew why, but I trust her enough to know that she has a good reason."

They turned together and made their way to the tower.

CHAPTER THIRTY-FIVE

Keltan could lay in bed with Bernadette for the rest of his days and be utterly content. He ran his fingers down her back as she snuggled against him, and he stared at the ceiling.

"Our time is up, isn't it?" she asked sleepily.

In fact, he should get ready. He expected Usaeil soon. "Aye."

Bernadette sighed loudly. "When will we get our time?"

"As soon as this is over."

They were both silent then, neither of them saying that there might be another outcome.

"You might not believe me, but what I felt when we made love didn't feel fake. It felt very, very real," she said.

He squeezed her tightly against him. "Aye, lass, it did."

"You don't believe me, do you?"

"I do," he insisted. "I just know how magic works."

She sighed and sat up to look at him. "When Usaeil dies, will her magic continue?"

He shook his head. "Nay."

"Good. Then you'll see that when she's gone, I'll still feel this strongly about you."

"I believe you," he said and pulled her back down to his chest.

"Remember when we were in the library, and you said it was Fate that I was supposed to be there?"

"Aye," he murmured and closed his eyes, thinking back to that day. It felt like months or even years had passed, but it was only a few days ago.

She caressed her hand over his chest. "I thought you were insane for saying that, but now, I can see it. All of this was supposed to happen. Just as I'm supposed to be right here in your arms tonight."

"I quite like you here."

"Good, because I don't want to be anywhere else."

He wished he could have another five minutes of just holding her, but Keltan knew he couldn't. He reluctantly shifted, and she sat up with him.

"You really think she'll come?" Bernadette asked.

Keltan shrugged as he climbed out of bed. He picked up the hand towel that he'd used to wipe his seed from her stomach. After what Usaeil had done to Claire and V, Keltan didn't want to find himself or Bernadette in that same predicament.

"I think there's a verra good chance she will," he said and tossed the towel into the dirty clothes hamper. "But there's also a chance that she willna."

Bernadette licked her lips. "I know it would help you if she does come, but I hope she doesn't."

"I know, lass," he said and bent to give her a soft kiss. "I'll be here to protect you, and doona forget, the house is warded. As are you."

"So, she can't hurt me?" Bernadette smiled. "That makes me feel a whole lot better."

Keltan, as well. After seeing her so ill, he didn't want to ever witness anything like that again. It had been one of the most terrifying things he'd ever been a part of.

"How long do you think this war will last?"

He reached for his clothes as she drew her legs up to her chest and wrapped her arms around them. "It could be over in a matter of hours. Or, it could be like the Fae Wars that went on for decades."

Bernadette's eyes widened. "Decades?"

Keltan finished dressing. "I doona think that will happen. Usaeil seems to have a plan, and I think she'll want to get to that sooner rather than later. Besides, a prolonged war means there will be more time for others to stand against her."

Bernadette shot him a forced smile. "It doesn't matter how long this takes, I'll be here waiting for you."

Just as Keltan was about to reply, Ryder's voice screamed his name in his mind. Keltan jerked his gaze to the doorway and then looked back at Bernadette. He had to get out—and quickly.

"Bernadette!"

The sound of Usaeil's voice was like nails on a chalkboard. Keltan winked at Bernadette before he gave her a nod. She flashed him a pointed look, reminding him that he was supposed to be outside.

Keltan shrugged. Things had changed, and he was rolling with the punches.

"I'm here," Bernadette answered and scrambled from the bed.

As soon as her feet hit the floor, Keltan used his magic to dress her. She stumbled when she found clothes on her body, then she smiled.

He loved that grin. He loved the way her eyes sparkled and crinkled at the corners. He especially loved the way the expression lit up her entire face as if she wanted the whole world to know that she was happy.

Keltan stayed in the bedroom and listened, waiting for an opportunity to strike.

She wasn't prepared for this. Though Bernadette had to admit that it didn't matter how many times she faced Usaeil now, she would never be ready.

Bernadette rushed from her room to find the queen walking around the kitchen, looking in Bernadette's cabinets. That seemed so . . . odd. "Can I help you find something?"

Usaeil spun around, her smile not quite reaching her eyes. "You changed up a few things."

"I did." Bernadette wasn't sure why that mattered, but more importantly, why had Usaeil been looking in her cabinets?

"Why?"

Bernadette blinked at the question. "Why what?"

"Why did you change things?"

"Because I wanted to," Bernadette said, suddenly wary.

Usaeil walked past her while nodding and headed straight for the desk. She touched the keyboard of the laptop to wake it and display the blank page she'd opened to write the article. "I see you've still not written anything."

"I will."

"How about you stop lying to me?" Usaeil said as she slowly turned her head to Bernadette.

Bernadette snorted and crossed her arms over her chest. "How about you stop lying to *me*?"

"About?" Usaeil prompted.

"The Dragon Kings."

At that, the queen smiled once more. Except, this time,

it was one of immense pleasure, as if Bernadette had walked right into a trap without even realizing it.

"Oh, the Kings are so predictable," Usaeil said more to herself than to Bernadette. "I wondered when you would tell me that you knew who they were."

Bernadette, for her part, decided to remain silent. Fear snaked down her spine when Usaeil smiled, and it took everything within her not to look toward her room for a glimpse of Keltan.

Usaeil tsked as she shook her head. "For so many eons, the Kings thought they could protect themselves from you mortals with a spell. And to my shock, it worked. Then, thanks to Ulrik, all that changed. One by one, the Kings found their mates. Don't you think it's curious that they're only just now doing it?"

Bernadette shrugged, preferring to remain silent.

"I do," Usaeil said. "Because it wouldn't have mattered if there were a spell or not. If one of their mates walked up, they would've felt it. It's a wonder that none of them have stopped to consider why all of this is happening now."

"Did you have something to do with it?" Bernadette finally asked.

Usaeil busted out laughing before putting her hand on her chest. "Me? Oh, you give me too much credit. I didn't have any part in it. Maybe no one did." Usaeil shrugged. "What I do know is that all those millennia when the Kings were unmated, they had no enemies. Then the first of them found their mate and look at all that has happened. Enemy after enemy after enemy. And now, the Kings have more than just themselves to worry about. They have their mates. It's why I chose you."

Bernadette's knees barely held her up. She had to grab

hold of the back of a dining chair just to remain standing. "What?"

"I'm not saying you're a mate," Usaeil hastened to add. "But I knew that since you're fairly attractive and have a vulnerability that draws men in, you were the perfect candidate. Even if it was just a quick affair, I knew you'd catch someone's eye. Imagine my surprise when it was Keltan."

Bernadette's stomach plummeted to her feet. "What?"

Usaeil rolled her eyes. "Did you really think I'd have you give a lecture and not be there watching? Of course, I saw it all. I witnessed the lecture, as well as Keltan coming up to you at dinner. Why do you think I said just the right things to get you to go to Dreagan?"

"You used me from the very beginning."

"Yep," the queen stated matter-of-factly.

Bernadette blew out a puff of air. "You have some nerve disrupting my life as you have."

"Oh, please. Don't play the hurt party with me. I know you've enjoyed the benefits of having a King pay attention to you. Trust me. I know all about it."

"What happens now?"

Usaeil walked to Bernadette and stopped before her. "You can tell Keltan that if he and the other Kings don't stand down, you'll die."

It was on the tip of Bernadette's tongue to tell the queen that she couldn't harm her, but she kept that part to herself. Instead, she made sure to show just enough fear that it was believable.

"Keltan will have a difficult time convincing the others, but I think he'll manage."

"You're awfully confident of his feelings toward me," Bernadette said.

Usaeil lifted a shoulder in a shrug. "Call it a hunch. I think he'll do whatever it takes."

"The others won't."

"I think they will," Usaeil said with a wink.

Bernadette shook her head, amazed at just how off her rocker the queen was. "You can't do anything to the other mates. They're at Dreagan."

"So they are," was all Usaeil said.

That worried Bernadette, but before she could ask for clarification, Usaeil was gone.

Bernadette turned to her room in the next instant, only to see Keltan walking toward her. "You heard all of that?"

"Every word." Keltan looked at one of the cameras. "As did Ryder. Even now, those who stayed behind at Dreagan are taking action. You doona need to worry. There is nothing that Usaeil can do to hurt you."

Bernadette smiled so he would know that she wasn't scared. "I remember. I wanted to throw it in her face, but I figured it'd be better if I didn't."

"Thank you for that. If we can get ahead of her on this, then we can stop everything."

"You don't need to stay here now. Go. Help your brothers," she urged.

His amber eyes softened as he pulled her to his chest. "I'm no' going anywhere."

"You're needed. Besides, Usaeil is finished with me."

"No' by her words, she isna."

"Yes, but I'm warded. The house is spelled. I'll be fine. I'd rather you go do what you need to do to win this war."

Keltan smoothed her hair back from her face. She briefly closed her eyes, enjoying his touch. "Ryder will be watching. If anything happens—"

"It won't," she insisted.

"If it does," he said sternly, "someone will be here to help you."

Bernadette realized that he didn't say *he'd* be there, but he couldn't teleport the way Eilish and Ulrik could. Still, it was enough that she wouldn't be alone. Ryder was watching. Maybe one day she'd get to meet him since he was seeing her private life.

"Go," she repeated. "I'll be here waiting."

He stared into her eyes for a long moment, then he lowered his lips and kissed her. It started slow but quickly became passionate.

She was breathless when he finally pulled back.

"I'll return as soon as I can," Keltan promised.

She didn't move as she watched him walk out the door and saw it close behind him.

CHAPTER THIRTY-SIX

"I'm not going to wait much longer."

Keltan walked into the cavern to hear Rhi's statement. He didn't slow until he reached Ulrik's side.

"What are you doing here?" he asked.

Keltan shrugged. "Waiting to fight alongside my brothers."

"I thought you were watching over Bernadette," V said.

Keltan turned his head to V. "I thought Ryder would've told you all by now."

"I was sorting through some things," Ryder said as he walked into the cavern. Everyone turned to look at him. He didn't say more until he reached the others. "Usaeil paid Bernadette a visit."

Ulrik's gaze snapped to Keltan. "And?"

Keltan shared a look with Ryder. "Usaeil said that if we doona stand down, she'll kill Bernadette."

"And you're here?" V asked with a worried frown.

It was Ulrik who answered. "We did ward both Bernadette and her home. If she stays there, Usaeil can no' touch her."

"Which is what Bernadette said," Keltan stated to the group. "Bernadette told me to come, and I'm only here because I know she's no' only protected, but Ryder and Kinsey are watching her."

Ryder raised a brow, his lips flattening. "Usaeil knew about the cameras. She blew one out. She seems to know everything that's going on at Bernadette's."

"That's no' a good sign," Rhys murmured.

Rhi rolled her eyes. "Who cares what Usaeil knows. She can't harm Bernadette anymore, and that was the main goal of us spelling the mortal and her home."

Ulrik slowly nodded before his gaze caught Keltan's. "What else happened?"

"She told Bernadette to make sure that I convinced all of you to stand down. Usaeil seemed confident that I'd do whatever Bernadette wanted, including convincing all of you no' to attack."

"Bernadette did say that we wouldna," Ryder added.

Keltan glanced at Ryder. "Aye. And when it sounded as if Usaeil was threatening the other mates, Bernadette reminded her that they were at Dreagan. Usaeil didna seemed fazed by that."

The cavern was silent as everyone took in the news. Finally, Kellan said, "Usaeil chose her words carefully. She suspects Bernadette is Keltan's mate, and we'll do anything to ensure our mates live."

"What of those who have already done the ceremony?" Rhi asked. "Usaeil knows those women are safe."

Keltan frowned at Rhi's words as he thought about the confidence that Usaeil had displayed while speaking to Bernadette. "Are they?"

"What do you mean?" Ryder asked.

Keltan looked around at the many mated Kings. "All of you believe that because you've gone through the mating ceremony that your women can no' be harmed. What if we're wrong?"

Guy crossed his arms over his chest. "Usaeil can no' get onto Dreagan. Con made sure of that."

"But she has Con," Rhi pointed out.

Ulrik shrugged one shoulder. "He wasna the only one. Even if Con reversed his magic, Usaeil still couldna get in."

Keltan ran a hand down his face. "There was something in Usaeil's voice. She didna seem at all worried about getting to the mates."

"Or perhaps it was just one mate she wanted to get to," Rhys said.

Every eye in the cavern turned to Keltan. He shifted his feet uneasily. "Bernadette isna my mate."

"Are you sure?" Ulrik asked skeptically.

Rhi snorted loudly and shot him a disbelieving look. "You sure do deny it often for someone who can't get to her quick enough."

Keltan sliced his hand through the air. "There's a verra good chance that Usaeil brought on the passion between Bernadette and me."

"You're such an idiot," Rhys said and looked away, shaking his head.

Keltan took offense and glared at Rhys. "What the hell is that supposed to mean?"

"Well, hot stuff," Rhi said, "it means that Usaeil could make Bernadette feel something for you, but she couldn't do the same with you. The conclusion is that if you feel strongly for Bernadette, then it's the real thing."

Keltan opened his mouth to deny it, but the words wouldn't come. Shite. Did that mean . . . ?

"Now he gets it," Rhys replied sarcastically.

Ryder caught Keltan's gaze. "Doona worry about Bernadette. Kinsey and I are watching her."

"He's right," Ulrik said. "Between the protection spells and wards, as well as the cameras watching Bernadette's every move, she's safe."

Keltan licked his lips and nodded. He'd deal with his feelings once the war was finished. At least, he hoped he could. Now that he'd seen the truth, he couldn't help but think of only that.

There had been women throughout the centuries who'd caught his eye, but none had captured his mind or his body quite like Bernadette did. He'd believed that he couldn't stop thinking about her because of the danger she was in, but now, he wasn't so sure.

He didn't want a mate. There had been a time before the war with the humans that he'd looked forward to finding his mate and having a family, but once the dragons were gone, he'd put it out of his mind.

Even when his brethren began falling in love, and he attended one mating ceremony after another, he'd never wanted to find love. If he could go back and change things, he . . .

Bloody hell, he couldn't even think the words. Keltan ran a hand through his hair and realized that Ulrik had been speaking. He forced his mind to stop thinking of Bernadette and focus on what was going on.

"—be alert. We know that Usaeil has already threatened V and Claire's unborn bairn. The queen has also made it clear that Bernadette and the mates are in danger. Those remaining at Dreagan need to be wary of anything and everything."

Warrick said, "We should shut down the distillery tours for a few days."

"I'll make sure it's done," Ryder added.

Ulrik nodded. "Dreagan is protected. The manor even more so. Eilish, Shara, Esther, Denae, and any mate who has training in either magic or battle will be on guard with the Kings remaining behind."

"Usaeil might not be able to get in, but what of the Others?" Keltan asked.

V mumbled something angrily, a muscle twitching in his jaw.

No one replied to his question. Keltan wasn't surprised. Every one of them believed that Dreagan couldn't be harmed, but the simple fact was that they knew next to nothing about the Others. What little they did know, didn't amount to much.

"I wish I had an answer," Ulrik said. "The fact is, none of us do. We know Usaeil is a part of the Others. We also know that she's killing Druids to help bolster her magic. Whether or no' she's found new Druids to help with the Others, I doona know. We need to be prepared for anything, but our main target right now is Usaeil. We take her out, we'll have made a big impact with the Others."

Rhi briefly met Keltan's gaze before looking around the cavern. "Usaeil will say a lot of things to make you think your mate is in danger. It's a lie. Everything she says is a lie."

"We know what to do," Rhys told her.

Her silver eyes swung to the King of Yellows. "Look, sweet cheeks, I know that you think you do, but Usaeil has been lying to all of us for centuries. We don't know what she's capable of."

"We do know she has several enemies," Ulrik added.

Rhi grinned at him. "That she does. Now, are we done talking? I'd like to get this show on the road."

"It is that time," Guy said.

Ulrik nodded and handed his silver cuff to V. "It's time you went to Balladyn and let him know the plan."

He turned his head to Keltan. "I'll give you the option of staying here or coming to Ireland."

"I'm going to Ireland," Keltan stated. He wanted a piece of Usaeil, and he was going to get it if it was the last thing he did.

"So be it." Ulrik looked around the cavern. "I doona know what awaits us when we get to the Light Castle. There's a chance Con will be there. Doona be surprised if he fights with Usaeil because we need to be prepared for everything."

No one mentioned that Con might also attack them. It was something they all understood, but none of them wanted to speak about.

Ulrik looked at Rhi. "Ready?"

"I've been ready for this," she declared, lifting her chin.

Ulrik, Keltan, Rhys, Sebastian, and Guy all touched Rhi. The six of them would make an appearance first while Shara and Eilish teleported the other Kings a short distance away. Usaeil knew the Kings were coming in force, but they wanted it to appear as if it were just the five of them delivering Rhi to the queen.

Keltan found himself looking into Rhi's silver eyes. A moment later, the cavern was replaced by green fields and a bright blue sky.

Keltan, Guy, and Rhys stood behind Sebastian and Ulrik, who each had a hand on one of Rhi's arms to make it look as if they were holding her. Within seconds of their arrival, the Light Army surrounded them.

The circle of Light Fae in their golden armor wasn't what kept the Kings from shifting. They had expected such a show from the army. It wouldn't be long now before Usaeil showed herself.

"You've come to deliver the traitor?" a female asked as she stepped forward.

Ulrik eyed her. "And you are?"

She removed her gold helmet with its large white feather. "I'm Sersa, Captain of the Queen's Guard."

Rhi snorted loudly and jerked her head to get the hair out of her face. "Is this Usaeil's way of telling me that Inen is dead?"

"You should know," Sersa answered. "You killed him."

Rhi gaped at her. "I didn't touch him. He was my friend. He was the one who warned me about Usaeil."

"She warned us that you would say such lies. It's sad, really. I looked up to you for years. Now, look at you," Sersa said as she shot Rhi a withering look.

"Do you want her or not?" Sebastian asked Sersa.

Sersa smiled. "Oh, we want her. Queen Usaeil has a special execution planned for her."

"We want to see Usaeil," Ulrik demanded.

Sersa shook her head. "She's otherwise engaged."

"Then we'll take back our prisoner," Sebastian announced.

"You won't be going anywhere," Sersa replied.

Keltan didn't take his eyes from the Fae staring at him even when he heard the note of amusement in Ulrik's voice when he said, "You think to stop us?"

"Yes."

That straightforward answer told them what each King had been dreading—Con was there and working with Usaeil.

Sebastian pulled Rhi behind him as Ulrik took a step toward Sersa. "We had an arrangement with Usaeil. We bring Rhi, and she doesna kill the bairn inside of Claire."

"I know of no such deal," Sersa stated.

Rhi threw back her head and laughed at Ulrik and

Sebastian. "You stupid fools. I told you Usaeil couldn't be trusted. She used magic to create V's child, and then she used all of you to bring me to her because she wasn't queen enough to find me herself."

Keltan knew that Rhi was putting on an act, making sure to toss in the facts as she did so, but they didn't have the desired effect, at least according to the Faes' faces he was looking at. It was as if, somehow, Usaeil had gotten the loyalty of her people back.

"Fuck," Keltan whispered.

Rhys raised a brow, silently questioning him.

Keltan made sure his voice was low enough so that only the Kings and Rhi could hear him when he said, "Usaeil has somehow gotten the Light back on her side. They willna believe anything we tell them."

Sebastian and Ulrik exchanged a look. Then Bast released his hold on Rhi. The Light Fae smiled as she held out her hand, and her Fae blade appeared.

"It's time you and I danced," she told Sersa right before she attacked.

CHAPTER THIRTY-SEVEN

"Is it how you imagined?" Cael asked from beside Erith.

She looked on from the top of a tower at the Light Castle to the battle below. It had taken Rhi all of two swings with her sword to cut down the new Captain of the Queen's Guard. By the time the Fae hit the ground, the Kings had shifted into their true forms.

"No," Death finally replied.

Cael took her hand in his and squeezed it. "Are you sure we shouldn't join in?"

Anger churned within her. "I should've forced Rhi to go after Usaeil before now."

"You told Rhi she needed to do it, but you couldn't make her. Mainly because you knew she couldn't do it alone. She needed help."

"Usaeil has Con." Erith swung her gaze to the Fae she'd loved from afar for thousands of years. She still couldn't believe that Cael was finally hers. The silver color of his eyes was gone, replaced by a dark purple after consuming some of her magic. Cael didn't like to admit it, but he was just as strong as she was now. Erith swallowed. "Usaeil never should've been allowed to do that."

"Con is your friend. I don't like that we couldn't locate him. Are you sure you don't want us to join the battle?"

Erith shook her head as she looked back at the skirmish. "No. I want to, but—"

"But what?" Cael urged. "The Reapers are Fae."

She sighed and faced him. "There's a reason I never allowed the Reapers to get involved with things on either the Fae Realm or this one. We're set apart, love."

"Maybe we shouldn't be. Not this time. It's not just Usaeil. She's killing Druids to take their magic."

"You say that as if I'm not aware."

Cael lowered his head to give her a soft kiss. "You're Death. I know you're aware, and I also think sending Rordan into the Light Castle to make the other Fae hesitant to believe Usaeil was smart. However, I don't think it's enough. All you have to do is look at the Fae below to see that they'll do anything for their queen."

"Against five Kings and Rhi, maybe," Erith said. "When Balladyn and his army arrive, along with the other Dragon Kings, things might be different."

"Might. Do you know what will happen if Usaeil wins?"

Erith nodded her head. "I will claim her soul."

"And both the Light and Dark will be left without leaders, Rhi will be dead, and who knows what will happen to the Dragon Kings."

Erith looked at the battle once more. Rhi and the five Kings finished taking out the last of the Light who surrounded them. That had just been a small skirmish. The real battle had yet to begin.

"Fintan spoke to me earlier."

Erith briefly closed her eyes. "He's already told me he wants to fight alongside Balladyn."

"All the Reapers want to stand against Usaeil."

"It may come to that. I fear we will be needed later in another battle. For now," she told him, "we watch."

Balladyn stood on the top of the wide stairs of the Dark Palace and looked at his army standing below him, their weapons in hand, waiting.

"I've not been your king long," he told them. "Previous kings ruled with fear and treachery. But we're more than that. To the Light, we're less than. Just because we embraced the darkness within us."

The Dark nodded, smiling at his words.

"I was once a general in the Light Army. I fought many of you in the Fae Wars as well as our civil war. But all that changed when Usaeil—my queen—betrayed me. She left me on the field of battle for Taraeth to kill. Instead, he brought me here, and I became a Dark."

The shock on some of their faces was what Balladyn had expected. But he didn't stop.

"Usaeil isn't a Light," he stated loudly. "She has killed her own family to become queen. She has killed her own children to make sure no one can rise up against her. She has betrayed and deceived many. What none of you know is that she set about those events because she wants none other than Constantine."

Just the mention of the King of Dragon Kings was enough to strike fear and unease in the Dark. He saw it on their faces as some even took a step back.

Balladyn smiled, getting ready to spill it all. "Usaeil is planning to ensure that the Kings marry Light Fae and produce children. Then they will wipe us out. Usaeil has used some powerful magic to kidnap Con and keep him with her. The Dragon Kings, as well as Rhi, have risen up against her. And we will be joining them."

There was a moment of silence before someone asked, "You want us to fight alongside the Dragon Kings?"

"The enemy of my enemy is my friend," Balladyn stated. "At least, today. Usaeil needs to be stopped before she can destroy us. We have as much right to be alive as she does. She's tricked the Light into believing she's something she isn't."

"She deserves to die!" someone in the far back shouted.

Balladyn watched as, one by one, the Dark started nodding, each agreeing. He could force them to go to war, but he knew all too well how much better an army fought when they wanted it.

"Today, we go to war!" he shouted, lifting his arm.

As one, the Dark lifted their arms, their war cry filling the air.

The Dark were still cheering when V and Kellan walked down the steps to stand beside Balladyn. He shared a look with the Kings and noted their smiles.

V leaned over and said, "Well done."

"You're a good king," Kellan said.

Balladyn appreciated the kind words, but he was already thinking of the battle. "Is it time?"

V's ice blue eyes met his as he grinned. "Aye."

Balladyn raised his arm and waited for the army to fall into silence. "We will line up on either side of the Dragon Kings and Rhi. The only ones we're after today are the Light who stand in our way and Usaeil. Am I clear?"

A loud, boisterous "Yes!" rang out.

"Then let's go kick some Light arse," Balladyn said as he teleported away.

Keltan flicked his tail, flinging off the blood from decapitating a Fae. He lifted his head and let out a roar.

The grass was stained with the blood of the Fae, but the Kings hadn't come out unharmed. The Light had managed to land quite a few blows with their orbs of magic. Even now, part of Keltan's wing was healing from being burned.

It hurt like hell, but he ignored it as he concentrated on more of the Light Army popping up around them. He briefly thought about Bernadette, but he didn't let his mind linger on her. He couldn't, not if he wanted to win. There would be time enough to see her. Until then, he kept a tight rein on his thoughts.

The whole of the Light Army soon stood before them. Keltan saw faces in the window of the castle, watching. He backed up and flapped his wings, eager to take to the sky. A dark shape flew overhead, and he spotted Dmitri's white scales. Right behind him was Arian, his turquoise scales bright in the sunlight.

It was the signal that the rest of the Kings were there. Keltan inwardly grinned as he saw the Light panic. He kept waiting for Usaeil and Con to appear. Keltan knew they would, but he wasn't looking forward to it.

Rhi walked in front of the Kings to stand between them and the Light Army. "Where are you, Usaeil?" Rhi bellowed. "You wanted me here, so show yourself! Come answer for the crimes of killing your family in order to gain the throne!"

"We're here," V announced in all their minds.

The Light took several steps back as the Dark Army appeared with the King of the Dark and two Dragon Kings.

"Look." Rhi pointed to them as she spoke to the Light. "The Dark have aligned with the Kings in order to fight Usaeil! That should mean something to all of you!"

"Stop with the lies," someone shouted.

Rhi stilled, her gaze moving over the many faces staring at her. "Lies? I'm not the one lying to all of you, Usaeil is. You don't want to believe me, fine. Don't. But the truth will eventually come out. Maybe I'll be dead when it happens, but the ones who will survive will look back on this moment and realize that you had the power to stop Usaeil. Instead, you helped her."

Keltan watched as a tall Fae broke away from the line. His helm was adorned, signaling that he had an upper rank. He removed his helmet and smoothed back his long, black hair as he approached Rhi.

He halted ten paces from her, but he didn't look at her. He looked at the Dragon Kings and the Dark Army. "This is your last chance to leave. If you remain, you will be killed." His silver eyes shifted to Rhi. "You will come with me to be sentenced by Usaeil."

Rhi let out a bark of laughter. "Do I look stupid to you? I'm not going anywhere. Usaeil made a deal with the Kings that she has since gone back on. Forget what she's done to me or anyone else, let the fact that she has betrayed the Kings mean something to you."

"The King of Dragon Kings is with Usaeil," the Fae replied. "That's all we need to know."

Rhi closed the distance between them until she was standing before him. "Then, by all means, bring Constantine out if he's man enough to face his own."

"We're not going anywhere!" Balladyn shouted. "It's time Usaeil answers for the things she has done. And we're here to ensure that happens."

A muscle in the Fae's jaw jumped as he took a step back and put on his helmet. Then he turned on his heel and rejoined the army. Keltan tested his wing, noting that it was fully healed. It hadn't taken but a few minutes to plow through the small group of the Queen's Guard that had initially tried to stop them.

They must have known they would all die, but he had to give them credit, they'd fought valiantly. It was just another reason to hate Usaeil. She sent good people to their deaths simply because she wanted to keep up a ruse.

And more would die. Many, many more. But it wouldn't be the Kings. It would be Light and Dark. Unless Con decided to attack. Which might very well happen.

Keltan glanced at the castle again and then did a double-take. He spotted Con standing in a window, watching. Instead of his usual suits, Constantine now wore a form-fitting white shirt and dark pants.

"*Con's here,*" Keltan told the others. "*He's standing in the window of the castle.*"

"*Well, fuck me,*" Merrill said.

Ulrik then replied, "*We knew he'd be here. Be prepared for anything.*"

Keltan itched with the need to get the battle going again. This waiting around was too difficult. Besides, the longer he stood there, the more time he was away from Bernadette.

Several Kings flew over them and circled the castle before returning. Keltan wanted to join them, but something told him to remain right where he was.

His gaze moved to Rhi as she began walking up and down the line of Fae. Every once in a while, she'd stop and stare at someone a moment before continuing on.

"I don't want to fight any of you," she told them. "I want Usaeil. All of us here want Usaeil. You don't even have to do anything. Just go home."

No one replied or even twitched. Keltan knew Rhi was trying to save as many as she could. It was too bad none of them appeared to be listening to her.

The male Fae who had stepped forward to tell them to

leave twirled his wrist, sending his sword dancing around him. Rhi locked her gaze on him.

Tension ran through the field like lightning. Everyone was on edge, waiting for it to begin.

The male Fae let out a bellow, and the army rushed in. Keltan hesitated for just a moment. He wasn't going to enjoy the bloodbath that was coming. But they had no choice if they wanted to stop Usaeil.

Keltan drew in a deep breath and opened his mouth, releasing dragon fire, scorching thirty Fae on the spot.

CHAPTER THIRTY-EIGHT

Bernadette gave up on the book she'd been trying to read for the past few hours and tossed it onto the sofa next to her. She dropped her head back and slid her fingers through her hair as she sighed loudly.

Her mind had been working overtime thinking of the battle and Keltan's involvement. Had it already begun? Was Keltan hurt? Who all was there? Did Usaeil yet realize how many people she had angered?

Those questions and dozens more ran through her head like lightning. She'd thought to give herself a break and read, but she couldn't concentrate on the words. She didn't even bother turning on the tele.

She dropped her arms and raised her head, her gaze going to the kitchen. She'd already organized the cabinets. Maybe she should clean the floor. Or scrub the bathroom. She had to do something other than just sit there. It was the absolute worst, not having any information. Fear, worry, and doubt continually crept in.

Bernadette rose from the sofa and went into her bedroom to stand in front of her closet. She'd meant to go through her clothes and get rid of things she never wore to give herself more space for a while. She didn't have that many clothes, and she had already gone through her stuff when she moved, but the closet was tiny, and she was tired of having to cram items in.

She turned on some music then pulled everything out and put it on the bed. Then she went item by item, putting them into piles for *keeping, maybe,* and *gone*.

There were quite a few articles of clothing in the *gone* pile. Bernadette removed the hangers and folded the items before putting them into a bag to take to a resale shop. Next, she turned to the *maybe* pile. It took more time to go through this one to weed out even more items.

Bernadette was pleased with the outcome, noting that everything she'd kept was something she felt good in and loved to wear. She also decided to get rid of a couple of jackets that she'd bought thinking she'd wear but never had.

Instead of hanging up the clothes, she turned her attention to her shoes. It became painfully obvious that she needed to do some shoe shopping. She tended to buy one really nice, expensive pair that would last her several years. And it had been that much and longer since she'd gotten new shoes. With her budget, she couldn't afford to replace all of them, so she chose the pair that looked the worst and decided to start with those.

By the time she'd finished with her shoes and resorting her closet, two more hours had passed. She sat back, pleased with her work, and a little excited about the few extra pounds she'd make in selling the clothing that she didn't wear.

She gathered the two bags of discards and brought them to the front door so they'd be easy to grab on her way out. Bernadette was on her way back to the bedroom when there was a knock on her door.

Her heart missed a beat. Her head jerked to the camera, and an instant later, her mobile phone rang. She rushed to answer it.

"Hi, Bernadette," said a female voice. "This is Kinsey, Ryder's mate. Just wanted to let you know not to answer the door."

She was a little startled to hear the Scottish voice on the other end of the line. "Thank you. Who is it?"

"Kids playing a prank. They're gone. I'm sorry I didn't get to meet you when you were here. I grew up in Glasgow, too."

Bernadette smiled and sat on the sofa. "Did you? Keltan didn't tell me that."

"They forget little things sometimes," she said with a laugh. "Is it weird that I'm watching you?"

Bernadette looked at one of the cameras and nodded. "A wee bit. But I'm thankful. If not, then I would've ended up answering the door to those kids."

"True," Kinsey replied, chuckling.

"Thanks for the ring. I'm going to order some food to be delivered soon."

"No problem. And just so you know, we're all worried and trying to find things to do. Just because we're here doesn't mean we know what's going on. The guys tend to keep that kind of stuff to themselves until one of us pries it out of them."

Bernadette grinned. "If you find out anything, will you tell me?"

"Absolutely."

They disconnected. Bernadette went ahead and placed an order for food on her phone, then went back to her bedroom and turned her attention to her small chest of drawers.

Drawer by drawer, she emptied out the contents, refolded and sorted the things she kept, and made a pile of the things that were going away. She was on the third drawer when the knock sounded on her door.

Bernadette waited a moment for her mobile to ring in case it was something other than her food. When her phone remained silent, she rose and jogged to the door. She grabbed her wallet from her purse and pulled out some money before she unlocked and opened the door.

The teenager before her still had his face covered in pimples and braces on his teeth. He gave her a bright smile and called out her order.

"That's it," she said and handed him the money. "Please, keep the change."

She took her food and was turning away when he said, "Let me give you your receipt."

Bernadette reached for it. At the last second, she realized it wasn't a piece of paper but a flash of metal she saw. The blade plunged into her stomach, violently. The teenager's smile was gone, replaced by something ugly and evil as he sneered at her. She was so stunned, she couldn't move.

For just a heartbeat, she didn't feel anything. Then the pain surged through her with a ferocious intensity that made her dizzy and light-headed.

"Usaeil did warn you," the boy said before he yanked out the knife and ran away.

Bernadette couldn't believe what had just happened. She grabbed the wound with her free hand and put as much pressure on it as she could. She took a step back, but her hands began to shake, and she dropped the carton of food, spilling it on the floor.

She looked down at the blood soaking her clothes and running through her hands, and all she could think of was Keltan. This couldn't be happening. She'd been warded, her house was protected.

Against magic, not mortals.

She swallowed and tried to keep her mind focused. She needed to get to a hospital, but as she stared out her door, she knew between the pain and the rapid weakness that was overtaking her, she'd never make it to her car. She didn't even know where her mobile was to call for help. Then she remembered that those at Dreagan were watching.

Bernadette's head turned to the nearest camera. "Help," she said.

She waited for Eilish or someone to come, but minutes passed without anything happening. If she didn't do something soon, she'd pass out from blood loss.

Bernadette grabbed her keys with a shaky, blood-coated hand and stumbled out to her car. She didn't close the door behind her. Nothing in her house mattered. She'd believed that she was safe, but Usaeil had once again proven that there was nowhere Bernadette was safe from the queen's reach.

It felt good to sit down but closing the car door was another issue. Bernadette had to keep one hand on her wound to staunch the blood flow, which made things difficult. Yet, she managed to do it. And then, somehow, she pulled onto the road.

"Something is wrong!" Kinsey shouted from the computer room.

Seconds later, Ryder came rushing in. "What is it?"

"Every camera in Bernadette's house froze," she said as she kept punching away on the keyboard.

Ryder calmly moved to his station and began rapidly pressing keys. A screen of code filled the monitor in front of him. He scrolled through it until he found what he was searching for and read over it. Kinsey watched as a frown formed.

"Someone tried to hack in," he said.

Kinsey rolled her chair to him and looked to where he was pointing. "You've got to be kidding. Why would anyone do that? It makes no sense that some random person would go after Bernadette."

"They're no'," Ryder said as he met her gaze. "We should've seen this coming."

"Seen what?"

"We assumed Usaeil would go after Bernadette with magic. She let us and Bernadette know that she was aware of our plans. We backed her into a corner."

Kinsey shook her head. "I'm still not understanding."

"Did anyone go to Bernadette's while I was away?"

Kinsey shrugged, nodding. "Some kids playing around. Then Bernadette ordered food."

Ryder turned back to the screen, his fingers moving so fast that they were a blur. Kinsey was one of the best hackers among the mortals, but Ryder far surpassed her. She'd learned much from him, but there was still so much for him to teach her.

She didn't press him for answers, just watched as he worked. She noted that he was searching for the origin of the attempted hack. It didn't take him long to find that the location was in Singapore. Instead of pursuing that lead as she'd expected, he turned his attention to unfreezing the cameras.

Kinsey grabbed her mobile and called Bernadette, but it went to voicemail.

"I need to go there," he said and pushed away from the screen.

Kinsey jumped to her feet. "You need to stay here, remember? Let me go."

He hesitated, his hazel eyes filled with worry. "Kin," he began.

"I know." She walked to him and put her arms around him. "She's not answering her mobile. I need to get there quickly."

"Eilish will take you. And be careful."

She smiled up at him. "Promise."

Kinsey ran from the room to find Eilish. In seconds, the two of them stood in Bernadette's home. The first thing Kinsey noticed was the spilled food and the open door.

"There's blood," Eilish said as she walked to the door and pointed to the smears as well as the large drops on the floor.

Kinsey let her deal with that as she went to the nearest camera. She checked the wiring, but everything looked fine.

"You can stop," Eilish said from behind her. "Bernadette isn't here. The blood trail leads out of the house, and her car is gone."

Kinsey turned to Eilish. "These are Ryder's cameras. They don't freeze."

"I'm sure magic was used. That doesn't matter now," Eilish told her. "We need to find Bernadette. Fast."

The worry in Eilish's tone hit Kinsey. She glanced at the fat drops of blood and swallowed. "She's hurt. We promised no one would harm her."

"Let's get to the hospital and see if she checked in."

Kinsey didn't even have time to agree before Eilish clicked her silver finger rings together and they teleported. Whatever hope they had of finding Bernadette at a hospital was dashed quickly enough.

"I don't trust them," Eilish whispered as she eyed the staff.

Kinsey frowned at her. "No one who came in recently fits Bernadette's description."

Eilish just gave her a flat look and disappeared. Kinsey looked around to see if anyone noticed the fact that a woman had just vanished in the middle of a crowded corridor. But it just went to show how no one paid attention to things because no one said anything.

Finally, Eilish returned, looking more upset than ever. "Bernadette really isn't here. Where could she have gone?"

Kinsey's heart sank as she realized the answer. "The only place she knew she'd be safe."

"Dreagan," Eilish replied with a frown.

In the next blink, Kinsey found herself back in the computer room, but Eilish was nowhere to be seen.

"What happened?" Ryder said from behind her.

Kinsey spun around and quickly filled him in as she went to her station. Together, they began searching CCTVs for any sign of Bernadette or her vehicle.

"Usaeil planned this," Ryder said angrily. "She fully intended to hurt Bernadette."

"Kill." Kinsey glanced at him. "She said she'd kill Bernadette."

Ryder's face set in determination. "That's no' going to happen."

CHAPTER THIRTY-NINE

"How does it feel to know that you've failed?" Usaeil whispered into Xaneth's ear.

Her nephew jerked, not from her words but from the torment of his mind. While she wouldn't admit it to anyone, she had learned many things from watching the Druid, Moreann, dole out punishment to others.

Usaeil hadn't realized how little magic it took for her to trap someone in their own mind. Then it was just a push to propel them into their worst nightmare.

However, for Xaneth, Usaeil had added her own special kind of spin to it. After all, he'd dared to try and deceive her. Not to mention, he'd sided with Death and the Reapers. As if any of that could go unpunished.

She straightened, staring down at Xaneth. As fun as he was to torment, she had a battle waiting on her. One that had been in the making for far too long.

Usaeil teleported to the Light Castle and walked to stand beside Con. "I told you they would come."

"So you did," he murmured as he watched from the tower window.

Her head jerked to him. "You're sad."

"I doona want to fight my brothers."

"You won't have to," she told him, though she secretly hoped otherwise. "You just need to remind them you are the King of Kings. They will do as you say."

He nodded before inhaling deeply. "I'm no' happy standing up here watching the slaughter of your people."

"That's war."

"You doona mind that your people are dying?" he asked as he looked at her.

She stared into his black eyes in an attempt to see if he was hiding something from her. The spell she'd used when she'd kidnapped him ensured that Con was hers forever. There had been a few days when he'd fought it, but eventually, the spell became too strong for him to overcome.

"Of course, I do," she replied. "I don't like to see anyone die."

"Then we need to get down there and stop it. The other Kings have arrived. As has the Dark Army."

She rolled her eyes at the mention of the Dark. "Balladyn is here because of Rhi."

"It doesna matter who is here or why. There's no need for death."

Usaeil raised a brow. She had grilled Con relentlessly about the Reapers and Death. Usaeil hadn't been at all pleased to learn that Death had befriended Con hundreds of years ago. Usaeil had even taken his gold dragon-head cufflinks and the pocket watch and thrown them into the Atlantic Ocean so she wouldn't have to look at them again.

"You think there's a battle now," Usaeil said. "Wait until they spot me."

"You're the queen. Stop all of this, now."

"They're here *because* of me, Con."

His gaze went hard. "I know. Do your duty and stop it."

For just a moment, she'd thought he was going to say that she should've stopped it before it all began. Then she remembered that Con was hers, and she didn't have to worry about him thinking like . . . well, like he used to.

The old Con would've figured out that she'd set this all in motion. The old Constantine would've tried to stop her. But he was no longer that male. The Dragon King who stood with her now was the one she'd always known he could be, the one who would rule beside her for eternity.

"I'll stop it," she told him. "Don't come out until I tell you."

He bowed his head. "As you wish."

Usaeil rose up on her tiptoes and pressed her lips against his. Then she looked into his eyes, her heart swelling with love. "This is where we're supposed to be. You know that, right?"

"I do."

"No one will be able to hurt us once we're mated."

He frowned, his hands grabbing her arms. "You're worried about someone."

Usaeil tried to shrug away his words, but he wasn't buying it. She blew out a breath. "I was going to tell you after the battle was over anyway. The Others, who have made your life difficult? Well, I'm part of them."

"I knew that."

"Of course, you did," she said, more to herself than him. She cleared her throat. "The thing is, they want the Kings gone. Not just from this realm, but from existence. All dragons, really."

"Why?"

Usaeil shrugged and stepped away. "They gave a big long speech eons ago. I don't really remember. I joined them because I liked the idea of finding a new home."

He crossed his arms over his chest. "The Others came to this realm before your world was destroyed."

"I know. I was with them," she stated.

Con's eyes narrowed on her. "All of this is a lie, then? You want us—*me*—dead."

"No," she said hastily and rushed back to him, her hands on his chest. "I did at one time, but that changed when I got to know you. The things you did to help end our civil war as well as terminating the Fae Wars was amazing. You were . . . brilliant. I knew then that I wanted you."

"Obviously, the Others are still around."

Usaeil nodded with a long sigh. "Unfortunately. I'm a bit concerned about the head Druid, but the others I can take on easily. Especially with you by my side."

"Why do the Others hate my kind so much?"

"I don't know, and it doesn't matter. We're going to end them once and for all."

Con took a couple of steps back from her. "Usaeil, you were part of the traps set up for my brethren. And me."

"I know where the Others are. I can stop all of it. I just need to kill Moreann first."

"Moreann?" he repeated the name, a question on his lips.

Usaeil didn't want to talk about the Druids, but doing so meant that she could prolong the battle taking place outside. "She's the leader of the Druids."

"On this realm?"

"She's from another realm. She and her people were the ones who brought the mortals here."

Con's frown disappeared. Usaeil knew that face. It was the one he used when he didn't want anyone to know what he was thinking, and that simply wouldn't do.

"Tell me what you're thinking," she demanded.

"I'm thinking I want to find this Druid and have a word with her."

Usaeil chuckled as she imagined the look of surprise on Moreann's face. "That'll never happen. At least not if Moreann knows you'll be there. She's scared of you, of all dragons, I think."

"We've never ventured from the realm until the mortals arrived and the war broke out."

She walked to him and took his hands in hers. "When this thing with the Kings, Rhi, and the Dark is settled, you and I will have a word with Moreann. Sound good?"

"You can contact her easily?"

"We meet on the Fae Realm."

Con jerked back, his face contorted with shock. "There isna much left."

"Which is why it's perfect. No one thinks to look there, and no one ever goes there."

"I'm eager to . . . meet . . . her."

Usaeil bet he was. She kept her smile to herself because the one being who could make sure that the Others never bothered her again was Constantine. "You will."

"Good. Now, let's take care of the battle."

She wanted to roll her eyes, but she stopped herself at the last minute. She was trying to be the kind of queen that Con admired. He didn't like some of her tactics. It was just that she had been doing them for so long that she didn't consider other ways. He was making her do that.

He was forcing her to look at everything differently, to see if there was another way—and if it benefited her more than what she would normally do.

Even a month ago, she would've scoffed at the idea of anyone changing her. But it was different with Con. He made her want to be better. He reminded her of the Light Fae she'd once been before she realized what she could accomplish with power—before she coveted that might and decided that no one would stand in her way of achieving it.

Now that she had it, she no longer needed to think like she once had. And now that she knew she and Con would be mated, she'd discovered a peace that she hadn't realized she needed—or wanted.

With Con, she could be the Fae she was supposed to be. She would unite the Light and the Dark. With their marriage, the Kings could look to the Fae to give them the children they hadn't been able to have before.

There was just one little hiccup in gaining everything Usaeil desired—Death and the Reapers. But Usaeil wasn't worried about the so-called friendship Con had with Death. He did whatever Usaeil wanted, and she wanted Death gone. Con would do it. And once Death was killed, then the remaining Dragon Kings could take care of the other Reapers.

The Fae would no longer have to worry about someone judging them and taking their souls. The only one they would have to be concerned with is her.

"I love you," Usaeil told Con.

He grinned and ran his fingers down her cheek. "The sooner we take care of this battle, the sooner we can be alone."

Now he was talking. "Then I'd better get to it."

"Aye," he murmured in that deep, sexy voice of his.

Usaeil shivered in anticipation of some alone time. She had been so preoccupied with Xaneth, Rhi, Bernadette, and the Others that she hadn't been able to spend the time with Con that she'd wanted. But if she were to keep everything on track, she didn't have a choice.

She winked at him before teleporting to the battle. Usaeil watched from a hidden spot. She didn't like to admit that Rhi was a truly gifted warrior, but she was. And even now, the Light Fae and Balladyn were fighting side by side.

Usaeil wondered what might have happened had Balladyn told Rhi of his feelings before she'd met her Dragon King. Would Rhi have loved Balladyn in return? The two of them could've produced amazing children.

But that wasn't what happened. If it had, Usaeil wouldn't be standing where she was, wanting nothing more than to cut Rhi down where she stood. That was coming. Usaeil couldn't wait to feel the relief when Rhi was finally gone for good.

Usaeil looked up at the dragons circling over her, their fire raining down to scorch the earth and whatever else was in its way. It was no wonder Moreann and her people were terrified of the dragons, but she'd gone about things wrong. Instead of making them an enemy, she should've aligned with them just as Usaeil was doing. What Moreann had failed to do worked to Usaeil's advantage.

While Usaeil was looking forward to killing Rhi to get rid of her, Usaeil could hardly wait to see Moreann's face right before Con ended her life. It would be glorious.

Usaeil wanted to draw out the battle, but she also wanted to start her life as Con's mate. That couldn't happen until the skirmish was over, which meant she had to make a decision. She'd pictured this day for so long, yet it didn't hold the joy she'd thought it would.

That was because she had Con waiting for her. Their new life together was just out of reach. With him, she could feel whole and loved like never before. She wouldn't have to watch her back because he'd do it for her. Just as she would watch his.

For the first time in her life, she wouldn't have to be alone. That was because Con was her equal in all ways.

He'd seen it. Otherwise, they never would have become lovers. It was Rhi's interference that had ruined it. As soon as Rhi was gone, Usaeil's revenge would be complete.

She called up her sword and armor and walked from her hiding place. It took seconds for Rhi's gaze to find her.

Usaeil smiled. "Let's finish this."

CHAPTER FORTY

It was becoming harder and harder for Bernadette to see, and to make matters worse, it had begun to rain. She kept blinking, trying in vain to make her eyes focus properly.

The attention she had to pay to the road and other drivers helped to keep her from thinking about her wound and the fact that the blood continued to flow. The pain, however, was unbearable, and she'd only driven for forty minutes. How would she ever make it to Dreagan?

She wouldn't. The realization brought tears to her eyes. Bernadette sniffed and gave herself a mental shake. There wasn't time to cry.

She spotted a hospital sign, but she didn't take the turn-off. She wasn't sure who she could trust. It was better if she got to Dreagan. *If* she made it there.

"I can't think that way," she told herself.

She had to stay positive. If she allowed the weak thoughts to pervade her mind, then she was already a lost cause. She thought about Keltan and smiled as she pictured his face. That's really why she was going to Dreagan.

Bernadette pulled off the road and put the vehicle in park. But Keltan wasn't at Dreagan. He was fighting Usaeil like she'd told him to. Not that she regretted it. Sure, she wished he had been there when she got stabbed, but he needed to be with his brethren, going up against someone as evil as Usaeil.

She glanced down at her wound. Her lower body was covered in blood, which had begun to soak into her seat, as well. She leaned her head back and closed her eyes. She had been so stupid to believe that she was untouchable. Well, to be fair, she *was* when it came to Usaeil.

It had never dawned on Bernadette that the queen would use a mortal, but it should have. Usaeil had used her to get to the Kings. Why wouldn't Usaeil use that same tactic to get to her? The queen had warned her that she would die if the Kings didn't back off.

And Bernadette had sent away the one person who could've helped her. Talk about irony. She was going to die alone, sitting on the side of the road. What an idiot she was. She could've been safe at Dreagan, which was where Keltan had begged her to go.

She should've done it. She'd gained nothing new from Usaeil that'd helped the Dragon Kings. In fact, Bernadette would argue that her remaining at her house had impeded the Kings. And that's precisely what Usaeil had counted on.

Even trying to think outside the box had landed Bernadette smack-dab where Usaeil wanted her. Bernadette began to wonder if the Kings could kill the queen. Usaeil seemed to know every move Bernadette made. Or, at least, Usaeil had been prepared for different scenarios. Not that it mattered now.

Bernadette closed her eyes and let her thoughts move to something much more appealing—Keltan. She smiled as she thought about the time she'd gotten with him. A real-life dragon, but not just any dragon, a Dragon King.

And he'd wanted her. She still couldn't believe that. For a few days, she had been someone special. That had never happened before in her life.

Tears poured down her face as she realized that her time was running out. She wouldn't get to see Keltan again or know if he'd won against Usaeil. She wouldn't get to look into his amber eyes and see them crinkle with laughter or darken with desire.

She wouldn't get to feel his arms around her again or have him hold her. She wouldn't know the taste of his kiss or the way his body moved inside hers.

She wouldn't know his love.

In that moment, as darkness began to close in around her, she knew for certain that she loved him. It didn't matter what had drawn her to him to begin with. Maybe it was Usaeil. Perhaps it was Fate. But the love that filled her now had nothing to do with magic or spells. It was real.

She held on to it tightly as it became more difficult to breathe. But the harder she tried to hold on, the more it slipped from her fingers, just like her consciousness and her life.

Bernadette felt it all fade away. Her last thought was of Keltan and the fact that she'd never gotten to tell him that she loved him.

Eilish appeared on the side of the road, instantly soaked by the rain storm as her gaze landed on Bernadette's car. She rushed to the passenger side and tried to open the door, but it was locked.

She snapped her fingers, using her magic to open it. Then Eilish moved into the seat. "No," she whispered when she discovered Bernadette slumped over.

Eilish grabbed Bernadette's hand and clicked her finger rings together to take them back to Dreagan. As soon as they appeared in the bedroom, others quickly gathered up Bernadette and brought her to the bed.

"This isn't good," Kinsey said as she looked while Esther and Denae quickly went to work on staunching the blood flow.

Eilish shifted on her feet. "It'll be fine. It has to be fine."

"You think she's Keltan's mate, don't you?"

Eilish looked into Kinsey's violet eyes and nodded. "I do."

"Me, as well. If she dies—"

"She won't," Eilish said before Kinsey could finish the sentence.

Kinsey wrung her hands. "I should've known something was wrong the minute the cameras froze. None of Ryder's creations go wrong."

"This isn't your fault. This is all on Usaeil. The bitch needs to die."

"Without a doubt. Bloody hell. I wish I was on the battlefield with the others."

Eilish fisted her hands. "You and me both."

"The thing is, you can go."

"I may want that, but I won't leave. I'm not sure Usaeil won't do something stupid and send others here to attack."

Concern clouded Kinsey's face. "You mean like mortals? Just like what happened to Bernadette."

"I wouldn't put it past her."

"Shit. I need to warn Ryder."

Eilish returned her attention to the bed. She hoped to get some kind of clue from Denae's and Esther's faces as to how Bernadette was doing, but she could tell nothing from their expressions. And there was no telling how long she'd have to wait before she found anything.

If only Sophie were there. But she was dealing with Claire, who had doubled over in pain before passing out. It was no coincidence that both Claire and Bernadette had been brought down nearly simultaneously.

Eilish sincerely hoped that Bernadette made it. No mate had died on the Kings, and she didn't want this to be the first. Keltan, for all his talk of wanting to remain single, was someone who needed to find a mate the most. His belief that he was better off alone needed to be smashed.

Oddly enough, it had happened with Bernadette. The couple was so sweet together. Their love was so pure and beautiful, it was amazing to watch. The way they looked at each other, the way they both feverishly wanted to protect the other.

Everyone at Dreagan knew they were in love. Eilish suspected that Bernadette knew, as well. It was Keltan who was dragging his feet. She didn't think it was because he didn't want Bernadette, but because he feared what Usaeil might do if he *did* fall in love with the mortal.

And Keltan was right to have such a concern.

If Bernadette died, Eilish wasn't sure what would happen to Keltan. The ones who shied away from love were the ones who fell the hardest. She should know. She'd been in his shoes not that long ago with Ulrik.

The battle raged endlessly. Keltan kept thinking that Con would show himself, but so far, the King of Kings had remained absent. Keltan was sure that had to do with Usaeil. No doubt she had some grand entrance planned for Con to cause shock and awe.

Keltan was surprised at how readily the Dark fought alongside them. He'd had to stop himself several times before he killed one, but that was because the Kings had fought the Dark for so long that it was ingrained in him to do just that.

Instead, he was slaying Light Fae. It boggled Keltan's mind that they wouldn't listen to anything being told to them. Whatever Usaeil had said to them worked. They were hers to control as she wished. The sad part was that the Light were dying for her, and she couldn't care less about them.

He tipped his wing, ready to make another sweep over the battle when he spotted Usaeil. His gaze immediately went to Rhi. By her sudden change in direction, she, too, had seen Usaeil.

"*Usaeil!*" he said to the others through their link.

Everyone wanted a piece of the queen, but none more so than V. He actually started toward her, but Keltan knew that Rhi would beat him there. A part of Keltan wanted to unleash dragon fire on her, but he knew she would evade it just as she had with Cináed's when he'd attempted it a few weeks ago during an altercation with her.

Keltan landed alongside Ulrik and shifted. He didn't call for his sword, at least not yet. He didn't need it to kill the Fae. He and Ulrik swept through a band of ten Light easily enough.

Even with the mass of people, Keltan could still pick out Usaeil. Her gold armor shone brighter than any other's. She didn't wear a helmet, but she did have a sword in each hand that she used with expert precision as she cut through the Dark who managed to get to her.

Just when Keltan thought he would get to see Usaeil and Rhi go head-to-head, the queen altered course at the same time a huge group of Light surrounded Rhi.

"Fuck," Keltan said when he saw Balladyn casually walking toward Usaeil, his sword dripping blood.

Ulrik looked to where Keltan was and let out a string of curses.

Keltan glanced at the window where he'd seen Con, but there was no sign of him. He then looked at Rhi, wondering if he should help her out.

"Rhi is fine!" Ulrik shouted as they both dodged a volley of Light Fae orbs of magic.

Keltan agreed with Ulrik, and just as he was about to say something about them helping out Balladyn, Ulrik shook his head.

"Balladyn willna appreciate any help. No' after what Usaeil did to him," Ulrik explained.

Keltan ducked a blade swung at his head before he reached out his arm and twisted his hand, breaking the Light's neck. "Rhi willna like it if Balladyn kills Usaeil before she does."

"Neither will V."

Keltan searched for V, only to find his friend doing his best to get to Usaeil.

"It doesna matter who kills Usaeil, as long as the bitch dies," Ulrik said via the mental link.

Keltan knew that Ulrik had said that to everyone, but it was really for V. Keltan felt for V, he really did. Bernadette might not be carrying his child as Claire was for V, but Usaeil had nearly killed Bernadette—and that was even worse, in his book.

He wanted nothing more than to go straight for Usaeil, but Ulrik was right. It didn't matter who got to her, only that she stopped breathing and her reign ended.

The Kings listened to Ulrik, but Rhi didn't get the message. She fought off the thirty Fae meant to stop her and ran straight for Usaeil and Balladyn, who were already engaged in battle—with Balladyn getting the upper hand.

Keltan saw the moment Balladyn spotted Rhi. It was the same time Balladyn swung his sword. He pulled up, stopping the blade just shy of cutting Rhi as she reached them. But in doing so, he allowed Usaeil to move and get free.

Before anyone could guess what would happen, Usaeil had her sword at Rhi's throat. The look on the queen's face as she cut her eyes to Balladyn told anyone watching that this was exactly what she'd wanted.

Then, the entire battle came to a standstill with a new arrival—Con. He walked over the dead and through the Fae to get to the Dragon Kings. He locked gazes with Ulrik for a moment, but Con didn't head their way.

"Did he speak to you?" Keltan asked.

Ulrik shook his head, a deep frown in place. "Nor would he answer me."

"Perfect timing, my love," Usaeil said as Con reached her.

Keltan winced when he saw Rhi's eyes widen in shock.

"Fuck me," Ulrik muttered.

CHAPTER FORTY-ONE

Just a few seconds earlier, the air had been filled with the sounds of battle. Now, you could have heard a pin drop. Keltan looked around at the other Kings to gauge their reactions.

They had expected something like this, so they hid their surprise well. Still, no matter what they had anticipated, to see Con choose Usaeil over them was . . . shocking.

And not at all something Keltan could comprehend.

"What did she do to him?" he whispered.

Ulrik lifted one shoulder in a shrug. "I didna think her magic strong enough. I guess I was wrong."

"This can no' be happening."

"Unfortunately, it is."

Keltan met Ulrik's gold gaze. "I'll no' stand with Usaeil. If I have to, I'll challenge Con myself."

"Every one of us will," Ulrik replied.

What irritated Keltan the most were the smiles the Light wore as they looked at Con as if he were their savior. The Dark simply stood, waiting for Balladyn to tell them what to do.

"What fools all of you are," Usaeil said to everyone.

"You dare come to my home and attack me and my people? Who do you think you are?"

"Those wanting revenge," V replied succinctly.

Usaeil didn't hide her smile as she swung her silver eyes to him. "I thought you'd be happy, though I did warn you what would happen if any Kings attacked me." Usaeil's gaze then slid to Keltan. "I also gave another such warning."

Keltan's heart missed a beat.

"Doona listen to her," Ulrik warned him.

Keltan knew that, but he couldn't help it. Without hesitation, he opened the mental link. *"Ryder? How is Bernadette?"*

When there wasn't an immediate reply, fear took hold of Keltan so strongly that his knees threatened to buckle. Nothing could be wrong with Bernadette. She was safe. They'd made sure of that. Usaeil couldn't touch her.

"Keltan, I'm sorry," Ryder finally answered. *"Bernadette was stabbed by a human. We have her at Dreagan, and we're doing everything we can."*

Usaeil started laughing. That's when Keltan knew that he'd let his distress show on his face. He took a step toward the queen, but Ulrik quickly moved in front of him, putting a hand on Keltan's chest.

"No' yet," Ulrik whispered tightly.

"Bernadette is hurt."

"I know. Ryder just told me. She's no' the only one."

Keltan frowned and looked at Ulrik. "Claire?"

"Aye."

Usaeil then said, "There will be more. None of you has any right to be here, attacking us. If you doubt me, look to your King."

Con had yet to say a word. Rhi's fury could've scorched Con where he stood, but he wouldn't look in her direction. Instead, he stared at Balladyn.

"Let Rhi go," Balladyn ordered Usaeil.

The queen raised a black brow as she turned her head to him "Why would I do that? She attacked my home, intending to kill me."

"Because you banished her simply because she quit her duties as Captain of the Queen's Guard."

"You don't really believe I'm that petty, do you?" Usaeil asked Balladyn sweetly.

Keltan shook his head. "Do none of the Light see Usaeil for who she really is?"

"No," Ulrik said sadly.

"They can no' be that blind."

But they were. Or at least they wanted so badly to believe their queen that they disregarded everything else. All they heard was hearsay. None of them had brought hard facts to the Light. If he were in the Lights' shoes, he wouldn't believe anyone either.

The standoff between Usaeil and Balladyn grew as the two glared at each other. Keltan looked around, waiting for the right moment to strike. He wanted the battle finished so he could get to Bernadette in case . . . He didn't even want to finish the thought.

Keltan saw red well up on Rhi's throat as Usaeil pushed the tip of the blade into her skin. The blood trailed down Rhi's throat and into her shirt. Rhi stood still as stone, her eyes locked on Usaeil before she kicked out her foot and connected with Usaeil's stomach.

The queen staggered backwards several steps before she gained her footing. Rhi ignored everyone who said her name as she advanced on the queen.

"You aren't fit to rule," Rhi told her. "I know none of the Light will believe me when I tell them that you created the Trackers who killed your family so you could take over. They won't believe me when I tell them that you murdered every child you conceived. They won't believe me when I tell them that you affiliated yourself with a group of Druids and Dark Fae to bring down the Dragon Kings. They won't believe me when I tell them that you killed Inen, or that you asked Taraeth to kill Balladyn— only the previous king turned him Dark instead. They won't believe that you went back to Taraeth recently and asked him to kill me. They won't believe me when I tell them that you used a spell to make sure V's mate conceived a child only for you to threaten that bairn's life, as well as Claire's, just because V stood against you."

Keltan smiled when he saw that the Light were beginning to frown as Rhi listed off some of Usaeil's crimes.

"They won't believe me when I tell them that you've been killing Druids and taking their magic to add to your own," Rhi continued. "And they won't believe me when I tell them that you're using glamour to hide the fact you're really Dark."

The last bit was the one that got the Lights' attention and made the Dark glance at each other in confusion.

Usaeil issued a dismissive wave of her hand. "All you have are words. There is no proof."

"It's a long list of crimes against you. I don't care if any of the Fae believe me or not. We both know the truth. And soon, so will everyone else," Rhi said and raised her sword. "I'm tired of talking. Shall we get on with things?"

Usaeil grinned. "Let's."

Everyone on the field watched as Rhi and the queen collided, their swords clanging in the silence. Keltan knew that Rhi was an excellent warrior, but he hadn't seen Usaeil in battle since the Fae Wars. He'd forgotten how good she was. In fact, it appeared they were equally matched.

That became apparent to everyone else, as well, including Usaeil. Her smile faltered, replaced by a determined frown. She tripped and went down on one knee, only to teleport behind Rhi at the last minute.

It was obviously a move Rhi was familiar with because she turned and raised her sword to block Usaeil's blow before the queen ever appeared.

The two continued sparring, one gaining ground, and then the other taking it back. And neither showed signs that they were tiring.

Usaeil with her white armor against Rhi dressed in all black. Every eye was trained on the duo as they waited with baited breath to see who would ultimately win the skirmish.

Then, Rhi managed to knock one of Usaeil's swords away. Two moves later, Rhi kicked Usaeil in the chest so hard that the queen landed on her back. Once more, Rhi turned, expecting Usaeil to appear behind her.

Instead, there was a quick intake of air. Except it didn't come from Rhi.

Balladyn fell to his knees, Usaeil's blade sticking out of his chest. He looked down at it, then slid his red eyes to Rhi. Usaeil yanked the weapon free of Balladyn and leaned over him to whisper something in his ear. Then she walked out from behind him and smiled.

Rhi rushed to Balladyn, catching him before he fell. Keltan and Ulrik quickly went to Balladyn's side, as well. Ulrik was slower, his gaze on Con, condemning him for not doing something. When Keltan reached Rhi and Balladyn, he could see that the Dark's wound was fatal.

"Con," Rhi called. She looked at him, beseeching him with her silver eyes. "Please."

Con hesitated but a moment before he started forward, but Usaeil moved to block him. "Where are you going?" she demanded angrily, her eyes flashing red.

"To help," Con replied.

"I don't want you helping him."

Con gave a snort. "I doona care what you want."

Keltan couldn't believe what he was seeing, but he wanted more of it.

"Did you honestly think I was yours?" Con asked her, his eyes cutting her where she stood. "Did you really think your magic could control me? That I actually *loved* you?"

Her outrage caused her face to mottle red as she bit out, "You are mine."

"That's the sad part. If you had paid more attention, you would've noticed I never told you that I loved you. I was never yours, Usaeil, and I never will be. It was all a lie so I could see what you were up to. And in case it isna clear, I willna be stopping my brethren from tearing you apart. In fact, I'll be joining them."

"You're making a big mistake," Usaeil called after Con.

Keltan wanted to send up a cheer. He smiled and found his gaze lowering to Balladyn to see the Fae gazing up at Rhi as she watched Con and Usaeil. There was such love in Balladyn's eyes that Keltan felt like an intruder watching something that shouldn't be shared with anyone.

"I love you," Balladyn said.

Rhi looked down at him. "I love you, too."

Balladyn smiled sadly. "Like a brother."

"I may not be in love with you, but I do love you," Rhi whispered. "If you don't believe anything else, believe that."

Balladyn took her hand as he coughed. "Kick her arse, Rhi."

"I'll make sure she pays for what she's done to you."

Balladyn coughed again, blood trickling from the

corner of his mouth as Con reached him. "Do it for everyone she's wronged, not just me. Do it for yourself. Do it for the love that was taken from you. Go now. I don't want you to see me die."

"But—" she started to argue.

Keltan understood what Balladyn needed. He touched Rhi's shoulder and urged her to her feet. "Con's here," Keltan told her. "Let Balladyn see you finish with Usaeil."

There were tears in Rhi's eyes as she looked from Keltan back to Balladyn. She nodded to the King of the Dark and gave him a soft kiss on the lips. "You will be avenged," she vowed.

Rhi softly lowered Balladyn to the ground and got to her feet without looking at Con. With her sword in hand, she turned to the queen. "You're going to pay for that."

"Pay for killing a Dark?" Usaeil asked with a laugh. "It's what the Light have done for generations. You, yourself, have killed plenty. What's one more?"

"That wasn't just any Dark. That was Balladyn. The most famous general of your army, the one who was the most loyal to you, the one who was my friend!" Rhi bellowed, her anger growing with every word. "And you didn't even give him the courtesy of an actual battle. You stabbed him in the back. Like a coward."

Usaeil laughed, but it was drowned out by chanting from the Dark, calling for her death. Keltan exchanged a look with Ulrik at the sound. It wasn't long before some of the Light joined in.

Keltan looked at Con, who was staring at the ground with a frown. Keltan then shifted his gaze to Balladyn to see how he fared, but the Dark was gone. He tapped Ulrik on the arm. "Where did Balladyn go?"

"I have a theory," Ulrik said.

Con drew in a breath and lifted his head, meeting Keltan's gaze.

Keltan started to ask Con if he'd seen what happened, then he realized it must be the Reapers. They wouldn't help in the battle, but that didn't mean they weren't there in other ways.

More and more Light started to chant for Usaeil's death. It was music to Rhi's ears as she and Usaeil circled each other. The darkness had been calling to her for the entire battle. Rhi had thought she could ignore it and win against the queen, but now she knew that wasn't the case.

Rhi had no choice but to embrace the very thing she'd been running from.

"Yessssssssssss," the darkness purred.

Rhi took a deep breath and welcomed it into her soul. There was no pain, but there was a surge of power that went through her. She was then able to see Usaeil in her true form. The queen's hair was nearly completely silver, and her eyes blazed bright red.

"You fooled us all for so long," Rhi said.

Usaeil smiled. "I'm not done yet."

"Oh, yes, you are."

Rhi heard someone shout her name. She knew the Kings were nervous. She could see herself glowing. But she had complete control over it. She couldn't tell any of them that, though. Not now—not until Usaeil was dead.

Usaeil attacked first. Rhi watched it as if in slow-motion. She was easily able to block all of the queen's attacks, including the magical ones. Rhi toyed with Usaeil for a bit as she realized that it wasn't a trick of her mind, she actually saw things in slow-motion.

"Feel the power I give you," the darkness whispered seductively. *"Now show Usaeil."*

Rhi reached up and grabbed Usaeil's right wrist before kicking the blade out of the queen's left. Rhi then swept Usaeil's feet from under her so she fell onto her back. That's when Rhi plunged her sword into Usaeil's heart. And twisted the blade.

CHAPTER FORTY-TWO

The hush that descended over the battlefield the moment Rhi's blade pierced Usaeil was bone-chilling. The Light could hardly believe that their queen was not only defeated but also dead. And the Dark, as well as the Dragon Kings, were more than a little shocked at how easily Rhi had crushed Usaeil.

Keltan was ecstatic that Usaeil was no longer alive, but he didn't want to celebrate with the others. He wanted to get back to Dreagan and Bernadette.

"Shite," Rhys murmured not far from Keltan's left ear.

Keltan glanced at Rhys with a frown, then turned to where Rhys was looking. That's when Keltan realized that Rhi was glowing—brightly.

That was never a good sign since it indicated that Rhi was losing control of her anger. She had accidentally blown up a realm before because she couldn't control the power, which meant that everyone was now on edge to see what Rhi would do.

To Keltan's shock, Con was the one who made his way to Rhi. But if they expected Rhi to listen to anyone, they were sorely mistaken. She turned away from Con, not even pretending to hear him.

"Rhi!" Constantine bellowed.

She kept walking, glowing brighter and brighter all the while. Fae—both Light and Dark—started teleporting as far from the area as they could. None of the Dragon Kings left. They remained, watching and waiting.

Rhi made her way to the spot where Balladyn had lain, bleeding out. She dropped to her knees without asking where he'd gone. She didn't utter a single syllable—but everyone who remained felt her heart-wrenching anguish, her soul-deep grief.

Keltan glanced at Con to see the King of Kings with a deep frown furrowing his brow. Con didn't take his gaze from Rhi, not even when Ulrik moved to his side.

Despite the confusion and more than a little worry, no King spoke a word. Rhys started toward Rhi when she suddenly threw back her head and released a bellow filled with such fury that Keltan could feel it on the air, cutting through everything like lightning.

More disturbing was the fact that Rhi's eyes kept shifting from silver to red and back again. Keltan wasn't the only one who noticed.

Rhi closed her eyes and dropped her chin to her chest as she put a hand on the ground where Balladyn had lain. Keltan spotted a tear roll down Rhi's cheek. But before any of them could go to her to comfort her, she straightened in one fluid motion and stalked back to Usaeil.

After yanking her sword free, Rhi lifted it over her head and sliced the blade through the air. Right before it severed the queen's head, Usaeil's body disappeared.

"Now, you take her soul?" Rhi screamed into the air.

She threw out her arms. "Is this what you wanted? Is that what you saw? Is this why Daire followed me all those months? You wanted to see this! But you don't let me take my revenge?"

Every word that fell from Rhi's lips was like a knife in each of the Kings. Keltan had known she was hurting. Hell, all of them had, but there wasn't one of them who truly understood how much until that moment.

Keltan's gaze moved to a certain Dragon King. Well, there was one of them who had comprehended Rhi's anger and resentment. He'd known from the very beginning. It was too bad that she wouldn't listen to him now. Not that Keltan could blame her.

If Keltan were in her shoes, he'd tell the King to kiss his ass. And Rhi might very well do just that. This was a side of Rhi that none of them had seen before. Frankly, Keltan wasn't sure what he could do to help. And it wasn't that he didn't want to assist, but his mind was on Bernadette.

"She let the darkness in," Rhys murmured in dismay.

Keltan drew in a deep breath. "Doona judge her."

"Rhi is judging herself." Rhys shook his head. "I never expected this to happen."

Keltan had always hoped that Rhi would best Usaeil, and they all knew that Rhi had power she hadn't yet tapped into. That's what she'd done today, and the result was in their favor. But what would it ultimately do to Rhi?

More importantly, who would rule the Light and Dark, since both their leaders were dead?

Rhi slowly let her gaze move over the Dragon Kings. Blood coated her as it did the rest of them. Rhi had a line of blood that ran diagonally from her right temple, over her nose, and down her left cheek to her jaw. With the gleaming white stone of the castle behind her and the darkening sky over her, it made for a striking picture. One Keltan would never forget.

"Ryder," Keltan called as he opened the mental link.

He expected an immediate answer, so when there wasn't one, Keltan grew frantic. He turned his head to Con, who bowed his head, acknowledging that Keltan could leave.

Without a word to anyone else, Keltan shifted and jumped into the air. His wings caught a current, and he soared straight into the clouds before flying swiftly to Dreagan. He wasn't the only one. V was right beside him.

The entire flight there, both he and V kept trying to communicate with anyone at Dreagan, but no one answered.

An eternity later, Dreagan came into view. That's when Keltan saw the smoke curling into the air. He and V exchanged looks before they split apart and went in different directions toward the manor.

"I doona see anything," V said a moment later.

Keltan's gaze scanned the ground, looking for anyone or anything that wasn't supposed to be there. *"Me, either."*

"Then Ryder should be answering us."

"I'm going in."

"I'll keep a lookout from above," V said.

Keltan dove toward the back of Dreagan Mountain. His keen eyesight didn't pick up any movement of humans or anything electronic. He spread his wings and glided into the mountain before landing. As soon as he did, he shifted.

He stood silently in the cavern for a full minute as he listened. Even when the Kings and mates were scarce, the manor hummed with a specific type of energy. There was none of that now. It was as if every living soul had left Dreagan.

"*Keltan?*"

He jerked at the sound of V's voice in his head. "*You should get down here.*"

It wasn't long before V stood beside him. They exchanged a look before heading toward the main tunnel that led to the manor. On the way, they stopped and checked on the Silvers. The four dragons still slept peacefully.

They continued on. Upon entering the house, it was as quiet as the mountain.

"Something isna right," Keltan said.

V shook his head. "Nay. It isna."

They both put a hand on the wall of the manor and pushed dragon magic into it. Almost immediately, Keltan felt a surge of Druid magic, one he recognized.

"Eilish," he said, looking at V.

V met his gaze. "And Shara."

Keltan tested the magic again, and sure enough, he also felt Shara's Fae magic. "Everything is warded and secure."

"Then where did the smoke come from?"

Keltan had forgotten about that after finding Dreagan deserted. "I'll check that out if you want to finish searching the house."

V walked off with a nod, while Keltan headed outside. He made his way around to the front of the manor to where he'd spotted the smoke. He found the rocks that formed a circle where flames erupted straight from the ground.

"Dragon magic," he murmured.

He followed the spiral of smoke upward until his gaze caught on the mountains. Keltan smiled as he realized exactly what had happened.

"*They're in our mountains, V,*" Keltan said.

V walked out of the manor, but he didn't wear a smile.

"That doesna explain why no one will communicate with us."

No, it sure didn't. Keltan's grin faded as he turned back to the mountains. "Either they can no' hear us, or they've used some spell to ensure they remain hidden."

"If Claire or the bairn is hurt in any way, I'm going to resurrect Usaeil myself just so I can kill her again," V said between clenched teeth.

Though all the Kings had suffered, V had endured much more than any of them except for Ulrik. Or maybe Con. No one had said it, but they all knew that the odds of V's and Claire's child surviving were slim. Still, Keltan held out hope for him.

After all, it would destroy V if Claire died.

No sooner had that thought gone through Keltan's mind than Bernadette filled his head. He had to find her. It didn't matter what he did or didn't want. All he knew was that she was in his life, and he liked her there.

So what if he fell in love? So what if he found his mate? Others had done it and managed to make it through each day. He could, as well.

"Bernadette," he whispered and shifted.

He jumped into the air and flew straight to the mountains that he'd seen behind the smoke from the flames. It wasn't a coincidence that the fire had been created there. It was a way for those who remained behind at Dreagan to tell the others where they had gone.

"*Con,*" Keltan called. Once the King of Kings opened his link, Keltan continued. "*No one is in the manor. It's empty. As is the mountain. Neither V nor I can get anyone to answer our calls.*"

"*Rhi isna in a fit shape to be left alone. We're still trying to get her to stop glowing.*"

Keltan wasn't surprised. *"Either V or I will alert you when we find out what's going on."*

"I just sent Merrill, Cain, and Vaughn your way," Con told him.

"We'll keep you posted."

Keltan severed the link and flew faster to the mountains. He and V circled one after another. They didn't roar because the sound would carry and attract the attention of mortals. But they kept trying to talk to Ryder and the other Kings who'd remained behind. To no avail.

Keltan had an idea when he flew over his mountain. He landed on top of it and slammed his tail down. V circled overhead as they waited. They didn't have to wait long. Within minutes, four Kings flew from different mountains.

Keltan called out Ryder's name when he saw the gray scales, but instead of answering, Ryder slammed a wing into him. Keltan shook his head to clear it. When he looked again, Ryder stood before him in human form.

"Doona use our telepathic link," Ryder stated angrily.

Keltan shifted as V landed behind them and also returned to his human form. Keltan frowned at Ryder. "What the hell is going on?"

"When Bernadette was hurt, and then Claire became ill, I noticed that every time any King at Dreagan communicated with those at the Light Castle, the women got worse. When I refused to answer or contact you, both Bernadette and Claire got better."

"That doesna make sense," V said.

Ryder threw up his hands. "I'm no' the only one who noticed. Sophie and Denae did, as well."

"I want to see Bernadette," Keltan demanded. They

could figure out the rest later. Right now, Bernadette was more important.

It wasn't lost on Keltan how his thoughts and feelings for her had changed.

CHAPTER FORTY-THREE

Something was wrong. Bernadette knew it, but she couldn't figure out what it was. Something had concerned her. She remembered that, just as she could recall feeling as if everything were falling apart.

But she couldn't recollect what had upset her so.

Maybe that was for the best. She didn't like that cold, empty feeling inside her when she was upset about something that was out of her control. It was better to let something like that go, to forget.

Yet it kept nagging at her.

"You need to wake up, Bernadette."

The voice wasn't hers, and Bernadette didn't recognize it either. She wanted to ask who it was, but she couldn't get her voice to work.

"Don't worry about me."

There was something distinctive about the feminine voice. There was a Scottish accent to the tone. There was also something else there, something that she knew she should recognize but didn't.

"Bernadette, listen to me. This is important. You're fading, and fast."

Fading? What the hell did the voice mean, she was fading?

"You're dying."

Oh. Well. Bernadette wasn't sure what to say to that.

"Do you want to die?"

Bernadette thought of Keltan, of the way his voice made her smile. No, she didn't want to die. And how did she get so sick in the first place?

"You can remember. It's right there, just on the edge of your thoughts. I'm not going to lie, it's going to hurt to recall everything."

But there was Keltan. He was worth any amount of pain. There was a smile on Bernadette's face as she followed the thread in her mind to the memories that were just out of reach.

They barreled into her with the force of a train. She gasped as she recalled the pain of being stabbed, of trying to make it to her car and then driving as far as she could to Dreagan.

She remembered the numbness that had taken over her body and the blackness that edged her vision. She'd been in her car thinking about Keltan and how she wanted to tell him she loved him.

The voice had said she was fading, but she wasn't dead yet. If she wished to live, then she needed to fight. She clung to thoughts of Keltan, to the love that had blossomed so beautifully, so surprisingly. She wasn't going to let that go without a fight.

Yet the more Bernadette clung to life, the more it felt as if someone—or some*thing*—were trying to stop her. Was Usaeil still not dead? Would Bernadette never be rid of her nemesis? And if Usaeil hadn't been defeated, then what did that mean for the Dragon Kings?

"Keltan. You're finally here."

Bernadette's heart leapt at the mention of his name. She knew the voice. It was close to her. She was supposed to know who it was, but she couldn't put a face or a name to it. Not that she was trying too hard since she couldn't open her eyes. That disturbed her the most.

She tried to hear what Keltan said, but she couldn't make out his words. Bernadette frantically clawed at the blackness that cloaked her. She wanted out of it and into the light. She needed to see Keltan's face and look into his amber eyes.

Suddenly, it felt as if something grabbed hold of her and yanked her down or away, she couldn't tell which. All Bernadette knew was that something was taking her away from Keltan. She screamed his name over and over in her mind, but none of it made it past her lips—at least that she knew of.

"Bernadette!"

She didn't know how long the voice had been yelling her name, but somehow, she heard it through her screams. Bernadette grew quiet, waiting to hear what the voice said, even while wondering if she should trust it.

"You've no reason to trust me, but I'm here to help. The Others used Usaeil's magic to connect with you. They have a hold of your soul, and they don't intend to give it back."

Bernadette was so stunned at the news that her mind went blank with shock. She didn't know that such things were possible, but she should have figured since it was magic. And anything was possible with magic—as she was finding out.

"I don't have long. They're going to notice me soon. The only way the Others can win is if you give up. If you have something strong holding you to life, then you have a chance."

Bernadette's eyes filled with tears as she thought of Keltan.

"Keep hold of Keltan. The Others will do anything to make you let go."

It was so hard. It felt like when Bernadette was a child, hanging on the bars on the playground with her fingers slowly—but surely—losing their grip.

"Love is stronger than anything, Bernadette. Even magic. You can't fail. Keltan needs you. Just as you need him."

Bernadette knew she was risking everything by believing the voice. For all she knew, it could be one of the Others, but for some reason, she didn't think that was true. There was something about the voice that she knew. She wanted to remember.

"Stop thinking about that. Focus on Keltan. Usaeil might have used you, but the joke is on her. She had no idea who you were, Bernadette. It was a secret kept from Usaeil for a good reason. Now, forget everything but Keltan. Think about your love for him. Think about the love between you. And remember . . . nothing can defeat love."

Bernadette didn't hesitate to do as the voice urged. She filled every fiber of her being with thoughts, images, and remembered conversations with Keltan. She then let the love inside her grow and grow, all the while imagining that it was like a giant bubble that surrounded her and pushed out anything negative or bad.

She became aware of other voices, of people touching her. It was distant at first, as if she were watching it happen to her body instead of actually feeling it. All the while, she kept listening for Keltan's voice.

Someone had said his name. He was there. She just needed to hear him. But the minutes ticked by with nothing. Others kept saying her name. It became louder and louder, the touches firmer until it was like she was being sucked back into her body.

Her eyes flew open with the pain that rushed through her. Her lips parted as she held her breath—a scream lodged in her throat.

On their own, her eyes went to the left where she spotted the head of a dragon looming over her. The citrine color of the scales mesmerized her. The large, silver eyes that stared at her with such intensity captivated her.

She knew those eyes. They might not be amber right now, but she recognized who they belonged to—Keltan.

The others surrounding her seemed to melt away as she let her gaze run over Keltan as he moved into the light so she could see him better. She'd seen the Silvers, but they had been curled together and sleeping. Catching sight of Keltan standing with his large wings tucked against him and his tail curling behind him was staggering.

She loved how the citrine scales grew finer and lighter around his neck and tail. Three rows of long spikes ran down his back. A mane of spines sprouted from the back of his head, and there was a bony ridge that separated his nostrils.

"Keltan." She winced at the hoarse sound of her voice.

He lowered his great head close enough that she could lift a hand and place it on top of his nose. She smiled when his warm breath fanned her body.

She'd waited so long to see him. She wanted to tell him how splendid he looked, how grand and terrifyingly beautiful he was, but she couldn't get the words out.

He shifted into human form and took her hand in both of his. "It's fine, lass. You can say anything you need to later. Right now, I need you to rest."

She shook her head. Bernadette didn't want to go back to sleep for fear of what the Others might do.

"You need to sleep," Eilish said from her other side.

Bernadette shook her head more firmly. "Can't," she got out.

Keltan's brow furrowed. "Usaeil can no' hurt you anymore. She's dead."

Bernadette wanted to celebrate, but all she could do was sigh. She licked her lips, and then with great difficulty, said, "Others."

"Oh, for fuck's sake," Eilish said.

Keltan put his hand on Bernadette's face. "Did they hurt you?"

"They tried. Used Usaeil's magic."

"That's how they got through our magic," a male voice said from behind Bernadette.

She couldn't see who it was, and frankly, she didn't care. She tightened her hold on Keltan. Bernadette was afraid that if she ever let go, she might lose him.

"I'm right here, lass. No one is getting to you," he vowed.

The promise in his eyes was so bright that she believed him without hesitation. She smiled as he stroked a hand from her brow over her hair.

"I'm sorry," he said as his face lined with regret. "I never thought Usaeil would use mortals. I never should have left you."

She put a finger on his lips. "I'm here."

"You doona know how close you came to no' being here," he whispered.

Bernadette looked into his eyes and said, "I do, actually." She paused to get her breath. "The Others had a hold of my soul. They were trying to take me."

"I really hate these people," Eilish murmured as she turned away.

Keltan's smile was forced as rage burned in his amber eyes. "You got free of them."

"I had . . . help."

"Help?" Keltan repeated, another frown forming. "Who?"

She tried to shrug, when that didn't work, she said, "I don't know. A woman. She sounded . . . familiar."

"Someone from Dreagan?" Eilish asked.

Bernadette glanced at the Druid. "I don't know."

"We'll sort it later," Keltan said. "The important thing is that you're here. With me."

She smiled when he kissed her fingers. "When I was bleeding out in my car, there was one thing I wanted to tell you."

"What's that?"

"I love you."

The smile that broke out over his face was so blinding, it would've overshadowed the sun. "Och, lass. I love you so much it hurts."

Bernadette wanted to throw her arms around him, but the pain in her abdomen hurt too badly to attempt it. Keltan pressed his forehead to hers as they stared into each other's eyes.

"I didna want a mate," he told her. "I never looked, and I honestly prayed I'd never find one. I feared it would make me weak."

She hated hearing that because she didn't want to make him weak.

"I was wrong," he continued. "I'm no' weak with you. I'm stronger than ever before because of our love."

"I'm yours."

"And I'm yours. It might be too soon to talk about it, and I'll wait as long as you want, but—"

She laughed, wincing at the throbbing it caused. "I want nothing more than to be your mate. Whenever you want."

"Now," he said with a chuckle.

She grinned, happier than she'd ever been in her life. It was amazing to feel as if you'd lost everything, only to then be handed the world on a platter. Not that she didn't think there would be more difficulties.

Usaeil might be dead, but the Others were just getting started. And, apparently, they didn't need Usaeil, after all. That didn't sound good, but if anyone could defeat them, it was the Dragon Kings.

Bernadette realized that now. Usaeil had known it, as well, which was one reason she'd wanted Con so badly. From what Bernadette had learned of the Dragon Kings, they bent over backwards for their friends.

Usaeil, had she gone about things differently, might have been able to align with the Dragon Kings to defeat the Others. Instead, she'd lost her life. Hopefully, someone better would step up to rule the Light Fae.

But that wasn't Bernadette's concern. The Dragon King gazing at her with such adoration and love was. Their path had started out rocky, and the climb had been perilous, but it had been more than worth it.

As she was drifting off to sleep with Keltan holding her hand, she remembered what the voice had told her—that she was special.

CHAPTER FORTY-FOUR

Henry stared at the backlit map on the wall in the cavern that had become something of an office for him. But he didn't really see the pins or the map. Instead, his mind was on Melisse.

The woman was different, that was for sure. Her beauty was enough to render anyone speechless, but it was something more. She exuded a confidence that went hand in hand with doubt and wariness, which she extended to everyone. At least to those he'd seen around her.

"Melisse," he whispered.

He loved the way her name rolled off his tongue. It was as exotic and striking as she was. The few words they'd exchanged weren't nearly enough. He had so many more questions he wanted to pose to her. And yet he also wanted to see her again. It was almost as if his eyes couldn't get enough of her.

He'd been trained to pick up every detail around him, but even if he hadn't, he knew he still would've noticed how the ends of her hair curled just a bit. He would've seen the chipped left pinky nail that she tried to hide.

What had she really been doing in Madrid? Not to

mention at the murdered Druid's house. She could be a Druid. Unlike his sister, Henry couldn't sense when there was magic near.

He pivoted and stalked from the cavern, nearly colliding with Banan as he did. "Sorry," he murmured and kept walking toward the manor.

Once inside, Henry made his way upstairs in the hopes of finding Esther and Nikolai in their room. He pounded his fist on the door, impatience riding him hard. Just as he was about to knock again, the door swung open to reveal his sister.

Behind her was Nikolai, sitting with a large pad of paper in one hand and a sketch pencil in the other. Nikolai's baby blue eyes locked on Henry, but he didn't say a word.

"Henry?" Esther asked with a frown. "What is it?"

"When you and Nikolai found me at the café, did you feel any magic?"

Her frown grew deeper as her nutmeg eyes narrowed on him. "Why?"

"Did you?" he pressed.

"Maybe. I don't know," she replied with a shrug.

Nikolai set the pad and pencil aside. "What is it, Henry?"

Henry rubbed a hand over his mouth and gave a small shake of his head. "Esther, please."

"Perhaps you should come in," Nikolai said and got to his feet.

Esther moved aside. Henry stepped over the threshold but didn't go any farther, even after Esther had shut the door. He glanced at Nikolai, but his gaze returned to his sister.

After a moment, she threw up her hands. "I was so worried about finding you that I wasn't paying attention, okay? I should've been, I know, but I knew we had to get back here immediately."

"It's not your fault," Henry said, trying to soothe her. "I just thought maybe you felt something."

Nikolai came to stand beside Esther and asked Henry, "Did *you* feel something?"

"I don't feel magic like my sister." Though he wished he could.

Esther tucked her brown hair behind her ear. "I only feel Druid magic."

"Someone made you think they had magic. Who was it?" Nikolai pressed.

Henry blew out a breath and put his hands on his hips as he leaned back against the wall. "I saw a woman outside the house we visited, and then again at the café."

Esther's brows shot up in her forehead. "Did you talk to her?"

"I did."

Nikolai gave Henry a pointed look. "And?"

Henry shrugged, his lips turning downward. "Nothing. She wouldn't tell me much. I did get her name—Melisse."

"No last name?" Esther asked.

Henry shook his head. "She's either naturally cagey—"

"Or she's been taught," his sister finished.

Nikolai blew out a long breath. "Talk to Ryder. He might be able to pick her up on the CCTV around Madrid. Maybe then we can determine who she is. Especially since she was around the house where Usaeil killed the Druid."

"Yeah, that bothers me," Esther said with a shake of her head. "Now, I want to know who this woman is."

Henry's arms dropped to his sides as he pushed from the wall. "No one talks to her but me."

"Hold up there," Esther began.

But Henry caught sight of Nikolai taking her hand to silence her.

Henry gave his brother-in-law a nod before he stalked from the room. He went directly to the computer room and spoke with Ryder. However, after an hour of searching near the café at the time that Henry had spoken with Melisse, they found nothing. The next three hours were spent combing the entire city, but once more, they came up empty.

By the time Henry returned to his cavern, he was more frustrated than ever. He'd thought that Esther might be able to tell him something. When that hadn't worked, he was sure that Ryder would give him answers. Ryder always found people.

"Unless they don't want to be found," Henry murmured to himself.

"I think you spend too much time down here alone."

Henry whirled around at the sound of the voice. He watched as Con stepped from the shadows of a corner to walk into the light. "I didn't realize you came in."

"I didna. I've been here waiting."

"My apologies. Did you need something?"

Con's black eyes studied him for a moment. "Is everything all right?"

Henry was a skilled liar, and while he knew he could get one past the King of Dragon Kings, he didn't want to. Con had given him a place at Dreagan. He wasn't going to ruin that.

"No," he finally answered.

Con's shoulders lifted as he took a breath. "Thank you for no' lying. Want to tell me what's going on? Or would you rather keep it to yourself?"

"You've been gone for weeks, and you want to listen to me?" Henry asked dubiously.

Con raised a blond brow briefly. "I've told you before that you're one of us. I listen to all who I consider family."

"I appreciate that, but I'm sure you have other things to take care of. I can't imagine what it was like pretending with Usaeil all this time. You could've left, right? She wasn't holding you."

"Nay, she couldna hold me there," Con admitted as he slid his hands into the pockets of his slacks. "I stayed because I knew it would gain us the advantage, which it did."

"Not to overstep, but how? You weren't in contact with anyone at Dreagan."

Con smiled as he nodded. "You more than anyone know the extremes a spy will go to in order to assure that those they want to get close to believe them. It didna take long for Usaeil to trust me. Once she did, she told me everything."

"Everything?" Henry asked, his head cocked to the side.

Con's smile grew. "Aye. I know who the leader of the Others is. And I know how to find her."

"That's great news. When do you go?"

"As much as I want to confront the Others, I'm no' going to rush into it. We need to be as prepared as we can."

Henry crossed his arms over his chest. "What do you need from me?"

"For you to tell me what's bothering you so badly that you didna even realize I was in the room."

Henry flattened his lips. "It's probably nothing."

"You're a trained spy for MI5. If your instincts tell you it's something, then it's something."

"Esther, Nikolai, and I went to Spain. Esther got a feeling, so we decided to go to Madrid."

"Good thinking," Con said with a nod.

"We found what had called to my sister. One of the Druids who Usaeil killed lived there before their death."

Con's face hardened at the mention of the Fae queen. "Usaeil willna be killing any more Druids for their magic."

"We can be thankful for that." Henry swallowed. "When we walked from the house, my gaze was drawn to a woman. She was staring right at me."

"Did you recognize her?"

Henry shook his head. "No, but there was something about her that drew my gaze. When I looked away, she disappeared. I asked Esther and Nikolai for a few hours to myself."

"To look for her," Con guessed.

Henry's lips twisted. "Yes. I walked the city for hours. I'd all but given up when I stopped at a café, and then she appeared."

"And?" Con urged.

"She was wary of me, but she did come to me. She said her name was Melisse."

Con said nothing, merely drew in a breath.

Henry hesitated a moment before he continued. "She was in the city to see where the murder took place."

"Did she say why?"

"Curiosity. There was more, but that's all I got out of her. She also knew me. I only gave her my first name, but she called me Henry North. Then she said that I wasn't what she expected."

Con's face was impassive as he said, "Is that right? Anything else?"

"She wanted to know about Esther and Nikolai. I explained that it was my sister and her husband. Then Melisse said I should leave. After that, she was gone. That's everything."

"But you want to find her."

Henry frowned and jerked back his head. "She knew who I was, Con. I've gone by so many aliases while working for MI5 that there are few people besides those I answered to who actually know my name."

"And you want to find out how Melisse knows you."

"Absolutely. Don't you?"

Con didn't answer as his black gaze moved to the map. "Do you have any ideas about who this woman is?"

"Not even a hint. It's a rare thing for someone to keep such things from me. I guess I'm getting rusty."

"Or she's that good." Con slid his gaze back to Henry.

Henry shrugged, realizing that was an option. "She could be."

"Ryder said he didna find a single camera angle with her face on it."

Henry issued a snort. "We're trained to make sure no cameras can pick us up if we want to remain hidden. If she went to those lengths, then she likely works for our government. She has a Scottish accent, so I might be able to call in some favors and see if anyone knows her."

"I doubt you'll find anything."

"You seem rather sure of that."

It was Con's turn to shrug. "Call it a hunch."

That got Henry's attention. "Do you know Melisse?"

"I do no'."

"Yet you don't seem surprised by what I'm telling you."

Con shot him a quick smile. "Henry, you've yet to understand that sometimes people are drawn to us for reasons we can no' understand at the moment. Then there is the fact that you're the JusticeBringer. Neither you nor your sister fully comprehends what your roles entail, and I doona think any of us will until it's time."

"You think Melisse has something to do with me being the JusticeBringer?"

"I think anything is possible. Tell me, if you were watching someone as she did you coming out of the Druid's house, would you stand in the open to be seen if you wanted to remain hidden?"

Henry shook his head. "She wanted me to see her."

"Aye. And she also came to you at the café. That tells me that she has an interest in you. I also think you'll be seeing her again."

"I hope you're right."

"I am," Con said as he turned on his heel and walked away.

CHAPTER FORTY-FIVE

"I've got you," Keltan murmured when Bernadette stirred in his arms.

She sighed and nestled against him. "Have I told you how much I enjoy waking up in your arms?"

"You can have it every day for eternity, lass," he said, smiling against her hair.

"You always say the right things."

He chuckled and kissed her head. "How are you feeling?"

"Like I was never stabbed. Con's ability is amazing. I can't remember if I thanked him or not."

Keltan smiled up at the ceiling. "Several times."

"In my defense, Denae had given me morphine." Bernadette raised her head from his chest to look at him.

"Verra true."

Her smile faded as she gazed into his eyes. "I realize how close I came to dying. Had Eilish not found me—"

"I know," he said and pulled her head down so he could hold her tightly. Every time he thought of how he'd nearly lost her, he became panicked. "But she did, and then got you here."

Bernadette swallowed, the sound loud in the silence. "You haven't said anything about the Others' attempt to take my soul."

"Each time I think of it, I get so angry, I want to destroy something."

"If it hadn't been for the voice in my head, I'm not sure I would've known what to do."

"We'll figure out who helped you, and we'll thank her."

Bernadette inhaled deeply before releasing the breath. "She said something that I can't stop thinking about."

"What's that?"

"That Usaeil might have used me, but she didn't know who I was. The voice said the Others kept it a secret from Usaeil."

That got Keltan's attention. He shifted so he could look Bernadette in the eyes. "I doona understand. Your identity was kept a secret from Usaeil?"

"That's what the voice said. I'm not sure I understand that since Usaeil knew who I was."

A knot of unease filled his stomach. "I think what the voice was trying to tell you was that you're far more important than Usaeil knew. Had she known exactly who you were, she might have used you differently."

"But I'm no one," Bernadette said with a frown.

"No' true. You're a Dragon King's mate."

The frown vanished as she smiled. "Do you think that's what the voice meant?"

"Nay." Keltan couldn't lie to her, though he wished he could to ease her mind. "I think there's more that we doona know."

"Ryder already looked into my past. Did he find anything?"

"Nay, but that doesna mean anything. We'll have to look in other ways."

Bernadette returned her head to his chest. "I thought that I'd feel better once Usaeil was dead. Why is it that I still feel as if there's a cloud over me?"

"Because there is. The Others." And Keltan was beginning to fear that Bernadette's identity was somehow tied to them.

"You think I'm part of them in some way, don't you?"

He adjusted his arms around her. "I think it's a possibility. It would explain why they fought for your soul so desperately."

"Why keep who I am a secret from Usaeil?"

"My guess is that they realized that Usaeil was deviating from their plan."

"What does that mean for me?"

"I doona know."

And that's what scared him. The truly frightening part was that Bernadette wasn't the only one of the mates who had a past the Kings hadn't figured out yet. There were several others, as well. And if Ryder, with all his incredible skills, couldn't find the information on the mates, then Keltan wasn't sure anyone could.

"I'm scared," Bernadette murmured.

Keltan held her tightly. "I've got you. Remember that. I'll always have you, and I'll always protect you. The sooner you become my mate, the sooner you willna have to worry."

"Did you ever think that perhaps that's exactly what the Others want?"

Keltan's breath froze in his lungs.

"I didn't think so." Bernadette leaned her head back to see him. "I'm not the only mate who has a past that hasn't been figured out, am I?"

"Nay."

"That should've raised major concerns for the Kings."

Keltan looked away, not wanting to go down this path—but there was no stopping it now. "When we find our mates, our only objective is to keep them safe from all harm."

"The mating ceremony that binds us to you," Bernadette said.

"Once we're bound, you'll be immortal."

Bernadette rose up on her elbow, her jade eyes meeting his. "I don't think we should do the ceremony until we know more about my past."

Panic seized Keltan, but he managed to calm himself enough to ask, "Why?"

"What do you know about the Others?"

He shrugged. "That they're Druids and Fae who joined together to destroy us."

"What else?" she pressed.

Keltan didn't want to get into this right now. "They set up traps and obstacles for us that have taken thousands of years to find. We know Usaeil was part of them, and we know that the leader of the Others is a Druid. Usaeil told Con about Moreann, stating that they often met on the Fae Realm to talk."

Bernadette lowered her gaze to his abdomen as she ran her fingers along his chest. "You know that the Others want to destroy you."

"Aye."

"And you aren't at all worried by the fact that I could be connected to them?" Her eyes snapped back up to his.

Keltan shook his head.

"You should be," Bernadette stated. "You should be very concerned. Because my guess is that the Others have plans for me and any other mate they happen to have a connection to."

He took the hand caressing him and brought it to his

lips, where he kissed it. "I'm no' worried, lass. Because I love you. Whatever happens, we'll get through it."

"It's because I love you that I won't go through the ceremony. You said dragons mate for life."

"We do," he said with a nod.

She raised her brows. "You would be tied to me forever."

"I doona see the problem in that since it's what we both want."

"Yes, I want it. More than anything. *But*," she said, raising her voice when he tried to speak. "I don't want you hurt. In any way. Whether it's something I do intentionally or not, I won't be a part of what the Others have planned."

Her words made him love her even more—if that were possible. "The thing is, whether we've gone through the mating ceremony or no', I know you're my mate. I'll never leave you, and it doesna matter what you do, I'll always love you."

"That's what terrifies me. I fear the Others will use me against you."

"You have the choice," he told her. "They can no' make you do anything."

Bernadette rolled her eyes and sat up straight before facing him. "Shall I remind you of what Usaeil did?"

"I know what she did, but now you have our magic protecting you, along with Druid and Fae magic. There's no way anyone can make you do anything you doona want to do."

She considered his words before nodding. "I hope you're right."

"I am."

Bernadette lay back down next to him to rest on his chest. "What does this mean for us?"

"Nothing has changed."

"Everything has changed, Keltan. You can't deny that."

He opened his mouth to argue, then decided against it. Mayhap she was right. Things had changed. Bernadette was now privy to all sorts of information she hadn't had before. Then there were the spells and wards protecting her, but he knew it was really about the knowledge she now possessed regarding the Others and her possible link to them.

"I'm no' denying it. I'm merely saying that despite everything that's happened, my feelings for you have no' changed. I still want you for my mate. I still want to go through with the ceremony."

"I can't allow that to happen."

"Because you think you're going to hurt me somehow?"

"Yes," she replied, her eyes wide. "Why don't you understand that?"

He smiled at her. "Och, lass. I do. Verra much. But the thought of you being killed isna something I can handle."

"And I want the knowledge that if somehow the Others force me to do something, or—I hate to even think it—I do it on my own, that you're not bound to me. I want you to be able to leave."

"That's just it. Now that I've acknowledged that you're my mate, I'll never be able to walk away from you."

She was silent for a heartbeat. Then, in a forlorn voice, she said, "Oh, Keltan. We are in a pickle for sure."

"Nay, lass. We're no'," he said and kissed her head. "We can no' predict the future, nor will I try. We have each other, and that's enough for me."

She looked up at him for a moment before her gaze moved away. "I have this stone of dread in my stomach that the Others are going to do something, and it's going to pit me against you."

He didn't tell her that she wasn't the only one with that concern. Instead, he said, "Do you remember when you fought them for your soul?"

"Yes, because the voice warned me."

"You did it because you didna want them to have you."

She blew out a breath. "Actually, the voice told me that the only way I could win was if I had something strong to hold on to. It was the love I had for you that I gripped tightly to and refused to let go of. The voice told me that I needed you, and you needed me."

"She wasna wrong. I do need you, Bernadette. I didna realize how much until you came into my life. Now that you're here, I doona want to contemplate a day without you."

Bernadette placed a kiss on his chest. "Neither do I. More than anything, I want to be bound to you. Actually, I already feel like I am, even without the ceremony."

"Then it doesna matter if we complete it."

"You won't change my mind," she informed him. "Not until we know for sure who I am and why the Others seem to know me."

He frowned, his chest tightening as he thought of all the ways Bernadette could be taken from him, her life wiped out in a blink. "That could take months. Years, even."

"I'll be beside you the entire time." She shifted her head to look at him and puckered her lips.

Keltan kissed her, even though several arguments arose that he could use to try to dissuade her. But he realized he was being selfish. Bernadette wasn't putting off the ceremony to hurt him. She was doing it *not* to hurt him. He had to respect that.

Even if he didn't like it.

"I willna speak more of the ceremony," he promised her. "No' until you want to, that is."

She flashed a smile. "You do understand that I'm putting it on hold to protect you, us, and everyone at Dreagan, right?"

"Aye, I do." Though it made him hate the Others even more.

She moved upward and gave him a soft, sexy kiss before whispering, "We'll be together, my Dragon King. We get to learn each other slowly, and then, one day, we will be bound together. I'll wear the tattoo proclaiming that I am yours."

"You know, we could be wrong. It might be the mating ceremony that protects the mates from the Others."

Bernadette bent her knee and moved her leg along his before she rocked her hips against his thigh. "Do you want to talk about that some more, or would you rather do other things?"

In the next instant, Keltan had her on her back, staring into her jade eyes as her black hair fanned out around her. "I think you know the answer to that."

She reached down and cupped his arousal with her hand. Bernadette grinned up at him. "Then why are we still talking?"

CHAPTER FORTY-SIX

With his gaze directed out the office window overlooking the valley as the rain came down in sheets, Con listened to Ulrik and Kellan behind him.

They had been going on for quite awhile about his remaining with Usaeil. He'd let them drone on, but he was growing tired of it.

"Dammit, Con, say something," Ulrik demanded.

Con turned his chair to face the two Kings. Both were furious. It blazed in Kellan's celadon eyes, while it showed in Ulrik's rigid posture. "What else would you have me say? I already explained."

"You explained verra little," Kellan bit out.

Con sighed. The last thing he wanted was to relive the weeks he'd spent with Usaeil, but he knew he had no choice. "I knew within moments of Usaeil taking me that it was the magic of the Others that shrouded where she had brought me."

"Do you know where that was?" Ulrik asked.

Con shook his head in regret. "She kept me in a windowless room. I doona think we were alone, however. She left often, and I could hear her speaking to others, but I never heard their reply."

Some of the tension in Ulrik eased. "Did she mention Xaneth?"

"Never. She would leave me alone for a few hours and then return and use magic on me. When I realized the Others' magic prevented me from communicating with you, I knew I had two choices. I could continue to fight her, or I could pretend to join her."

"It was a fucking brilliant idea," Kellan admitted with a nod. "I just wish we had known that's what you were doing."

Ulrik snorted loudly. "We knew that Usaeil's magic couldna hold you."

"After everything Usaeil did, you were right to worry about why I wasna contacting you. Her magic did nothing to me, though I allowed her to believe otherwise. It was a slow process, but eventually, I convinced her I was totally hers."

Kellan shook his head. "What did she say to you?"

Con shrugged one shoulder. "That we were meant to be together, and I was making things difficult. That if I just gave in, we could be happy."

"I'd pity her if I didna hate her so much," Ulrik declared.

Kellan glanced at him and nodded. "I think we all feel that way."

Con wanted to hate her, but he couldn't. "She wanted love. She craved it as much as she needed power. I do pity Usaeil. When she thought I was hers, she was a different person. Soft, you might even say."

Kellan's brows shot up in his forehead. "Soft? I doona think so."

"We didna see it," Ulrik said sympathetically.

Con met his friend's gold eyes and nodded. "In the

end, when the battle was taking place, I kept hoping I might be able to change her mind and stop her. I thought I might be able to help her. Right up until she plunged her sword into Balladyn's back. I have no love for him, but he didna deserve that."

"Some might disagree," Kellan said.

Ulrik swallowed and looked down at the floor. "Balladyn was a great many things, but in the end, he turned out to be someone I trusted. Usaeil betrayed him, and Balladyn's Fate was changed forever. I can only hope that Death and the Reapers have him."

"We may never know," Con said.

Kellan quirked a brow. "You could ask Erith."

"I could," he agreed. "And I may. He did stand against Usaeil."

"I doona like that no one could find you," Ulrik said.

"I wish I could have told you where we were, but I never saw anything other than the room I was in. It was only recently that she moved us to the Light Castle, and I didna leave her chamber until the verra end."

Kellan leaned forward in his seat and rested his elbows on the arms of the chair. "Please tell me you learned something valuable from her."

For the first time, Con smiled. "Oh, aye. The name of the leader of the Others—Moreann. She's a Druid."

"Shite," Kellan murmured.

Ulrik frowned as he looked at Con. "A Druid? No' a Fae?"

"Moreann isna from the realm. It was she and her kind who brought the humans here."

Kellan got to his feet as he said, "Fuck me."

Con waited until Kellan had poured three glasses of Scotch and handed them out before he continued. "Usaeil and Moreann met on the Fae Realm to talk."

Ulrik tossed back his whisky. "When are we going to start planning that battle?"

"Right now," Con replied.

Kellan set his empty glass down and swallowed his drink. Then he looked sheepishly at Con. "No one has said her name, so I'll be the first. What about Rhi?"

"Rhi will be grieving Balladyn," Ulrik said. "She willna be seen until she wants to be."

Con had known the subject of the Light Fae would come up, but he wasn't ready to discuss Rhi just yet. He'd seen her eyes flash red, and he knew that could only spell trouble for all of them.

"She willna turn Dark," Kellan said.

Con swirled the whisky in his glass before he took a sip. "I doona know what will happen to or with Rhi. She's no' the same Fae that we knew before."

"It would be impossible for her to be," Ulrik retorted angrily. "Rhi has been bombarded continually for months now, and she managed to stay on her feet—albeit wobbly at times. The battle that she'd been preparing for, the one she eagerly went into was also the one she didna want. Why do you think she didna fight you hard when you kept putting it off, Con?"

Con lowered his gaze, because he knew Ulrik was right.

"She had to face off against her queen, against the friend who betrayed and banished her. Then she watched Balladyn die." Ulrik shook his head. "That would fuck anyone up. We've taken her for granted. So many times, we turned to her for help and counted on her being there."

Kellan blew out a long breath. "We should be there for her."

"She willna want us," Con said.

Ulrik closed his eyes briefly as he shook his head.

"Con's right. She willna want us. She willna want anyone."

"I'm sure we all remember the last time she was by herself when she was suffering so."

Con felt their gazes on him. He finally looked up and met them. "She willna listen to me."

"There is someone she might listen to," Kellan said.

Ulrik gave a nod. "Phelan."

Con jerked his chin to Ulrik's silver cuff. "Mind if I borrow that?"

"No' at all," he said. "What happened to your cuff links and pocket watch?"

"Usaeil," Con replied.

Kellan and Ulrik grunted in unison.

Con was absolutely fuming that he'd lost both precious possessions. And not just because the watch allowed him to teleport. It was because they were gifts from Erith, who had taken the time to visit him when he needed a friend the most. Now, they were lost to him.

Erith had been the only one to ever give him a gift. He'd treasured them dearly. Usaeil taking them from him felt like a knife twisting in his gut.

Ulrik tossed him the cuff. Con put it on and thought of Phelan and Aisley's house near the loch. Then he touched the cuff and transported there.

Con stood outside the home, looking at the coziness of it. It wasn't a grand manor. It was quaint, but that's why he liked it so much. The flowers surrounding the dwelling were in full bloom, the colors as bright and glorious as the sun that beamed down on them. There were dark clouds on the horizon, but the storm hadn't reached them yet.

The door opened, and a tall form stepped out onto the porch. Con looked into Phelan's blue-gray eyes and gave a nod. "I'm sorry to intrude."

"It must be something important to bring the King of Dragon Kings here." Phelan walked from the porch, shoving his hand through his long, dark brown hair.

Con waited until the Warrior was near, then he said, "I wish I didna have to come."

"What happened?"

"So verra much." Con bit back a sigh. "I doona know what you've heard or no'."

"Then perhaps you should come in and tell us," Aisley said from the door.

Con bowed his head to her. "I'd be happy to."

The three of them walked into the house, and Con began telling them everything that had happened to Rhi over the last year while Aisley heated water for tea. Some of it they knew, but the majority, the couple wasn't aware of.

When Con finished his tale forty minutes later, Phelan's face was taut and pale. "Why did she no' tell me?"

"You know why," Aisley told him. "She doesn't like disturbing your life."

Phelan's features were pained. "She's my friend."

"Which is why I'm here," Con said.

Aisley's fawn-colored eyes met his. "You want Phelan to talk to her, don't you?"

Con nodded slowly. "Someone needs to. She doesna need to be alone."

"Is this like when her King broke it off? Is it that bad?" Phelan asked.

For a moment, Con couldn't answer. He wondered if Phelan knew his involvement in what had happened in Rhi's past, and then he realized it didn't matter. "It has the potential to get there. Rhi was in a verra bad place during that time."

Aisley moved next to Phelan and rubbed her hand on his back as he placed his forearms on his knees. "She watched Usaeil kill Balladyn. While I know the two of them had their differences, they were friends, and Rhi knew that he loved her."

"And she cared for him," Phelan said.

Con nodded because he knew just how deeply Rhi had felt for the Fae.

Phelan looked up at Con. "I'll call to her, but she probably willna answer."

"Then you need to go to her."

The Warrior frowned as he looked at Con as if he'd lost his senses. "How am I supposed to do that."

"You know Rhi better than most. She's come to you in times of crisis. I'm sure during those instances, she let something slip about where she might go," Con told him.

Aisley sat up straight as she turned her head to Phelan. "Rhi said something about her island, remember?"

"Vaguely," Phelan said slowly, as if trying to recall the conversation. "But do you have any idea how many islands there are?"

Con rose to his feet and handed Phelan Ulrik's cuff. "Please return this to Ulrik when you're finished. He willna mind you using it."

"How are you going to get back to Dreagan?" Aisley asked.

He smiled at her. "I'm going to fly."

Con walked outside. He barely made it two steps from the porch when Phelan's voice stopped him.

"Are you all right?"

Con halted and turned to look at the Warrior. "Of course."

"You were with Usaeil for a long time. You watched as she hurt your Kings, their mates, and Rhi."

Con drew in a breath and released it slowly to control the rage that threatened to break free. It took all of his power to hold it back, to look at things as dispassionately as possible. Because if he let his emotions get in the way, then he would make the wrong decisions. "There are many who think because I doona show my emotions that I doona feel. They would be wrong."

Phelan stared at him for a full minute before he nodded. "Aye. I can see that now. I'll find Rhi."

"We want to make sure she'll be okay. Please let her know that she has friends, and we're all worried about her."

Phelan said, "I'll do that."

Con turned and shifted then. For once, he didn't care about his ripped clothes. His heart hurt at the prospect of not having to think about his cuff links or the pocket watch, but he put that out of his mind. There were many, many more things to worry about.

He spread his wings and took to the sky, shooting straight up into the clouds that would hide him on his trip back to Dreagan.

CHAPTER FORTY-SEVEN

The manor was buzzing with excitement. It was the only word Bernadette could use to describe it. The joy felt in the wake of Usaeil's death and Con's return was only dimmed by the fact that none of the Kings had heard from Rhi.

Yet, they didn't let that stop them from celebrating. Bernadette had been in the kitchen with Sabina, Claire, and Gemma, helping Keltan get the food ready for the big party later that night.

"I'm so excited for Eilish and Ulrik," Gemma said, her light blue eyes filled with delight.

Sabina nodded, her dark brown curls bobbing with her head. "Yep. And I'm not at all jealous."

"Ditto," Claire said with a wink.

The four of them looked at each other and then busted out laughing. Bernadette glanced at Keltan to see him grinning, though it faded quickly. She knew he was thinking about the mating ceremony that Roman, V, and Cináed would have with Sabina, Claire, and Gemma once Ulrik and Eilish had theirs.

If Bernadette would agree, it would also be the time

she and Keltan would be mated. She wanted nothing more than to be his for eternity, but she couldn't stop the worry that grew with every hour.

Usaeil had been unpredictable, and Bernadette seemed to be the only one who was worried about Usaeil's body disappearing. Keltan had said that the Reapers and Death probably had her, but Bernadette wouldn't believe the queen was really dead until she saw the corpse herself.

"Just a few more days," Bernadette told the women. They had become fast friends. In fact, Bernadette had become close to all the women at Dreagan.

It was odd to have so many who were family, sisters even, but she enjoyed it. Despite there being so many people at the manor, everyone seemed to know when it was time to be alone and when it was time to gather as a group.

Sabina quickly cut her eyes to Keltan before she leaned close to Bernadette and said in her Romanian accent, "I still don't understand why you two aren't joining us."

"She's worried that the Others have something in store for the mates," Gemma said.

Sabina's dark gaze grew troubled. "The Others won't be able to hurt us once we're mated."

"Bernadette thinks that's exactly what the Others will use," Keltan said as he wiped off his hands and turned to shoot a smile at Bernadette.

Claire looked between them, then asked Keltan, "Do you think the Others will be able to make us do something to harm you?"

He shrugged. "The Others have done a great many things that I never expected."

"I know that for certain," Sabina replied.

Gemma's lips pressed together. "Aye."

Bernadette walked to Keltan and rose up on her toes to give him a quick kiss. Then she faced her friends. "I want to be mated to Keltan more than anything, but I have this feeling that I can't ignore."

"Then don't," Sabina said. "Coming from a long line of women who have the gift of Sight, always follow your feelings. They won't lead you wrong."

Keltan's arm around her tightened. "And I'm prepared to wait however long I need to in order to make Bernadette mine."

"You two," Claire said, sniffing and wiping her eyes. Then her face crumpled. "These damn hormones make me cry at everything."

Gemma looked at Sabina and said, "We need to make sure we have a lot of tissues at the ceremony."

Claire buried her face in her hands as her shoulders shook. Then she lifted her head, her face streaked with tears. "I don't want to embarrass myself or V. I want to stand up there and be . . . you know, proper."

"You'll be perfect in whatever you do," Keltan said. "Because you'll be up there with V. All he wants is you."

Bernadette looked at Keltan, his words cutting through her. She wondered if she was making the right decision in holding off on the ceremony. Then the same churning in her stomach she felt each time she thought about the future reminded her that she had to follow her feelings, regardless of where they led her.

Though she knew they wouldn't take her from Keltan.

What she worried about was what the voice had told her when she was fighting for her soul. The Others had kept who she really was from Usaeil. Just who was she, really? And did Bernadette even want to know?

"I must get ready," Keltan said as he turned her to face him.

She cupped his face and smiled up at him. "I'll be here waiting. Always."

"I love you."

"I love you more," she said.

He pulled her against him and claimed her lips in a fiery kiss. Then he said, "I love you most."

Before she could reply, Keltan was gone. She had to grab hold of the counter to stay on her feet.

"Damn," Sabina said, waving her hand in front of her face.

Gemma nodded, her eyes wide. "I second that."

"You're good for him," Claire told Bernadette.

Bernadette smiled at them, happier than she had ever been in her life. She wished she could just forget about the outside world, but she had caused too many waves with her lecture. She needed to rectify that. Already, she and Ryder had come up with ideas to do just that. Bernadette had finished writing the first of five columns she would publish. Ryder would then put them in all the right places.

It wouldn't happen overnight, but it was going to happen quickly. Bernadette wanted to make sure that the Kings and the women who lived at Dreagan were safe from anyone who wanted to dig into them. And she was prepared to do whatever it took to ensure that.

She might not be mated to Keltan, but these people had taken her in. They had found her when she was dying and helped her. They were, in fact, her family. And she would do anything for them.

"She's coming," Sabina said from the kitchen doorway.

Gemma, Claire, and Bernadette hurried to Sabina in time to see Eilish coming down the stairs. She glided down the steps with her long, black hair left to fall in waves down her back. The sides were pulled back just enough to show her face.

The dress—silver to match Ulrik's dragon color—molded to her body like a glove. The sleeveless, halter neck A-line gown had silver sequins that added just the right amount of sparkle.

She wore no jewelry except for the platinum teardrop earrings that dangled from her lobes. Eilish smiled at Con, who walked her down the stairs.

"So, the earrings are his gift to her," Sabina said.

Bernadette waited until Eilish and Con were out of sight before she asked, "Who? Ulrik?"

"Con," Claire said.

Gemma's eyes bugged out. "Con gave her a gift?"

"He gives one to every mate right before the ceremony," Sabina explained. "It's always in the color of the King, and somehow he manages to find the piece that's most perfect for the intended mate."

Bernadette smiled. "I like that he does that. Almost like his way of welcoming the women into the family."

"That's exactly what it is," Claire said.

The three women went quiet, and Bernadette knew they were each thinking of the day that they would walk down the stairs with Con toward their own ceremonies.

One day, it would be Bernadette's turn. She had no doubt about that. For now, she was content just being with Keltan. He was the love of her life. Whether they were mated in a dragon ceremony or married in a human one, they were together. And that's what really mattered.

Keltan walked up beside Cain in the cavern. Ulrik stood at the front, waiting for Eilish. Everyone was quiet, anticipating the event of the century.

Ulrik, the one who had been lost to them, the one who had sworn to destroy the Dragon Kings, had not only returned to Dreagan but he had also found his mate. There wasn't a King in attendance that hadn't wondered if this day would ever come.

Con appeared and stood next to Ulrik. Suddenly, Ulrik's face split into a wide smile as he looked toward the entrance. Keltan turned his head and caught sight of Eilish in her flowing silver gown, making her way toward Ulrik.

Keltan wished with all his might that he could be in Ulrik's place watching Bernadette walk to him in the next week, but he knew she was his. He just wanted the ceremony so that she would be immortal and unable to be harmed by the Others.

But he had to respect her wishes. One way or another, Bernadette would be protected because she was at Dreagan. That's all that mattered.

Except Usaeil had been able to get to her and Claire, and then the Others had used Usaeil's magic to cause their own harm. Dreagan was supposed to be impenetrable.

Once everyone returned from the battle, they had made sure all of Usaeil's magic was wiped from Dreagan. It had taken all of them days going back and forth over all sixty thousand acres. Even though Usaeil was dead and her magic no longer held power, there was still the potential for the Others to use it.

Dozens of additional wards had been added. The Kings mixed their magic with Druid and Fae to keep the Others out. They weren't sure if it worked or not. Neither Bernadette nor Claire had been struck again, but that didn't mean anything. The Others could very well be biding their time.

Keltan shut off his thoughts as he listened to Ulrik and Eilish exchange their vows, the love between them was so obvious that everyone could feel it.

A moment later, Eilish winced as the dragon eye tattoo, signaling that she was mated to a King, appeared on her left shoulder. The couple kissed as the cavern erupted in a loud cheer.

Keltan worked his way up to Ulrik to congratulate him. As soon as Keltan did, he left the mountain and returned to the manor. He found Bernadette coming down the stairs as he was halfway up.

He let out a whistle as he raked his gaze over his woman. Bernadette's hair was pulled away from her face without any adornment. She wore a black, sleeveless dress with a cutout back. The hem reached her knees in the front and hung longer in the back.

"You're stunning," he said when she reached him.

Her smile could have outshone the sun. "Thank you. I'm also liking this."

Keltan didn't bother looking down at his kilt. It was nothing compared to the beauty of the woman before him. He held out his arm for her to take. "Shall we go to the party?"

She took his arm, but she held him back when he started down the stairs.

"What is it?" he asked with a frown.

Her jade eyes held his. "I love you."

"And I love you."

"We will be mated."

He sighed and pulled her close. "I've no doubt."

"But you wish it was now."

"I do. I also understand your reasoning. It's valid, lass, but even if I didna think it was, I would still stand by your decision."

Her lips tilted in a smile. "You're an amazing man, Keltan. I'm so glad you came to that lecture."

"I rather think I'm the lucky one for being told to go.

You shook up my life in just the right way, showing me how wonderful love can be."

"Here's to the beginning of our future."

"Aye," he said and sealed it with a kiss.

EPILOGUE

The Fae Realm

The grief was devastating, crushing. Rhi could feel it pushing against her from all sides. It was only the darkness within her that kept her on her feet.

"I will always protect you."

It would be easy to believe the darkness, but Rhi wasn't a fool. She knew the only one she could truly depend on was herself. But even she could admit that it was all she could do to put one foot in front of the other.

She hadn't been able to stay on Earth. It wasn't just the Light Fae or the Dark. Or even the Dragon Kings.

It was *everything*.

She should be rejoicing that Usaeil was dead, but all Rhi could see was Balladyn's face as his life drained from him. If Rhi killed Usaeil a million times, it wouldn't come close to what the queen deserved for murdering Balladyn.

Rhi stumbled and then fell. On the ground, she dropped her chin to her chest. Try as she might to hold them back, the tears came anyway.

"Oh, Balladyn," she whispered as she cried for her friend.

For the man who had been with her for most of her life, the man who had loved her from afar, the man who had been betrayed because he loved her. He had suffered terribly.

Because of her.

And how had she repaid him? She had made him believe that they had a future together, then ended it. She was worse than Usaeil because she had given him hope.

If anyone knew how badly unrequited love could cut, it was her. And yet, she had done the same thing to Balladyn.

She covered her face with her hands and let the tears fall. She cried, the sobs wracking her body. She thought of nothing but the pain that consumed her.

"It will make you stronger," the darkness whispered.

Rhi was tired of being weak. She wanted to be strong, to be able to control her emotions instead of having them control her.

"I can give you that."

It was an offer too good to pass up.

Edinburgh, Scotland

Melisse opened her eyes and took a deep breath. She rose from the bed and walked to the window of the Balmoral Hotel to look down at the city streets teeming with tourists.

She was bolstered by the fact that Bernadette had listened to her and fought against the Others. But things were just getting started. It wouldn't take long for the Others to realize that she was involved.

It was as if she wanted the Dragon Kings to win. In fact, Melisse didn't care what happened to the Kings. But she wanted the Others to fail. And she would do whatever it took to make sure that happened.

Henry North would help her—though he didn't know it yet. She hadn't been able to believe her luck when she'd seen him outside of Dreagan. Unfortunately, their discussion in Madrid had been cut short. Partly because his sister was looking for him, but also because she hadn't been prepared for his line of questioning.

She should've been, though. After everything she knew of Henry, she should have known that he would confront her directly. It was her mistake in thinking that she could lead him down a particular path of questions.

He was smart. And very observant. Of course, that's what spies were, but he was . . . more so. It was no wonder he'd been so good at his job. It was a shame he no longer worked for MI5, but she understood why his attention had shifted to the Dragon Kings even before his sister became involved.

"We shall meet again soon, Henry," Melisse said before turning from the window.